*Previously published Worldwide Library titles by*
*PRISCILLA MASTERS*

THE FINAL CURTAIN
GUILTY WATERS

# CROOKED STREET

## PRISCILLA MASTERS

**W🌐RLDWIDE**

TORONTO • NEW YORK • LONDON
AMSTERDAM • PARIS • SYDNEY • HAMBURG
STOCKHOLM • ATHENS • TOKYO • MILAN
MADRID • WARSAW • BUDAPEST • AUCKLAND

**W❂RLDWIDE**™

Recycling programs for this product may not exist in your area.

ISBN-13: 978-1-335-40191-5

Crooked Street

First published in 2016 by Severn House Publishers Ltd.
This edition published in 2021 with revised text.

This edition published by arrangement with Harlequin Books S.A.

For questions and comments about the quality of this book, please contact us at CustomerService@Harlequin.com.

Harlequin Enterprises ULC
22 Adelaide St. West, 40th Floor
Toronto, Ontario M5H 4E3, Canada
www.ReaderService.com

**Printed in U.S.A.**

# CROOKED STREET

*The world's a city with many a crooked street*
*And death's a marketplace*
*If life was merchandising which men could buy*
*The rich would live*
*The poor alone would die.*

Taken from a Staffordshire jug, circa 1820

*I'M NAMED AFTER a princess, so my mother told me. A princess? Well, we all have our dreams—our nightmares and our problems. My mum said that I was and always would be a princess and when I was a child I was fool enough to believe her. I guess that was her dream and it permeated into my mind so I believed I deserved the life of a princess. Mistake number one. I had a lot to learn.*

*These days I have another dream. Not the Martin Luther King sort about kids of different colours all playing together. That happens already, doesn't it? I mean, look at any street in any part of the UK. Kids all playing together, black, white, brown, yellow, Muslim, Christian, Hindu, Sikh, Buddhist. What's the difference anyway? They all believe in being good. Just in different ways. Nah. My dream is much more impossible than world peace. My dream is personal, purely for myself: a cottage. A pretty, cream-washed cottage with roses climbing up the walls like the cottages on old-fashioned boxes of chocolates. My cottage is somewhere in the country where I can open my door and see lambs playing around. Never mind children. I've seen plenty of them. No, what I want to see is cows and sheep. Fields. No cars. Just miles and miles of fields rolling towards the sunset while I sit there with a glass of cold white wine. I don't ask for love. I had that once and look where it got me. Bloody nowhere. I want this house. I don't care if it's not in great condition or if it's a bit old fashioned. I want it and I want no one to come knocking on the door every Wednesday night.*

*There is something else I want that's every bit as impossible as my quiet cottage. I'd like to have some money in my bank account. To go to the ATM, ask for a balance on screen and not have the letters DR after the figures. I don't mean I want a lot of money in there. I don't want silly money for a private jet or designer clothes. Not for posh holidays and a big flashy car. No, I just want to be able to go to the ATM and for it to give me some of my own money instead of laughing, embarrassing me and amusing the queue behind me by displaying rude messages. 'You're friggin' jokin', darlin'.' All right, it doesn't actually say that but you know what it's thinking—if it can think at all. Maybe it's just my paranoia that believes that behind an ATM is a malevolent and malicious brain.*

*What do I want the money for? Oh, just luxuries like food, or rent, or the electricity bill. Maybe the odd bottle of wine and a couple of cigarettes a day. Nothing excessive. Keep my car on the road—legally. Not to have to worry, worry, worry all the time. Those are my dreams. Not much, is it, compared with being a princess? More than anything, I want a life free of debt.*

*But I can tell you now my dreams are about as unattainable as me climbing Mount Everest tomorrow or having a weekend trip to the moon and back.*

*That's my situation.*

*Sometimes I confess I get down and I worry about my future. Unlike when I was three years old, wearing my plastic crown and believing my mother's fables, I now know I'm never going to be royalty or anyone important. I'm just me. At school one of my teachers said I would never make anything of myself or my life.*

*She was right.*

*But what am I going to do about it?*

# ONE

*Wednesday, 5 March, 10 p.m.*

DI JOANNA PIERCY was late home. Investigating an alleged fraud by a local garage, she and Mike had felt the exhilaration of nearing their quarry for importing fake parts and lost track of time. When she had looked at her watch it had read 9.45 p.m. 'Time to go home,' she'd said, stretching her arms. Working on a computer is not a healthy way to spend a few hours. She'd felt cramped and stiff. With a feeling of guilt she'd logged off the machine and together they'd headed for the car park and their separate vehicles.

When she arrived at Waterfall Cottage Matthew was asleep on the sofa, his hair tousled, his mouth slightly open, breathing deep and regular. Dead to the world. She bent forward to kiss the top of his head, caught the scent of whisky on his breath and then drew back, alert. Matthew only hit the whisky when he was troubled. Her gaze moved to the coffee table and she picked up a bottle of Glenlivet—half empty. Not simply asleep then.

'Matt?' she said softly.

He stirred, mumbled something as he surfaced slowly to consciousness then finally sat up, his fingers still grasping the whisky tumbler.

'Matt,' she said again.

He tried to smile but it came out as a troubled frown.

She sat down beside him. 'Bad day?'

He drew in a deep sigh and nodded, staring ahead of him. 'Bloody awful,' he said, not meeting her eyes, and took another sip of whisky. 'Really bloody awful.'

She waited.

'Little kid,' he enlarged. 'Accident.' Then, putting his glass down: 'No accident. It wasn't an accident and it wasn't the first time the kid had been hurt.'

She didn't even try to untangle his words but waited for the explanation.

'Just a kid,' he said. 'Four years old, Jo.'

She sat down beside him. It was something most pathologists dreaded, performing a post-mortem on a child. Unavoidable but always distressing. Particularly when...

'His name was Rice.' Matthew tried to smile and failed, just looking more distressed. 'Where do they get these names from? Maybe he was meant to be Rees. Or Rhys.' He bunched his shoulders together. 'I don't know. Social services' case. Slipped through the net, they said. Little kid, four years old, weighed fifteen pounds. He'd been starved, beaten.' He lifted his troubled eyes. 'How can people do it, Jo?' he asked. 'How can they be so cruel? To a child?'

There was no response to this except, 'Was it the mother?'

He shook his head.

'Father? Mother's partner?'

Again he shook his head. 'Grandmother,' he supplied. 'Mother...' He shrugged. 'She wasn't there anyway and there is no father or father figure. No. It was the grandmother who...' He couldn't say any more but slurped down another mouthful of whisky.

# TWO

SHE RANG THE POLICE STATION just after twelve. She had sat, anxious when ten o'clock came and went, watching the news, then a comedy show, increasingly uneasy, watching the minutes tick by and absorbing the silence—no car in the drive, no footsteps, no key in the front door. No shout of '*Hi there*.' Nothing. So she set a time when she would finally acknowledge that something was wrong and watched the minutes tick by on her laptop, telling herself that she would wait until just after midnight when she picked up the phone and dialled 101.

'My husband hasn't come home,' she said in her clear voice when the phone was finally picked up by the central line before being transferred to Leek.

DC Danny Hesketh-Brown smothered a grin, at a loss for what to say, every comment seeming inappropriate. 'Umm.' He started by taking down her details. 'What's his name, love?'

'Jadon.'

'Surname?'

'Glover.'

'And what time did you expect him home?' He looked around him, making a face at his colleague, the traditional eyebrows raised, palms displayed, the non-verbal equivalent of, *You what?*

Eve persisted. 'He's usually home by nine. He's three hours late.' Her voice rose. 'He's *never* late.'

'Well…' Hesketh-Brown was still at a loss. He began with an inoffensive, 'How old is your husband?'

'Thirty-two. We've been married two years. He's never been late before. He's *very* reliable.'

'Have you tried his mobile?'

Eve was affronted. Did he think she was an idiot?

She replied with dignity: 'It goes straight through to answerphone. I've left messages.'

'When did you last speak to him?'

'Six. I rang him,' she raised her voice, 'at six to ask him to pick up some…stuff…on the way home.'

'Is he in a car?'

'Yes.'

'Tell you what,' Hesketh-Brown said. He was a soft-hearted guy and the woman sounded distraught. 'Give me the make and number of your husband's car and I'll see if anything's come in.'

'J4DON. It's a black Mitsubishi Shogun Warrior.'

Hesketh-Brown winced and continued, 'When you spoke to him did he sound all right?'

'Yes. Fine. Absolutely as normal. He said he was running late and not to bother with tea.'

'And where was he?'

'I didn't ask. Probably in his office in Hanley. Or out visiting clients.'

'What does your husband do?'

'He works for Johnston and Pickles, an accountancy firm in Hanley, as a financial advisor.'

Hesketh-Brown drew breath. Financial advisor? He could do with one of those—not that he had any bloody money to be advised about.

'Tell you what,' he said cheerfully, 'give me all your details—your names and phone numbers, home and mobiles.' He was scanning his screen as he spoke. 'Nothing's come in so far on his car but we'll look out for it.' He couldn't resist adding, 'It shouldn't be too hard to find.'

Eve Glover sniffed.

'I'll let you know the minute anything turns up, Mrs Glover. In the meantime, you ring me back on this number, direct dial, mind, if he turns up. If he's just had a flat tyre it'll save us a lot of bother. How about that?' He tried to sound cheery but already Hesketh-Brown's mind was thinking of the four 'S's': sex, sozzled, smash-up, sanity (loss of).

'Thank you.' She seemed reluctant to put the phone down.

IT WAS A busy night in Leek. Plenty for the depleted force to deal with. Burglar alarms going off when they shouldn't; a shop window smashed by drunks. A couple more having a sing song in the square and a report of a cat burglar which turned out to be a teenager who'd forgotten his keys and thought he'd access his friend's house balanced on a wheelie bin via the bathroom window. Unfortunately he'd not only forgotten his keys but also, apparently, which house his friend lived in. He went to the wrong one and alarmed a middle-aged retired couple into dialling 999. And then, to top it all, at four a.m. there was a nasty car accident in Bottomhouse which necessitated the attendance of the air ambulance and shut the road for two hours. But the car was not the missing man's, which would have wound up the problem nicely. It all took time and needed written reports, scenes sealed off and so on, but to his credit Danny Hesketh-Brown did run a few checks on the missing man and his vehicle. No accident report. In a quiet moment he ran a few more checks. Mr Jadon Glover appeared to have no criminal record. Hesketh-Brown tried his mobile phone number and left a message asking him to get in touch with the police and his wife who was concerned at his late return.

At 6.30 a.m. he spent roughly five minutes again running through the likely scenarios. Car breakdown? Not so far. Another woman? Possibly but a bit silly not to cover his tracks better. He was in for the rolling-pin treatment if and when he did turn up. A drink or six with his mates? Yep, maybe he was slumped somewhere, possibly blotto on a friend's sofa. Hesketh-Brown chuckled to himself, the mockery of the sober towards the inebriated. And in the morning? A blinding hangover plus an angry wife to face when he woke up.

If that was the case he didn't envy Mr Glover. His wife sounded very certain of herself. Mrs Eve Glover, he believed, was not expecting to be side-lined.

*6.45 a.m.*

Matthew was finally asleep but his mind was not resting. He was tossing and turning and Joanna knew from previous experience that he was probably having troubled dreams and the little boy with the strange name would be somewhere in the tangle of her husband's mind. She laid her head against his shoulder and put her arm round him, trying to calm him, reassure him, reaching out for his hand. He grasped it and his breathing deepened and gradually became more regular.

# THREE

JOANNA DREW BACK the curtain and knew she could cycle in to work this morning. It was fine and dry. Get back on the saddle, pump up those legs. After the storm of last night the sun beamed down on them, promising a warm spring then summer nights... Just around the corner.

Matthew stirred and sat up. 'Ouch,' he said, rubbing his temples. 'Remind me not to drink whisky again.' He looked a little shame-faced.

She sat on the bed and ruffled his hair. 'It's nice to know you're not quite perfect,' she said, kissing him. 'So what's for breakfast, whisky-breath? Alka-Seltzer?'

'Yeah,' he said, wincing and touching his temple with tentative fingers. 'That and coffee. Lots of cups of strong coffee.'

'And Matt,' she said when she came out of the shower, a towel wrapped around her hair, 'don't beat yourself up over this. You've done the best you can. The little boy isn't your responsibility, you know. At least you know the grandmother will never do anything to any child again and she will be convicted on your evidence.'

He blew out his cheeks and met her eyes. 'It's up to

the police,' he said. 'I can document his injuries and point the finger. It's up to them to present the case.'

She kissed the top of his head and he continued, 'I know what you're saying, Jo. And thanks. But I can't say I feel much better.' He ran his fingers down his face. 'Well, hey, today I have to face another day.' He grimaced. 'They always say pathologists shouldn't have feelings. Little Rice wasn't the first and he won't be the last but that pathetic body.' His face was twisted in pain. 'Those tiny, skinny, helpless arms.'

He fell silent and Joanna simply held his hand and kissed the top of his head again. 'Coffee,' she prescribed.

*8.30 a.m.*

SHE'D BEEN RIGHT ABOUT the weather. It was cold—she was glad of her gloves and leggings—but there was a bright optimism in the air which sparkled in rain-washed freshness. A new day. She almost felt like singing, though with her dubious voice she'd better not. 'Don't sing, Joanna, you'll scare me and the birds and make it rain,' her father used to say, but ultimately it wasn't her voice that had frightened him away.

Her legs seemed to spin round the pedals, hardly slowing even on the inclines. On her bike she felt alive. She bent over the handlebars, relishing the feeling of power. Energy seemed to flow through her body. The ride in to Leek across the moorlands was spectacular, the sun causing steam to rise from the water-logged land. There was something clean about this newly washed landscape that seemed to put the world to rights. And it always felt good to be on her bike. She took the hill with extra vigour, pedalling in a fury, panting at the top but loving it.

She arrived at the station half an hour later, pleased with her time, locked her bike to the railings then went to the cloakroom for a shower and change. Cycling shorts were hardly *de rigueur* for a detective inspector of Her Majesty's police force.

Instead, she changed into dark blue trousers with a cotton shirt and wedge-heeled boots. There—dressed and ready for action. 'Morning.' She greeted Hesketh-Brown who was manning the front desk and looked as though he was ready for a good day's sleep.

'Hi,' he said back, understandably not mirroring her jaunty tone after such a night.

'Anything much to report—before you get some shut-eye?'

The traffic and pub incidents didn't take him long. They would be the responsibility of the uniformed boys anyway. Then he told her about the missing husband.

And like Danny, she didn't take it seriously. 'So…? What's the story?'

'Jadon Glover. Age thirty-two. Wife, Eve, rang in,' he stated. 'Her husband was expected home last night around nine. Never turned up. Still not back this morning. I've checked,' he added before she asked the inevitable. 'Mobile phone off. No sightings of the car.' He grinned. 'And it's the sort of vehicle that would be noticed.'

'Oh?'

'Mitsubishi Shogun Warrior. Black. And wait till you hear the reg.'

'Go on. Try me.'

'Ready for this?'

She laughed. 'It's too early for me and too late for you to play guessing games, Danny.'

'J4DON. Get it?'

'As you say,' she said, 'not a car to go unnoticed.' Her mind was quickening. 'Is there anything suspicious about this man's no show last night?'

Hesketh-Brown grinned and leaned across the desk. 'They've been married two years. According to his wife there's been no arguments, no disagreements. I wish,' he said.

'Hmm. Go on. I'm not getting much of a clue here.'

'He doesn't have any health problems. Not a drinker, not a gambler.' His eyes flicked up to hers. 'His wife says he's as reliable as clockwork. Never home late. She describes him as a perfect husband, Jo.'

She couldn't stop herself laughing. 'Perfect husband?' she echoed, rolling her eyes and recalling her own husband's bleary red eyes this morning. 'That's suspicious in itself. There's no such thing, Danny Boy.'

He yawned. 'Oh, yes there is,' he said. 'Ask my Betsy.'

'Exactly.' She couldn't resist pulling his leg. 'I rest my case.'

He gave yet another cavernous yawn. 'Well, it's over to you now. I'm off for some shut-eye, if Tanya will let me.' Tanya was his small daughter, a child who made her presence known at every occasion, according to her doting Daddy. He handed Joanna the note with Eve Glover's contact details and she took it without enthusiasm.

'Cheers,' she said.

Once in her office she dialled Eve Glover's number herself. The voice that responded was high pitched with anxiety tinged with disappointment when she realized it was not her husband on the other end.

Joanna took it gently. 'Mrs Glover, it's Detective Inspector Joanna Piercy here, Leek Police. I understand your husband's missing?'

It had been the wrong word to use. Eve Glover drew in a sharp breath. 'I wouldn't say that,' she said, panic making her voice tight and stressed. 'He should have been home last night around nine but…' She sniffed. 'He's not *missing* exactly.'

Joanna heaved a sigh. Tripped up by semantics. 'OK,' she said wearily. 'He hasn't turned up?'

'No.'

'Has he ever been so late—stopped out—before?' *Is this a habit?*

'No.' A pause. 'We've only been married for two years. Jadon's completely reliable. Never ever been late before. Not even half an hour late. I can't understand it.' Her voice was rising towards hysteria. 'And why is his phone off?'

'Maybe a dead battery?'

That didn't impress the wife. 'Please, listen to me. Something's happened to him.'

Joanna picked up on the note of desperation. 'Why do you say that?'

'Because it's so out of character. He's *never* late.'

Joanna began to wonder: *was* there something more to this?

'OK,' she said slowly. Her office door had opened and closed again. Korpanski had entered and was watching her, his antennae quivering, wondering what she was doing on the phone. 'I'll come over and see you later this morning, Mrs Glover. You'll be in?'

'Yes. Yes. I'll wait in for you.'

'Good. I'll see you later. Please let me know if he turns up.'

She put the phone down and looked up. 'Morning, Mike,' she said.

He grinned back at her. 'Hi, Jo.'

She studied her sergeant. He was looking really well these days. Hours at the gym gave him a muscular, beefy build, well suited to a detective. Loyal as a Staffordshire bull terrier, he was not only her colleague but also her good friend. And he looked extra happy today—almost glowing. His two children were rapidly growing up and his wife had a job with more sociable hours as a nurse so family life was making him contented. He and Ricky, his son, had a shared love of football and followed Stoke City in father-and-son bonding trips and Jocelyn, Mike's daughter, now a teenager, had the petite build of her mother and the dark good looks of her father. She was a stunner. Added to that, she had a sharp intelligence. Mike proudly boasted of her grades at school. Oh, yes, Joanna thought. Detective Sergeant Mike Korpanski was a happy family man these days. And there was more to come.

'You're not going to believe this,' he said, dropping into his chair and swivelling around to face her, grinning from ear to ear.

'Believe what?'

'Ricky's been offered a place at Birmingham University. Three Bs.'

'Wow,' she said. 'To do what?'

'French,' he said, laughing, 'of all things. There's nobody French in our family. I speak a bit but I'm no great linguist.'

'You managed OK with the French families in the autumn.'

'Just about but I can't even speak more than two words of Polish, to my dad's disgust. We're not good at languages in our family.'

She laughed too. 'Well, you are now. Ricky'll probably end up working for the EU, Mike,' she said, still laughing, 'if we're still a member state.'

He laughed too and it seemed a good work environment. Two happy detectives.

He finally came down to earth. 'So,' he said, 'anything exciting happening? Who were you talking to on the phone?'

She sidestepped his question by turning it into one of her own. 'Tell me, Mike,' she challenged, facing him. 'Is there such a thing as a perfect husband?'

'Besides me, you mean?'

She lifted her eyebrows in response.

'Well, I would have thought Levin,' he continued grudgingly, giving her a sly sideways look. Between the two men who were closest to her existed an uneasy truce. When they met they skirted around each other like wrestlers new in the ring preparing to lunge but never quite making contact.

'Levin,' she confided drily, 'was half sozzled on whisky last night when I finally got home.'

'Oh?' Korpanski looked up. 'Is that a habit he's going to develop?'

'I don't think so. He'd had to do a PM on a four-year-old and it'd upset him.'

'Funny,' he remarked. 'You don't think a pathologist would get upset at a post-mortem.'

'He does—when it's a child.'

'That little Rice guy?'

She nodded and he continued, 'I read a bit about it in the paper but I have to admit I turned the page over quickly. I hate reading stories like that.'

'Yeah. Nasty business.' She turned back to her computer. 'And we have enough to deal with here.'

'So what's all this about a perfect husband?'

Briefly she told him about the disappearance—unexplained—and the wife's assurance that this was out of character, that her husband was beyond reproach. 'I thought I'd go round there later, give Mr Glover a chance to turn up and make his excuses. Speak to her.'

Korpanski waited and finally she admitted: 'There was something in her voice, Mike. Something panicky as though she'd half expected something to happen. I just wondered why.' She glanced through Hesketh-Brown's notes. 'Financial advisor, married two years.'

'It's a good job we don't get called out for every husband who fails to arrive home,' Mike said grumpily. Always mercurial, his mood had quickly dampened.

'Just what I thought.'

'So what did you tell her?'

'Took down her details. What else could I do? Promised we'd go round there some time in the day and asked her to call if he turns up.'

'Yeah. That'll do.'

'So…' She searched through the computer. 'Nothing else much interesting happening, is there? We've nailed the garage owner. It's up to Trading Standards to take him to court. Apart from that Leek's getting quite law abiding.'

'Well, it won't last,' Korpanski said, positively gloomy

now and with one eye on Joanna. 'Rumour has it that the Whalleys are coming up for parole.'

'All of them?'

'More or less.' Mike's face changed. 'Mum and Dad I don't mind too much. They're just a couple of stupid burglars who pretty well always get caught. And Tommy—well, he's so stupid he'll never be much of a problem. Besides, his MO is so obvious you can always tell it's him. I ought to tell him not to bother to wear gloves—he leaves a trail of DNA all over the place.' He laughed. 'I practically know his bar code off by heart. No, it's Kath that I worry about. She's got a wicked streak in her that I find unnerving. She's plain nasty—the sort that sets cats alight by the tail. She nearly blinded that old lady—all for twenty quid. No...' Mike was shaking his head. 'She's bad.'

'I know.' Joanna sighed. 'We don't want her back on our patch.'

'Well, rumour says this is where she'll be heading, straight back to Leek—and you.' Korpanski's face was tight with concern. 'She's sworn vengeance on you, you know?'

'Yeah, I know, Mike, but there isn't a lot I can do about it, is there? This is my patch. My life. I can't move. Even if I did she'd follow me. Anyway, surely she's more likely to head for a big city: Manchester, Glasgow, London, Birmingham?'

'Let's hope so.'

She frowned. 'How come she's out after so short a time? She's only been in for what...'

'Eight years,' Korpanski supplied.

'Doesn't seem long for robbery with violence. She must be...early thirties?'

'Somewhere round there.' Korpanski half smiled. 'A social worker described her day-to-day life inside. She got a lot of sympathy and boy is she a good actress! She played the victim to perfection in the witness box. Did a really good job convincing the jury that *she* was the real victim.' He looked at her curiously. 'How come you don't remember all of this?'

She flushed. It had been in the days when Matthew was still married to Jane, his first wife. 'I think I was going through turbulent times, Mike,' she said quietly. 'I'd taken my eye off the ball for a bit.'

He nodded. 'Well, it all ended well, Jo, didn't it? I mean, you're a happily married woman now, aren't you?' He couldn't resist smirking.

Oh, for the days of a desk charged with missiles. She could have thrown a rubber at her sergeant. But these days there was little more than a mouse mat. No good at all.

So she contented herself with making a face at him and returned to the business of the day. 'So we're reduced to searching for errant husbands. There's bugger all else interesting going on. You're right. Leek is getting boring. Perhaps we should look forward to the release of the Whalleys. At least they'll give us something to do that's a bit more like proper police work than looking for the…' she wiggled her fingers in quotation marks, '…husband who didn't come home at night.'

'Yeah, we sure want a crime-wave from our burgling family,' Korpanski said sarcastically.

Joanna sighed and logged on to her computer. 'Well, we'd better get on with filling out statistics and crime reports on that nasty little pranger that happened on Brook Street yesterday. That guy, I can tell you, deliberately turned out from Aldi in front of the Ford Focus. A witness said he'd accelerated right into it. It's an insurance fraud so let's look into what else Billy the Basher's been involved in.'

It took them two tedious hours but in the end they had eight cases where William Arthur Stratton had been involved. Joanna frowned into the screen. 'I don't know this guy,' she said. 'Is he new to the area?'

'We've got a previous Stafford address.'

'So he's moved up here to create trouble in a new patch.' She grinned across at Korpanski. 'Forgetting, I suppose, that it's still Staffordshire. Maybe we should be paying *him* a visit instead of our mystified wife. Or, Mike, we can alert the insurance company and let them do all the hard work.'

'Sounds like a good idea to me.'

'And now…' she stood up and reached for her jacket, '… I suppose I'd better call round to Mrs Glover's and see what's happening.'

'Want me to come?' Korpanski was already on his feet.

'No, thanks, Mike. I'll take Phil Scott. He's coming up for his sergeant's exams so it'll be good training. You can speak to the insurance company and then I want you to dig around and find out why this guy is *not* a perfect husband.' She gave him a wicked leer. 'Find his flaws.'

'Yeah, all right. Sounds fun.'

But at the door, Joanna hesitated. 'I'll just ring her again. I don't want to drive round to…' she looked again at Hesketh-Brown's notes, '… Disraeli Place and barge straight into a domestic, a sheepish husband rolling in halfway through the morning.'

But the phone connected with an anxious voice and

when Joanna asked if her husband had turned up she said, in some distress, 'There's still no sign of him.'

'His mobile?' Joanna asked hopefully.

'Still straight through to answerphone. Mind you,' Eve Glover continued as though desperate for a rational explanation, 'he's not great at keeping it charged up.' She sounded as though she was trying to convince herself.

'OK. We'll be round.' Joanna put the phone down and jerked her head at Korpanski. 'Just look him up,' she said, 'before I head off.'

Korpanski blew his cheeks out and leaned back in his chair as he scanned through Hesketh-Brown's notes and searched on the computer. 'Name, Jadon Glover. Age, thirty-two. Works as a financial advisor in the Potteries. Where, presumably, Eve probably thought he was working last night. No police record apart from speeding over thirty miles per hour.' He grinned at her. 'And who, I wonder, hasn't got one of those? It'd be more suspicious if he was squeaky clean.'

But Joanna was distracted, already tracking towards a series of questions. 'I wonder if he often works late.'

Korpanski shrugged.

She continued, 'I'm not sure whether I'm suspicious at the description of him or just sceptical in general. Basically I think already that this man cannot be for real.'

Korpanski simply shrugged again.

'No children?'

He glanced back at the screen. 'No.'

She leaned forward. 'Hang on a minute,' she said. 'He works for?'

'Johnston and Pickles. Hanley. You already told me that.'

'I take it he hasn't turned up for work yet?'

'Just about to check.'

She frowned. 'You miss my point, Mike. Why didn't his *wife* ring his workplace?'

'Mmm.' He was alerted. He found the telephone number for Johnston and Pickles and dialled. But the conversation did not go as anticipated.

It began as expected with Korpanski introducing himself and asking if a Mr Jadon Glover was at work.

That was when the conversation changed. Joanna watched as Mike's shoulders stiffened. He glanced across at her, his eyes wide. 'What?'

Joanna's skin prickled.

Then: 'Are you sure?'

More words, then: 'Can you just check your records, please, sir?'

That produced an angry roar which even Joanna could hear. Every word. 'It's not exactly a forgettable name, is it? I *know* who works here.'

She watched, bemused, as Korpanski's face looked confused. Finally, after a polite apology, he ended the call.

'What was all that about?'

'Apparently,' he said, 'our missing financial advisor doesn't work at Johnston and Pickles at all.'

'What?'

Korpanski simply nodded.

So instead of heading out she paused in the doorway for some thinking time.

If asked, Joanna would have described the job of detective as being one that consisted of asking questions.

Questions unearth anomalies and lies. More interesting than the lies themselves could be the reasons *behind* the lies, if you could home in on them. Does there always have to be a reason? No. But… Whatever, this was lie number one. The perfect husband didn't work where he said he did. How many more lies would they unravel? Why had Jadon Glover lied about his place of work and did this have any bearing on his current disappearance?

To Mike, she said, 'This is beginning to sound a little more interesting. Let's put out a general search for the Mitsubishi and see if we can get a lead from that.'

Korpanski nodded. 'It's a start, anyway—give the lazy buggers in Traffic something to do.'

'Judging by the general congestion in the town and the problem they dealt with last night in Bottomhouse they're not exactly dying of boredom,' she responded. But privately she agreed with Hesketh-Brown, who was by now, hopefully, tucked up in bed and fast asleep, that it wouldn't be long before the vehicle was found. Strange, she reflected as she finally left the room, that a car is so much easier to find than a person. But there is no Automatic Number Plate Recognition for human faces. They are the proverbial needles in haystacks. Descriptions are vague. Medium height, medium build, brown hair, aged between thirty and forty. Last seen wearing…

It was not precise enough. They could melt into any crowd from John O'Groats to Land's End taking in London, Birmingham, Manchester and all the other big cities and small towns in between. With so many cameras acting like watchful public eyes it was likely they would find the car before the man.

But thinking was not going to find him. She needed action.

Three minutes later she'd picked up DC Phil Scott and was heading out of the station.

# FOUR

*Thursday, 6 March, 11.00 a.m.*

As SHE DROVE JOANNA asked DC Phil Scott to try Jadon Glover's mobile number one more time. She took her eyes off the road for a moment to smile encouragement at the young DC. There was something heartening about these young detectives still wet behind the ears but willing to have a go at preserving law and order in a changing world. 'Maybe he's turned up, tail between his legs, a lame excuse between his teeth and we can turn the car around and all go home.'

But Scott hit the same result, straight through to answerphone. Glover's phone was switched off so all he got was an irritating message. Scott looked at her, understanding that if Glover's phone was switched off they couldn't track him using Cell Site Analysis. However, clever though these gismos were, they weren't infallible. He left a message on Glover's answerphone anyway and the number of Leek Police Station. But, as he disconnected, Joanna had the oddest feeling: Glover never would be returning that call. It was the strangest feeling that the, '*Hi, this is Jadon Glover. Leave a message,*' would be all they ever heard of his voice. Already it sounded like a voice from the past. The voice of a dead man?

She shook herself. In this job there is no place for

spooks. And it wouldn't do DC Phil Scott any favours either. Feelings and superstition would not help him pass his sergeant's exams.

She pondered for a while, turning over the possibilities. And, like Hesketh-Brown the previous night, she ran through the same likely options…mistress, girlfriend, out with mates, drunk, car breakdown, accident, amnesia (not that she believed in that one). Then there were the other, stranger stories—less common and harder to pull off: John Stonehouse, Canoe Man John Darwin or, in fiction, Reggie Perrin, faking their own death only to reappear later. Phil Scott was watching her. 'What percentage of missing husbands are never found?'

'It's surprisingly high,' Joanna said, her hands on the wheel, stuck in traffic again. Leek, these days, was so congested maybe it would have been quicker if she'd come out on her bike, Scott jogging beside her. She smiled and turned her attention back to him. 'If they don't want to be found,' she said soberly, 'they usually aren't.'

But he pushed her. 'So you don't think anything bad's happened?'

She studied him. Young, keen. He'd make a good detective because, exams aside, he asked questions. That was why she'd requested his transfer to her. Besides, she liked him. With his habit of earnestly scribbling everything down he reminded her of herself a few years ago now.

'Put it like this, Phil,' she said. 'There are…anomalies in Jadon Glover's case.' Again, she fell silent, reflecting.

There were disappearances that never were solved,

people who simply vanished off the face of the earth, never to be seen again and no clue as to their fate. So which one of these would Jadon be? Had living up to the perfect husband image just got too much for him and he'd done a runner? Or would his lie about his job match up with another deceit—another woman or a man. Perhaps another entire family?

It was all possible.

She caught Phil Scott grinning and read the excitement in his eyes as his thoughts probably matched hers. He couldn't hide his pleasure at being asked to accompany her. Once she'd been like that. Now she'd grown up but she'd never quite lost her buzz.

And now they'd arrived at the small, modern development on the Ashbourne road, the road that ran due east out of Leek towards the high ground, Thorncliffe and beyond. The town was trying to creep into the surrounding moorland tortoise-slow so nobody noticed. But in the years since she'd been here, she had. No big developments, nothing too obvious or controversial. Lip service must still be paid to the sacrosanct green belt and the protection of the National Park less than five miles away, but here and there the odd field had been swallowed up to provide eight or nine smart houses, with the cheeky selling point that they were surrounded by some of the most beautiful and unspoilt countryside in England. But the muddy fields bordered with dry stone walls and the ancient trees and hedges had vanished to be replaced by nice houses for nice people, and with it some of the character of Leek was leaching away. One day, Joanna wondered, as she turned into Disraeli Place, would there be no moorland? No wild green lungs for the inhabitants to breathe? Well after her time, she hoped. Take away the moorland which cocooned Leek, wrapping it in wild country as though it was a precious pearl, and it would lose its identity to become just another small town. The same as any other.

Perhaps it had been as a means of pleasing the people and avoiding controversy that the few roads had all been named after prime ministers—hence Disraeli Place, Gladstone Avenue and Wilson Rise. There was no Thatcher Park, Joanna noted. That would have been a step too far, guaranteed to make furious headlines in the *Leek Post & Times*. Thatcher had been just too controversial, someone who polarized opinion, particularly among the largely Liberal moorland farmers and other businesses in and around Leek.

Number 8 Disraeli Place was as neat and well maintained as the other seven houses in Greenland's select development. Outside there was a matched pair of pink flowerpots sporting yellow pansies and purple crocuses and tarmac space for two cars. A navy Mini was parked to one side of the drive. The space for a second car yawned empty.

The door was opened as they pulled in and Eve Glover stood, waiting, on the doorstep.

Joanna had always had a problem with people who veneered their teeth and sported orange skin. It might look OK on television but in the flesh they looked like some sort of genetic mutation instead of real people. Apart from that Eve Glover was a petite, attractive woman of around thirty, long blonde hair with fashionable dark roots tied back loosely in a ponytail. She was wearing a pink V-neck sweater and tight-fitting skinny jeans with black leather pumps. She had a movie-star figure; curves everywhere. She was very attractive.

Joanna heard even DC Scott give the sort of guttural grunt that men make when they have to acknowledge a sexy, beautiful woman. The sound always reminded her of apes, particularly as she didn't think that men were aware they had made any noise at all. It was a sort of feral instinct. But, as Joanna faced Jadon Glover's wife, she wondered. Eve was attractive enough without morphing into something so bizarre. She was blessed by nature. Joanna studied her, searching for the woman beneath the veneer. Her face was perfectly made up but strained, her expression anxious. Her blue eyes were beseeching and puzzled and frightened. In spite of the fake suntan and teeth she looked a vulnerable innocent. A babe in the literal sense rather than someone streetwise.

'Mrs Glover.' Joanna flashed her ID card, introduced DC Scott and studied the woman further. 'Can I come in?'

Eve's shoulders twitched. 'Yes, yes. Come inside. Have you heard anything?' Her voice was Marilyn Monroe breathy.

Joanna shook her head and took it as said that Jadon Glover had not been in touch with his wife either.

Eve Glover led Joanna into a soulless room with a huge television and everything else beige. Sofa, carpet. Even the picture over the mantelpiece of one solitary dark red flower had a beige background. The place was spotlessly clean and smelt of fragranced candles or a plug-in air freshener—something every bit as artificial as Eve herself. Joanna looked around. The room was an enigma. There was no obvious sign of a male occupant. It seemed like a house whose sole inhabitant was a woman. It was as though Jadon did not live here, had no role here, no function and no personality either. It made him a curious void. An absence—someone difficult to picture. All Joanna had heard of him, so far, was a fairly brusque voice on an abrupt answerphone message. Even here, in what was supposed to be his own home, it was difficult to conjure up his physical presence. So, did this perfect husband spend so little time at home, with his new wife, that he left no mark? Or did he simply sit on a corner of the immaculate sofa and watch television with his equally perfect wife?

Joanna's frown deepened. Questions. As a detective, the minute you stepped inside a case there were never-ending questions, anomalies, hidden secrets. Questions with too few honest answers. In her experience everyone had *something* they wanted to hide. A public front behind which hid a truth they were anxious to keep hidden. Sometimes they were so anxious they would commit perjury—a further crime—simply to conceal evidence. And it all wasted police time and resources and provoked police suspicion.

DC Scott stood by the sofa and she sat down, opening the interview in neutral territory. 'I think it's best, Mrs Glover,' she said gently, 'if I begin by explaining what we do in cases like this, in general, rather than referring specifically to your husband's apparent disappearance.' She spoke very slowly and clearly, avoiding ambiguity, giving Eve Glover plenty of time to digest the content and ask questions before she continued, 'First of all, has he ever been missing before?'

Eve Glover winced at the word, steadying herself by studying the polish on her nails. 'No, Inspector,' she said heavily and deliberately. 'He has not.'

'Right.' Joanna paused. 'Was he on medication?'

Eve was too angry this time to do anything but shake her head.

'Any history of mental illness?'

'No.'

Joanna scooped in a deep breath. Mrs Glover was not going to like her next statement. 'Now then, obviously, while we are concerned about your husband's disappearance, the level of concern is not as high as if he were a vulnerable child or an elderly person.' She was going to keep the anomaly of her husband's workplace a secret for now, a hidden card up her sleeve.

Anger flashed through Eve Glover's eyes as charged as lightning. 'I think that's wrong,' she said, quickly suppressing the emotion with an effort by tightening her lips. She probably perceived, quite perceptively, that hostility would not further her cause.

Joanna continued, still in the same calm voice. 'We will of course search for your husband's car and continue trying his mobile phone. If necessary we'll gain access to his phone records. Now you can help us, Mrs Glover. But first I have to ask you some more questions.'

Eve Glover braced herself, hands either side pressing into the cushions, knees together, body tensed. 'Ask away,' she said. Then added as she leaned forward, 'You can *ask* what you like but I can tell you, Inspector, something very bad must have happened to my husband. Jadon loves me. *I* am his first priority.' Her words were delivered with the flourish of a bull fighter's cape. 'First and last. His instinct, *whatever* has happened, would be to come home. To me.' She was close to tears now but Joanna was intrigued by the word *whatever*. What on earth was going through this woman's mind? What horrid scenarios was she cooking up? She would have liked to have asked her whatever it was that she thought her husband might have done. Questioned her in more detail, put her under pressure, but as it was she needed to stick to the guidelines. She could practically *feel* Chief Superintendent Rush's dried-up talons sticking into her bones as he peered over her shoulder, checking whatever it was that she was doing. She couldn't afford to make any *more* mistakes.

'As I said,' she repeated, very calmly, 'there are certain questions I must ask. Have you any financial difficulties?'

Eve Glover looked surprised at the question. 'No. He had a good job.'

*Not working at Johnston and Pickles, he didn't.*

Joanna tucked the rogue fact away—for now, wondering where it would lead. 'Ah, yes.' She picked up. 'Where did you say he works?'

'Well, it's really his own company.' There was a hint of conspiratorial pride in Eve Glover's statement. 'Johnston and Pickles. Financial advisors. He's one of the directors,' she said, adding comfortably, with the first touch of humour they'd seen, 'Jadon is a financial advisor, Inspector Piercy. He wouldn't be a very good one if we had money worries ourselves, now, would he? No. Jadon is very good with money. We're comfortably off. No problems there.'

*Smug.*

Joanna tried not to let her eyes betray her and she didn't dare even glance at Phil Scott. 'How long has he worked there?'

'Since before we were married.'

'OK. And you say he had no health problems?' Joanna looked up. 'And was not on any medication?'

Eve Glover leaned right forward and locked her eyes into Joanna's to give her words emphasis. 'My husband is thirty-two years old,' she said. There was the glimmer of a smile and more than a hint of pride. 'He's as fit as a flea, Inspector. Goes to the gym at least twice a week.'

Joanna's ears pricked up. First place to start asking questions. You wouldn't believe how many romances start up alongside the running machine or the weights bench. No better place to admire or display a nice body. She kept her voice casually neutral to ask, 'Which gym?'

'Pecs.' That was when the first tiny note of doubt crept into Eve Glover's voice.

Joanna ignored it, her own mind too busy to be diverted. Will the real Jadon Glover please stand up? She was struggling to recognize his identity while at the same time mentally drawing up a list of where to begin her enquiries. Already she was intrigued.

She looked up. 'Pecs. Is that the gym on Southbank Street?'

'Yes.'

'Does he go on regular nights?'

Eve was answering more slowly now, weighing up her responses warily before responding. 'Usually a Monday and a Thursday. He's there for about two hours, generally comes home about nine thirty.' Joanna glanced towards the door wondering whether Phil Scott had, like her, picked up the note of doubt in Eve's voice, the first hint that maybe all in the garden was not newly mown grass and fragrant roses. But as quickly as the doubt had arrived it flew out of the window and Jadon Glover's wife recovered her confidence with a stunning smile.

Joanna waited, knowing she needed to ask the next question delicately.

'Has he ever stayed out overnight before?'

Eve simply tightened her lips and there was a blaze in the china-doll eyes. She'd already given her answer.

Joanna bulldozed forward. 'Does he have friends he might have stayed with, maybe if he'd had one over the limit so decided not to drive? A work celebration or something?'

The answer was predictably haughty and at the same time oddly dignified. Eve Glover sat up straight and met Joanna's eyes full on. 'That isn't Jadon, Inspector.' Her trust was touching. 'It isn't my husband. It isn't his way. When I say he is a perfect husband that's exactly what I mean.' Her eyes challenged Joanna. 'He's reliable, Inspector.'

Joanna was silent. She was going to get nowhere here. 'His business partners?'

She looked up at the pause which greeted the question, sensing something that Mrs Glover was not quite so certain of. Shaky ground? She almost repeated the question verbatim but instead changed it to, 'Have you rung his business partners?'

Eve Glover looked awkward. 'No,' she said flatly and Joanna's automatic response was why not? It was the obvious step. So why hadn't she?

She felt a familiar prickling along the back of her neck.

Eve supplied an answer of sorts. 'I don't have their numbers.'

Joanna was incredulous. *What?*

Her next was a trick question. 'You've rung his office?'

Again, there was a pause then a variation on the response. 'He doesn't like me bothering him at work.'

*I'll bet he doesn't. Because he doesn't work there.* Joanna was beginning to smell a stinking big rat somewhere and by the wary expression on DC Scott's face she suspected he shared the same feeling. This enigma, this paragon of husbands, wasn't ringing true. He'd been lying to his wife at the very least about his job. And what else? Did his wife suspect all was not as it seemed? Was that why she had been so twitchy and nervous when he had been late home, ringing the police after just five hours? Did she know her husband was deceiving her? Had she known this and wanted to close her eyes to it? Act blind? It was either that or she was naive enough to swallow his lies without the most basic of checks. Unless… Joanna's mind was tracking down another path. It was possible that she had rung the police to alert them to this anomalous man. Joanna smothered a smile. So many possibilities.

Call me a suspicious copper, Joanna thought, but I wonder what this guy really did do all day. Then she exhorted herself. Tread carefully, Piercy, or you're going to fall through thin ice. And God help you swimming around in freezing cold water without Colclough to throw you a lifebelt.

So she had to skirt around the lie Jadon Glover had told his wife. And that was what she knew so far. She kept her voice politely curious. 'Have you ever called in to the office to see him?'

'Oh, no…' Eve said, defensively adding, 'because he does quite a lot of calls—out to clients, you know. To their homes. He's not always there,' she finished lamely.

After the aggressive defence a sweet little confidence

came next, spoken with a shrug of the slim shoulders and a sugary smile. 'He's not really the sort to sit in an office all day.' Now she seemed to be apologizing, trying to get them on her side. Eyes wide open, explaining?

Joanna's thought was: so if he wasn't *that* sort what sort was he?

She was making mental notes of the responses and from DC Phil Scott's intense expression she could see that he was doing the same. There was a deep line between his brows as he puzzled over the exchange.

Joanna stopped asking questions for a moment, looked across at Eve Glover and wondered about her, about the real woman beneath the orange skin and perfect teeth and nails who was so incurious about her husband's life outside the home. So happy to accept him at face value. Never asking questions. How much did she know; how much did she care? She'd *never* been to her husband's place of work? Really? Never *rung* him at work? Again, really? Had rung the police when she was worried rather than wait for morning and check first with his colleagues or workplace? Didn't appear to have his workmates' or their partners' numbers. Why not?

For a loving wife Eve Glover was singularly incurious about the great big gaps in her knowledge of her husband's life. It was all *bloody odd*, Joanna thought. Surely your husband's workplace is the first place to start asking questions, particularly if his evening's events had been connected with his job. She frowned at something else that had snagged her from the beginning. Why had her first port of call been the police? Simply the hour? Or…?

She put the question to her. 'Why did you ring the

police rather than your husband's place of work—or his colleagues?'

The blue eyes flashed their warning signal again. *Don't go there.*

'It was the middle of the night. Besides, as I've just told you, Inspector,' she said impatiently, 'I don't have their numbers.'

'Right.'

It was no answer.

Put together with Jadon's apparent deceit her curiosity was pricked. Why the subterfuge? What had Jadon been hiding from his wife? Why? And, looking at Eve Glover, what in turn was his wife hiding from him?

She checked again. 'Can I just run over a couple of points with you, Mrs Glover?'

Eve turned towards her with a smile as enigmatic and unreadable as the *Mona Lisa*'s. Only not quite so guileless.

'Of course.'

'You've *never* been to your husband's place of work?'

'No.' The answer was flat and invited no challenge.

Joanna was incredulous and from the wary expression in DC Scott's eyes so was he. 'And your husband's work colleagues?'

'I've met them. They came to our wedding.' There was a defensive flicker in her eyes which Joanna couldn't interpret. She liked them? She didn't like them? Joanna couldn't pick up on which.

Considering the Glovers were an apparently devoted couple this was a curious setup. Alerting the police before checking with her husband's workplace and colleagues struck Joanna that this was like going to hos-

pital instead of seeing your GP. Which reminded her...
She bit her tongue and proceeded.

'Do you have the address of your husband's office?'

'Of course.'

She gave them an address in Hanley. Joanna's eyes
flickered over it. This was not the address Korpanski
had been contacting. It was not the address of Johnston
and Pickles. She frowned. Rather than being an object
of fun, a silly little distraction in an otherwise quiet day,
this was turning into a full-blown case. It had all the
hallmarks, anomalies and inconsistencies of something
much deeper. And the questions kept on pricking her.

Why had Eve been so convinced something awful
had happened to her husband when he had simply been
a few hours late home from work?

'When did you last speak to your husband?'

'Around six.'

'He sounded all right?'

'Yes. As normal. He sounded fine.'

'Why did you ring him?'

'Just to ask him to pick up a bottle of wine on his way
home. That's all. I thought he'd be back at nine and I
waited. I thought he'd ring, maybe say he'd broken down
or had an extra call to do. But he didn't. He'd said he'd
be home just after nine and that was it.'

'Had you cooked a meal for him?'

There was the first hint of embarrassment. 'Jadon's
very pernickety about food,' she said, looking away. 'He
usually does himself an omelette or a steak or something or gets a takeaway.'

'You don't eat together?'

Eve Glover smiled and shook her head. 'I tend to
eat earlier.'

Nothing more than 500 calories.

'Right. OK.'

Joanna bounced Eve's sweet smile back to her. 'Would you like to look for the names of your husband's colleagues and I'll find out their numbers? We'll take it from there.'

Eve left the room, returning with a notebook, and slowly and methodically copied out three names. Joanna took the sheet of paper from her. Eve Glover was, it appeared, dyslexic—unless one of her husband's colleagues had the unusual surname of Wolsin. There was someone called Stoc and another called Jitt. She looked up. Eve Glover quickly dropped her eyes, embarrassed.

'Sorry,' she said, took the sheet of paper back and very carefully copied out the names again. Leroy Wilson, Jeff Armitage and Scott Dooley.

That made more sense.

'Do you have a photograph of your husband we can borrow?'

'Yes.'

Eve delved into a drawer in the beige-painted sideboard. Wedding picture not up, Joanna noted. Not on display then? Unlike the wedding picture of her and Matthew, taken minutes after they had been pronounced man and wife. It stood proudly framed on their dresser, their arms around each other, laughing into the camera as though they had just shed all the cares in the world. She in her midnight-blue dress, the scatter of crystals flashing in the sharp winter sun and Matthew in a grey morning suit, grinning from ear to ear. He had what he wanted and it showed. His arm had encircled her. She smiled at the memory, returned to the present, focused on the job in hand and studied the picture Eve had just handed her.

Jadon Glover stood alone, in the centre of a patch of grass. Their garden?

Her first impression was that he matched the image she had started to build up of him. A good-looking guy with a confident smile, around thirty years old, a bit shorter than she had expected and very slightly stocky. His features were regular. He had nice teeth and very short dark hair. If it had been his wife who had taken the photograph Joanna sensed no affection bouncing back. His smile into the lens was ironic and impatient. Impatient for the picture to be taken. Impatient with the person who was clicking the shutter. Perhaps. He was standing up straight and self-consciously in a sleeveless vest, the muscles he'd worked for at the gym bulging. He stood half sideways, showing off a toned, heavily muscled body. He was confident of his image. He liked posing. There was more than a hint of mockery in his expression. Perhaps mockery for the wife he was so successfully deceiving—or not. How much did she really know?

Joanna studied his face closer for a moment or two, trying to gain some insight into his fate. What had happened to him? Where was he now? He looked like someone who could take care of himself. So why was he missing? Surely he must have known he risked exposing the tissue of lies he had fed his gullible wife? Why build them up in the first place? Why the duplicity? At some point he was going to get found out. He couldn't have kept up the deceit for ever.

If a picture is worth a thousand words and this photograph was a true portrayal, she didn't think she'd like him.

There was something weasel-like about his narrowed eyes, something cruel in his thin lips and something calculating in the expression. He looked too sure of himself. Men like that sometimes misunderstood situations, reading them as safe when they were not. And because they were unconscious of any danger around them they lost awareness. But the picture had told her two things: this man would make enemies, and if Jadon Glover remained missing there was a good reason. She looked up to see Eve watching her.

'Can I take this?'

'Yeah. Sure.' Eve Glover hesitated before asking what must have been filling her mind. 'Inspector…' She paused. 'What do you think's happened to him?'

'Most probably,' Joanna said slowly, 'nothing serious. He's just been held up, Mrs Glover. Perhaps an accident.'

It wasn't going to satisfy the devoted wife. And she wasn't that stupid either. 'But you said you'd contacted the hospital and he wasn't there. Besides…his phone,' she objected.

Joanna countered quickly, 'And *you* said that he was sometimes a bit careless. Left it out of charge. Maybe broken or stolen.' She tried to make light of it. 'You know how unreliable mobile phones can be, Mrs Glover—signals going down and batteries going flat, particularly when we're relying on them.'

Dissatisfied, Eve Glover gave a deep, heartfelt sigh.

Joanna felt some sympathy for her but at the same time the woman irritated her for her blind acceptance of her husband's porous stories. 'We'll run some checks,' she said again. 'And be in touch.'

Eve Glover didn't answer but narrowed her eyes as though evaluating Joanna's forced 'jollity'.

Joanna stood up. 'Well, I'd better get back,' she said. 'Here's my number. If anything happens let me know.'

Eve Glover smiled and responded politely if automatically. 'Thank you.'

'Will you be here or at work?'

'I don't work,' Eve said, again with a hint of that irritating smugness. 'I used to have a beauty parlour and hairdressing salon but I gave them up when we married. Jadon didn't want me to work. He likes having me at home.'

'Oh.' Again it was a strange insight into an unusual twenty-first-century marriage. Joanna stood up, shook Eve Glover's hand, promised to keep in touch and asked that she do the same. And they left.

Joanna quizzed DC Scott on the way back to the station. She wanted to see how much he'd picked up on the interview.

'So what did you think, Phil?'

'I think it's an odd setup,' he said, 'but some blokes do like to keep their mates and their work life separate from their private life, don't they?'

'Korpanski's been in touch with Johnston and Pickles,' she said. 'They deny that our Mr Glover even works there. And the business addresses are different, Phil. Near enough but not the same. So if Jadon Glover didn't work at Johnston and Pickles, where do you think he might have worked? Why would he lie to his wife?' She wanted to challenge the detective, see how much he could work out for himself.

'Some guys just do lie,' Scott said, smiling a little

sheepishly. 'Pretend they're brain surgeons when they just dig the road.'

She smiled too. Matthew had never had to pretend anything. She'd known from the start what his job was.

'So where would you go from here, Phil?'

He responded cheerfully. 'I don't know.'

'OK. What about we have a look at the list of Glover's work associates? We have a Leroy Wilson, Jeff Armitage and Scott Dooley. We'll have a go at their numbers when we get back to the station. OK?' She decided to set DC Scott a further challenge. 'What do *you* think's happened to Mr Glover, Phil?'

He shrugged. 'Done a runner, I think.'

'OK—think that one through. What do you do now as an investigating officer?'

He gave her a swift, uncomfortable glance. 'Look into his life, friends—bank account, gym membership, car, stuff like that.'

'Good,' she said. They'd turned into the station car park. 'So get on with it. Work with DS Korpanski.'

Back in the office she could speak freely to Mike. 'Weird,' she said. 'Glover's wife doesn't ring his work colleagues or his place of work. And you say he doesn't even work at Johnston and Pickles?'

'Not according to the CEO.' He grinned at her. 'And you'd think he would know.'

She laughed. 'So what have you found out so far?'

'The car hasn't turned up yet. He's not short of funds. No criminal record. Nothing really.' He looked at her.

'Bank cards? Has he been withdrawing money?'

'Not in the last twenty-four hours and his mobile records show that his last call was received at about

six yesterday evening. Looks like he was on the out-
skirts of Leek.'

'That fits in with his wife's account that she rang
him to ask him to pick up a bottle of wine.'

'I'm guessing that's why she was so angry when he
was late. Never a good idea to keep a lady waiting for
her vino.'

'Is that a dig at me, Korpanski?'

'Perish the thought.' But Korpanski looked interested. 'What's she like?'

'Just your sort or any man's. Very glammed up.'

Korpanski raised his eyebrows but made no further
comment.

She reached for the phone. 'So let's try his buddies.'

They all went straight through to answerphone. Joanna left messages on all three, sat back and looked at
her sergeant.

'So where's his car?'

Korpanski shrugged. 'We've nothing on it so far.
Come on, Jo,' he said gruffly. 'It could be anywhere.
*He* could be anywhere. Not even in the country.'

'Well, we've got no reason to detain him. Being
home a bit late is hardly a case for Interpol.'

She looked at her sergeant, mischief in her eyes,
stared at the screen for a moment, then: 'Mi-ike.'

He knew that wheedling tone.

'I know we can find out stuff from the PNC,' she
said, 'but I feel far too fidgety to just sit in front of a
computer all afternoon.'

His response was guarded. 'What are you suggesting?'

'Why don't we go to Johnston and Pickles? See what
they've got to say. We've got an address. They're just

round the corner from each other. We can go into his real office and kill two birds with one stone. Come on, Mike, let's go.'

Korpanski, similarly happier active than sitting at a desk, was already on his feet. They commandeered a car and tried to convince themselves this was work and they weren't simply playing hooky.

# FIVE

*Thursday, 6 March, 12.10 p.m.*

THEY WERE HALFWAY to Hanley when her mobile phone rang, caller ID one of the three numbers on her list. '*Leroy,*' Joanna mouthed when she read the contact. 'Hello, Detective Inspector Joanna Piercy here. Mr Wilson?'

Leroy grunted. 'What's this about?' The voice was suspicious. Wilson was already on his guard.

Joanna wasn't going to tell him straight away. She grinned at Korpanski, inverted her outstretched hand, pressed her thumb and forefinger together and wiggled them as though she was a puppeteer. Thinking: I've got you dangling on a string. 'We understand you work with a Mr Jadon Glover?'

'Yeah.' He sounded guarded.

'Where exactly *do* you work?'

'We've got our own business.' He sounded Afro-Caribbean with a hint of Birmingham.

'Together with Scott Dooley and a Mr Jeff...?'

'Armitage,' he supplied reluctantly.

'Yes. *Jeff* Armitage.'

Mike was watching her.

At last Leroy showed some concern. 'Look, what is all this about?'

Joanna ignored the question. 'What exactly is the nature of your business, Mr Wilson?'

'Financial advice,' he supplied. Then added quickly, 'Mainly to do with debt.'

'Associated with Johnston and Pickles, the Hanley firm?'

'Sort of,' he said.

She knew that heavy, groaning sigh. She was going to have to drag it out of him. 'How sort of?'

He wasn't going to tell her. Instead, he got stroppy. 'Look,' he said, 'what *is* all this about? Why are you harassing me?'

Joanna almost groaned. Not the old harassment card—per-lease.

'Mr Glover, your fellow *financial advisor...*' she knew the sarcasm in her voice would elude him but pressed it in anyway, 'didn't quite make it home last night; neither has he turned up this morning. His wife is naturally anxious.'

Leroy's response wasn't quite what she'd expected. He didn't even affect concern but gave a loud, sceptical guffaw. 'He's a big boy,' he said. 'He can look after himself.'

'Well, we'll see about that, won't we? Do you have any idea where he might be?'

'Not a clue.' He wasn't simply unconcerned—he was bored.

'If he doesn't turn up soon we'll be in touch again, Mr Wilson.'

'Yeah. Right.' And he ended the call.

'Well, Mike,' she said, 'we'd better just wait and see what happens.'

Mike was focusing on manoeuvring his way through the traffic.

'I'll ring Mrs Glover again,' she said after a few minutes. 'See if Jadon's reappeared.'

But this time there was no answer from her phone either—not her landline or mobile. If her husband was still missing she wasn't exactly waiting in for him. Or did this mean that he had turned up? Joanna gave Mike a swift, puzzled glance. He simply shrugged, grinned and focused on his driving. She tried Jeff and Scott's numbers again. No answer from either of them.

In fact, the three buddies were having a discussion in their offices in Hanley.

Leroy was scowling. 'So what the heck's going on, man?'

The other two shrugged.

'Where's he gone off to?'

Again this drew no answer.

Leroy's face changed. 'How much money did he have on him?'

'Depends.' Scott was a big guy and a man of few words.

'Yeah, depends on what?' Jeff's sour character had distorted his features years ago so his face was fixed in a permanently asymmetrical sneer.

Scott was undeterred by the challenge. Of the three of them, although his thought processes were slow, he was actually the most intelligent. Jadon had been their smarmy front-line man. Good with the clients. Convincing. Suited and booted, in designer shades, his bullying Mitsubishi with heavily tinted windows and bull bar, he had acted the part of a New York heavy when really he'd been nothing like it. Inside Jadon was a wimp and the others had known it.

Scott was the one who could work out the exact finances down to the last percentage, the last penny. 'I'll tell you what it depends on, Jeff,' he said. 'It depends on how far he'd got with his round. If he'd finished maybe eight, nine hundred quid?'

He spent a moment calculating, his head nodding as he totted up the numbers and revised his estimate. 'It wouldn't have been more than a thousand. Not enough to justify doing a runner unless he'd been salting stuff away for a bit, or else he had bigger plans,' he finished slowly. Scott was the one with the brains. He was also the most suspicious. A product of a violent home and youthful abuse, he had no faith in human nature. Absolutely none. Zero to minus.

Jeff spoke next, his eyes narrowed. 'Did you talk to Eve, Leroy?'

'Yeah, I did.' Leroy Wilson spoke quickly, jerkily. 'As soon as the detective got off the line. I rang her. Asked her what was going on.'

Scott showed curiosity. 'What did she say?'

'Nothing. She just burst into tears.' Far from being sympathetic, his expression was one of disgust.

Neither of his two colleagues had anything like an appropriate response to this either so after a pause Leroy held his hands up. 'I tell her, you go out shoppin' for a bit.' He looked at his two mates. 'Well, that's what works for women, innit?'

Jeff and Scott rolled their eyes. They didn't think much of this plan.

It was Jeff who started to move forward. He gritted his teeth. A small man with a naturally sour and paranoiac nature, he trusted no one. And that, in this business, was a virtue.

'We need to find him, don't we?'

Scott laughed, tipping back in his chair. 'We can let the police do that. They're on the job.'

The other two simply shrugged and Scott continued, 'Let's be practical. One of us has got to take up the round,' he pointed out reasonably. 'We can't let them get away with it. It's our living. We can't afford to lose money ourselves.'

'So, what's happened to him?' Jeff Armitage looked at each of his buddies in turn. Leroy's response was typically confrontational. 'What do *you* think's happened to him?'

They looked at one another.

'He has to have done a runner,' Jeff said, but with hesitation.

Scott was scornful. 'You think? You really think?'

Jeff dropped his eyes and looked uncomfortable.

THEY TOOK THE ring road round Hanley. Mike was fishing. 'So what's she like?'

'Who?' Inwardly she was smirking. She knew perfectly well who her sergeant was referring to.

'Eve. Mrs Glover.'

'You'd like her,' she said, meeting his dark eyes. 'She's glamorous, an ex-beautician. Petite. Very pretty, actually. Perma-tan and pearly white teeth.'

Korpanski played up to the role. 'Oh. So when do I get to meet her?'

Joanna turned to look at him. 'Soon,' she said, 'unless her devoted husband turns up.' She was silent for a moment, her mind working through the sparse facts she knew about their missing man.

'Mike,' she said, 'which gym do you go to?'

'The Fit Factory. I thought you knew that. Why?'

'Our missing husband was a member of Pecs.'

'That place?' Korpanski snorted. 'Full of psychopaths pumped up on anabolic steroids.' He was chortling to himself. 'The only reason it hasn't been raided is if it was it'd be closed down and then you'd have a load of psychos at a loose end five nights a week.'

'I see.'

Joanna wondered whether that described their missing man. Not a perfect husband but a psycho?

But she had no time to ponder that point. They'd arrived.

Johnston and Pickles was a smart, square, modern and characterless building on the edge of Hanley. Purpose built and easy to find with plenty of free parking all around for clients and the threat of an expensive wheel clamp for anyone misusing the privilege. The board announced its business modestly with a small and unobtrusive sign advertising 'Accountancy and Financial Management'. Everything about the building and its ambience was uninspiring, as anonymously beige as the house in Disraeli Place. But then, Joanna supposed, maybe it was better if accountants and financial managers weren't too flashy but merged into the background without attracting attention from HMRC or anyone else for that matter. She pushed open the door.

Surprisingly the person behind the front desk was not a glamorous young woman but a youth—maybe aged twenty—in a chain-store suit with Justin Bieber hair who rose as they approached. 'Can I help?' His manner was guarded. He'd already sussed out they were police.

Joanna flashed the Open Sesame ID card and he flushed. Instinct confirmed.

'Can we speak to your CEO?' Korpanski asked bluntly. 'Just for a minute.'

Joanna was watching him carefully. His fingers on the telephone keypad were not so much shaking as vibrating. He was either pumped up on too much caffeine or he was nervous about something. Just the presence of the police?

But Joanna had met this before—people who had a guilty conscience even though they were innocent. It didn't necessarily mean anything. But still...

The youth spoke quietly into the phone, hand over his mouth, eyes fixed on them both as though they were likely to nick the vase of flowers that sat on the desk. 'It's Simon, sir. Front desk. The police are here.' Well, at least the lad was brief. He flicked his glance over Joanna and Mike. 'Couple of detectives,' he added. 'They're asking to see you, sir.'

Something was barked down the phone and the youth responded. 'Yes, sir.'

They noticed the CEO had not asked what a couple of detectives wanted to see him about. A lack of curiosity or did he already know?

'He'll be down in a minute.' His training must have kicked in then. He smiled at them, the charm switched on to max. 'Can I make you a drink or something?'

'A coffee would be lovely,' Joanna said. Give the kid something to do. Mike merely nodded.

The next few minutes were taken up with the supplying and drinking of coffee from a machine served in Styrofoam cups. But the flavour wasn't bad.

The CEO of Johnston and Pickles was much as expected, plump but brisk, in a smarter suit than his office boy, with thinning hair, a wide smile and anxious eyes.

'Karl Robertson,' he said, holding his hand out for a firm handshake. 'Do you want to come to my office?'

'Thank you, sir,' Joanna answered politely. No point antagonizing him.

Like the CEO himself, Robertson's office was much as expected. Top-of-the-range computer and an abstract painting on the wall—a blur of greens, blues and reds. A phone, cream walls, beige carpet and a lovely view over the hilltop centre of Hanley on the horizon completed the picture. Joanna crossed to the window, picking out two stumpy bottle kilns. Robertson picked up on her appreciation of the view. 'Shame there aren't more of those left,' he said. 'Would give the city a bit more of a unique identity.'

She turned back to face him. 'Yes. It would.' For the briefest of moments there was a connection. They were not police officer and potential informant but two people who could appreciate the city's heritage.

Then abruptly the atmosphere cooled. Robertson settled behind his desk and Mike and Joanna perched on two black leather armchairs opposite. Now there was no mistaking their roles. They were CEO and police. Robertson leaned forward ever so slightly, conspiratorially, almost indulgently. 'Now what *is* all this about?'

'Do you know a Mr Jadon Glover?'

Robertson looked annoyed. 'No, I don't,' he said. 'I've already been asked that. I don't know the man.'

Korpanski shifted slightly in his chair and Joanna

flipped the photograph on to the desk. 'This is Mr Glover,' Joanna said. 'Do you recognize him?'

Robertson did her the courtesy of looking carefully at the photograph before shaking his head. 'Nope,' he said with certainty, looking up now. 'I don't recognize him.'

'He claimed to work here.'

There was a pause before Robertson asked the obvious question. 'Why would he pretend that?' His frown could have been interpreted as puzzlement or it could simply be an affectation. It gave Joanna time to provide some alternative answers to herself.

To hide what he really did? Why would he do that? And why pick on this little mouse of a business? Purely because it was geographically near to his real base? Or was there some other reason?

She studied Robertson and wondered. Was there a connection between the two?

Not having received an explanation, Robertson was frowning. 'I know all my employees,' he said, a crisp challenge in his voice. 'This isn't a big firm.' He couldn't resist tacking on a small plug. 'Although we do handle a great deal of important business. This man,' he jabbed at the picture with an aggressive forefinger, 'does not work here, I can tell you. He is not on the firm's payroll.' Then something else struck him. 'What is your interest in him?'

'He appears to have gone missing,' Joanna said.

'Well, I'm sorry,' Robertson said tightly, 'but I can't help you.'

Joanna was about to get up, thank the man and take their leave but surprisingly Mike spoke up. 'Do you know *Eve* Glover?'

'No,' he said quickly. 'Should I?'

'She's this man's wife.'

Robertson shifted in his chair, hinting that it was time for them to go. 'I'm sorry,' he said. 'This seems to have been a bit of…'

Joanna anticipated. 'Not a bit of it,' she said. 'We just thought we'd check up, you know.'

'Quite, quite. Well, I'm sorry I can't help you but…'

His face changed. Froze. 'Wait a minute,' he said. 'Eve Glover wouldn't be Eve Sutherland, would she?'

Korpanski spoke out of turn. 'I don't know her maiden name. Why?'

'Possibly,' Joanna said, caution in her voice.

'If it is her she used to have a hairdressing salon and beauty parlour in Russell Street, Leek,' he said. 'A few years ago now. She used to do *my* hair.' He looked a little sheepish. 'When I had a little more. And she did my nails. I think she sold up just about the time she got married.' His eyes narrowed. 'So you mean that this'— slight pause—'Jadon is Eve's husband?'

'It's possible, sir.'

Joanna shifted in her seat. The long arm of coincidence? The short arm of something else or the beginnings of a sticky snail-trail?

She gave Mike a swift, grateful glance. They had established a connection between Mr Jadon Glover and the firm of Johnston and Pickles. Admittedly through his wife and it was a pretty tenuous one—hair and nails…she must have had lots of clients—but it was a definite connection and it interested her.

'You haven't seen her since her marriage?'

'No. I've had to go somewhere else…' another embarrassed smile, '…for my beauty treatments.'

Joanna resisted the temptation to smile at the image. 'Right.'

'Is there anything else you can think of that might help us find the missing husband?'

Robertson shook his head.

As they were leaving the accountants Joanna touched Mike's shoulder. 'So where did that bit of inspiration come from?'

He looked sheepish. 'His nails.'

She stared at him, astonished. 'And since when have you made a study of men's manicures?'

His response was a loud, slightly embarrassed guffaw. 'You're not the only one who notices things, puts two and two together and makes five, you know, Jo. I put his tidy appearance together with what you told me about Mrs Glover. Anyway, I hit gold, didn't I?'

'You certainly did,' she said. 'Well done, you. But the thing is, Mike, who *is* Jadon Glover? What's his real job? Why has he gone missing? Where is he?'

'Oh, just a few questions, Jo,' he mocked. 'Nothing too much, eh?'

For answer she gave him a wicked grin. 'Shall we take a look at Jadon's *real* offices, Sergeant?'

But they proved hard to find. They cruised along the street, past closely packed terraced houses, a few foreign food shops and a newsagents, but nothing proclaimed any business premises. It was invisible.

Joanna rang Leroy from the car. This time he picked up straight away and recognized her number. 'Inspector.' His tone was polite. Wary.

'I'm in your street.'

'Ah.'

'Where exactly are you?'

'In my office.'

'Which is?'

He gave a little chuckle. 'Park by the Chinese food shop. Turn to your right and walk back down the street a hundred yards. Do you see a doorway painted black?'

'Yes.'

'Then come straight up the stairs. We'll see you in a minute.'

They walked and found it. Unobtrusive, almost furtive, painted black as Leroy had described, set back from the street, hidden from view. Nothing on the door to advertise what was inside.

It led to a steep, narrow staircase, poorly lit. The door at the top had frosted glass and a light was visible beyond. Again, no business title. She knocked and pushed it open without waiting for an answer, Mike right behind her.

They were in a surprisingly spacious office, a big dormer window at the end with, like Johnston and Pickles' offices, a panoramic view over the untidy city: rows of steely roofed terraced houses, a couple of stumpy bottle kilns and the spire of St Martin's Church recently saved from demolition. Hanley rose up in front of them. Three pairs of eyes regarded them.

Leroy was a handsome big black guy with dreadlocks. Obviously Afro-Caribbean—very striking and memorable. He had a beautiful wide grin stuffed full of big white teeth, set in a face full of fun and merriment. It was hard not to like him. Not so hard not to trust him. Behind the giggles was a formidable scowl and a hard stare. Something cruel lay behind the laughter. He was the sort of guy who would laugh all the time he was kicking or punching.

Joanna turned her attention to the other two. Jeff Armitage proved to be less charismatic: a skinny, mean-lipped and shifty-eyed guy with a suspicious manner and a twist to his mouth while Scott—well, Scott was just big and beefy with a large pot belly and surprisingly perceptive eyes. All were superficially polite, standing as they entered the room. Joanna wondered where exactly Jadon had fitted into this bunch of ne'er-do-wells.

Leroy seemed to take the lead initially. 'Inspector Piercy,' he said, holding out his hand and with a quick glance to the other two. 'Nice to meet you.'

Korpanski took up his usual stance, arms akimbo by the door as though he was expecting trouble: one of them trying to escape. He looked like the genie of the lamp, waiting for it to be rubbed and given his instruction. Joanna communicated with a swift look. DS Korpanski looked uncompromising. No one was going to get past him.

'OK,' Joanna perched on the desk, crossed her legs and addressed them collectively. 'I don't know quite where to start,' she said, pursing her lips. 'What is all this about? Where's your colleague? Why have you hidden your business behind Johnston and Pickles? Why is there no name on the door? Why did Jadon lie to his wife about his place of work and his job? Why conceal your address and what is your true business?'

The three looked at each other as though wondering who was to answer the flurry of questions. After a minute or two Leroy sucked in a deep breath. 'We ain't done nothing illegal,' he protested.

'We'll be the judge of that.'

In the end it was Scott Dooley who started answering in a surprisingly cultured accent. 'Jay didn't want to tell Eve what he really did.'

'Because?'

'He thought saying he was an accountant would give him a bit more status.'

'Than?'

Scott drew in a deep, wheezy breath. 'You could say,' he said pleasantly, 'that we're sort of financial managers.'

Joanna didn't have time for this. 'What are you?'

'Sort of payday lending,' Leroy said with a broad grin.

'Doorstep lending?' It was Korpanski who'd spoken with a hint of anger and accusation in his voice.

Leroy stared him out. 'It's all perfectly legal, Sergeant.'

'Yeah.' Korpanski took a threatening step towards them. None of them backed off. They were a tough load of old chickens.

Joanna continued, 'So you have clients who owe you money and whom you charge exorbitant interest rates. Where was Jadon off to on Wednesday night?'

'He would have been doing his regular round, collecting from the clients.'

'The same ones every Wednesday?'

'Yeah.'

'I'd like a list.'

Scott shuffled his feet. 'Uuumm.'

Joanna was not in the mood for playing games. 'Is there a problem with that?'

'No. No. I'll sort it.' For a big guy, his movement was quick and agile.

'How many clients do you have round Leek?'

'Forty, fifty—somewhere round there.'

'And altogether?'

'Phooph.' Leroy blew his cheeks out. 'Thousands, Inspector, love. Leek, Hanley, Burslem, Stoke, Fenton, Longton and all the areas round about. The Potteries and Leek are not exactly Mayfair, you know. People need money.' He spread out his big hands. 'Things are expensive and wages aren't exactly high round here. You're lucky if you get the bloody minimum.'

'Right. And I suspect you have eye-watering interest rates?'

It was Armitage who responded to this in a wheedling tone. 'We got to make a living.'

'OK. So where is Jadon?'

The three looked at each other.

'Truth,' Joanna prompted.

'We don't know.' Scott had decided to play honest with them.

'Did he have a mistress?'

'You must be joking.' Leroy was quick to defend his chum. 'He was devoted to Eve. They'd only been married…'

'Two years,' Korpanski supplied.

'Yeah, so no, he was not playin' around.'

'Would he have been carrying a lot of money last night?'

Scott averted his gaze, obviously uncomfortable at the question. 'Depends what you call a lot,' he mumbled.

Joanna took a step nearer Scott. 'Don't play funny games with me,' she warned.

'Under a grand,' he supplied quickly.

'Has he been fiddling the books?'

'We're checking up but we don't think so.'

'Have any of your clients threatened him?'

All three shook their heads. Scott supplied the truth. 'Goes with the job a bit. Nothing serious.'

'Right, so from you,' Joanna said, 'we want his likely movements last night and then a list of the clients he would have been visiting. All right?'

It was Scott Dooley who nodded for them all.

On the way back to the station they decided to keep the known connection between the missing man's wife and Johnston and Pickles to themselves—just for now. It possibly had nothing to do with the situation but in Joanna's mind coincidence was a rare occurrence. Her curiosity had been well pricked. The real question was what did it have to do with Glover's disappearance? If anything?

Korpanski was still chewing over Glover's deceit regarding his career. 'I suppose an accountant does sound a bit better than a blood-sucking leech.' To her surprise he suddenly grinned. 'Sometimes blokes do want to make out they're more important than they are.'

She turned to look at him and registered an unusual sight. Korpanski blushing? Now that was worth a picture. In colour.

'In my youth I've been a brain surgeon a couple of times,' he admitted.

Joanna burst out laughing. She couldn't imagine anyone looking or sounding less like a brain surgeon than Detective Sergeant Mike Korpanski. Well-muscled and bull-necked, even if his tattoos had been covered up no one would swallow the fable that he was a brain surgeon. Copper was written all over him right down to his size eleven feet. She recalled Phil Scott's take on the situation, reflected how they had both gone down that road and lied about their careers. Then she remembered something else. 'When I was about fourteen I did meet an astronaut at the local club.' He had been shorter than she, pimply and pale, very unhealthy looking. Maybe he really had been orbiting the earth for a few weeks.

'But you weren't married to him for two years,' Mike pointed out.

'No. That might have been a bit more difficult to keep up.'

'Exactly.'

'At least I knew what Matthew did for a living.'

Korpanski hesitated before he responded, 'But you didn't know the most important thing about him, Jo.'

'Which was?'

'That he was married.'

She was silent. She hadn't *known* it—not for certain—but she had guessed. Married men have a certain stamp on them but she hadn't pursued the subject. She had kept her blinkers firmly fixed on either side of her eyes, ignoring anything on the periphery of her chosen field of vision.

'Well, whatever we think of doorstep money lenders there's a place for them today. Jadon Glover was obviously making a reasonable living—his wife not working, nice house, expensive car. What's to be ashamed about? Do you really think Eve would have cared how he put the bread on the table or the wine in her glass?'

'I don't know, Jo.' Korpanski was trying his hardest not to sound aggrieved. 'I haven't met her.'

'Yet. Don't worry, Mike,' she said. 'If her husband doesn't turn up you almost certainly will.'

They were turning into the station car park when Joanna spoke again. 'There is another alternative,' she said. 'That it wasn't simply the money lending that's led to his disappearance. Maybe our Jadon was doing something *else* underhand or illegal.'

'Like what?'

'I don't know—drugs or something.'

'Or maybe he knew his wife would disapprove of money lending even if it wasn't illegal.'

'And you think that's the solution? That she found out what he did, didn't like it and he didn't dare come home? I don't think so, Mike,' she said sceptically. 'I don't think that's why he's gone AWOL. For now I'm sitting on the fence, hovering between nothing's happened to our man and he'll walk back into his wife's life with minimal explanation and we can let whatever it is go and get back to our policing.'

They had finally battled their way through the congestion that always seemed to typify Leek these days. Maybe they did need a bypass. The debate would swing on and on maybe never reaching a conclusion. In the meantime, the residents and visitors to Leek would continue to sit and fume in the traffic. What an appropriate verb.

The first thing Mike did when they returned to the station was ring Eve Glover again. But even from across the other side of their office Joanna could hear the tone of the conversation and knew that Jadon, wherever he was, was not at home. She left the room to have a chat with some of the other officers. When she returned, Korpanski was putting the phone down, looking awkward. 'I, er…'

She faced him. 'Let me guess,' she said, her arms folded. 'You've agreed to go round and comfort her. Mike,' she said, 'we haven't got anything to give her except the fact that her husband's been lying through his teeth about where he works and appears to have vanished. Now why would you want to spend time visiting someone with nothing to give her? Huh? Except that you can't wait to meet her?'

'I just thought I'd check her out.'

'Because?'

He shrugged. 'Well, from what you say she's every man's fantasy.'

She smiled.

'I just thought I'd check her out, *Inspector, love*.' He managed to pull off Leroy's accent to a 't' and it made her smile. Then she moved on. 'Haven't we found his car yet?'

'Don't look like it.'

'Then we need to keep looking,' she said wearily.

Across the moorlands, beyond the barren hills, damp, mossy ground and empty landscape, a cottage stood stark and neglected against the grey sky. The wind whispered softly through gaps in the windows, entering cold rooms and empty bedrooms, stirring the vegetation outside in what had, until a few months ago, been a well-tended garden. Dividing the plot was a row of concrete stepping stones which led to an outside privy. The door rattled a little in a slight breeze. Chilly air moved around. A plank of wood dropped to the floor, startling a brown rat into watchful alertness.

# SIX

*Friday, 7 March, 8 a.m.*

MONICA PAGETT WAS lying in a hospital bed thinking over
the unwelcome news that had been given to her that
morning. She could hardly bear to think it. She closed
her eyes, closer to tears than she had been for many
years. Ninety-five years old and life had been reduced
to this? If she could have she would have stamped her
foot. But that was denied her.

'I'm sorry, Mrs Pagett.' It was a deputation of a
nursing-home owner, social services and the consultant under whose care she had been since the fall had
broken her hip two months ago.

The consultant had been kind but his words had not
been. 'You're going to need residential care.' Politely
he had waited while she absorbed his words.

And she had. 'You mean I can't go home,' she said
bluntly.

The woman from the SS had spoken next. 'In such an
isolated house and with such…' she paused delicately,
'…basic amenities. We've taken a look there. Done an
assessment. Even your toilet is outside.'

Monica protested. 'I've managed with that all my
life.'

'Not with a broken hip.' This time it was the man-
ager of the care home who spoke.

Monica looked from one to the other and read only a steely kindness in their faces. But they didn't understand her character. She was a tough moorlander. She'd been stuck behind snowdrifts, waited for hours in the rain for a bus that never came, lived on food dug from frosty ground and broken the ice to draw water from a well when the pipes were frozen. 'And if I refuse?'

The consultant drew in a long, reluctant breath. 'We have a few options,' he said. 'We could refuse to discharge you. We could detain you under Section Five, the nurses' holding power. Or...' his blue eyes were as transparent as the sea, '...we could let you go with some support and see what happens. But I don't recommend that.'

'Why not?'

It was turning into a challenge. 'Because you could be stuck in bed, fall, hurt yourself and lie there for days. We can have carers come in.' He stopped. 'Look, Mrs Pagett, you're a tough and independent lady. I respect that. But I have experience of what can happen in cases like this. Why don't we reach a compromise? Initially go to the residential home for a month. See how you go and we'll reassess after your hip has healed and you've had some physiotherapy.'

She'd looked at him sharply. Oh, he was a clever one.

And she'd had no option but to agree.

JOANNA KNEW AT some point she would have to speak to her Chief Superintendent, Gabriel Rush. She planned to give Jadon twenty-four hours to see if he turned up or, alternatively, if anything happened to arouse their suspicion, but she still hesitated. In the old days she would have gone straight to Chief Superintendent Ar-

thur Colclough. They would have discussed the likely
possibilities and formed a plan together. But Gabriel
Rush was a different kettle of fish. He lacked a sense
of humour. They'd had a shaky start and things hadn't
got much better. Not yet anyway. She'd decided he'd
been prejudiced from the beginning against the detective whom he had seen as Superintendent Colclough's
little pet, token senior female officer in the Leek station, appointed as a sign of progressiveness. She smiled.
Token female? Maybe when she had started but these
days women outnumbered the serving officers in Leek.
Besides, what Rush had failed to realize was that Joanna
had been genuinely fond of her superintendent and he
of her. What might have started out as a political statement years ago had morphed into mutual respect. But
that affection had had its fallout. If Rush resented her,
Joanna, in turn, resented him taking the place of the
senior officer she had been so fond of, and from the
beginning she had been apprehensive about her new
boss. With Colclough she'd known exactly where she
was. He'd supported her ideas and protected her from
the very worst of herself, slapping her wrist when she
stepped out of line. But nothing worse. Even on the odd
occasions when she had, frankly, broken the rules with
very nearly tragic results—not to herself but to her sergeant. Colclough might have been indulgent but Fran
Korpanski had never forgiven her. CS Gabriel Rush
was still an unknown quantity. So, that morning, before
braving the office, almost in desperation, she checked
yet again whether Jadon Glover had turned up. Again
she met with a negative from an even more distraught
wife. So she made her way reluctantly along the corridor
towards the chief superintendent's office. She was not

relishing the thought of consulting with him but at the same time she didn't have the authority or the budget to proceed on this without his support and agreement.

As she walked at a snail's pace she knew the argument only too well: damned if you do; damned if you don't, with the added bonus of a public outcry if it turned out there was a case to investigate and she'd dragged her feet.

She found Rush in his office, scowling into a computer screen, head down, glaring. Without even looking up, he spoke. 'Sit down, Piercy,' he said. 'I've just got word that one of our…' he looked up and there was an unexpected gleam in the pale eyes the colour of boiled peppermints, '…more infamous families will soon be on their way home from Her Majesty's favourite hotels.' He looked back at the screen. 'Fred from Winson Green, Hayley from Drake Hall, Tommy…' He looked up, pale eyes cold as Arctic ice meeting hers, '…from Stoke Heath and Kath from Winson Green. Quite a family,' he finished drily. 'Can we expect trouble from the Whalleys?'

She heaved out a sigh. 'I don't know, sir. Maybe.' She thought for a moment and added, 'Probably.'

Rush's lips tightened. 'Between them they've done quite a stretch,' he said. 'Surely prison will have reformed them?'

She looked at him incredulously. *And if you believe that*. Then suspiciously. Was this a joke? She still didn't know how to take him.

'I wouldn't count on that, sir,' she said flatly, her voice neutral.

'No,' he agreed. 'It rarely does. Now to what do I

owe this social visit, Inspector?' She searched his face for a glint of fun, found none and spoke.

As concisely as she could she explained the circumstances of the never-before-missing man, his wife who held him in such esteem and his false claim to work for a firm of financial advisors who didn't appear to know of his existence. She added his real occupation and saw his face darken. Well, now she knew one thing about CS Rush. He didn't approve of doorstep money lenders.

'Hmm,' he said, unruffled. 'Financial advisor. Payday lenders.' He heaved out a sigh and wafted his words away with a wave of his hand, 'Whatever you want to call them. Interesting lot. Wonder who the clients are that they have in their stranglehold.'

Was it deliberate or accidental that her shoulders twitched? She felt her entire body stiffen. Consciously or unconsciously, with that one word Rush had put his finger over a throbbing pulse.

Stranglehold.

'I'm waiting for a list of his clients,' she said. 'Apparently he had a regular run on a Wednesday evening. We have no bank account or mobile phone activity since six p.m. on Wednesday evening.'

He looked straight at her and quickly put his finger on another pulse. 'And his car?'

'We haven't found it yet, sir.'

His mouth twitched. 'Then I suggest you try the new Sainsbury's,' he said. 'Car park's big enough to swallow up a jumbo jet.'

She tried not to grin. The image was funny. But he was right. Where else would you hide a car except in a car park? 'We will, sir. And I'd like to further interview the men that Mr Glover claimed he worked with…dig

around a bit. Mobile phone records. Nothing heavy,'
she added quickly, reading correctly his look of alarm,
'unless we find something untoward but… We're going
to need your permission, sir.' Then it burst out of her.
'Why would he build up a tissue of lies to his wife, sir?
She had no telephone numbers for his colleagues; she
didn't have the address and their business premises are
difficult to find. If she had rung Johnston and Pickles
she'd have found out they'd never heard of him.'

CS Rush's mouth bent in an almost-smile. He looked
*almost* kindly. Only almost. 'Don't waste too much time
focusing on that, Piercy,' he said, 'and don't neglect your
other work. Keep the Whalleys in mind and these insurance scams need to stop. Focus on finding Glover's
car. That's my advice. If you find that we can at least
make a start, get the forensics boys to look over it. That
should help you.'

She smiled. The first time she'd ever smiled at Rush.
'Thank you, sir.' She wanted to say so much more, to
thank him for his support and direction. It was the second time he had acted as her superior. But he was absorbed in his computer screen and somehow, she felt,
thanks would appear creepy. She still longed for Colclough though the longing was not quite so strong.

# SEVEN

BUT THE DAY proved disappointing and, like many early days of investigations, yielded nothing of use until 6 p.m. Rush was right. In the corner of the new Sainsbury's car park stood a black Mitsubishi Shogun Warrior. A car that was the diametric opposite of a vehicular wallflower. It stood more like Brad Pitt as Achilles in *Troy*. A big, black, stroppy-looking vehicle. It screamed and shouted and yet it had stayed invisible for forty-eight hours. Planted right in the middle of the car park, no one had noticed it until the vigilant PC Jason Spark.

Joanna and Mike zoomed in a noisy squad car, scattering a couple of tardy supermarket trolley pushers. 'So he didn't do a runner in this,' Joanna mused as they pulled up in front of it.

'Locked?' she asked Jason. PC Jason Spark, whom she had privately nicknamed PC Bright Spark. He was no pinup, with ears that stuck out, very irregular teeth, carroty hair and an inexhaustible supply of bouncy enthusiasm. When she'd turned the tight corner into the car park and seen Jason standing there, on guard, self-conscious and patently proud of himself, her heart had done a little skip. She'd always known he'd make a good copper, right back to the days when he had been an unwaveringly optimistic police cadet. PC Spark had recently fulfilled his dream of being a regular officer of the law.

And here he was.

The Mitsubishi was already cordoned off when they arrived and Jason hardly relaxed his stance as they approached, Joanna making observations as she slipped her gloves on and examined the exterior. 'No marks. No dents. Neatly parked, square in the space.' She tried the door. 'And locked.'

PC Spark grinned broadly, waiting for his pat on the back.

She addressed him. 'I take it our missing man hasn't lost himself up the aisles of Sainsbury's?'

Spark got the joke and laughed dutifully. 'They have CCTV, ma'am,' he said. 'I've taken a peek. Looks like he was on his own. Walked back towards the exit. It's quite a flashy car,' he observed with reverence and a tinge of envy. 'The guy who wheels the trolleys back to the entrance says he's noticed it before on a Wednesday evening. Usually parked here for a couple of hours.'

Joanna looked around her. 'If he was heading towards the exit I wonder where he was going.'

The supermarket had been built in a dip off the main Macclesfield road. Turn left out of the car park and there was a mill which made sports clothes. Beyond that was Mill Street which had a row of shops: fish and chips, newsagents, hairdressers and a pet food outlet. Over these shops were pensioners' flats. Straight ahead was the steep climb back into town. On the right-hand side of the road was a beauty salon, a restaurant, another huge derelict mill called Big Mill and behind that jumbled rows of terraced mill workers' cottages. Leek had once been a flourishing mill town and evidence of this peppered the entire area. Some of the old mills had been converted into antiques warehouses, others into flats. A couple had been demolished but many of them, including the biggest of them all, Big Mill, remained derelict, loosely boarded up, a magnet for dossers and drug users or anyone who wanted to hide. Big Mill towered over the road. Six storeys high, with blackened bricks, it dominated the area, as sinister as a huge black crow. Joanna's gaze looked up at it with misgiving. Leek police knew it well. Her mind moved beyond to the area behind the mill and further up the steep hill to the cramped, crooked streets of Victorian terraced houses. A brief walk and a couple of hours parked up here would give the missing man plenty of options. And, according to their observant trolley man, who was watching initially from a distance but soon came forward, he had seen this car here before.

'Always on a Wednesday,' he said. 'Round about six till eight thirty.'

'But you didn't think it odd that it's still here?'

'Thought it must have broken down or something,' the trolley man said, glancing enviously at the car. 'He's a nice guy, polite. You know. Wouldn't want to get him into trouble. Hand out a fine. I knew he'd come and collect it.'

*Except he hadn't.*

'Do you know where he went on a Wednesday?'

The trolley man shook his head and scanned the enormous car park. 'This here's my patch,' he said. 'I don't bother what folks is doing unless it comes on my patch. Outside isn't none of my business.' He gave her a hard look. 'Understand?'

'Yeah.' She drew breath. 'Was he alone?'

'Yessir.'

'Always alone?'

The trolley man nodded. 'Didn't never see him with anyone,' he said.

She had a quick word with Mike who was standing at her shoulder, watching the trolley man's antics with amusement. 'So,' she said, 'this was a regular occurrence. Not his gym night. Anyway, Pecs is the other end of town. Eve Glover mentioned home visits as part of her husband's work. For my money this is the answer so we need that list from his colleagues.'

Korpanski nodded. 'If he walked from here what the heck's happened to him?'

She wished he hadn't finished the sentence with a glance over her shoulder at the big square building up the road.

Joanna spoke to Spark, who was watching. 'Can we get inside the car?'

PC Spark's grin stretched from one ear to the other. Another gold star in his book was imminent. 'Got a bloke coming,' he said. 'Apparently it's quite easy. You just got to…'

Joanna peered in through heavily tinted windows. The driver's seat was empty. He could be inside, in the back, but she could not make out a body. However, it was difficult to be certain because the tint was so deep. In fact, she was unsure whether it was darker than was legal. Well, it was hardly a priority. They could deal with that sometime in the future. But, with the tinted windows, the Shogun looked menacing.

'A drug dealer's car,' Joanna muttered and Mike agreed with a jerky nod and a spluttering laugh. 'Don't say that too loud, Jo,' he warned. 'The manufacturers will sue you.'

She gave him a look that was meant to be withering but had absolutely no impact on her sergeant. She allowed herself, for one second, to reflect on the pleasure of working alongside him. What a long way they had come, she from the prickly new inspector and he from the sergeant resentful at working beneath—as he saw it—a woman. Korpanski was the archetypal male chauvinist pig—or had been—then. They had both moved on.

She regarded the car for a further minute. 'So he's been missing now for forty-eight hours. He parked up expecting to return probably within the usual two to two-and-a-half but he didn't. I guess the car's been here all that time.'

Spark interrupted. 'We've got some CCTV footage, ma'am. Soon check it out but it's still wet underneath the car. Wednesday night was heavy rain. Since then it's been dry.'

She was still thinking. 'What are these sorts of cars worth, Korpanski?' He was the petrol head.

'A little over thirty thousand,' he said. 'And that's one of the basic models. This one's all singing all dancing.'

'So he's pretty unlikely to have just left it here.'

She addressed PC Ruthin who had just joined them. Any drama soon attracted backup. 'So what do you think, Paul?'

'Put it like this: I wouldn't just abandon the love of my life in a supermarket car park. Not safe. And it's not just in danger from the joyriders or organized crime who steal to order. No, the real threat comes from the bloody trolleys, their unpredictable wheels and rubbish drivers bashing into you.'

'That's right,' she said thoughtfully, 'I wouldn't leave

it here either. And the phrase *love of my life* could be applied to Mrs Glover too.'

She was silent. Something had happened to Jadon Glover. The question was what, how, why, when, where and where was he now? *Why* was the easiest question to answer considering his occupation. His career was hardly the pathway to making friends. And *when* almost answered itself. Between 6.15 p.m. on Wednesday evening and 9.30 p.m. when he had failed to return home.

The other questions posed more of a problem.

A car pulled up. The scanner had arrived. Within minutes she had slipped a pair of gloves on and the door was opened.

Inside stank of air freshener and was obsessively clean. The Shogun had been left in gear, the handbrake on. No keys in the ignition. Nothing suspicious. The seats were in order, in the right position for Jadon Glover to drive. There was no visible blood or hair or anything else that might suggest foul play. Nothing out of place.

It did not look like a crime scene.

She crossed to the passenger side and opened the glove compartment. Nothing there except the log book. But the car was fitted with a SatNav so they could retrace his travel history back to his last destinations, if he'd used it. DC Alan King could sit and play with that one. He was the tech king.

She opened the boot. Just the usual: spare tyre, jack. Again, all in order. Jadon Glover, she was fast realizing, was a very tidy man. Methodical and careful. He'd left nothing personal behind, just the car. Like his home, it was anonymous; there was no clue as to his real character except that he was tidy. Tidy, she wondered, or

careful? Obsessively careful usually meant something
to hide. Leaving the car here simply to vanish was careless and out of character, and so it was at that precise
point that Joanna knew Glover's disappearance was
sinister. She was glad now that she had pre-empted
this discovery and discussed the case with CS Rush,
quite apart from him pointing his finger in this direction. She could have the car on a low loader in half an
hour and down to the forensics lab in Stoke. Then they
would wait for developments.

She authorized removal of the Shogun, gave the
officers a few requests and requirements, asked PC
Ruthin to remain with the vehicle, had the immediate
area sealed off and she, Korpanski and Jason Spark entered the store to commandeer the CCTV tapes from
the supermarket. A couple of Specials could watch them
over Coke and crisps. It was a boring job but necessary.

Their next unenviable task was to speak to Eve again.
Korpanski had planned to visit anyway this evening but
finding the car had changed the situation. They should
both go. Joanna authorised a preliminary search of the
surrounding area including the derelict mill. It wouldn't
do to find Jadon injured somewhere, awaiting their discovery and help. In the morning she would tackle the
missing man's business partners again, get that list of
clients and look into Glover's movements on Wednesday evenings.

It was dusk by the time they arrived at 8 Disraeli
Place. It looked deserted, as did the entire street. It
seemed no one lived here or in any of the other houses.
Had the field been swallowed up to form a street of
houses where no one lived? What a waste.

They knocked anyway.

This time Eve was dressed more soberly in a short black skirt and cream mohair V-neck sweater that set off her blue eyes to perfection. Her blue eyes looked disturbed and, once or twice, as they spoke, filled with tears.

She was very quiet when they told her they had found her husband's car. Her face was pale and shocked. She looked frightened. Joanna looked at her closely and was convinced this was no act. The woman was genuinely heartbroken.

'He loved that thing,' she said, smiling through her tears. 'I used to tease him about it. Used to say, "Love it more than me, you do".' And then the hollow, brittle show of bravado completely crumbled. Her shoulders shook. Even Mike looked moved by her distress, as though he would put his arm around her. Joanna shook her head.

'What's happened to him?'

'We don't know.' Joanna let that sink in before she spoke again. 'Look, Eve,' she said, 'I'll be quite honest with you. We don't know where your husband is. We don't know what's happened, why he's gone missing. We are looking around the area…' Unbidden, Big Mill loomed in front of her eyes, black and forbidding, throwing its huge shadow over the entire area like a cloak, its rows of broken-blind windows staring out over the steep hill, watching the road that led out to Macclesfield. She knew the building was poorly secured. Anyone could get in with minimal effort—and they did with regularity. To date they had found one corpse, a drug overdose and three more comatosed would-be fun seekers. She recovered herself, hoped that Eve hadn't picked up on her sudden silence and involuntary shudder. She picked up the conversation. '… The area around where his car was found. If we find anything you'll be the first to know. In turn, if you learn anything you do the same. Let us know straight away.' She tapped her mobile. 'I'm on the end of this twenty-four seven. Or you can phone the station.'

Eve nodded.

'The car was found at Sainsbury's car park,' Joanna continued. 'It appears that this was a regular slot for Jadon. Most Wednesdays he parked there and was gone for an hour or two. This time he did not return. That's as much as we know at the moment. Do you know anything about the people he visited regularly on a Wednesday?'

Eve shook her head. 'He didn't talk about his business.'

*Not surprising under the circumstances.*

'So you'd better ask the others,' Eve said.

'You mean Leroy, Scott and Jeff?'

She nodded.

'But you can't add anything?'

She shook her head.

Mike and Joanna exchanged a swift glance. They'd worked out their strategy on the way there and that did not include telling Mrs Glover the anomalies they had already learned about her 'perfect husband'.

Joanna tried to steer the conversation. 'How long did you say you've been married?'

The innocent opener went down completely the wrong way. It tipped Eve Glover into defensive manner. She flushed. 'Are you suggesting my Jadon's having an affair? That he's gone off with another woman?'

*Don't tell me it hadn't crossed your mind?*

Joanna tried to smooth the wrinkle out. Maybe she should have left this to Korpanski after all. 'No. I'm not, Mrs Glover. I'm just collecting background information.'

*And don't be so damned prickly.*

'Sorry. You can understand.' A loud sniff. 'Obviously I'm not myself.' A brave smile now. 'Two years.' Another bright, toothy smile. Tombstone white. 'We got married in Italy,' she said brightly.

Now why didn't that surprise Joanna?

'Have you got a wedding photograph?'

'Yeah. Yeah.'

She crossed the sterile room to the enormous television set and handed Joanna a wedding photograph which had stood on a shelf behind it, unnoticed until now.

Joanna gazed at it. There are some couples for whom glamour is the most important aspect. And Jadon and Eve certainly fitted into that category. Pukingly Glover was even wearing a white suit and had matched his skin tone to his wife's exact shade of orange. And his wife's dress was a froth of sparkling white chiffon topped by a tiara. Diamond or paste? The dress looked hugely expensive.

To Joanna he didn't look like an accountant but a flashy criminal. A clean frontman for a dirty little business. She peered closer at the picture and picked up something else—something she hadn't expected, something a bit less predictable. Rather than looking cocky at his wedding, Jadon Glover looked uncertain. His smile didn't quite ring true. She wondered about this. Was his uncertainty about his nuptials or something else? Was there a hint of defiant bravado about the tilt of his chin but a sense of panic behind the eyes? A challenge thrown out carelessly to his guests? She'd seen this look before. There was something in his expression which she recognized but could not identify.

She continued looking. Ostentatiously on his third finger on his left hand he sported a gold ring with a large diamond. Unless it too was fake, the size of the diamond chilled her further. Diamonds that big cost big money. A few grand a carat. More money than any honest accountant would make. And even though the syndicate charged astronomic interest rates it represented a lot of people paying him and his mates back—for ever. A lot of lives damaged and hurt. To a detective, big diamonds mean one of two things. Legitimate fame and fortune or law breaking, cheating, drugs, thefts and lies. The murky world of the Big Diamond. They'd already discovered one little lie and, like weeds blown in on the breeze, little lies spread.

And that was how big diamonds came to nestle on cheating fingers.

Behind the big lies and cheating fingers could be a whole host of dangerous, cruel enemies.

The case was beginning to intrigue and worry her in equal measure because she had the feeling that at some point not very far down the line she was going to be breaking some very bad news to the devoted Mrs Glover. She glanced across at Eve. Staring down at the picture seemed to be having a calming effect on her. She was smiling into it, only recalling the presence of the two detectives when she looked up and her face instantly hardened.

'Is there something you're not telling me?' She searched her mind. 'Something about the car? Was it bumped—damaged in some way? Was there blood in it?' She put her hand to her throat. 'Dear God, is he hurt?' It was a theatrical gesture but Joanna did not doubt it was genuine.

So she answered bluntly but kindly. 'I'm sorry, Mrs Glover, but we really don't know—yet.' Then she took pity on her. 'We didn't see any blood in the car but we'll get it checked out all the same.'

Eve nodded and couldn't resist tacking on, 'Where do *you* think he is? Why do *you* think he's not getting in touch?'

*Why do you bloody well think?*

Joanna sidestepped the question. Enough time had been spent on this. It was time to progress. Now how could she put this? 'Do you remember a Mr Karl Robertson at your salon?'

Eve searched her mind then shook her head. 'I don't think so.'

'Middle aged, balding.'

The smile Eve gave was ever so cynical. 'Loads of men who looked like that came in wanting a makeover. Why do you ask?'

'He claims to know you.'

'Oh.' She tossed her head in the classic gesture of a beauty dismissing the beast. 'Lots of men do that— pretend they're my friend when really they're just a client.'

*Just a client with a tenuous connection to both you and your missing husband.*

'Jadon was glad when I gave it up. Too much male attention, you know.'

Eve gave a self-indulgent smile, the equivalent of a woman patting herself on the back for her flawless physical attributes. It was the smile of a woman spoilt and coddled by an adoring husband.

An adoring husband who deceived the wife he adored? Or was the story behind Jadon's lies something a little more complicated? A little more connected to the size of the diamond he wore on his muscular finger?

Eve hadn't quite completed her little soliloquy. 'He likes me to be a stay-at-home wife.'

'Right.'

Joanna was getting sooo bored. She needed to move in, find some answers and get back to real policing, using police time and budget in a more constructive way.

'You're sure you've never rung your husband at work?'

Eve gave a small shake of her head. 'Why would I go through all his secretaries and stuff when I can just dial his mobile? He's always got that switched on and he's always got it with him.'

*All his secretaries and stuff?* Joanna gave Mike a swift, *I don't think so* glance. There had just been the three guys. No secretaries and stuff. What tales had Glover been spinning? 'Have you ever visited him at work, met him for lunch, maybe?'

'I don't go to Hanley much,' Eve said. 'I'm not fond of the place. There's not a lot of designer stuff there anyway. *We* tend to go shopping in Manchester or Birmingham, sometimes London. Take in a show, you know.'

Joanna knew she was meant to look impressed. She tried and probably failed.

Suddenly Eve Glover cottoned on. She looked from one to the other. 'Why do you keep asking me all these questions about Jadon's *work*? What's that got to do with his disappearing? He didn't vanish from *work*.'

Mike stepped in. 'Well, you said he was working late on Wednesday night so we wondered where he might be working late? Who he might be with?'

Inwardly, Joanna groaned. Mike had put it so clumsily.

Eve Glover turned her rather beautiful blue eyes full on Mike and spent a minute assessing the burly policeman with his powerful build and ready grin. Sensing the missing man's wife was about to go all girly on them, Joanna braced herself. But while Eve's attention was diverted it gave her the chance to focus her mind in another direction. What if Jadon wasn't having an affair but his beautiful and probably bored wife was? Might that be a reason for his disappearance? A rival lover? Might the little white lie Jadon had fed his beloved be no more than male bravado? Considering the insecurity she had sensed from the wedding photograph Joanna thought it was possible.

She watched the woman warm towards her detective sergeant and wondered. She was not above taking advantage of women's instinctive trust in her sergeant. Sometimes it brought results.

But Eve soon turned back to her and her voice was cold. 'Jadon has private clients,' she said with extreme and careful dignity. 'They pay a great deal for his expertise in finance. Some of them he has to visit every week. Clients with money,' she added. 'He has to keep them sweet.'

'Do you know any of their names, love?' Korpanski was really milking this one.

'Oh no,' Eve said, with cleverness adding, 'it wouldn't be professional for him to discuss business or clients' names with me. It would break confidentiality.'

*Where had she picked this one up from?* Joanna wondered.

Mike was still in pursuit. 'Jadon didn't socialize with his clients?'

'No.' Said firmly.

'You never met any of them?'

Eve frowned at him. '*No*—I'm sure in time I would have but no, I never did.' She pressed her lips together, still frowning, then repeated, 'I never did. It was just what Jadon told me.' Another bright smile. 'He'd keep me really entertained about his work.'

'I'm sure.' But Joanna was thinking, *We don't have time for this. Not now. Not yet, anyway.*

'Did he stay out late sometimes entertaining clients?'

'Very occasionally. But it was business,' she insisted.

'Did he mention any venues—restaurants, hotels, clubs they went to?'

Eve shook her head. 'Not especially,' she said. 'And the latest he was ever home was ten and he'd always let me know.'

'What about your husband's other friends?' Joanna asked. 'Family? Old school friends? Anyone apart from his work colleagues?'

'Only Jeff, Leroy and Scott,' she said reluctantly.

'I've spoken to Leroy,' Joanna said. 'He didn't seem to have a clue where your husband was.'

Eve opened her mouth and closed it again. 'We did sometimes…' sounding as though she'd just remembered something and was trying to be helpful, '…socialize. The three of them came to our wedding with their partners. And we've been for a drink with them all a couple of times. I get on really well with Leroy's wife.'

'What's her name, love?' Korpanski couldn't resist a quick grin at her.

Joanna braced herself for a flamboyant name but was disappointed.

'Pat,' Eve said. Then added: 'She works in the council offices.'

'Here,' she said, with pride, passing her phone to the DS to read off her contacts. 'That's her number. She rang me yesterday and told me to keep in touch.'

Korpanski took a note of it and passed the phone back to Eve. He would love to have taken the phone and retrieved all the data it would hold—calls made, calls received, text messages. Oh yes, he sighed. Mobile phones held life's information—if you could get hold of it, legally.

'Thanks,' he said, holding her gaze for just a little longer than necessary. She giggled then put her hand up to her mouth.

'Any time, Sergeant,' she said, and Joanna had great trouble not rolling her eyes at him. Like Mrs Glover the DS was a huge flirt who used his undoubted physical attraction to obtain maximum information from the fair sex. What none of the women realized was that DS Mike Korpanski was a very happily married man with two children whom he adored. He just wasn't going to be playing around however tempting the offer. It was all a game to him and a means of extracting information.

'OK,' Joanna said. 'Do you know where they all live?'

Eve looked upset and a little confused. 'No. We always met them out somewhere and they'd sort of talk about work.'

*Sort of?* Joanna looked innocent. 'Anything specific?'

Eve looked at her sharply, her head jerking around and Joanna rephrased the question with a smile. 'Anything that will help us find your husband?'

Eve looked even more confused.

'What about *your* family, love?' You had to give it to Mike—he could charm the birds off the trees. If anyone was going to winkle information out of this featherhead it would be the DS.

'*My* family?' She put a hand up to her throat but it didn't stop them seeing the ruby flush that blotched her neck. 'My mum and dad are separated,' she said quickly, as though rinsing out some dirty underwear. 'We don't see much of them.' She frowned. 'They were both a bit nasty about Jadon so we didn't make much of an effort to see either of them.' She gave a watery, damaged smile. 'New partners, you know?'

*A bit nasty about him.* What had they picked up on that Eve, obviously, had not?

'What about Jadon's family?'

Eve looked awkward. 'He doesn't really have any.'

Joanna frowned. *Everyone* has a family. She, Matthew, Korpanski. They all had family. As, undoubtedly, did the missing husband. He hadn't been dropped from the sky. Somewhere there must be a mother, a father, possibly siblings. Something else to put on the *to do* list. Look into another question. Who was Jadon Glover?

If he didn't turn up soon the list of areas to explore could be as long as Pinocchio's nose—and growing.

She had to ask it. 'So who else was at your Italian wedding?'

'Just Leroy, Scott, Jeff and their partners and two really good school friends of mine.'

'Oh.' It all sounded a bit sad to Joanna and it appeared the same to Eve. She looked down at her fingernails, long, professionally manicured, Red Gel with small daisies painted on them. 'We wanted just close family and friends,' she said in a whisper.

Joanna didn't point out that none of these people actually was family, close or otherwise. Neither her mother nor her father had attended, new partners or otherwise. The intrigue surrounding Jadon Glover's disappearance was compounding.

She stood up. Then a thought struck her.

'Exactly when did you last *see* Jadon?'

'When he left in the morning,' Eve said. 'Day before yesterday. He usually leaves quite early. Round about seven. It was nearer half past on Wednesday.'

'Any particular reason he was a bit late?'

Eve shook her head. 'No,' she said, patently wondering why the question. 'It just happened that way.' Then she flushed an even brighter red and Joanna knew. They'd been making love. Oh, wow! But as with other statements it told her something. If Jadon had been making love to his wife the morning he went it was unlikely he was anticipating running off with a mistress. In fact, everything in his disappearance suggested it had been unexpected. Car parked in the usual place, routine Wednesday visit. Not *impossible* but *unlikely* he'd gone with another woman…

'Look,' she said, awkward now and embarrassed for the woman. 'We have work to do, people to talk to. Keep my number and get in touch if you hear anything.'

Eve grabbed at her arm and asked again. 'What do you really think's happened to him?'

'I don't know,' Joanna said honestly. 'And I'm not paid to make guesses. It's my job to look into it and that, I can promise, will be done. We'll be examining the car but all appeared in order there.' Something struck her then. Just a small detail. 'He parked at the supermarket every week. Did he do your shopping there?'

'No. I didn't even know he knew it existed,' Eve said with a cynical smile. 'Jadon doesn't "do" supermarkets.'

It didn't surprise Joanna.

# EIGHT

WHILE JOANNA AND MIKE were interviewing Eve Glover
other officers had divided into two teams fanning out
into the area around the supermarket. Their brief was
to make a cursory search of anywhere where Jadon
Glover might be, hurt, alive or dead. At the same time a
board had been erected in the car park asking if anyone
had seen him. They had also contacted local media and
had started a house to house. Joanna was directing the
operations and kept coming back to the deserted mill.

It seemed the obvious place to start.

Big Mill dominated the area, standing over Macclesfield Road like an unwanted guest at a birthday party.
Built in 1857 by William Sugden, it had once homed a
thriving weaving industry. But as the mills were no longer working the buildings had been abandoned. A few
had been turned into antiques centres but as that industry too had hit the doldrums they had gradually closed
down and fallen into disrepair and dereliction and now
they radiated an air of doom. They were a living testa-
ment to work and jobs long gone; a film set for a violent
thriller, a backdrop for minor crime… Six storeys high,
twenty-one bays long and five bays deep, Big Mill was
huge, the largest in the town. There had been plans to
turn it into residential flats but the developer had fallen
on hard times and now it was boarded up though hardly
villain-proof. Lead thieves had clambered on to the roof

and helped themselves. It was a miracle that no one had fallen through to their death. Like many derelicts it was a magnet for the homeless and drug dealers, runaways and the odd couple wanting illicit sex.

The result was that it was well known to the police and the people who lived in the surrounding houses were frequently picking up the phone to report suspicious activity. Two teams of four officers couldn't hope to do more than a cursory job of searching the entire place but they worked their way through as carefully as possible. By the end they could be pretty certain that Jadon Glover was not here.

Alive or dead.

There were other areas near to the Sainsbury's car park that warranted a sift through: patches of wasteland, a child's play area. Nothing yielded anything obvious. If Glover didn't turn up or they had some other clue as to what had happened to him they would have to do a more thorough job. Joanna listened to the reports coming in and wondered. Had he been picked up in another car?

But so far they had drawn a blank. And the list of Jadon's Wednesday evening clients helpfully emailed through by Scott Dooley didn't help much except give them a focus for the house-to-house enquiries.

*Friday, 7 March, 9.30 p.m.*

MONICA PAGETT WAS SITTING up in bed when Stephanie Bucannon came in. She had been transferred that very morning and now found herself in Brooklands Nursing Home in Leek, in a small but private room. And she had found a familiar face. She looked at the girl with affection. 'I'm thinking,' she said. 'Wondering whether the doctor's right and that I'll never be able to live in my cottage again.' She heaved out a long sigh. 'It isn't what I want but…' She gave a mischievous smile at the health care assistant. 'I thought I'd live in that cottage for ever,' she said. 'I thought someone would find my body frozen to death one year in late March two months after I'd met my end.' Her face twisted as she recalled one of the doctors' and social workers' most powerful arguments. 'If you were in trouble who would hear you shout that distance when the wind howled loud enough to drown out any scream and the snow was banked up six feet either side of the road?' And, 'How would the emergency services reach you, Monica, if you fell again and the weather was bad? How would anyone even know you were in trouble? A slip. A fall. It was fortuitous that your neighbour rang that morning and when she got no answer called round to find you on the floor.'

Monica had not gone down without a fight. 'It's the way we do things out there on the moors. We look after each other.'

Now all she recalled was the social worker's sceptical silence.

And she had to accept what it meant. 'I'm not going to get back there, Stephanie, am I? I may as well sell it.'

The girl perched on the bed and touched her hand. 'It must be hard for you. You were born there, weren't you?'

'Lived there all my life.'

'So to sell it must be a terrible wrench.'

'It is,' Monica said stoutly, 'but I don't have much choice, do I?'

'I'm not even going to try and answer that,' Stephanie said, trying to put a smile back on Monica's face.

Monica was silent for a moment, reflecting. Truth was Brooklands didn't seem to be as bad a place as she had imagined. The staff seemed kind, the lunch and tea she'd had were better than she ate at home and it was so warm here. Warmth, except on a very few summer days, was something she was unused to. Winters spent on the moors had been cold from October to March. It was just that Brooklands wasn't home. She smiled at the girl. Stephanie's grandfather had been a moorlands farmer. Eric Bucannon had been a neighbour of hers, living only four miles away, practically on the doorstep in the sparsely populated area. Neighbours were few and far between in the Staffordshire Moorlands so she had known Stephanie from a little girl. Monica had always liked her even if her dad had broken the mould and was a poncey solicitor somewhere in London—a foreign country to her. But Stephanie had returned to Leek which endeared her to Monica. Also, the girl had treated her with dignity when she had arrived, calling her Mrs Pagett instead of jumping in with her Christian name. She treated her as though she was only physically infirm rather than mentally gaga.

And she realized that Monica would find it hard to adjust. She understood her real home circumstances: used to an outside loo, a solid fuel Rayburn that had to be stoked with wood and coal, being cut off by snow for weeks at a time and the isolation of a house where her nearest neighbours were a mile away across muddy fields. And now this: central heating, hot water, an en suite, meals cooked for her. Company.

But the moors still called her back.

# NINE

THE WEEKEND HAD passed without Jadon turning up or any clue as to his fate.

Scott, Leroy and Jeff were having a pow wow in their office.

'Tasha's got a friend who works at Sainsbury's,' Scott was saying. 'She told me that the police have been down there sniffing around a black Shogun Warrior. It was removed by the police on a low loader. She didn't catch the number but it's bound to be his.'

His two friends gawped at him.

Jeff spoke for them all. 'What the heck's going on?'

'Come on,' Leroy said. 'Bloody obvious. He's done a runner.'

'What,' Jeff said scornfully, 'with just a few hundred quid? When our income's steady and topping a hundred grand each? Not worth it.'

Scott spoke again. 'How do we know it *is* just a few hundred? He's the one that meets the clients, drums up new business. He could have been filching money away for years and we didn't know.' Scott had planted the cat firmly in the centre of the pigeons.

Jeff narrowed his eyes, looking feline and sneaky. 'He wouldn't have left that pretty little missus of his behind. Come on, you two. He bloody well worshipped her. He'd never leave her. He just wouldn't.'

'Maybe he hasn't. Maybe she's playing a double game too,' Scott continued. 'Maybe they're off to Spain or something taking a load of *our* money with them. Maybe she's planning on joining him.'

Leroy looked concerned. 'You think? You really think?'

Scott sat back in his chair, folded his meaty arms and spoke to his colleagues. 'Look, you dimmocks, his car's here. His missus is home. The police have been called in. Put two and two together. He's run off with money. We'd better check our records and start cleaning stuff up.'

'We're legal,' Jeff Armitage pointed out.

Leroy laughed. 'Some of the time, sure. But the rest—hey…'

The other two were silent at this then Scott said slowly, 'He could have been set on, robbed. He always had a pocket full of cash, didn't he?'

'Who'd dare do that with us three ready to sort anyone out who went for him? We watch each other's backs. We'd protect him.'

'Maybe some barmy druggie or something. Someone off his head.' It was all Leroy could think of.

'So where's the body? The police have checked the hospitals. He ain't there.'

'If some smackhead's bumped him off when they was off their heads they wouldn't exactly be at their cutest hiding the body, would they?' Scott said. 'If that's the case the police'll soon find him.

'OK. OK.' Scott, as their leader, was anxious to focus their attention on what was important. Now. 'What about now, all the money we're still owed. We can't just drop the business, let it all go. We can't afford to. We've got to pick up the strands.'

*Come on, my pretties. Send another into the ring. I'm ready for you.*

*It's all about the money, love. Money, money, money.*

KORPANSKI SPENT MONDAY afternoon dealing with Billy the Basher's insurance fraud, liaising with a nice guy called Roger from the insurance company who was only too glad to have events and dates from the DS. Roger was happy to let the police take care of it and conduct a civil case to recover costs. As for the criminal case, the wheels of law ground slowly but in the end they would grind exceedingly fine, a fact which gave Korpanski a feeling of warm happiness. Billy the Basher might not end up in prison but he would be cleaning the streets of Leek and its surrounds for a few months and his fine would be hefty. Better—if Billy didn't play ball they could put him away. And—this was a nice touch—he would be unable to find an insurance company to cover him so would not be able to drive—legally—for a long time yet. And if he broke the law—again—they would soon pick him up—again. Yeah. Korpanski felt this was a good day's work.

Joanna had had word that Kath Whalley was due out on the following Monday and she sat and thought. She wouldn't say she was scared or nervous of the girl but she was very wary. She recognized the kind of mad evil that was at the core of the worst criminals. Kath was the wildest member of a criminal family notorious in the Staffordshire Moorlands. OK, not quite the Krays but they'd caused havoc in their day, the family business being burglary, handling stolen goods and a few other talents. But at some time some knobhead had introduced Kath, already bordering on psychopathy, to crack cocaine and it had made her even more dangerous and unpredictable. She had assaulted an old lady late at night on the streets of Leek, slashing at the terrified woman across the face—almost blinding her—all for twenty pounds, which had led to Joanna putting her away. She knew that Kath Whalley had sworn vengeance on her. She was not afraid of pain or the law. She was one of those who would always bully and survive. Joanna was prepared but she hadn't told Matthew about her fear. Matthew was protective of her and would worry. He might hide it from her but it would show in a hundred little fussing ways: extra phone calls, him at the door if she was late home, maybe even a quiet word with Korpanski. Joanna smiled. She'd always thought of herself as a tough cookie, physically and mentally strong. There was something so sweet about Matthew fussing over her as though she was some sort of female wimp.

Besides…

There was the future to think about.

She might have assured CS Rush that she was not nervous but, knowing Kath Whalley as she did, she would have to be insane not to keep a watchful eye out for her movements. When Joanna had had her sent down almost ten years ago now Kath had sworn vengeance from her cell, from the dock and from the remand centre. The flame of hatred had burned bright. Joanna knew that she was the focus of that hatred. She had been the senior investigating officer who had largely been responsible for cleaning up Leek's streets and ridding them of the pesky family who had been responsible for burglaries, assaults, car thefts, shoplifting and frauds. All nuisance crimes, until Kath's vicious assault. That had changed everything. When the Whalleys had finally been sent down the town had practically cheered. And the crime rate had plummeted. But it had all come at a price.

And now they were out and Joanna knew that Kath Whalley would waste little time in returning to her previous career. She stood in the way.

She closed her eyes and pictured Kath, who was a bulky girl, heaving a meaty fist right into her face.

She stood up quickly. She couldn't afford to let this image stick.

Back to the missing man.

*2 p.m.*

SUPPLIED WITH COKE and crisps, a couple of Specials sat watching the CCTV videos from Sainsbury's superstore. They were mind-numbingly boring: cars pulling up, trolleys laden with produce, children, pushchairs, baby carriers. Cars coming, cars going. People hurrying.

And then they saw the Shogun, sliding into view like a monstrous black whale, being driven carefully, pulling into a parking space. With the tinted windows it was impossible to see who was inside. Someone got out, looking around. It looked like Jadon Glover. They freeze-framed, noted the date and time. Wednesday 5 March, 7.01 p.m.

Dressed against the weather, he walked quickly away from the car, head down against driving rain. It was impossible to be absolutely certain but it would ap-

pear that, so far, this was the last known sighting of
their man.

They leaned forward, mesmerized. There is always
something chilling in this, a last known sighting. They
watched as he strode out of the car park, away from
the supermarket, until he turned left, out of their view
and vanished. They looked at one another. There had
seemed nothing untoward, nothing odd, furtive or hurried. According to the supermarket car park attendant
this was a routine event—happened on a weekly basis.
But this time he had vanished.

They watched for hours more, focusing on the Shogun, waiting to see if he returned. But he didn't. There
was no further sighting. Jadon Glover had parked his
car, locked it, left it and vanished.

Last sighting 7.01 p.m., Wednesday 5 March.

They called Joanna in and watched for her reaction.
She was as puzzled as they were. She watched to see
if anyone was following Jadon but no. In the blustery
weather, rain sheeting down, everyone seemed to be
going about their business. No one appeared to be taking any notice of their missing man. No one had probably noticed the figure, dressed against the rain, hurrying
away from Sainsbury's. Everyone else was intent on
getting on with their shopping and getting home.

Mike wandered over and they watched the sequence
through again then looked at each other. 'Seems like,'
Mike said slowly, 'we ought to follow up his Wednesday
evening itinerary. He obviously wasn't doing the shopping or just getting the wine for his wife. He was using
the supermarket car park so…he was headed somewhere
within walking distance?'

'Seems logical.' Joanna produced the list of Jadon's

clients, finally emailed through, asterisks marking those he visited on Wednesday evenings. She had the feeling Jadon's colleagues had dragged their feet as long as they'd dared. 'Have the house-to-house team come up with anything?'

'Not so far. I wonder, Jo…' Korpanski hesitated.

They looked at one another. 'Work or a mistress?' she supplied and Korpanski nodded.

'So…' With a sinking heart she knew she must speak to CS Rush again, keep him up to date. Another trip along the corridor.

*3 p.m.*

'PIERCY.' HE LOOKED up as she entered, his face unreadable. She would have found it easier if he had displayed some emotion, even something negative—impatience, irritation. Anything but this blank, bland expression that always left her wondering: what was he really thinking?

'Sir, I thought…' She felt awkward. With Colclough he'd always invited her to sit down and it had seemed a natural exchange. Here she felt wrong-footed and uncomfortable. Defensive.

'Sir,' she began again. Their eyes met. His hard and sharp as boiled peppermints, hers stormy and resentful.

'The missing man,' he prompted impatiently.

'Still missing,' she said. 'It's been more than five days now. We have the car and some CCTV footage taken from Sainsbury's car park. He parks up and walks out of the supermarket, turning left towards the town. According to the car park attendant it was a regular spot for him. He's not been picked up on any other cameras. We have a list of his clients and are checking up with them.'

'OK,' he said, 'take me through them. Describe the area.'

'If you turn left out of Sainsbury's car park there's a row of shops with flats. It's called Mill Street. Jadon Glover had six clients who lived there.'

Rush appeared preoccupied.

'If you then cross the road there are another thirteen families he visited.' She wasn't sure how familiar he was with the town and its geography and felt the need to explain. 'They're Victorian mill workers' cottages, terraced, not great for parking—particularly a big SUV, and his last road ends in a cul-de-sac so it would make sense to park in the supermarket car park and walk on his rounds.'

He looked up. 'Even though the weather was foul?'

She shrugged. 'We're kind of used to it round here. He was wearing a mac.'

'And the rest of the area?'

'Includes a derelict mill, sir. Big Mill.'

He frowned, so she enlarged, 'Six storeys high. It covers a massive area. We've checked that out superficially but nothing so far.' She hesitated. 'And there's a child's play area too right in the middle of the streets he would have visited.'

'Which are?'

'He would have started with Wellington Place then gone up to Britannia Avenue. The child's play area is at the end of Britannia Avenue. He would probably have moved to Barngate Street, cut through a passageway and finished at Nab Hill Avenue before returning back to his car.'

'So your plan is…?' Eyebrows raised. Waiting.

'Speak to his work colleagues, focus on his Wednesday evening schedule. We'll continue with the house to house in the area, find out which he visited and do our best to pin down precisely at what point he abandoned his normal schedule. Then we'll look at other possibilities—his connection with Johnston and Pickles.' She paused. 'We've established a connection between Mr Karl Robertson, the CEO of Johnston and Pickles, and Mrs Glover, the missing man's wife. We'll check out his gym, his family, his clients. Look further into his financial affairs.' Inside, she was cringing. None of this sounded exactly inspirational. Even to herself she sounded like an uninspired plod.

Rush looked almost bored.

And she was missing Colclough even more. He would have talked around the subject, questioned her about her instincts, trusted her gut feeling, but looking at Chief Superintendent Gabriel Rush's stony face she couldn't see him fishing.

She dismissed herself.

She detailed four teams of PCs to continue with the house-to-house search including a more thorough look at the mill while she and Mike focused on Glover's business interests, not forgetting Johnston and Pickles. Why had he used that particular business? The simple geographical proximity of a real accountancy business? Was it nothing more than a name he had picked up through his wife's connection with the CEO? Or was there something else behind it? Was it of any significance anyway? Or was she doing her usual—barking up the wrong tree?

*5 p.m.*

USING THE LIST OF clients forwarded to them the teams
had split into three groups and fanned out from the
supermarket car park. Paul Ruthin and Bridget Anderton took the Mill Street area, two floors of sixties
flats over the row of shops. A team of officers combed
Big Mill for a second time and Jason Spark and Dawn
Critchlow took the four streets to the right of the main
road. For Jason and Dawn this entailed a steep climb up
to Wellington Place then along Britannia Avenue, which
rounded the back of the mill. They then cut through
the children's play area to Barngate Street, ending up
in Nab Hill Avenue which was a cul-de-sac to traffic
though not to pedestrians:

Apart from the empty dereliction of the mill the area
was densely populated with rows of terraced houses
crammed together, higgledy piggledy, cars parked either side further narrowing the streets and little room
for anything much bigger than a Smart car to squeeze
through.

They would start with the list of names given them
by Jadon's colleagues but house-to-house enquiries
could take days. Even weeks. And great care must be
taken to collate and store the facts. You never knew in
such extensive enquiries when you might find a nugget
of information. The trouble was knowing which facts
were of significance. But Jason Spark, as he trotted
along the streets, was nothing if not optimistic. Even
if the weather *had* been foul that night surely *someone*
would have seen *something*? Hopefully.

Joanna and Mike, in the meantime, were back at
Johnston and Pickles and Karl Robertson was no more

delighted to see them the second time around than he had been on the first.

'Look,' he said, practically gritting his teeth, 'I'm a very busy man. These are not easy times, you know, for accountancy firms. Businesses going bust and the government wanting more and more information, accusations of aiding money laundering and tax evasion. Eve was a good beautician and a lovely girl. I liked her. Since they married she hasn't been working and I don't see her anymore. I don't even *know* her husband. I've never even met him.'

'Do you have any idea why he used your name, in particular, to pretend that he worked here?'

'I haven't the faintest idea.' He looked slightly flustered, his top lip sweating.

'Do you recognize any of these names? Leroy Wilson?'

He shook his head.

'Jeff Armitage?'

Another shake of the head.

'Scott Dooley?'

Robertson frowned. 'Dooley?' He appeared to think for a minute. 'Someone called Dooley used to work here as a janitor keeping the building sorted, hiring cleaners, being on call for the burglar alarm. That sort of thing.'

'Does he still work here?'

Robertson's response was slow. 'He left…a year or two ago.'

'Was there any reason why?'

'I believe he was setting up his own business.'

He flicked his phone. 'Simon, come in here a minute, will you?'

The youth appeared as though by magic, standing as smartly as an officer on parade.

'Sir?'

'Scott Dooley.' There was an air of bemusement in his voice. 'When did he leave?'

'Eighteen months ago, sir—not long after I came.'

'You don't know where he is now?'

'No, sir.'

Next Joanna showed them both the picture of Jadon Glover. Robertson looked at it impassively, Simon too. Both shrugged. 'Sorry.'

'OK,' Joanna said, sensing a continuation of this blind avenue. Nothing here, at least nothing they were giving away. And yet, her copper's nose was twitching. She didn't believe that Glover's choice of employer had been random. But was Scott Dooley really the connection?

They made their exit.

Joanna was slowly realizing the scale of the operation when she looked again at the list of Jadon Glover's clients, the amounts loaned and the money handed over, not just on Wednesday nights but other nights of the week as well as the days. 'He can't have vanished,' she said. 'It isn't possible. Someone knows where he is.' She jabbed a finger randomly on the list of Glover's Wednesday evening clients. 'For my money one of these people.'

Scott, Leroy and Jeff were treading the same path, looking down the same list of their colleague's clients. 'Let's just run through it.'

Leroy answered. 'Six in Mill Street. Across the road, four in Wellington Place, three in Britannia Avenue, three in Barngate Street and another three in Nab Hill

Avenue.' He looked at Jeff, who appeared to be the figures man. 'How many's that?'

'Nineteen.'

'So one of these nineteen must know something.'

It was ironic that the police and Jadon's colleagues were walking in each other's footsteps. Almost on each other's toes.

'He visited the same clients every Wednesday?'

'Yeah.'

'So,' Scott said, a hint of cruelty now in his voice, 'that's where we start looking.'

The other two didn't argue. When Scott Dooley was in this sort of mood no one ever did.

*6 p.m.*

HAVING LEFT JOHNSTON and Pickles, Joanna and Mike hadn't travelled far. 'Well,' she said, looking mischievously at Mike, 'just look where we find ourselves.'

As they pulled up outside the offices she put a warning hand on his arm. 'Go easy, Mike,' she said. 'We'll learn more about their business if we tread very gently, act just a bit dumb. OK?'

'OK.' He grinned. 'Shouldn't be hard.'

They found Jadon's three colleagues having their pow wow, which ceased immediately when they opened the door.

They looked at the three of them: Scott, big, beefy and bright; Leroy, patently the bad boy of the business who looked like trouble; and Jeff, sneaky as a weasel. Yes, they had needed Jadon as a smooth front line operator to deal with the customers and give their business credence.

Joanna perched on the corner of a desk and crossed her legs. 'Tell me,' she said encouragingly, 'how it worked after you left Johnston and Pickles.'

Scott regarded her with dark eyes pouched in fat. He hadn't even twitched when she'd mentioned his previous employer.

'It's just to do with debt,' he said, speaking reluctantly, the words dragging out. 'I realized when I worked at Robertson's place that people in debt are desperate.'

Korpanski butted in, his voice harsh and, in spite of Joanna's warning, truculent. 'So you prey on them.'

'I don't put it like that.' Now it was Leroy who was taking the lead, defending their business.

'So how *do* you put it?'

Scott took over then, his voice cold and careful. 'More like,' he grinned, 'giving them a helping hand. These are people going through hard times. Get it?'

'How do they learn about you?' Joanna was genuinely curious.

'Website, word of mouth. Usual ways.' Scott was nonchalant but his eyes were watchful. He was no fool. 'Look,' he said, 'what's this got to do with Jadon going AWOL?'

'We don't know yet,' Joanna said.

There was an awkward silence, no one wanting to risk the next sentence.

'So tell me,' Joanna continued, 'you don't seem bothered by the fact that your mate, your colleague, your business partner, has gone missing?'

The three of them looked at one another, almost sheepish. Leroy's big shoulders shrugged for them all. 'He's a big boy. He can look after himself.'

'Sure about that?'

Scott put his pasty face near to hers as though sharing a confidence and they were the best of friends. 'We're more bothered by the fact that he'll have been working all day as well as the evening and he'd have had close on a thousand quid on him in cash and now he's missing.' His expression was ugly, his meaty arms, well decorated with tattoos, tensing across the desk. 'That's money that rightly belongs to all of us.' He looked around his mates. 'Shared equally,' he emphasized. 'Get it?'

Joanna stood up, folded her arms and challenged them. 'So what do you think's happened to him? Where do *you* think he is? You really think he's done a runner, abandoned home, colleagues, a good living, his wife, all for a thousand nicker? I don't think so.'

The three guys looked foolishly at one another. Joanna couldn't work out whether any one of them had an answer. She waited. Then she ran out of patience.

'Come on,' she prompted. 'You must have discussed it. He hasn't been seen since Wednesday evening when he was collecting money. It's getting on for a week now. Where do *you* think he is?'

Again, no answer. They all looked steadfastly at the floor. Leroy's eyes flickered up to her, across to Korpanski then quickly back to the floor. Scott's jaw was clenched so tight she could hear his teeth grinding. And Jeff Armitage was frowning, his lips no more than a thin, bloodless scar.

She tried again and spoke pleasantly. 'For instance,' she said conversationally, 'do you think Jadon's absconded without his car, without using his mobile phone or using his credit cards? Not a word to the wife he's so devoted to?' Worryingly she caught the faintest huff of mockery from Armitage so she pursued the point. 'When they've only been married for two years and appear so happy?'

They all looked shifty then. Tried to bluster. Jeff spoke up, talking steadily, but there was no mistaking the confrontation. 'It's your job to find him, Inspector,' he said, tight-lipped, holding his thin shoulders rigid. 'Not ours.'

'OK,' she said. 'Is there something else you're not telling us? Anything about…' she fished in the deep, '…perhaps one of the clients he visited on a Wednesday?'

There was not even a hint that she might have hit on something.

Behind her, she felt Mike take a step forward. She tried again before he exploded on to the scene. 'Look, you might help us out here. It's your mate, your colleague, who's missing. We're doing our best to find him. This is taking up a lot of police time and money that could be better deployed.'

All three stifled sniggers. She could read their mind. Doing what? Handing out traffic offences, helping old ladies cross the road, issuing parking tickets?

She tried one more time. 'Please?'

'He'll turn up.' Jeff Armitage this time.

Joanna made no response but looked from one to the other. 'Well, perhaps you'll get back in touch with us if you hear anything?'

All three responded to this with fake enthusiasm until she added, 'We already have some uniformed officers interviewing the clients that Jadon visited regularly on Wednesday nights.' She handed them a card. 'If you think of anything else either phone, text or email it through as soon as you can, please.'

Scott Dooley grabbed the card, glanced at it then tossed it down on to the desk. It was an act of rebellion. So she hadn't exactly won them over.

She and Mike left then. They would get nothing here.

As SOON AS the door was closed behind them the three cracked into action, Leroy kicking off. 'OK, so now we've got the *police* interested in our business. Great.'

'It's legal,' Jeff responded.

Scott intervened. 'Yeah, but you know what they're like. Once they've got their eyes on you they'll find something that isn't. We need to take this seriously. Find him.' His chin jutted out with absolute determination. 'Find out what he's bloody well playing at. Still, at least we've learned something. He hasn't used his mobile or taken money out of the bank. So where is the little bugger?' He searched his two mates suspiciously. 'Do either of you two know anything?'

Their response was quick. 'No.'

''Course not.'

And because Jeff Armitage's mother had drummed into him that attack was the best form of defence, he bounced the same question back to Scott. 'Do you?'

'Don't be daft.'

After a lengthy pause, during which they could almost feel the static of fury rip through Leroy, he continued, 'How much money *exactly* is missing, Jeff? You're the numbers man. Has he been sneaking bits and pieces for a while? Where exactly *was* he going on Wednesday night?'

'Just the usual,' Jeff mumbled. 'He just had some

money to collect from round the town. Same as every other bloody Wednesday.'

'Except it wasn't.' This from Scott, whose eyes were now watchful. 'I'm going to be doing some checking.' He was thoughtful. 'So if it was the same as any other old night why's he gone missing then?'

Leroy shrugged. 'I don't know. Maybe he upset someone?'

Dooley's response was scathing. 'Upset someone? One of those saddoes who owes us money for ever, one of the little bleeders who's mortgaged their souls? What do you think those fucking victims would do? Listen…' he jabbed his finger on the desk, '…they was born poor. They was born bloody unlucky and they was born careless. It's only *us* that lifts them out of their miserable lives and abject poverty.' He wasn't sure what abject meant but it seemed to go well with poverty.

Jeff Armitage looked at him. 'You think?'

'Yeah.' But his response was less sure.

Jeff continued, 'You really think they're grateful?' He was incredulous.

'Well, they ought to be.' Dooley's voice was less sure.

Leroy took over. 'Listen, you two. Get sensible. Get reasonable. Nobody, *nobody*,' he emphasized, 'would be so stupid as to take us on. Those wimps? They wouldn't dare.'

Scott and Jeff simply looked at each other, doubts crawling into their minds, sucking out confidence like hungry leeches.

'Perhaps,' Leroy continued, leaning forward, 'one of *us* should do the Wednesday round, find out who he saw and who he never got to see.'

'I can do that.' Jeff Armitage had already stood up, ready for action. Anything but inactivity.

It was Scott who stopped him. 'Hang on a minute, Jeff. That's what the police are doing.'

Leroy chipped in. 'We can see what they turn up.'

'Yeah,' Scott contributed. 'Wait to see if they come up with anything.'

But Jeff's worry wouldn't go away. 'If they come round here again sniffing around for trouble, looking into our books and such, what shall we say?'

Scott Dooley laughed and slapped his hands flat on the desk. 'We're doing *nothing* illegal,' he said. 'In fact, we're doing society a service, helping the poor and needy. *They* should be giving *us* a medal. Just think of the misery we're preventing. Children going hungry, cars being repossessed, jobs lost, homes being taken back by the mortgage company. All of them gagging for money. Money no one else will give them.'

'Not spent on fags or wine or drugs,' Leroy put in, laughing now, feet up on the desk and hands behind his head.

Jeff joined in. 'Yeah. *We're* the ones what produce the goods. We should be gettin' the OBE or something.'

Even Scott was laughing now. 'Services to humanity.'

'Yeah, well, exactly.' For once Jeff had summoned up a smile without rancour.

And then Scott brought them right back to basics. 'Well, somebody ain't giving us a medal. Or at least not Jadon. You think he's with the queen now having it pinned on his chest? You think that's where he is? Not bloody likely.'

'What do you mean?' Jeff would be the first to crack. He was the weakest link.

Scott looked at him pityingly. 'Use what little brain you've got, Armitage. If Jadon hasn't done a runner why would he go missing? We know Eve meant everything to him.'

'Yeah,' Jeff put in spitefully, 'but was *he* everything to *her*?'

Leroy was astonished. His feet slammed back on the floor. 'Now where's your twisted little mind going off to?'

'You think she just sits at home and waits for her beloved to come home?'

His two mates looked at him. 'You what?' Scott said. 'Eve? She bloody adores him.'

Jeff Armitage backed down grumpily. 'Just saying. That's all.'

But the other two weren't letting him go. 'What *are* you saying exactly?'

'Just that I don't think she's everything she seems. That's all. I think there's something…' he paused, '…funny about her.' The other two were tempted to ignore him. Bitter and twisted. That's what he was. Suspicious of everyone.

Now the three of them eyed each other suspiciously. Trust? Among thieves? But of course they weren't thieves. They were…philanthropists.

Leroy reined them in. 'How much money exactly's gone with him?'

'Near enough a grand,' Jeff said. 'Wednesday was always a busy day but it's not enough to make it worth his while walking out on us, the business, the wife, his house, car, everything. It doesn't make any sense. Something must have happened to him.'

'Like what?'

They were all three silent then Scott said very slowly, 'You don't think one of our clients has got a bit miffed with our "not very competitive" interest rates and gone for him, do you?'

The other two shook their heads but doubt was beginning to creep in like mustard gas seeping beneath a door.

Scott Dooley sat and tried to work it out. He was a tousle-headed guy with some Arabic writing tattooed up his arm. He didn't know what it said—he'd just liked the look of it so he'd had it done. When the tattooist had asked him if he wanted a translation, he'd said, 'Nah. Don't bother. It's OK.'

'But what if,' the others had joked, when they'd seen it, 'it says something really rude or offensive?'

He'd looked a bit anxious then. 'I did say when he was doing it that I didn't want nothing that would make trouble.'

'Yeah, right. They'll only behead you.'

For weeks afterwards he'd had nightmares about this. He'd be walking down the street, someone walking towards him. They'd read the writing on his arm and then whoosh. Big sword.

But now the nightmares had faded. And he didn't want them replaced with any more. He didn't want to think about what had happened to Jadon. Jadon was slick, smart, clever. He'd been the one to dream up the idea. He and Scott had worked it all out, employed Leroy because he was a thug and Jeff Armitage because he was wary, suspicious and good with numbers. Jeff was their bookkeeper. For three years now they'd made money. Real money. Their clients were completely cowed, terrified of being evicted, terrified of starving or not being able to keep up the payments on their cars, not being able to get to work. Between them they'd heard every single sob story in the world: death, disease, destruction. But most of all bad luck. The people who borrowed, digging themselves into a bottomless grave, blamed everything on bad luck. That was the way it went.

They'd lent money for weddings and funerals, divorces and engagements, parties and wakes, houses, rentals, deposits. Everything, they sometimes reflected when they went to the pub after work. Everything in life and death needed one vital ingredient—money.

And they could supply it.

Only once had someone tried to pull a fast one. Leroy had dealt with it and since then they'd had no more trouble except… Scott shoved it out of his mind.

Scott was not only the most twitchy of the three, he was also the most aware. Leroy might take the lead in threats but he acted first and thought later and Jeff was so sour and suspicious of everybody that he couldn't sort out facts from products of his warped and paranoid mind. But Scott was smart. The business had been his idea: the name, with its double entendre, the subtle advertising, the exorbitant interest rates, the weekly rounds. When he'd worked for Johnston and Pickles he had learned about money, or rather, something more important—the need for money. The love of money. The desperation for money. He knew exactly how desperate people were when they were really skint and had no access to credit. He knew where the pressure points were and he knew how to apply exactly the right amount of persuasion.

*Come on, missus, you wouldn't want your daughter to be evicted, would you?*

*And without a car how do you think you'll get into work?*

*You deserve a holiday, love. You've earned it. You owe it to yourself.*

*He was a good bloke. He should have a good send-off. You'll want to say goodbye properly.*

Then there were the little levers:

*You'll soon pay it off.*

And last of all the little lies:

*It isn't that much interest once you've started to nibble away at the capital.*

And you could always use terms to confuse them:

*Yeah, well, it's* compound *interest, you see.*

*The* APR *works out at a very advantageous rate.*

And the beauty was he'd learned it all from Johnston and Pickles. Legit.

And his meeting with Jadon? Pure, beautiful, designed chance. Robertson had asked him to cancel an appointment one day with his beautician and Jadon had answered. He'd immediately recognized the oily suspicion in the man's voice and followed it up.

Bob's your uncle.

SCOTT DOOLEY KNEW precisely where they'd crossed the line once or twice. Maybe more than once or twice—coerced people who hadn't really needed to borrow, at least not from them at their 'advantageous' interest rates. And when people couldn't or wouldn't pay up they had two options: either extend the loan so their clients were locked in even tighter or take something to cover costs. Tellies, cars, jewellery. Anything really. And when that didn't work it was a matter of bringing on the heavies. Always a last resort but the sight of Leroy was usually enough to sort out any problems. He terrified them. So now, when Scott started pacing around, his own mind was beginning to work things out. Whatever had happened to Jadon he had been a good, steady worker—reliable. It was out of character for him to have gone missing. And Scott didn't believe for a minute that Jadon had done a runner with under a grand in his pocket. More likely, someone had gone for him. This was dangerous territory. He had a sort of premonition of them being picked off one by one.

Shove it, he said to himself.

But in this he was a step ahead of the police. He knew Jadon Glover and he knew Eve as well. He also knew that the police would be sniffing around them for a bit longer yet. He just hoped it wouldn't have too much of an impact on the business.

'We need to delete some files,' he said. 'Take them off our computers.' Then when the other two raised objections about losing money and what they called leverage he qualified with a, 'We'll keep a copy of who owes what. We won't lose out but we need to take this seriously.'

'Yeah.' Jeff was already pressing keys.

'We'll go round and see Eve,' Leroy suggested. 'She's bound to know something.'

Jeff was scornful. 'All three of us? We'll frighten her.'

Scott took over. 'Not you, Leroy. Just me,' he said.

His two colleagues were used to leaving most of the thinking to Scott. They were happy.

'No time like the present,' he said with a false jauntiness, heaving himself out of his seat.

COINCIDENTALLY, THIS WAS exactly where Joanna and Mike were. Even as they turned into Disraeli Place they sensed a sombre, quiet feel to number eight. There was no sign of anyone in the road, even peering from behind curtains. The entire place was deserted. Although the day was dull and cool there was no light on. Joanna looked at Mike. 'Think she's gone out?'

'Whatever,' Korpanski said unhelpfully.

Eve didn't come to the door straight away and as they waited on the doorstep they looked around at the ghost estate. Did anyone actually live here? There were no cars in the drives, no lights on, no noise. It was eerie.

Then a white face appeared in the downstairs window and quickly disappeared. They heard a security chain rattling. So Eve was nervous?

When she finally opened the door they had a shock, wondering for a moment whether they had the right house. She was barefoot, wearing a baggy grey bloke's sweater and pink jogging pants. Her face was nude which made her look anaemic, younger and vulnerable. She looked frightened and very, very tired. Pointless to ask her whether she was all right. They did anyway.

Her eyes asked the desperate question and Joanna shook her head. 'I'm sorry,' she said.

They needed to tread carefully now. This wasn't a simple case of a misper, a husband going AWOL. It was a something else. Something deeper and more sinister. On the way over she and Mike had discussed the case. Plenty of people would have had reason to dislike Jadon. Hate him even for locking them into the trap of poverty, never paid off debt because of interest rates high enough to make your eyes water. As soon as the reports started coming through from the uniformed house-to-house interviews they would be asking questions.

But not her.

They followed her into the soulless sitting room. What did she do all day? There were no books, no magazines. The television was switched off. There was no radio on. Did she simply sit around and look at four beige walls? There was no clue as to the real Eve.

Joanna opened the questioning, feeling awkward. She was going to have to share with Jadon's wife the fact that he had lied about his career. And what else? She must dig deeper.

'Mrs Glover, Eve,' she said cautiously, 'you said that your husband worked for Johnston and Pickles. Well, we've been there.'

Had Eve Glover had bristles they would have quivered.

'Mr Robertson, Karl Robertson, the CEO, says Jadon doesn't work there.'

The blue eyes were confused now. 'I don't understand.'

'We've spoken to Jadon's colleagues, Leroy, Jeff and Scott,' Joanna continued. 'Their office is, in fact, just round the corner from Johnston and Pickles.'

'Oh?' She was frowning.

'Do you know Mr Robertson?'

She thought for a moment then smiled. 'I used to know *a* Mr Robertson a few years ago before I was married. He used to come to my salon. Is it the same man?'

'It would appear so,' Joanna said cautiously, only too aware that the connection between Jadon, his wife, Karl

Robertson and his happy comrades was tenuous. They still knew so little about Jadon Glover. 'You didn't realize that this Mr Robertson is the CEO of the firm your husband said he worked for?'

'Well, no. I mean, I'd have thought he would have said.' She was picking at the grey sweater, worrying at it. Plucking at the wool. 'Might have mentioned it.' She thought for a moment before looking at them.

'So if Jadon wasn't an accountant working for Johnston and Pickles, who did he work for and what *did* he do?'

Joanna exhaled. The first question was easy to answer. 'He worked for himself. He, Scott Dooley, Leroy and Jeff ran their own business.'

'Doing what?'

Joanna glanced very briefly at Korpanski then took the plunge. 'Have you ever heard of doorstep lending?'

Eve shook her head.

'Or payday loans?'

'I've *heard* of them.'

She took a while to jump across the chasm from fiction to fact using deduction as a bridge. 'Are you saying…?' She stopped abruptly as though she had just reached the edge, was teetering and wasn't sure whether she wanted to take the next big step, diving over the cliff. 'Is that what they did? Is that what *he* did?'

Joanna nodded then glanced at Mike. He was looking intrigued, almost fascinated at the metamorphosis taking place in front of their eyes as the alteration in her husband's status sunk into Eve Glover. They were watching her unravel.

She was initially quiet as she digested the information. 'So the clients he was meeting…?'

'People who owed money to the firm.'

Eve frowned. 'People who were really hard up?'

'Yep.'

Eve swallowed. 'I've heard that those loans can never be repaid,' she said quietly and slowly, 'because the interest rates are so high.'

'It's how they make their money.'

Eve worked her chin, clearly upset. 'So Jadon…'

Korpanski butted in. Joanna could have killed him. 'I wouldn't be too hard on him, love.' But Eve's eyes were hard and unforgiving as she faced the sergeant. 'He *said* he was in financial management.' Again, for some inexplicable reason except, maybe, male loyalty, Korpanski tried to defend the missing man. 'Well, he was…' he caught Joanna's eye and ended lamely, '…in a way.'

Joanna couldn't even be sure Eve had heard him. Her face was frozen. And she was angry. 'Do you think this has any connection with his disappearance?'

'It's one theory we're working with.'

'Someone who owed him money and was…desperate?'

'Well, now we know the truth it's one possibility we'll work with. We already have uniformed officers doing house-to-house calls.'

Eve stood up, agitated, and crossed to the window. 'Kidnap?'

'It's a possibility,' Joanna repeated awkwardly, not pointing out the obvious fact that there had been no kidnap demand and there was another possibility. Eve's mind was tracking away, trying to place facts in order, one step in front of another.

'He was lying,' she said finally. 'Just lying.' Then she

turned around and spoke with, considering, surprising dignity, smiling. 'I stuck up for Jadon,' she said. 'I tried to be exactly what he wanted me to be, at some cost to myself. I sacrificed…' And here she stopped, her blue eyes wide open, horrified.

Joanna imagined then that she understood. Eve had sacrificed her beauty salon business for her marriage.

Eve continued, 'I thought, when I married him, that I was really very lucky.'

Mike Korpanski took one heavy step forward. 'It's just the job he did,' he said. 'It doesn't change the man.'

Her eyes were full on him as she responded. 'Doesn't it, Sergeant?'

Maybe the question was just too deep for any of them to answer.

# TEN

MONICA PAGETT WAS deep in thought. Over the weekend she had been handed a list of activities. Brooklands, apparently, offered sherry and quizzes, Scrabble mornings, shopping trips, even a concert or two. She didn't like to admit she was tempted.

She recalled fetching in a bucket of coal and slipping on the icy path. She recalled the bitter cold and frosty mornings, the trips into Leek to Wednesday's market day, trips which became increasingly difficult.

She missed her cottage high up on the moors, 500 metres above sea level, exposed to the most brutal of elements, summer and winter alike. In Brooklands, she mused, one would not know the seasons, would be unable to tell whether it was summer or winter, hot or cold, wet or dry. The place would maintain a year-round temperature and atmosphere. Out there the seasons dictated your activities—sheep dipping and shearing, apple picking, bottling and pickling, harvesting the fruit, the silage and haymaking. There was always something to do. In here she would simply be filling in time between today and the grave.

She sat immobile. Then she rang her bell.

'Stephanie,' she said decisively, 'no time like the present. In the morning I want you to contact someone called Wendy Bradshaw. You'll find her telephone number in my diary. Go on, dear,' she said. 'My diary's in my handbag. Just get it. I know you're not going to be pinching my purse.'

JOANNA WAS PORING over the list of the nineteen clients Jadon Glover visited regularly on a Wednesday night. She pictured the small flats over the shops, the huge mill, the narrow streets and small terraced houses. She studied the map of the area, taking in the child's playground, surely deserted last rainy Wednesday night. Had the weather been fortuitous? She read through the list of names, none of which was known to her—a good sign. Not a petty criminal among them. These were the families under their radar—honest, decent, hardworking people who paid their taxes, insured their cars and worked. And were poor.

She tossed the list over to Mike. He went through it as carefully as she had and agreed, looking back at her, his face dubious. 'Don't see anything obvious here.' He tried to lighten her mood, grinning. 'No known serial killers, Jo.'

She folded her arms and sat back in her chair. 'I don't know what you've got to grin about, Korpanski. All I see ahead is a great long list of people to question and not one sodding answer.'

His grin simply widened. These days it was hard to ruffle his feathers.

The initial report had come through on the Mitsubishi. It was clean. No blood or any other signs of assault or trouble. 'So,' Joanna said, sitting back in her chair, 'the car was parked, locked and left. He expected to return to it. Whatever happened to Jadon Glover happened after he left the vehicle.'

It was what she'd expected.

The lab was waiting for further instruction. 'Fingerprints?' she asked without much hope.

'Just Mr Glover's and his wife,' the lab responded. 'So what now…?'

'Just hang on to it,' Joanna said and put the phone down.

*9 p.m.*

FOR ONCE SHE WAS first home and when she rang Matthew he was still half an hour away. He'd been delayed. 'Just enough time to make some supper,' she said and rifled around in the fridge. She started chopping onions and peppers, slicing bacon, opened a tin of tomatoes and put the pan on for the pasta. Just cheese left to grate. She heard Matthew's car outside and pulled the cork from a bottle of Rioja.

'Hey.' He looked tired but happy. No trace of the traumas of the other night. It was always difficult to know whether to bring up a sticky subject so she searched his face and found only placid contentment as he ate his supper. They both needed to unwind so they sat together on the sofa and watched a film.

The little boy with the strange name, Jadon Glover and his cronies, Eve, Karl Robertson, the inhabitants of the crooked streets, even Kath Whalley were so very far away.

*Tuesday, 11 March, 8 a.m.*

BUT NOW JADON HAD been missing for almost a week. It was time to get serious, step up the enquiry. Time to get focused.

She called a briefing to collate at least some of the

information gathered by the teams who had been working their way around the area. A map was pinned to the wall so they could trace Jadon's usual route, starting with Mill Street. The families in the flats over the sixties' shops were largely pensioners. The flats belonged to a housing association and the rents were affordable.

The houses on the other side of the road were different—terraced mill workers' cottages privately owned and well maintained. Joanna knew the area though not well. Little of their work was centred around these streets apart from one incident almost three years ago which had changed the geography of the place. A child had been knocked down on Nab Hill Avenue, which had then been used as a chicken run by drivers wishing to take Macclesfield Road to avoid the town centre. Since then Nab Hill Avenue had been blocked off with concrete bollards and was now a dead end.

In most other respects the streets were the same as they had been in Victorian times. Their families were proud of them. They were uniform, a door, one window to the side and two above, and yet they were individual, each one sporting something different—a hanging basket, a UPVC front door, neatly draped curtains, French blinds. Some had been rendered with stone, others painted gaily. Some were obsessively neat, others less so. In general, this area where Jadon Glover would have collected his dues was not somewhere the police visited. These were reasonable, hardworking families who caused little trouble—not even the odd domestic. Poverty or a struggle to survive might well be a feature of their lives but crime was not.

PCs Paul Ruthin and Bridget Anderton gave their report first. They had visited all six of the Mill Street people on Jadon's books, ending with a lady called Astrid Jenkins who told them Glover generally put her last on the Mill Street list and he had called, as always, at 7.25 p.m. 'He apparently whizzed round his clients,' Bridget said.

'She originally borrowed eight hundred pounds to help her granddaughter put a deposit down on a house. She didn't tell her family she'd borrowed the money. At the time she worked as a cleaner in the clothing factory but eight months ago she had a stroke and since then she's no longer been able to work.' She hesitated. 'She's been paying it off for nearly two years.'

'At a rate of?' Joanna asked sharply.

'Fifteen pounds a week. And she hasn't quite paid off half of it yet.'

Among the assembled officers there were a few dropped jaws but just as many set faces. This was the reality of life below the wire, under the radar and in the crooked streets.

'What did she think of him?' Joanna was curious.

PC Paul Ruthin took up the answer. He was a relatively new officer who still lived at home with his widowed mother. A mother who was not above ringing the station and complaining if she thought her boy was being worked too hard. It didn't do a lot for his reputation. 'Nothing,' he said. 'She just reported events without really showing any emotion.'

'No resentment? No anger?'

'No. She was just factual. It was as though that was what she paid and that was that.'

'Did she have any idea when the debt would be paid off?'

'She said it was under review but that as interest rates were changing all the time it was hard to work out.'

Joanna let out an expletive. 'Arithmetic is hardly my

strong point, Paul, but even I can work out this simple
sum. She's already paid off twice her original debt.
Surely it's coming to an end?'

The PC's eyes were hard but he was smiling. 'I don't
think that's how it works. She just said that he helped
her out, came to her rescue when she needed it. No
one else would and her granddaughter was expecting
a baby.'

He and Bridget gave brief descriptions of the other
families in Mill Street. Astrid Jenkins was, it appeared,
typical of Glover's clients, and as she'd been the last to
see him on Mill Street they quickly moved on.

Joanna turned to Jason Spark and Dawn Critchlow.
'And after that?'

Dawn Critchlow moved forward to use the whiteboard. 'We worked on the other side of Macclesfield
Road. We didn't find everybody in, ma'am,' she said,
'so our facts are patchy. We don't know in what order
Jadon called on his clients last Wednesday; neither do
we know whether he visited in the same order each
week. Geographically the logical order would be to
pass Big Mill, turn into Wellington Place,' she moved
her finger up the map, 'up to Britannia Avenue, cut
through the children's play area, turn into Barngate
Street, cross through to Nab Hill Avenue and then return down the hill back to Sainsbury's. He could have
done it the other way around—started at Nab Hill Avenue and finished at Wellington Place, or even swapped
the order round a bit.'

'Right,' Joanna said, glancing at the sheet.

'Because the story is a bit patchy,' PC Dawn
Critchlow continued, 'we thought we'd spend tomorrow trying to collate all the information and then make a

fuller report in the morning briefing?' She looked anxiously at Joanna who was nodding, her attention still on the list of names and the geography of the streets. Finally she turned to look at them, still nodding and frowning. 'That seems a good idea, Dawn and Jason,' she said. 'Continue with your house to house and get back to me if you find anything that seems to hold a clue as to what's happened to Jadon Glover and at what point he vanished from view.'

She took a good look at Jadon's photograph. How would she describe him? Bold, audacious. He looked smart but she had the feeling that his apparent superconfidence was only skin deep. Scratch the surface and you would find something and someone quite different. The question was: what? And who? Was it vulnerability she was sensing or something else?

She threw the next question wide open to the floor. 'Did any of you get closer to learning at what point Jadon disappeared?'

Dawn Critchlow tried to answer. 'According to our clients' statements,' she said, 'it appears that he got at least as far as Britannia Avenue. There is CCTV of someone crossing the children's play area towards either Barngate Street or Nab Hill Avenue but we can't be sure whether it's Jadon or not, and none of the inhabitants of those two streets confirm that he visited them on that night.'

'OK.'

She threw the next question wide open to the whole room. 'Have any of you unearthed anything suspicious in Jadon's disappearance?'

Again she looked at a sea of blank faces and shaking heads. 'Right,' she said, 'keep on with the investigation of Glover's known movements, focus on this area…' she put her hand over the map of the four streets, '…and let me know at once if you find anything out.'

They shuffled out.

But when the officers had left she shared her thoughts with Mike. 'Both Eve and Jadon seem to be an enigma,' she said. 'I just can't get a handle on either of them. They seem unreal—plastic. Where did they come from? We have no background. No family. Only a few friends at their wedding? Two of hers and his dubious colleagues with partners? That big flashy wedding in Italy. So where were their family? Why do neither of them appear to have a past? Where are their previous relationships, children, ex-partners? Were Jadon's colleagues and their partners in on the secret? Were they sworn to secrecy to keep Eve from knowing what her husband really did? That far from being a professional man, a financial advisor, he was scum, preying on people on their beam ends?' She could feel her anger rising. 'Were Scott, Jeff and Leroy's partners kept in ignorance too? Did they share Eve's naivety? Or was it only Eve who was left out and why? Why was she singled out? Was she so vulnerable? Or so fickle that her love, admiration and devotion for her perfect husband depended on him being a financial advisor rather than a Shylock?'

Korpanski, too, was frowning. 'Maybe our Mr Glover thought she'd dump him if she found out what a shit job he did.'

'Maybe…' She sensed there was more depth to this story and struggled to grasp it. She looked squarely at Mike. 'Was he so very vulnerable? Is she so *very* beautiful?'

Like all men Korpanski knew when he was caught out. He looked embarrassed. 'We-ell,' he said. 'There's a lot of paint.'

She giggled, took pity on him, let him off the hook and moved back to her topic. 'Maybe instead of focusing on the exact point where Glover disappeared from view we should be delving a little more into backgrounds.'

Korpanski made a face.

'Rather than focusing on where he is perhaps we should be asking where he's come from? Where does she come from?'

'If you think so, Jo.' Mike was patently dubious. His usual approach was less circumvent, less subtle. He liked to charge in, blast out questions, bully his suspect into submission, caution them, charge them, secure a conviction and move on to the next case. Slap hands together. Job done.

Unlike his senior officer he didn't spend hours merely thinking, musing, tossing 'dumb' ideas around. DS Mike Korpanski was a man of action. 'What that might have to do with things I don't know. I mean, what does it matter, Jo?' he grumbled. 'What's it to do with all this?' He wafted his hand around the maps and diagrams, timelines, photographs, questions.

She followed his gaze and felt a quick moment of apprehension. She always felt that CS Gabriel Rush peered over her shoulder, ready to criticize any unnecessary or spurious action—or lack of. And he was more likely to share Korpanski's methods than hers.

Everyone in the force knew that it was all too easy to waste thousands on a red herring in an investigation. It happened all the time. 'I don't know,' she said slowly. 'I'm just confused. This man's disappeared from practically the centre of a busy market town. OK, it was a rainy night. It was dark. It seems nobody was around but we've lost trace of him as though he's dropped through a wormhole.' She frowned. 'We'll see what Jason and Dawn dig up from the other side of the road when they've revisited and found a few more people in. Then we'll try and piece it together.' But a vision of Big Mill swam, unwelcome, into view. 'Then there's that bloody big derelict factory sitting like a trap plumb in the middle of our search area.' She took a sly look at Korpanski who was scowling, shoulders tipped forward as though he was about to enter the wrestling ring. Could she risk a joke? 'Don't suppose the Tardis is parked somewhere inside?'

Korpanski didn't laugh. But his face softened.

So she continued, 'Is he in there? Have we missed him? Tripped over his body?' And when she still had no response, she carried on musing. 'What do you really think's happened, Mike?'

He didn't even hesitate. 'Bloke like that, Jo? Has to have done a runner. None of these…' He turned and looked at the board. 'These people were made monkeys of, intimidated by our money lenders for a couple of years. I just can't see one of them committing cold-blooded murder all of a sudden and successfully disposing of the body. Why now? No,' he said, even more certain of his opinion. 'Glover's probably been setting it up, salting bits away. He'll be in Spain or Turkey or somewhere.'

'Without his wife?'

'She might be planning to join him when this has blown over.'

'So if that was his plan why draw attention by alerting us?'

Again Korpanski shrugged. 'Part of it? Who knows?'

But Joanna was still shaking her head. She turned back to the board, to the list of names and addresses of the families from the five streets, studying the names, trying to stimulate her mind. Trying to think. In what order had Jadon Glover visited them? That night, had he started with Wellington Place or Nab Hill Avenue? Who last saw him and where? Was the CCTV footage of a figure crossing the small playground him?

Damn the weather, she thought, then realized. It had aided and abetted, helped to conceal the circumstances.

She spoke almost to herself, running her eyes down the list of names. Widnes, Stanton, Murdoch, Ginster, Madeley, the three women in Nab Hill Avenue, and wondered who, out of these names almost picked out of a hat, knew anything about Jadon's disappearance.

'Does one of these people have him, do you think?' Korpanski shrugged.

His sceptical silence brought her to a decision. 'Well, if we don't have an answer soon I'm going public on this.'

Korpanski's eyes were as black as his hair which made him completely unreadable. But she could guess his thoughts. Somewhere between *waste of time* and *OK, get in there.*

But he was a sergeant. He could afford to be neutral. She could not.

And in the meantime, Jason Spark, Dawn Critchlow and their teams of officers continued knocking on doors.

# ELEVEN

*Tuesday, 11 March, 8 p.m.*
*8 Nab Hill Avenue*

THEY OFTEN MET for a glass of wine—or six—and a take-away on a Saturday night, the three of them. They'd laugh about ex-boyfriends, gossip about the other people in their lives, swap celebrity chatter. Sometimes they'd watch a box set, the three of them as close as pickles in a jar. Their differing ages and backgrounds made absolutely no difference. They were women; they had that in common. It was enough. They'd had their struggles which had bonded them as close as sisters.

Men? They didn't need them in their lives, they all said. Men were a complication, a nuisance. An expense. They dragged you down. Back into the gutter.

Grandma Charlotte was the oldest. She lived in number six and was in her early sixties. Grandma Charlotte held the record for men, having had four husbands but out of that only one daughter—Irina, having gone through a communist-loving phase in her forties. It was then that she'd stopped cooking husband number two's breakfast because she'd had morning sickness. He had scuttled away the moment Charlotte had given birth and, following in his father-in-law's footsteps, Irina's husband had subsequently beaten even that record by doing a runner the minute she'd shared similarly good news with him. Irina had two children herself now and she and Grandma Charlotte brought them up between them. Their father had made a brief reappearance—just enough to fertilize a second embryo—and then disappeared for ever.

To the Nab Hill Three men were the arch enemy. Their mantra was: men—who needs them?

Every now and again Erienna or Charlotte would meet someone of the opposite sex and regale Yasmin with their stories of awkward, drunken fumblings and unsatisfactory love-making.

Erienna Delaney was Irish, fiercely so, with bright blue eyes and dark hair. She was far too independent to even consider having a husband or children. Had the IRA still been around she would have been a bomber or a spy but as it was she was a zealot without a cause. Except to run men down.

She lived in number eight.

Yasmin was the most different—the daughter of a Turkish family who had a restaurant in Cardiff, it was hard to work out how or why she had landed in Leek— not that her two great buddies had ever asked. They accepted the fact that she was a Muslim who didn't appear to currently have a boyfriend or husband but one could never tell with Yasmin. She was—or could be—enigmatic.

She lived alone in number four.

One day, they had promised themselves, they would go on holiday to Yasmin's country, Turkey. She spoke the language. She could be their guide and they would travel around and see the cities and the people, the mosques and the beaches. Oh, yes, the beaches. When they talked about it they could almost feel the heat of that Turkish sun, see the blue of the sea, the yellow sand and imagine sipping *elma çay*—apple tea—which Yasmin said was nectar, sweet and fruity, just like them and, spoken with a giggle, an aphrodisiac.

Being a Muslim, Yasmin had to be very careful to keep her head down and she never told them anything about her previous life. She was secretive but very beautiful with big brown eyes, heavy black eyebrows, an infectious giggle and, beneath her hijab, a naughty sense of humour. When the others spoke about sex she would simply giggle without giving anything away. Erienna and Charlotte had learned not to ask Yasmin about her life and loves so they focused on their own adventures and enjoyed hearing her giggle at the more risqué bits. As for children, that was another taboo subject. They didn't know whether Yasmin had any. For some reason Charlotte and Erienna felt she did have offspring but if she did she never talked of them. There were no photographs of any family around her neat but spartan house.

Yasmin wasn't supposed to drink any alcohol but, as she said, when she downed her first glass of cheap white wine, three for ten pounds at Asda, 'Who's to know?' It was one of her favourite phrases.

It wasn't really very funny but after a couple of glasses of the sharp wine it had the effect of making the other two shriek with laughter.

'Who's to know?'

Naturally the talk that night was of the disappearance of the one person who had helped form their initial bond—their creditor—who landed on their doorstep every single Wednesday evening.

Without fail.

Yasmin spoke first. Being unused to alcohol, the wine had loosened her tongue faster than the others.

'What do you think's happened to him?' Her big eyes sparkled with merriment. All she knew was she'd had a week off paying. A blessed week when she had an extra twenty pounds to spend all on herself.

'I don't know.' Charlotte took a long swig. 'Maybe he's run off with another woman.'

'Well, *we're* all here, so it's not one of us,' Erienna responded, chortling while the others exploded at her wit.

'Seriously.'

'Listen, love,' Charlotte said, 'I don't know and I don't care either. I just hope he never surfaces again, smarmy little bloody worm.'

Erienna held her glass up. 'I'll drink to that.' They clinked glasses.

'But,' Yasmin said slowly, 'if he doesn't appear again someone else will only take his place. They won't let us go.'

The words were almost enough to sober them up. Defiantly, Charlotte opened another bottle of wine. This week they had money to spare. They had a third bottle to go but tonight they didn't feel like drinking it. It was starting to taste sour.

The knock on their door sounded ominous even through their alcohol-induced state of relaxation.

It being Erienna's house, she was the one to get up and answer it after an anxious glance at her friends. She looked so pale and suddenly frightened that Charlotte almost stood up and offered to answer it for her but Erienna being Erienna, Charlotte didn't think the gesture would be appreciated.

She heard the conversation, albeit one-sided, and glanced at Yasmin, worried.

'It's not convenient,' she heard her friend say. 'I've got a couple of pals round for the evening.'

The person on the doorstep spoke again and she answered. 'Yeah, he did use to call.'

More talk, then, 'Yeah, I heard. No. No. He didn't come last Wednesday.'

*There, it was said now. He didn't come last Wednesday.*

Erienna answered another question. 'Sometimes early-ish. Sometimes later. In between half seven and nine.'

The person on the doorstep spoke again and Erienna responded, 'If we was out?' A cynical laugh. 'If we was out he'd charge double the following week. With interest.'

And for the first time during the interview Charlotte heard it in her friend's voice. A hard, bitter note of resentment. 'Jadon? Forget? Never. He never forgot. A mind like a spreadsheet, he had.'

Then they both heard her sarcasm. 'My pleasure, Sergeant.'

A mumble corrected her so she scooped up the compliment. 'Sorry—Constable.'

*Wednesday, 12 March, 8 a.m.*

THE DAY WAS BRIGHT and blustery. Matthew was subdued and Joanna knew that the murder of the oddly-named child might recede in the evening's distraction but this morning it stuck with him. She could see it in his face.

He looked…hurt. She sat on the side of the bed and planted a kiss on his cheek.

He smiled at her abstractedly. 'What was that for?'

'Because sometimes you take the cares of the world on your shoulders, Matthew Levin.'

His smile broadened. 'You too, I think.'

'Yeah. I just don't have it planted in front of me in such graphic detail. I don't have to…'

He held his hand up to stop her. 'I'll get over it, Jo. Until the next time I see a child… I don't know. Knocked down, diseased, hurt.' He stared across the room, eyes unfocused. And his voice, when he continued, was bitter. 'I wish I came home to something of my own, something I could cuddle and love.'

Hurt, she bit back the words that had landed on her tongue without thought. *So I'm not enough?* She knew they would sound petty and selfish. Instead she got off the bed, moved into the bathroom and started brushing her teeth.

But when she came back into the bedroom Matthew still looked troubled. He was still in that horrible place. 'I hated it, Jo. The poor little thing; he just didn't stand a chance.'

'What about the mother?'

'The little scrap spent most of his time with the evil grandma. I don't think she wanted him any more than the mum but apparently Mum's new partner didn't like kids.' The glance he gave her was almost an appeal. 'How can anyone not like children, Jo?'

There was a time when she could have answered this rhetoric but her brain had scrambled since they had married. She'd changed. She could hardly believe how much. Her own ambition and desires seemed to have merged with Matthew's. What was more, he knew it. He wasn't saying anything but the way he looked at her, with a mixture of humour, sympathy and understanding, told him that he was only too aware of her metamorphosis.

*Wednesday, 12 March, 10 a.m.*

JASON SPARK AND DAWN CRITCHLOW were continuing to knock on doors with their allotted team. And finally they were gaining a clearer picture of Jadon Glover's movements last Wednesday night. Dawn was a hard-working officer whose husband had a failed garage business. He currently stacked shelves in one of the local supermarkets so she was the main breadwinner. In some ways she was unsuitable to be a police officer. She rarely saw harm in anyone, always seeming to peer beneath the surface and find some good, somewhere. She grinned at Jason. 'If there were sinkholes in this part of Leek,' she said slowly, 'I'd like to think Jadon Glover had fallen down one.'

PC Spark chortled and the pair of them continued with the pretty fruitless house to house. Either no one knew anything relating to the disappearance or else they simply weren't talking. The overwhelming response of the debtors who denied having seen the money collector on the previous Wednesday was relief at having a week's grace from paying.

But the two officers did their job. They took statements from everyone and pored over the results, made an attempt to tabulate them.

At eleven a.m. they would have a brainstorm and briefing and pool their knowledge with the rest of the investigating officers, try and pinpoint the exact moment when Jadon Glover had dropped beneath the radar. And they knew DI Piercy would expect them to be concise and precise. Then someone would have to make the decision whether to escalate the investigation or scale it down. It was an unenviable responsibility and would depend on their findings.

Joanna had begun the day with yet another phone call to Eve Glover which she already knew would be fruitless. But there was some point to this. The first and most sensible reason was that as SIO she was supposed to keep relatives informed of any progression in their case.

Some hope, Joanna thought as she picked out the number.

The second reason for the call was even more futile. But there was just the vaguest of possibilities that Jadon might have turned up.

After all, if he had reappeared, tail between his legs, or even if he had contacted his bemused wife to explain the inexplicable, it would no longer be a police matter. Lying about your place of work was nothing to do with them. It was an uncomfortable lie between husband and wife, something they could sort out privately. No point having egg on your face if Glover had simply been sleeping off the mother and father of all hangovers but, as before, she could tell from the tense tone when the phone was picked up that none of these scenarios had happened. Jadon was still missing. And, she expected, he would remain so.

Today Eve displayed a mixture of hysteria, grief, worry and absolute confusion. Her voice alternated between flat and hysterical.

'Something bad *must* have happened to him,' she said, her voice stiff and—frankly—flaky. She sounded so strange Joanna wondered whether she had been pre-scribed tranquilisers. 'I don't understand, Inspector. Where is he? Why hasn't he come home? Why hasn't he rung? What's wrong? I wonder if I even knew him. Who is he? What is he? Has someone…' Her voice, high and hysterical, finally trailed away.

The phrases sparked an emotion which resonated in Joanna's copper's mind. Who is he? The real Jadon Glover. Who was he?

Joanna tried to put herself in the woman's position and understood only too well. Had it been Matthew who had vanished she would have been beside herself. But this was an unusual disappearance. Later today, she promised herself, she would do a little more digging into Jadon's identity. The lab had found nothing untoward in the car so far, so Joanna had no further information for Eve except to reassure her that police enquiries were ongoing and they would be making an appeal later today on local radio and television. Apart from that everything she could say with assurance was negative. *None* of Jadon's credit or debit cards had been used; *neither* had there been any activity on his phone. 'For the moment,' she told her, 'it seems unlikely that your husband has been abducted or assaulted. We've found no evidence of any assault in your husband's car or in the area from where he disappeared.' She hesitated before exploring her thought. 'I take it no one has contacted you?' She left the word ransom out of the question.

'No.' Eve's response was snappy.

'And you can't think of anyone who had a grudge against him?'

*Apart from the people whom he was robbing hand over fist.*

A sniff was Eve's response.

'So all we can do, for the moment, Mrs Glover, is exactly what we *are* doing—ask questions and wait.' Her meant-to-be reassurance was greeted with silence.

Joanna tried again, to reassure the upset wife that in cases like this there was every chance that Jadon would turn up with his own explanation but when, minutes later, she put the phone down, Joanna was very reflective. She didn't believe her own words, neither did she think for a moment that she had hoodwinked Jadon's wife. They might not be saying it but they both knew that there was something rotten at the core of this scenario. It wasn't simply the deceit that had lain between them but Jadon's insistence his wife leave her career. It smacked of almost pathological insecurity and a need for control. Perhaps stemming from Jadon's past? And Joanna knew another thing: he wouldn't have got halfway through his evening's work. Everything screamed against it.

It was only as she put the phone down that she really chewed over the possibility of kidnap. And that opened another entire recipe book of issues. But, unless Eve was lying, the contraindication to that shouted at her. No ransom note.

So what would be the point?

Joanna couldn't resist smiling to herself. There had never been a kidnap in Leek. Maybe the first? She shook her head.

WHEN MIKE ARRIVED back ten minutes later they began to dismantle Jadon Glover's life brick by brick. He had, it appeared, been a careful, even thrifty man. His bank account was OK. Regular payments in which easily covered his outgoings. Paid in in cash. Unsurprisingly no monthly cheques, no debt. All cash. Household bills paid by standing order. Mobile phone records showed that most telephone calls were to his three colleagues or to his wife. He'd led a carefully controlled life. A tidy life. Apparently no family. He was a mystery. Almost a shadow existence. Was this deliberate? What was behind the shadow?

# TWELVE

*Wednesday, 12 March, 11.20 a.m.*

JOANNA LOOKED AT the list of names in her hand. There were more than forty. They had cast their net wider. Forty families in Leek affected by debt and hardship, desperate enough to need payday loans or something that would eke out their existence. For ever an albatross around their necks. And if this was the list of people in one area of one small town, how many more families were affected in the Potteries? Hundreds? She scanned the list again and homed in on the nineteen families who lived in the immediate area around Sainsbury's, the families that Jadon Glover visited on a Wednesday night, walking up from the car park in heavy rain, shrouded by the hood on his waterproof, invisible and unidentifiable to passers-by. Anonymous.

Well, there was only one thing for it. She would listen to Jason and Dawn's account and then she and Mike would have to visit each and every one of these families and try and pinpoint the moment and place where Jadon had vanished into thin air. At what point had he ceased to be a visible human being? They needed to home in on that exact time. It would mean further extensive house-to-house interviews. She had forty officers assigned to her and now divided the list of people up so each and every one of them was visited.

At the back of her mind she still had the troubled vision of Big Mill, of empty room after empty room. It would be so easy to hide a body there. If they got no further they would summon sniffer dogs to the mill and search again. What a human eye might miss a dog's nose might find.

THE HOUSE-TO-HOUSE FORMAT had been the same in every case, the roads and houses divided up into grid references, each person asked the same set of questions and their answers documented.

Did Jadon Glover call on you last Wednesday? At what time? Did you give him money? Did you notice anything unusual in his manner? Do you know anything that might have a bearing on his disappearance? Do you know where he went next? Did he ever mention being followed? Threatened?

Over and over the questions were asked, the responses documented so that by the afternoon they could be collated, at least those who had been at home to answer. The rest would be more evening calls and another briefing in the morning.

The officers had worked through the weekend to collate the facts. They'd made a second cursory search of the mill and interviewed some of the people Jadon had been visiting. So far nothing really stuck out as she scanned the results, trying to divine the message beneath. She glanced across at Korpanski, who raised his eyebrows. She read their message. Nothing there either.

There had been no other major developments. So what minor discoveries? She crossed the room and stood in front of the map for a recap.

'If everyone's account was correct, collating that

with their indisputable CCTV evidence, he parked in the supermarket car park at a little after seven p.m. As was his habit, he visited his six clients in Mill Street, last of all Astrid Jenkins, leaving her at a little after seven twenty-five. That much was already known from Paul Ruthin and Bridget.'

Bridget stepped forward to speak for both of them. 'They all said he visited at the usual time and that he seemed as normal.'

'OK,' Joanna said, checking, 'so up until seven twenty-five it was business as usual.'

'Yeah.'

'Then?' She turned to Jason and Dawn, who had done a really good job. They'd always called Jason 'Bright' Spark and now he was proving himself worthy of the name. He stood at the front, explaining his approach, and Joanna was really impressed. It was methodical. Typically Dawn was standing back, allowing the young PC to take centre stage.

'He crossed the road and started at Wellington Place.'

Wellington Place was a little upmarket—between-the-wars semis rather than the Victorian terraces further up the bank. There was off-street parking for one—at a squash two—cars. Joanna was a little surprised that these people had needed to resort to payday loans from notorious doorstep money lenders. She would have thought their finances more secure. She was obviously wrong.

Dawn took over, speaking out in her clear voice, interrupting Joanna's thoughts. 'We did ask what sort of a guy he was and the majority said he was business-like, that he took "no shit from anyone", but was basically polite.'

'What if they were late with their payments?'

'He would threaten them.'

'What with?'

'He'd just say they had one week to cough up. If they couldn't manage it he'd take jewellery or goods to the value of.' Dawn looked unhappy. 'He didn't mess around.'

Jason Spark spoke up next. 'I suppose,' he said thoughtfully, 'he couldn't afford to go soft on them.' He must have heard the murmurings around the room and felt his fellow officers did not agree or understand this opinion. 'I mean,' he continued, going red now, but sticking bravely to his guns, 'if he let one of them off one week's payments the whole business would go down the chute. They'd all plead poverty.'

There was a ripple of resentment round the room. Policeman's pay didn't always stretch quite far enough. However foolhardy and unwise it might have been, many of them had been tempted to go down this road— just till they got paid. So there was a natural empathy towards the victims here rather than the missing man.

The criminal here, in their eyes, was Jadon, the whole enterprise fuelled by pure greed. Not one of them was fooled by the claim of altruism put forward by Glover's colleagues.

Joanna frowned. 'Let's concentrate on the facts,' she said, 'rather than sympathise or not with the victims.' Even as she spoke she wondered: who was the victim here? 'Let's start with the timeline. The families in sequence. The last person to see him before he crossed Mill Street and climbed the hill up to the other thirteen families was Astrid Jenkins, who saw him as normal at around seven twenty-five.'

'So then he crosses Macclesfield Road, passing Big Mill, to the other thirteen families who lived on the north side of the road?'

'He didn't always visit in order,' Jason said, 'but that night it appears he went first to Wellington Place.'

'Time?'

'Round about seven forty-five. No one could be sure of the exact time. Then he went to Britannia Avenue and visited the families there. That's all confirmed. Then he would have crossed the children's play area into Barngate Street, which is where we think we picked him up on the CCTV but we can't be sure it's him even after enhancing the images. Then he would have proceeded to Nab Hill Avenue.' He paused. 'But that night it appears that he didn't arrive at Barngate Street and never visited Nab Hill Avenue at all.'

'So the last sighting of our man is a possibility on the CCTV and the last definite sighting was on Britannia Avenue.'

'Yeah. It seems like it. We've put some signs up by the swings just in case he was spotted there but it seems unlikely considering the weather.'

'Any more CCTV cameras round there?'

'Only the one mounted on one of the houses on the corner of Britannia Avenue.'

'So if he was abducted was the weather opportune or coincidence?' She stopped musing. 'Go on, Dawn.'

'We worked on the assumption that he normally worked his way along Barngate Street then went through the passage into Nab Hill Avenue but he didn't always stick to that. Sometimes he did it in reverse.'

Joanna studied the map. Whichever path Jadon had

taken, his route would have been a giant loop. He would have got soaked.

'So let's say it is him hurrying through the play area. That would mean he disappeared somewhere round here.' Her hand spanned the two streets. Again, she thought: how? People, windows, eyes, cars. Had no one seen anything? How had that been achieved? As the night was so nasty he would have wanted to finish his round as quickly as possible. Get back to the car.

'The clients along Wellington Place say they saw him as usual around eight-ish and gave him the money they owed. One family, the last to see him along that street, admitted that they didn't have the money.'

Joanna glanced at the board. 'Time?'

'They think about eight thirty.'

'And their names?'

'Carly Johnson and her partner, Stuart. They live in number eight.'

'Why didn't they have the money?'

'Apparently Stuart had been ill. He's a diabetic and things had gone wrong. He'd been fired from his job as a delivery driver because he went a bit funny.'

Dawn Critchlow continued, speaking in a flat, un-emotional voice, but when she looked up her eyes were gleaming. 'He called it a hypo. Low blood sugar. It made him a bit dizzy. He had to inform the DVLA. They stopped him driving. Anyway, they didn't have the money and it was the second week they'd missed. Apparently Jadon told them if he didn't have the money this week there was to be no grovelling. They either lost the car or the telly. And like most people they had to have the car for Carly to get to work. She works in the Potteries' Shopping Centre in Hanley,' she added.

'So what happened on the doorstep that night?'

'Jadon wasn't too pleased they didn't have the money—again. Carly promised she'd have it by the following day and would drop it in to his office in Hanley.'

'How much did they owe?'

'A thousand—originally. They'd been desperate—took an emergency holiday to Benidorm in September. They'd taken out the loan for six months paying a hundred a week. They managed until Stuart lost his job. They were living on the edge,' she said. 'And Stuart didn't get another job.'

'So where was she going to get the money from by the next day?'

'She was going to ask her mum for it. Apparently she promised Jadon she'd get the money to his office by midday.'

'How did he respond to that?'

'She said he was none too pleased, that he chuntered a bit but in the end said OK. What they want is the money—in cash. Goods are more trouble, aren't they? Have to be got rid of—and they never make as much as you think.'

Joanna felt her skin prickle. 'Did she actually *go* to her mother on the Thursday and ask for the money?'

'I haven't checked yet.'

Joanna knew she didn't need to say any more but it was possibly a crucial point.

'Anything particular about the other three debtors in Wellington Place?'

'Just one. A couple called Paul Ginster and Christine Maundy. She's expecting. They seemed pretty desperate too.' She frowned, finding it hard to say why she had picked this couple out. 'Scared,' she said.

'Right, so...' Joanna turned back to the map. 'Britannia Avenue. How many clients there?'

'Three. One family—the Murdochs—said they were out.' Jason Spark made a face. 'Hiding behind the curtains, more like.'

'Names?'

'Josie and Vernon Murdoch.' He hesitated. 'Josie stank of cider when I interviewed her.'

'What time was that?'

'Just after ten.'

'So even at that time in the morning she'd been drinking?'

He nodded. 'She was pretty drunk and abusive.'

'And her partner, Vernon?'

'No sign of him.'

'I wonder what our debt collector made of that.'

PC Spark blew his cheeks out. 'A black mark,' he said. 'At the very least.'

'And the next family?'

'Said they gave him sixty quid a week including interest.'

'Name?'

'Karen Stanton.'

'OK...' Joanna turned back to the map. 'She saw Glover at what time?'

'Some time after eight thirty.'

Dawn hesitated. 'She was the last person to see him. Or at least,' she added with characteristic literalism, 'she was the last person to *admit* to seeing him. The other family—the other *person*,' she corrected, 'said she didn't see him. She said he didn't call that night.'

'Name?'

'Marty Widnes. She's a widow.'

'And she says he didn't call?'

'She said sometimes he let her off paying.'

The ripple around the room was heavy with scepticism. Joanna made a mental note to follow this one up.

Joanna turned back to the map. 'So the last person to admit to seeing him was Karen Stanton. After that… nothing.'

Dawn nodded.

Joanna waited. Dawn was clearly uncomfortable about something. 'The person he was supposed to be collecting money from, Marty Widnes…her husband, Frank, hanged himself a year ago. Rumour is it was connected with debt. There was a suicide note that came out at the inquest. Marty herself was in a terrible state after Frank's death. There was an elaborate funeral apparently—plumed horses, a carriage.' Dawn looked around the room. 'It was quite a sensation.'

A few officers were already using their smartphones and tablets to look up the newspaper articles covering the coroner's report. There were pictures of a funeral which looked high Gothic Victorian: prancing horses sporting black plumes, a horse-drawn hearse, open carriages and undertakers walking in front, solemn and with top hats bordered with black crepe.

Joanna was silent for a minute. If the newspaper reports were to be believed Marty Widnes had plenty of motive for wanting Jadon out of the way. But there was something which intrigued her: Jadon hardly struck her as a man with a big heart or someone who suffered with guilt or empathy for the fates he had a hand in. And yet this one woman claimed he sometimes 'let her off paying'. So who paid her weekly share? Jadon himself?

She addressed Dawn Critchlow. 'Is it possible…?' She didn't need to finish the sentence.

Dawn shook her head. 'I don't think so. She's a small woman, not overly strong. Jadon was a member of the local gym. Not exactly a heavy, but… No, she couldn't have assaulted him.'

Joanna looked at Mike, almost holding her hands out in frustration. Same old story: motive but no opportunity.

'So we have him tracked to Karen Stanton. Did she see in which direction Jadon was headed?'

'No. She said the weather was so vile she just handed the money over and shut the door on him quickly.'

'Did she notice anything else? Anyone hanging around, following him, cars nearby? Anything unusual?'

'No.'

'OK, talk us through Glover's next movements.'

Dawn looked at Jason Spark. 'The play area,' she said. 'It's just a small area, a triangle with two swings and a slide. There's nowhere to hide there.' She was thinking. Nowhere for a would-be murderer to hide or conceal a body.

Spark nodded. They all knew the area, a tiny sop to the cramped streets, an alternative to dangerous trespass in Big Mill. Somewhere for the children to play safely, watched by the dumb eye of a CCTV camera.

Joanna turned to DC Phil Scott. 'Take me through that CCTV again?'

'We see someone cross it,' he said, 'just before nine o'clock, who fits Glover's description, but he's hurrying and wrapped up against the weather. We can't be certain it is him.'

'Let's assume it is,' Joanna said. 'Cutting through the child's play area, he would have gone next to Barngate Street and then on to Nab Hill Avenue, which is blocked off to vehicles but not to pedestrians.'

'Yeah.'

'So how many families are on his books in Barngate Street?'

'Three. But they say he never got there. Not one of them saw him.'

'And Nab Hill Avenue?'

Dawn shook her head again.

'So he vanished somewhere between Britannia Avenue and Barngate Street. We're not sure whether the person seen crossing the play area is Jadon or not.' She paused. 'And we don't know whether he intended going next to Barngate Street or Nab Hill Avenue. How many clients does he have in Nab Hill Avenue?'

'Again, three. All women.'

She raised her eyebrows. 'Yeah.' Jason grinned. 'Bit of a coven if you ask me.'

'But none of these women say they saw him last Wednesday.'

'No. Not one of the six clients in those two streets admits to seeing him last Wednesday night.'

'He never got there, Joanna,' Mike repeated.

She turned to face him. 'So they say.

'OK,' she said slowly, 'so the last definite sighting is Karen Stanton. The Murdochs say they were out and Mrs Widnes claims he didn't call. So,' she said, 'we'll start with turning a searchlight on these people.'

Again, she studied the map. Somewhere in these cramped streets, Jadon Glover had achieved the impossible. He'd vanished.

Something in her toes tingled. 'Tell me about the people who live in Barngate Street, the ones who deny seeing him.'

'Petula Morgan, number twelve,' Jason read from his notebook, 'Roberta Slater, number five and a lady called Sarah Gough who lives with her son in number sixteen.'

'The son?'

'A strange lad.' Dawn took up the story. 'A bit funny in the head. He has learning difficulties.'

'History of violence?'

Dawn shook her head, her maternal instinct coming out now. 'No,' she said, laughing. 'He's a big softie. Nice chap actually.'

Joanna moved her finger across to Nab Hill Avenue. 'So what about the Nab Hill Coven?'

A couple of officers managed a smile. It was a feeble joke but it lifted their mood and encouraged them in a case which seemed so difficult to grasp.

Dawn took over. 'There are three of them. All single, all live alone. I suppose the ringleader is a lady called Charlotte Parker. She's about sixty—very outspoken.' She smiled. 'Quite a tough character. She was the one who led the campaign to have Nab Hill Avenue blocked off when that little boy was knocked off his bike and killed. Motorists were flying up the road as a shortcut between Macclesfield Road and Newcastle Road.'

Joanna put a hand up to pause her. It was an aspect of the case they had so far not explored. She homed in on DS Hannah Beardmore. Reliable, patient, thorough Hannah. 'Look into the circumstances of the accident, will you, Hannah? Just see if there's any connection with any of our debtors or creditors.'

Hannah simply nodded. A woman of few words, she

had been brought up in the area, her parents moorland farmers. She was used to the ways of the people who lived in the area around Leek and was an invaluable source of information.

Jason Spark took over. 'Charlotte's a tough cookie who's had a few husbands. She's fairly hard boiled,' he said, smiling at the memory of the woman who had reduced him and his uniform to a first-former standing in front of the headmistress.

'But no criminal record.'

He shook his head.

'Family?'

'One daughter and two grandchildren that she looks after for ninety per cent of the time.'

'The three women seem to spend a lot of time round each other's houses with a bottle or two of wine,' Dawn put in.

'Then there's a Turkish lady who was all veiled up. She was very quiet, a bit subdued. She was wearing a headscarf round her face so I couldn't really see her expression.'

'Name?'

'Yasmin Candemir. I couldn't tell you how old she is,' Jason said awkwardly. 'I couldn't see enough of her to guess. By the sound of her, thirty-something. Quietly spoken, very polite, speaks quite good English.'

'And the third?'

'An Irish fireball called Erienna. She let rip all right. Not shy of saying where Jadon Glover could stick his debt.' He grinned around the room. 'Where the sun doesn't shine.' There were a few rolled eyes but most of his colleagues managed a snigger.

Joanna dragged them back to the present. 'OK, let's

take a minute to run through this. Glover parks up at around seven p.m. in Sainsbury's. He collects the money from the six families at the back of Mill Street. So far, everything normal.'

'Yep.'

She narrowed her eyes. 'Is there anything there we should go back to?'

Paul Ruthin and Bridget shook their heads.

'He crosses the road, passes Big Mill and goes to Wellington Place. He collects money there as usual apart from one person, Carly Johnson, who says she'll bring the money to his office on the following day.' She focused on Dawn. 'Did she?'

Dawn flushed.

'You need to ask that question,' she said gently. Joanna continued, 'He leaves Wellington Place at around eight thirty and moves up to Britannia Avenue.' As she spoke she was tracing his movements with an index finger moving along the map. 'The Murdochs at number four say they were out and missed his call. Jason, you think they might have been hiding in the property to avoid paying?'

He nodded. 'She's an abusive drunk,' he said. His face was comical as he shuddered. 'Horrible woman.'

'Right. Apparently he doesn't call on Marty Widnes, whose husband apparently committed suicide connected with debt. Let's find out if the debt-collecting agency was this one or another. It would appear she's the one who has the best reason for wanting Glover dead, except that physically Mrs Widnes wouldn't have been capable. So next in line is Karen Stanton, who says she gave him sixty pounds. It appears that Karen is the last person who admits to having seen him, at around eight thirty p.m. At some point Jadon steps outside his routine. His next port of call is one of the two remaining streets and his last six clients, in which case he'd have taken a diagonal route through the children's play area. We see someone cross the area but can't be sure it's him. All we know is, according to these clients, he never makes those last calls, either to Barngate or to Nab Hill Avenue.' She scanned the room. 'At least that's what we're told.' Her eyes drifted across the map and she knew precisely why she had felt uneasy. Britannia Avenue curved around the back of Big Mill. It would have been all too easy for someone, on that night, to drag Jadon Glover, unseen, into this dark and hidden place. She pointed to it. 'If he never did reach the children's play area let's wind back to Big Mill.' She addressed DC Alan King. 'You've searched it?'

'Just a cursory search, Joanna. No dogs.'

'I take it you found nothing?'

He shook his head.

'Was it locked, hard to gain access?'

'Absolutely not,' King said. 'You could just walk in—and that's through the front door. All the windows are broken.'

'And the rear access?'

'No better. If anything a bit worse.'

'But nothing there?'

Again, Alan King shook his head and waited.

'OK,' Joanna responded. 'We'll take the dogs in and do a more thorough search. But if he isn't there we need to track back.' She thought for a moment and reverted to the people in Britannia Avenue and PC Jason Spark. 'So the last person who *admits* to seeing him alive is Karen Stanton. Tell me more about her.'

'She's nice. Quiet, polite, contained.'

'And what's *her* sob story?'

'She just got behind on the mortgage when her husband left her last year.'

They were all sad stories. One after another avalanching straight into the money lenders' greedy little laps. 'Does she work?'

'Yeah. Doubles up. Teaching assistant at Saint Edwards Primary School and a carer for an elderly lady early morning, before she goes to work, and in the evening when she puts her to bed. It's a private arrangement.'

'Children?'

'A daughter aged ten who lives with her father and his new partner.'

Joanna looked up. 'That must rankle.'

'Yeah. I got the impression it did. The little girl is ten years old but that's where she wants to be, with her dad. Not a lot you can do about it these days, Jo. The wishes of the child are paramount. Dad and new wife have plenty of money plus the added bonus of new wife having a daughter Shona's age. The two have bonded and are, according to Karen, like sisters. She's very bitter about it. Says the woman stole her life, her husband and her daughter. Not only did she have to borrow to cope with the mortgage but in the summer she borrowed some more.'

'More?'

Jason Spark's face dropped. 'Yeah, but it didn't work. She offered to take Shona to Disneyland, Paris but Shona said she wouldn't go without Carys so the whole thing fell through. Quite honestly, Karen's just given up. Since then she says she's nearly paid it off.'

'Really?'

Joanna took another look at Jadon Glover's movements. Suddenly Britannia Avenue looked like a hotspot vibrating with debt and tales of woeful drama. 'Have we had any response from the board we put up in the play area?'

It was Dawn who answered. 'Not so far but it was such a horrible night even the dog walkers were staying inside.'

So did Jadon walk, did he run or was he taken? The question was impossible to answer with their current evidence. They needed more. There were plenty of people who had reason to dislike him but reason and dislike did not vaporise people. Would they have hated him enough to abduct and kill him? Joanna's mind was whirring. If someone had wanted poetic justice out of this miserable anthology of sad stories they would have kidnapped Jadon and demanded enough of a ransom to pay off their own and their neighbours' debts. But realistically, what would that achieve? There was Leroy, Jeff and Scott to take his place. Possibly even some other greedy little villain waiting in the wings for an opportunity to cash in on the business. No one could fight them all. Someone else would soon take Jadon's place. Killing or kidnapping him wasn't worth the risk. The debt wouldn't disappear as Jadon had. It was there and would have to be repaid.

So if there had been no ransom demand what would be the point of abducting Glover? Where would they keep him? Joanna's thoughts stopped in their tracks, causing a *bump, bump, bump* of a collision. None.

Then her mind tracked sideways. What if by focusing on the missing man's unsavoury career choice they were making a mistake? What if the answer to this was personal rather than connected with his work?

She turned aside to voice her theory to Korpanski, who listened intently. 'Mike, should we be looking into his personal life more? Check out his perfect wife? Remember her response to his career change?'

Korpanski nodded.

'Some women,' she said thoughtfully, 'need to be able to look up to a man. You could almost see her love and respect for him slide down the scale. Maybe we should look a bit harder at his perfect marriage rather than concentrating on this morass of troubled people?'

'It's a thought, Jo. Probably worth a look.'

'And we never found out about either his or his wife's past,' she said, concerned now by their omission.

'True. But Jo…' He put a hand on her arm. 'There're lots of threads of enquiry we can follow. We can only take one strand at a time.'

She nodded. 'And whatever the answer to his disappearance, his last sighting was still in that area.' Her eyes flicked towards the board. 'So we'd better get some teams out, focus on the area between Britannia Road, Barngate Street and Nab Hill Avenue and seal off the children's play area.'

'You're going to be popular.'

At one point she would have barked back at him: *I'm not in this job to be popular, Korpanski.* Or, *I can't help that.* These days she simply smiled, met his eyes and knew he was reflecting on the change in her.

They had both changed.

So now, decided in her direction, she addressed the assembled teams. 'Right,' she said. 'We have a few lines of enquiry here which will all be followed up.

As an adjunct to the enquiries connected with Jadon Glover's work DS Korpanski and I will be looking into Jadon Glover's private life. In the meantime, I want you to focus on a few points. I want to know a bit more about Carly Johnson's failure to produce the money and what happened subsequently. Did she borrow it from her mother on Thursday the sixth? Did she turn up at the offices in Hanley at twelve o'clock, as promised, Dawn? If she didn't, why not?'

Dawn nodded.

'Hannah, look into the child's accident that resulted in the blocking off of Nab Hill Avenue. Find out who paid for the funeral, who he was related to and what he was doing in that area. Look, in particular, for any connection, even if it's tenuous, with any of our debtors or the money lenders. Jason, you and Dawn check out Frank Widnes' suicide. See what lending agency he was indebted to. Lastly, we'll be looking again more carefully at the CCTV footage of the child's play area between Britannia Avenue and Barngate Street and carrying out a fingertip search.' She paused for a moment. Because of the low index of suspicion following Jadon's disappearance the area had not been sealed off straight away. She could only hope that would not prove to have been a miscalculation. 'DC Phil Scott, you can enhance the images. Pay particular attention to your subject's height and build. Are there any distinguishing marks on the person's clothing? And then see what he's carrying, even his gait. We may be able to get Eve Glover to take a look and see if she recognizes the subject as her husband.'

In spite of the situation she was smiling to herself as she spoke. She would have recognized Matthew's blond hair and his long-legged, loping stride anywhere, however fuzzy the image, let alone the way he held his head and focused straight ahead, the speed of his steps and the clothes he wore. That, she decided, is familiarity, and she allowed herself a swift vision, feeling momentarily wifely smug. *My husband.*

She was being watched. 'I want a team examining both Jadon and Eve's past,' she said. 'Where have they sprung from? Why no family? And last of all,' she said, 'look into any further connection between Karl Robertson and our debt collectors.'

Korpanski eyed her. 'You'd better clear it with you know who.'

And, reluctantly, she had to agree.

# THIRTEEN

*Wednesday, 12 March, 12.45 p.m.*

As COLCLOUGH HAD said when he'd promoted her, planning a case, working out budgets, focusing on some lines of enquiry while ignoring others was all part of the job. That, Piercy, he'd said, is what you're paid for. On the other hand, she didn't feel any salary could compensate for this aspect of being a DI. Facing her new and antagonistic chief superintendent was an ordeal. It was the bit she dreaded most. She knocked on his door and pictured his thin mouth in the tight-lipped, 'Come in.'

He looked up as she entered. CS Gabriel Rush was sitting behind his desk, frowning into the computer screen. But… Was it her imagination, wishful thinking or was there really the hint of a smile around his face?

*Imagination. Don't be stupid.*

'Sit down, Piercy.'

He didn't prompt her but waited for her to offload. Briefly she outlined the conundrum that was Jadon Glover's disappearance. She listed the anomalies and her proposed lines of enquiry then watched as he absorbed it all. He listened, making not a single facial expression until she'd finished speaking and a heavy silence had fallen between them, a silence which lasted for seconds but seemed like hours. Then he said tightly, 'So what are your immediate plans?'

'We're sealing off the area, sir. Taking the dogs into Big Mill to check it more thoroughly.' She wasn't sure whether he'd realized the vast size of the place. 'It's a huge place, sir. It will take a team a couple of days to search it thoroughly and we'll need sniffer dogs. Korpanski and I will be interviewing the last people to admit to seeing Mr Glover and I'm going to interview Mrs Glover again.' Had it been Colclough, she would have been able to share her scepticism of the woman's description of a perfect husband. How much had Eve really suspected that Jadon was not all he seemed? Were they one of those couples who kept secrets from each other? And now she had found out his true career what difference would it really make? But she found it hard to ruminate on this level with Rush. He didn't invite confidences or supposition, just firm evidence—something that could be entered into a box on a computer.

He nodded sagely, seeming to think for a while, then looked up and surprised her. 'And your gut feeling?'

She was open-mouthed. She hadn't tagged Rush as being one of the imaginative sort. More a doer, a rule-keeper, someone nicely lacking in imagination. But then, maybe, you never could tell.

She hesitated. 'I think,' she said, licking dry lips, 'someone has abducted him.'

He raised his eyebrows. 'Abducted him?'

Shit. He'd just asked her that to make a fool of her.

'Taken him, sir.'

'So is there going to be a ransom demand?' He *was* mocking her now.

She looked at the floor and cursed it for not swallowing her up. 'It's possible, sir. This is, surely, all about money?'

'What you mean is he is screwing these people to the ground. Cheating them, he and his…cronies. This is a villainous man. He's got enemies, Piercy. Enemies.'

'Yes, sir.'

'But I agree with you. This is about money so kidnapping and a ransom demand would seem likely. So you look closely and find the crime scene. If he was abducted he was probably grabbed from somewhere. Speak to the wife again. Make sure she hasn't been approached and is keeping quiet out of a misguided sense of protection.' He shook his head in mock despair. 'You know how sometimes relatives are told that something will happen to their loved one if they tell the police?'

'Yes, sir.'

'You've told me how devoted his wife appeared. Check up on her finances, make sure there are no large withdrawals from *her* or rather *their* account.'

She nodded.

'And remember, if there is no ransom demand in the next few days it's equally possible he's either done a runner or been killed.' He hesitated. 'For revenge or…' Even Rush was running out of ideas, but he continued his advice with, 'I take it he isn't the sort to just vanish, do a runner, go on the streets?'

'I've seen no indication that that's what's happened, sir. I can't see any reason why he would. He appears to have had a comfortable, stable home life. His wife is distraught.' She paused. 'I've arranged to meet with the media tomorrow and appeal for help from the general public.' Anticipating his disapproval, she finished lamely, 'Just in case someone did see anything.'

She'd misjudged him. He smiled—he definitely smiled. 'Rather you than me, Piercy, though I expect they'd rather have your pretty face in front of them than mine.'

She was thrown by the comment. Confused, she stood up and found his uncomfortable eyes on her as though he had X-ray vision. He stared at her for what felt like minutes but was again probably just a second or three, then made an odd noise at the back of his throat—part cough, part chortle.

'Oh, and by the way,' she said, speaking from the doorway, 'you were right about the car. Sainsbury's car park.'

His smile widened, then, 'OK,' he said. 'Off you go.'

She shot off.

They had to wait for the sniffer dogs to arrive from the kennels in Newcastle-under-Lyme. Appropriately if unimaginatively named Holmes and Watson, they were a pair of German shepherd dogs trained to follow a trail and find people dead or alive.

The delay gave Joanna the perfect excuse to visit Eve again.

*2 p.m.*
*Back at 8 Disraeli Place*

THERE WAS SOMETHING VERY strange about Eve on this third visit. She was icily calm, controlled and something else. Calculating. She'd changed. No longer the devoted wife but furtive, looking as though she realized she'd been taken advantage of.

What Joanna couldn't work out was the backstory. When she made her request Eve climbed the stairs and returned with a slightly soiled shirt, white with a faint blue check, a rim of faded brown around the inside of the collar. 'Will this do?'

Joanna looked carefully at her face as she handed it over. 'Yes,' she said. 'It's fine.'

What was going on there? But Eve Glover was good at keeping secrets.

'Do you think we could also have a toothbrush, a hairbrush?'

'Of course,' Eve said, still icily controlled. 'DNA, I suppose.' Joanna stared after her. The words had seemed almost casual. And it wasn't just in her manner.

Today Eve was dressed in a clinging black dress, smart high heels and all her make-up was in place.

'Excuse me asking,' Joanna said, bemused, 'but are you going to work?'

'A friend's asked me to help out,' Eve said with dignity. 'Afternoons, early evenings. I start at two thirty.'

'Right.' Joanna bagged up the samples. 'Umm, Eve,' she said, 'I need to ask you something and I need an honest answer.'

Eve sat down, knees tidily together, ankles crossed, hands resting on her lap, her face all attention. It was a classic pose. There was nothing natural about it. Her eyes were wary.

Joanna paused before she spoke, trying to get a handle on this woman, but she failed. The sheet of ice calm was too thick to penetrate. More than ever she was curious and noticed that although she'd left a pause and Eve Glover was due at work soon, she didn't prompt her.

So Joanna dropped the stone into the pond. 'Has anyone been in contact with you about Jadon?'

Slowly Eve shook her head, bemused.

'There's been no ransom demand?'

'No.' She thought for a moment before adding incredulously, 'You think he's been kidnapped?'

'It's a possibility.'

'No.' This time there was a note of regret, of sadness. 'No, Inspector,' she said. 'No one has contacted me.'

'OK.' Joanna stood up to leave, her head still confused with Eve Glover's reaction.

It was only as she drove away that she wondered if she'd found the handle. Some women need a man around. It's as simple as that. If Jadon wasn't there Eve would just have to find someone else.

*3 p.m.*

WENDY BRADSHAW WAS A solicitor based in Leek with an office plumb in the middle of the market square. She'd worked with her father when first qualified and since he had retired had run the practice with two other partners. Many of the clients she worked with today had been her father's which had led to some lively and helpful discussions with him over Sunday lunch. Monica was one of these—an inherited client.

And she had been summoned.

Wendy parked her Audi tidily in the staff car park, picked her briefcase off the back seat and approached the entrance of Brooklands Nursing Home, ready to do her client's bidding. She had served Monica Pagett for the last five years, ever since her father had retired. When he had finally relinquished her he had given his daughter a quick description.

'She's an intelligent woman, in her early nineties but with all her marbles. Just because she's not educated to a high standard and has lived all her life in the isolation of the Staffordshire Moorlands doesn't mean to say that she doesn't have a handle on her own finances or people's character. She is very astute. Just unmaterialistic.'

'How did the cottage get its weird name?'

'Bit of a sad story, really. It was her grandmother who named it. It used to be called Sky Cottage.'

Wendy had laughed. 'That's a more apt name, surely?'

'You didn't know the old woman. She was a tartar. Anyway, she had a pet bird—a crow.' His eyes had held a mischievous twinkle, 'As you might have guessed. It lived in the house with her, apparently scaring the living daylights out of anyone who called. It would swoop down on them, peck their heads. They would even cover their eyes. Crows have very powerful beaks, you know, and it was an evil bird. But unfortunately, of course, this evil bird was completely domesticated. So when the old lady was snow bound in Leek for ten days…'

'The bird starved to death.'

Her father had nodded. 'The old lady was heartbroken. That's when she changed its name.'

She returned to the present circumstance. 'And now Monica's slipped on the cobbles outside the Butter Market. Broken her hip. She's in a nursing home. Apparently it's unlikely she'll ever return to Starve Crow Cottage.'

'Oh dear,' her father said. 'That'll break her.'

Wendy had taken to Monica straight away and been flattered that the elderly lady with a fierce intelligence and iron character had accepted her almost straight out of law school. In fact, Monica had appreciated the young solicitor's modernist views though not always falling in with them. They had had some great discussions on factory farming, GM crops, antibiotics for dairy herds, even on grazing management. Wendy had learned much and had begun to have some insight into the difficulties of managing the high and almost barren land, the barter that ducked below the tax system: a dozen eggs for a piece of lamb or some pork; a fleece in return for silaging the field. With each conversation Wendy's respect for the elderly woman had grown and she had been really sorry when Monica had broken her hip, quickly recognizing it as the beginning of the end of her independence. And sure enough Monica never had returned to the cottage where she had been born and had lived her life out. Wendy knew the moorlander missed the open spaces and was feeling claustrophobic in the nursing home. Brooklands was as good a home as could be but the old lady simply didn't belong here. Her habitat, like the kestrels and buzzards, rabbits and hares, stoats and weasels, was scampering around the moors, drinking at pools, striding across boggy marshes, sticking to trails, sheltering from hostile winds. She just didn't belong here in this small, overheated room with an en suite shower. And so Wendy decided she would stay a little longer than was necessary, bring a breath of fresh air into the stuffy little room. Like her client, she enjoyed these encounters with a sort of relish and excitement. One never quite knew what Monica would say or do next. She was wonderfully unpredictable. And challenging.

The nurse showed her to room nine.

'Monica. How are you?'

But the old lady didn't waste time. 'No time for all that, Wendy, dear,' she said. 'We've got things to do.'

'I'm sorry. Anything I can do?'

'The bloody lot,' Monica said with spirit. 'I've realized I'm not going to get back home. My nursing home fees have to be paid. I want you to put Starve Crow up for sale.'

Wendy felt the bleakness of the situation. 'You're sure about that? It's early days yet.'

'Certainly I'm sure.'

Monica reached out a liver-spotted wrinkled hand and touched the young solicitor's. 'I want you to handle it.'

'You sound as if...' Wendy was at a loss what to say.

'Like a thief in the night,' Monica said, urgency making her voice hoarse as she quoted, 'We know neither the day nor the hour.'

'Are you telling me you're...?' The words stuck in her throat.

'No. No,' the old lady said impatiently. 'I'm not going to die yet. It's just that it's too important to leave to chance. I'm in my nineties. What if I have a stroke or a heart attack? What I'm telling you...' She seemed to soften and reached out to touch her solicitor's hand with a gentle stroke. 'What I'm trying to say is that this is too important to leave to chance.'

She sat, shaking her head.

*3.15 p.m.*

THE DOGS WERE COMBING through the giant premises of Big Mill. Room after room, floor after dusty floor, sifting through debris—cigarette ends, the odd syringe or two, ancient newspapers, some used as toilet paper. It was a filthy job with much to distract Holmes and Watson. The place had been used by the homeless and drug addicts but there was nothing that placed Jadon

Glover here and after a sniff at his worn shirt the dogs' tails remained down, their barks staccato yelps of the disappointed. After three hours they left, dejected in spite of the treats their trainer slipped them anyway. If it wasn't there they couldn't find it. The teams of officers looked at each other. However tempting and appropriate the large derelict building might have appeared it was not a crime scene. So they must return to the crowded streets, the higgledy piggledy cram of terraced houses and the unlikely backdrop of a children's playground with the usual misplaced CCTV.

Joanna was aware that her date with the local TV and radio was for five o'clock, in time to be aired on the news. Local and even, possibly, national, if no other story stole the day.

She'd learned this lesson the hard way.

Prepare your statement and then prepare it again. Wear plain clothes so as not to distract your audience from your message. She'd chosen a navy turtle-necked sweater and black jeans which would be hidden by the table. She'd brushed her hair and applied a pale pink lipstick. Again, nothing too garish. Keep your facial expression neutral. Mentally she practised her words as they prepared the lighting and sound.

The bank of cameras and microphones didn't faze her now as they once had. She waited.

It had been suggested that Eve make an appeal. It usually worked better if the wife played her part. But Eve had declined the opportunity. Joanna couldn't quite work out why except that Eve was distancing herself from the husband who had deceived her.

As Joanna waited to be given the go ahead she ran through other possibilities.

Some people find the media daunting but Eve didn't strike her as one of those.

Surely she was desperate to find her husband? Get him back?

The cameraman gave her the signal, Joanna cleared her throat and began.

'We are concerned as to the whereabouts of Jadon Glover, a thirty-two-year-old man, who has not been seen since last Wednesday evening.' She paused. 'Mr Glover was connected with the money-lending business and was on his rounds when he vanished. It is possible that his disappearance is somehow connected with his work.' Again she paused and fixed her gaze on the camera. 'We have CCTV footage of a person crossing the children's play area from Britannia Avenue walking towards Barngate Street at around eight thirty p.m. but we cannot be sure if this is Mr Glover.' DC Phil Scott cued in the footage. 'As you can see this person is wearing a mac, hood up, and you can't see his face. Mr Glover was a devoted…' she stumbled on the word as though it wasn't quite in context, '…husband and has only been married for two years. Naturally his wife is distraught.' The word felt false, penned without truth or thought, simply fitting neatly into the sentence. 'Please, if you can help in any way to find out where Mr Glover is, contact us.' She read the number out for listeners as it was displayed at the bottom of the screen for the TV watchers.

'Also, please let us know if you are the person picked up on that CCTV footage. I would remind you that last Wednesday was a very wet and windy night—not a night to be out for a stroll.'

She finished with a polite, 'Thank you.' Got the

thumbs up from the presenter, thanked her lucky stars for media training and wondered whether the appeal would bear any fruit.

## 7 p.m. briefing

AT THIS POINT THERE were still more questions than answers and focusing their enquiries with maximum efficiency was proving difficult.

DC Alan King was their computer man so he was asked to delve into the couple's past while Paul Ruthin and Bridget Anderton headed the team continuing with their house to house and Jason and Dawn followed up their original enquiries. At some point Joanna intended to meet the players on the field herself but she was staying back for now. Bank enquiries and mobile phone records had still turned up precisely nothing.

But now it was getting late and she had an early start in the morning. Joanna headed back to Waterfall.

The evening was dingy and cold and the lights of Waterfall Cottage seemed to sparkle an invite out to her. Inside would be Matthew, almost certainly either reading or more likely perusing his tablet, searching through papers and articles on anything—absolutely anything—to do with pathology which was both his work and his passion. She had never known anyone study so consistently as her husband. He seemed to soak up facts like a piece of blotting paper.

She climbed out of the car, tempted to peep in and spy on him through the lit but un-curtained window. But she didn't. She simply locked the car and let herself in through the front door.

He looked up from his book. 'Hey, you,' he said

with a big smile and she leaned over him and kissed his mouth. No whisky this time.

Just coffee.

She sat opposite. 'How did your starring part go in The Mystery of The Missing Man?'

She giggled. 'Not exactly Cate Blanchett,' she said, 'but at least I didn't fluff my lines.'

Matthew lifted his eyebrows in an expression of mock admiration which she took with a bow.

He moved forward to put another log on the fire though the room was already warm.

'Aaagh.' He sat back on the sofa and held his arm out for Joanna to rest against. 'This is the life,' he said.

She never quite knew whether to bring up the subject when Matthew had had trauma at work, whether to encourage him to talk about the child and his role in the forthcoming conviction of the grandmother or wait and see whether he mentioned it first. The court case, she knew, was looming and would be harrowing enough. He could appear so professional, dealing with injuries and symptoms, evidence of trauma or disease. She'd watched him prepare his cases, taking hours of trouble, then his appearances in court. She'd listened while he gave his evidence, slowly, factually, hardly ever leaking out any emotion.

*Extensive bruising to the throat. A deep wound to the neck. A penetrating wound to the chest. Death would have been slow—instantaneous. A tumour which had infiltrated...*

Lists of bones which had been broken, lives ended.

It touched her when he revealed this vulnerable underbelly of his work. She looked at him. His face was relaxed, his demeanour happy and contented. He'd recently had his hair cut so it was less tousled than before and yes, he looked slightly older, the small lines around his eyes and mouth a little deeper, a little more troubled than when they had first met. Life had not been easy.

He caught her scrutiny. 'What are you looking at so hard?'

'Just wondering if you're OK.'

He knew exactly what she was talking about. His arm tightened around her. 'Yeah,' he said. 'The case will come to court and I'll give my evidence, put the old bag behind bars—for ever, I hope—so she can never ever do that to a child again.' He was staring into the fire now. 'If I succeed in my bit and the prosecution in theirs I shall feel I've done my best.' His face darkened, as though a sad, damaged memory had passed across his light source. He looked at his hands as though they had the memory of their work imprinted on them. 'After all,' he said, 'I never get to see them until they're dead or…' always literal, '…very *rarely* do I see them alive. I am OK, Jo,' he said slowly. 'Really.'

There was silence between them.

She leaned back against him and he stroked her hair. 'Jo,' he said tentatively. And she stiffened. She knew Matthew. He was a restless character, often wanting something else. Something more. Something different. His periods of peace and tranquillity tended not to last for very long.

'I was thinking,' he continued, still stroking her hair. 'If we are going to have a little one this place really isn't big enough.'

He could have no idea how uncomfortable this simple statement made her. On both counts.

'You want to move?' She ignored the *if*—pretended he had not referred to it.

'We-ell, yes. You know that.'

'Where?' She swivelled her head around to look straight into mischievous green eyes. Yes, he *had* recovered. 'Into Leek?'

'Yeah.' Then he couldn't hold it back any longer. 'I've got the details of a lovely place on the Buxton road,' he said, speaking quickly. 'One of those Victorian houses.' He stopped speaking, waited for her to absorb his statement.

She'd known they would, at some point, be moving, and though she loved their cottage in Waterfall, she would accept it. Matthew had had itchy feet for a while; it had been inevitable even if her own so far barren state was less predictable and more difficult to solve. She held her hand out. 'Let's have a look at the details then.' And somehow, miraculously, Matthew produced them from, apparently, nowhere or rather from behind a cushion.

It was, as he had said, a large, five-bedroomed house with Gothic revival black and white half timbering. The interior shots looked slightly old fashioned with dark, antique furniture and dated wallpaper. But that was simply cosmetics.

Matthew was watching her anxiously. 'What do you think, Jo?'

She was scanning the size and aspects of the rooms. Large, square, many south-facing.

The garden looked amazing—a huge, rectangular lawn and flower beds all around. Some mature trees. There were apples on the ground.

She glanced at the price. Reasonable. They could

afford it though not if it needed extensive structural alterations. She looked at him. 'It's sound,' he assured her and her mind began to adjust. There was another advantage to moving into the town: she would be nearer the station. Cycling in in the morning would take her ten minutes not forty-five. And she could probably do it in all weathers, except snow. Snow and cycling was a bad mix. It wasn't just your own slithers and skids—it was the cars that could hardly be controlled. Like novice ice skaters, their direction was totally unpredictable, which meant they could easily slam straight into you.

Curtains.

'We'll take a look?'

'I hoped you'd say that.' She loved the eagerness in his voice and his face.

'Tomorrow? In the morning?'

'Yeah.' In spite of herself, she felt excited. It was the sort of house they could do a lot with. A home. And to live on the edge of the town instead of in the village seven miles out could have distinct advantages.

Matthew couldn't stop talking about it. 'It's an elderly couple who are moving into sheltered accommodation,' he said. 'They've got somewhere lined up and are ready to move. So it's vacant possession on completion.'

She looked around her. 'We'll have to sell here first, Matt.'

'Yes, but the estate agent said these easy-to-manage country cottages in village locations are going like hot cakes these days. Often as second homes or holiday lets.'

He was leaping ahead. She scrutinized him. 'How far have you gone in this pursuit, Matthew Levin?'

'Not all the way,' he said, sliding his hand down her back, bending and kissing her mouth. 'Not quite all the way.'

He was hard to resist in this boyish optimistic mood. And actually, why should she?

It was an hour later. They had made love and now dozed contentedly. It was ten o'clock. Too early to go to bed. They could have watched the television but there was nothing that interested either of them. They sat and talked some more then Matthew went quiet. 'Actually, Jo,' he said, 'there is something else I should tell you.'

Her heart dropped. She was instantly alert. She knew that tone. Either Eloise or…

Matthew plunged in. 'Mum and Dad. Well, now they're retired. And if we do manage to have a family…'

*Glad you said if and not when.*

'What is it?' she said. 'You're making me nervous. They're not going to come and live with us, are they?'

'No,' he assured her. 'No.'

And then she could guess. All too easily. Matthew's parents, who had disliked her from the start, blaming her for their son's marital breakup and granddaughter's subsequent unhappiness. Even now she felt indignation bubble up inside her. As though Matthew had played no part in events.

'They're moving down here, aren't they?'

He nodded and she was thoughtful. She and Matthew had had an affair while he was still married to Jane. Things had got messy, as they do, and Matthew's parents had naturally taken their daughter-in-law's side and been very hostile towards Joanna. She'd been surprised they'd come to the wedding but they had, sitting frosty and quiet in the front row, obviously holding her responsible, adoring him but resenting her, loving their granddaughter. To them she was the scarlet woman. A temptress Matthew had not been able to resist. Evil to the core, and that stung Joanna as being a very lop-sided view. But Matthew really loved his parents and, as he was with his daughter, Eloise, he fiercely defended them, even to her cost. Which made the situation ran-kle even more.

His father was a retired GP and they would spend hours discussing medical breakthroughs and cases. Fa-ther and son—and granddaughter—were close.

'They want to be near me...' he paused before fin-ishing the sentence, '...and any grandchildren we might have?'

He was watching her anxiously. 'If—when—we do have a child they want to help.' He gave her a sly glance. 'It'll be useful for us—if we both want to continue with our careers.'

He'd thought this one right through, tying her hands behind her. She couldn't explain how trapped this made her feel.

'It'll be all right, won't it?' he asked nervously.

She couldn't answer. It was the next step in their lives, a step right out there into the unknown.

# FOURTEEN

*Thursday, 13 March, 8.30 a.m.*

RUSH HOUR IN the moorlands was two cars—one heading towards Buxton and the other in the opposite direction towards Leek. After that there was silence. As the sun climbed up the sky the moors were illuminated, the sunshine reaching even the darkest corners. The cottage sat, motionless, a few sheep venturing timidly into the yard, munching their way through the spring grass, their bleating sounding like complaints. A buzzard flew overhead searching for his breakfast, a kestrel hovered and swooped and two hares gambolled, paws up ready for a boxing match. The ivy almost covering the door shivered in a chilly breeze but all else was still.

Joanna was standing in the driveway of a large, detached Victorian house looking up at the bedroom windows. So far so good. Briarswood looked in reasonable condition and she liked the name. She slipped her hand in Matthew's and gave him an encouraging grin.

They were let in by an elderly gentleman with a shock of white hair and a lovely, polite manner. 'Doctor and Mrs Levin,' he said formally. 'Welcome.'

Joanna smiled as she crossed the threshold. Mrs Levin sounded nothing like Detective Inspector Joanna Piercy. And in some ways they were two different people.

*11 a.m.*

ACROSS THE OTHER SIDE of Leek Fred Whalley was preparing to meet his wife and son again. They had done shorter terms 'inside' than he so they had had time to get the celebrations under way. It was funny, he reflected. It had been a family business yet Hayley and Tommy had got four years, he seven and Kath nine. But for once his daughter had learned to behave herself so she would be out sooner.

For now he would be content with a few friends, a bottle or two of wine, some lagers and crisps. Then they'd have to have a family meeting—without Kath, of course, who was due for parole in a couple of months. Fred drew in a deep breath. Kath. Now there was the problem. Kath had a tendency towards violence or extreme violence depending on her mood or what she'd had for breakfast, how much she'd had to drink the night before or even whether her victim was wearing red or blue. Unpredictable was her middle name and that was why she'd got the longer sentence. The judge and jury had all sensed it. Fred was a happy-go-lucky sort of guy who went with the flow and was more than content to continue in the same sort of line he'd been in before. A 'stretch' or two was just an occupational hazard—a bit like getting asbestos lung damage if you were a builder, falling and breaking a leg if you were a steeplejack or getting a chair thrown at you if you were a teacher. Most careers, in his opinion, carried some sort of danger. Sometimes when he wondered about what he would have done if he hadn't been a thief he'd consider the alternatives and quickly got stuck. He couldn't imagine being anything else. In fact, being in-

side wasn't so much of a problem. It wasn't so bad really—not if you kept your head down. You got used to
it. The only thing he really missed when he was inside
was his family. He was devoted to Hayley and Tommy.
OK, Tommy wasn't exactly the brightest button in the
box but he was a lovely boy. But Kath… Fred wouldn't
have admitted it to anyone but deep down inside he was
frightened of his daughter. His own daughter! Once or
twice she'd turned on him and it had been him who'd
backed down. She had a nasty streak in her, that one.
She'd come to a bad end one day.

So he wasn't sure about having Kath along on his
future little jaunts. It had been the violence that had
got them the custodial sentence instead of a rap on the
knuckles and a bit of community service again from
the judge. After all, they hadn't made it a habit to get
caught; neither had they kicked their victims in the
head until they lost consciousness. That had been Kath's
contribution.

So as his mate dropped him off outside the modest
front door of their small semi, Fred was anxious. Until
the door opened and Hayley threw her arms around
him. 'Surprise,' she said.

The room was full.

Half an hour later Fred, happy as anything, lager in
one hand, fag in the other, was talking to two of his oldest mates, his eyes wide open. But the same problem:
what to do about Kath.

'She's sworn vengeance, you know,' Fred said, troubled. 'She's said she'll 'ave that policewoman that put
her inside.'

Chad Newick looked troubled. 'Piercy?'

'Yeah.'

Newick scooped in a deep breath. 'That's not a good idea, mate,' he said.

'So, you going to tell her?'

Newick dropped his eyes.

'Or you, Angus?'

And then Fred knew that it wasn't only him who was nervous about Kath. They all were.

Newick finally spoke. 'She gets us in too much trouble, mate,' he said.

Fred looked thoughtful. 'She don't care about that.' Then, almost with a hint of pride, he followed it with, 'She ain't frightened of anything. Not the law. Not Piercy. Not anything.'

Angus spoke up then. 'Sort it,' he said, 'before we go back into business.'

Fred looked even more troubled. 'Easier said than done, mate.'

*11.15 a.m.*

NOW THEY HAD EXCLUDED Big Mill from being a crime scene the team was spreading out to further interview the inhabitants of the five streets which had been on Glover's Wednesday night hit list. Now it was time for Joanna to explore the area herself. While officers interviewed the players, Joanna and Mike made their way to the small area bordered by low metal bars and surfaced with damp bark on which stood a slide and two swings and passed as the children's playground. The gardens of the terraced houses were small so it was somewhere for the children living in the cramped streets and small houses to let off steam, meet and play. The day was grey and cold, the play area uninviting—even less so surrounded by police tape. Spring had retreated back into its fleece jacket and hardly even peeped out from behind it. The 'fun' area didn't look much like fun today.

The floor consisted of bark chips—not the easiest surface on which to conduct a fingertip search. The officers moved forward in a line, picking up debris: a couple of condoms, a few cigarette butts, sweet papers and the ubiquitous polystyrene fast-food boxes. Joanna watched. They couldn't test it all for Jadon's DNA. She turned to Mike. 'Does Jadon Glover smoke?'

'We'll soon find out.' He moved away from her to speak to, presumably, Eve, and was back with her in minutes, grinning. 'He wasn't supposed to but she'd smell it on him and found a packet of fags in his glove compartment.'

'What brand?'

'Silk Cut.' He'd anticipated the question. These days they both knew the routine well enough to foresee each other's moves and decisions which meant that many cases progressed in preordained moves as classic as a game of professional chess.

'OK.' She stepped forward to speak to Baxter Cornell, one of the new breed of civilian SOCOs. They would begin with any Silk Cut cigarette butts found and DNA test them. Take it from there.

'Do we know if this area is cleaned on a regular basis?'

'Tuesdays,' he said. 'Same day as the bins are emptied. But not this Tuesday,' he said with a grin. 'We asked them not to. Just as a precaution.'

'Good.'

She cast her eyes over the swings, dripping from the heavy rain, then at the bag which now held a sodden, half-smoked cigarette butt. The ground would have been cleaned the day before Jadon disappeared. If it showed Jadon Glover's DNA it would probably confirm the CCTV sighting, though they hadn't seen their person either smoking or throwing away a butt. At least it could fix him up to here, confirm the time and place and allow them to focus on the debtors from the two other streets, Barngate and Nab Hill Avenue. The CCTV footage had shown only one figure cross the area. No one had come forward to say it was them. So if the cigarette butt could be linked to Glover they could assume he had been heading towards Barngate Street unless he had changed his order and visited Nab Hill Avenue first. Always assuming, that is, that the council cleaners did a thorough job and the cigarette butt had only been there since last Wednesday.

Too many variables. But then, that was police work, and at least it narrowed their search area.

'Have you found anything else?'

Cornell shook his head. 'Not so far.'

It was now heading towards early afternoon. Joanna and Mike decided it was time to speak to the clients on Jadon's round for themselves. Junior detectives and the uniformed boys often did very well but there was nothing like seeing it for yourself.

For now they left the six families on Mill Street. Too many people had seen Jadon after he'd left. They knew where he'd been right up to 8.30 p.m. so they had decided to focus their investigations on the four streets beyond Big Mill. According to Astrid Jenkins, who had been the last person on Mill Street to admit to having seen the debt collector, she had seen Glover cross the road towards Big Mill at around 7.25 p.m. Big Mill had been cleared as a crime scene. So assuming the figure crossing the playground was him they could shadow his movements up until then.

Following in Glover's footsteps, they parked in Sainsbury's car park, sure the two-hour rule would be waived for a squad car. As Mike and Joanna retraced Glover's steps Joanna was aware of how many stories lay behind each and every one of his debtors. All of them different and yet tragically the same. Desperate people. Desperate measures.

They started with Wellington Place and number eight. Carly Johnson proved to be a slim, anaemic-looking young woman with dyed blue hair and a tired expression. Even opening the door seemed an effort to her, her shoulder straining to prop it open. She raised drooping eyelids and sussed them out straight away. 'I suppose you're here about Jadon?'

Joanna nodded while Mike kept his eyes on her. Carly kept them on the doorstep and made a mild pro-test. 'I've already been interviewed.'

Mike stepped forward then, charm at the ready. 'We just wanted to know,' he said, 'how he responded when you said you didn't have the money.'

'As always, Sergeant,' she said wearily. 'None too pleased.'

Joanna had an impression of extreme lassitude.

She continued, 'But he just wanted his money so when I said I'd bring it to the office—'

Joanna jumped in. 'And did you?'

Carly frowned, not understanding. 'Did I what?'

Then she got it—a split second too late. She gasped and her face went red then deathly pale. Her hand reached out for the doorpost to steady herself.

'Did you ask your mum for the money?'

That was when Carly gave up. 'I couldn't face it,' she said. 'I just couldn't ask mum for money again.'

'You'd had to do it before?'

She nodded.

'So what was your plan, Carly?'

Her response was so quiet it didn't even qualify as a whisper. 'I didn't have one.'

Joanna shrugged her shoulders and glanced at Mike. This was a woman who had given up. Giving up implied there was nothing to lose. Someone who has nothing to lose takes risks. Her mind was threading it all together like a string of seashells. Carly was on her list of suspects. You couldn't hide from these people. You couldn't just wipe out your debt with a lame excuse. Joanna knew that and so did Carly Johnson.

'Where did Jadon go after you?'

'I don't know. I didn't look. It was a shitty night. I just shut the door on him.'

*As I'd like to do on you.*

From inside the house, someone was calling. 'Carly?'

'Carly.' The voice was male, petulant.

Joanna looked at Mike, her eyebrows raised. *Mr Madeley, I presume.* 'I take it that's your partner?'

The blue eyes rested on her. Carly nodded, a curve of cynicism at last giving her face some animation.

'That's him all right,' she said.

Joanna smiled and they left.

THEY VISITED THE two families Jason and Dawn had deemed to be of no interest and agreed with the assessment. They seemed kosher, each one telling their story without emotion or self-pity and verifying the facts surrounding Jadon Glover's final visit. Joanna found their mixture of optimism, that they would one day finally get out of debt and pessimism that they never would, touching. 'Get out of debt?' Fay Langton in number seven said, her face twisted. 'Rob the boys of their easy regular income? That's not the name of the game, love. No, this is a millstone which will hang around my neck until after I'm dead. I'll never get out of debt, Inspector Piercy. I just don't have the means. Income too low, expenses too high. Get it? Maybe it'll even be inherited by my children like my blue eyes and dark hair or if you'd rather just like some terrible genetic disease.' Her face was challenging Joanna to disagree. Joanna didn't even dare ask her how much she'd initially borrowed, what for or how much she still owed.

The Ginster family at number sixteen were typical but had something extra to add when she asked him how the situation had begun.

'My best friend at work,' Paul Ginster said, a thin man with a worried face, the lines creasing his forehead scored too deeply to ever be erased. 'It was him who recommended I take out a loan. We worked in the same place, a little engineering company on the Ashbourne road. It went through bad times in 2008 with the recession and that and we was all put on short time. At the same time Christine was expecting.' His face looked even older. What should have been a happy time in their lives had turned into a nightmare. 'I didn't know what to do.' His anger burst then like a boil, sudden, hot, infected, painful. 'We couldn't afford a fucking thing for the baby. Not a pram or a cot. None of the essentials.' And then the bitterness melted. It was as though the sun had come out from behind a cloud.

'Scarlet's two now—child care's expensive so we still haven't paid off the two grand we borrowed for stuff even though I'm working all the hours God sends. And you know what? I don't think we ever will. That's their plan. They know we'll give them money for life. There's only one way to break free of it.'

His face changed again. The wind had blown something else in. Gritty, determined and unutterably sad. 'Frank—the guy who told me about them.' He drew in a deep breath. 'He hanged himself last year. He left a note for his widow. You know what it said?'

They could guess.

*'It's the only way I'll ever get free.'*

Joanna knew then. Silken threads, sticky as a spider's, were beginning to form a recognizable pattern. Here was a connection. Frank Widnes, who had hanged himself a year ago, had borrowed money from Glover and his cronies. He had worked with Paul Ginster and Ginster had borrowed money too. She looked at Mike and knew from his expression that he too was seeing the pattern emerging.

'Just remind me,' she said. 'What's Frank's widow's name?'

'Marty.' Another glimpse of a smile, of the sun emerging from behind a cloud. 'Think it's a sort of substitute for Mildred?'

Even Joanna failed to suppress a smile. 'Mrs Widnes is still in debt?'

Paul Ginster nodded. 'Oh, yeah,' he said, almost casually. 'Death doesn't wipe it out.'

Something crossed Joanna's mind then. If these debtors were connected not only by common debt but other threads—being neighbours, loyalty, friendship—was it possible this was not a single assault but a collective one? Had they all plotted this? Was it possible that they, the police, were being fed a tissue of lies constructed by a network of debtors?

She affected innocence. 'Does Mrs Widnes still live in the town?'

'Yeah. Still lives in the same place. Just round the corner. Britannia Avenue.' There was no guile behind his response. 'Paid off part of the debt with his life insurance.' His face was set now. 'Even that didn't cover it all.'

'You must have felt very bitter against the firm.'

Slowly, Paul Ginster nodded. 'Every time that bastard knocked on our door,' he said, 'I wanted to bloody well kill him.'

Joanna cleared her throat. Considering the fact that Glover was currently missing these were not wise words.

'Well,' she said, 'he's disappeared now.'

'He'll turn up,' Ginster said pessimistically. 'Bad pennies don't just vanish. They turn up.'

*No. They don't—at least, not alive, not unharmed. Not always.*

'So where do you think he is?' Joanna asked curiously, affecting complete stupidity now.

'Recruiting more clients,' Ginster said sourly. 'He's too canny to have got caught out by any of his victims. Look at us.' There was a flame in his eyes now. 'We are the poor suckers here.'

Joanna felt awkward. Her sympathy might be with these debt-ridden people who had been taken advantage of but her job was to find out what had happened to the missing man. And behind Jadon Glover, she was beginning to realize, was not simply a story of greed and exploitation but a web of people connected. So where did it all fit in and where was the missing man?

She and Mike left Wellington Place and threaded their way between a long snake of houses, cars parked on either side, narrowing the road to the size of a small vehicle. Many of the drivers had parked sensibly, tight to the kerb, their wing mirrors folded in. Probably from experience. Constantly replacing wing mirrors could prove expensive.

They walked to the junction with Britannia Avenue, a long row of terraced houses built in the early part of the twentieth century when the mills were busy, shuttles rattling across the looms providing a constant background clatter. There had at least been full employment then if not a fair and decent living wage. Again, cars were squeezed in all along the road with no visible space. They walked. Each house consisted of one small ground-floor window, a door which opened straight on to the pavement, two windows above, original sash windows now mostly replaced with UPVC. The replacement windows gang must have had a field day here. House after house had had their attention. In between every fourth house was a narrow passage leading through to the back.

Three more debt-ridden families lived in Britannia Avenue: the Murdochs, cider-scented Josie and her partner, Vernon—the pair who had claimed to be out when Glover had called for his Wednesday money. The second person was the hardworking, abandoned Karen Stanton and the third person on Jadon Glover's books was the widow of Frank Widnes, Marty.

'We'll speak to the Murdochs first,' Joanna said.

Vernon Murdoch opened the door. He was an

effeminate-looking man in his forties, slim and with floppy brown hair which he pushed out of his face with a theatrical gesture as he opened the door, releasing a waft of cigarette smoke. 'Gosh,' he said, eyes wide open. 'You've just got to be the police.'

'That's right.'

'I'm really sorry—my wife is out at the moment, working.'

'But not you.'

Vernon jerked his head back towards the living room where they could hear the sound of a TV. Something inane with tinkly music and sporadic bursts of canned laughter. 'Someone has to mind the kids,' he said with a brave smile, displaying nicotine-stained teeth.

'OK,' Joanna said. 'You probably know why we're here?'

At her side she could feel Mike bristling. As a traditional male he didn't respond well to house husbands.

Vernon pushed the flop of hair out of his eyes. 'Yes,' he said. 'Of course. I do.' He grinned. It was a mischievous expression, oddly endearing. 'How strange,' he mused. 'Really odd. Jadon Glover's about the last person I'd have expected to just vanish.' He followed this with a terrible joke. 'He's hardly the traditional magician's assistant in sequinned dress and spangled tights, is he?'

'We didn't know him,' Joanna said, not responding to the humour.

'No—quite. Well, all I can say is that if you didn't know him you're one of the lucky ones.'

Joanna put a foot forward. 'Might we come in?'

'Yeah. Sure, but you won't learn anything. Neither me nor Josie knows a thing about what happened to

Jadon.' He couldn't resist tagging on, with bravado, 'and we don't care either.'

As he led them into the narrow hall he turned and pressed a finger to his thin lips.

'*Pas devant les enfants*,' he said in a convincing French accent.

There was no problem there. *Les enfants* were far too engrossed in the huge screen spewing out noise and colour to take any notice of the three people sitting, talking in low voices around the small table at the back of the room.

'You know that nobody has seen Jadon Glover for over a week now?'

'Yeah,' Vernon said, again pushing the lock of hair out of his eyes. Joanna could almost read Korpanski's reaction. *Why didn't he buy a bloody hair grip?*

'Weird, isn't it? I wonder where on earth he could have got to.' His expression was suitably bland. Beguilingly innocent.

When neither Mike nor Joanna responded he gave a nervous laugh. 'I mean, he must be somewhere, mustn't he?'

There was no argument against this.

'You were out last Wednesday?'

'Yeah,' he said, a bit too quickly. 'Ellie had a swimming lesson and we all decided to go. We took Nat.' His eyes flicked from one to the other to see whether he was being believed.

It would be easy to check with the pool attendants.

'But…? If you defaulted with your loan and didn't pay, didn't it cause problems?' Joanna asked innocently.

'Well, yeah. But…'

'We understood that defaulting on a payment wasn't an option. Had you missed before?'

'Once or twice.' He added hurriedly, 'We just paid double the following week.' He sniffed. 'He knew us. He knew we'd pay in the end.'

Unspoken words rang loudly in Joanna's ear.

He knew we'd *have* to pay in the end. What Joanna was realizing was that for the debtors or clients there was no escape. They were rats caught at the bottom of a concrete-lined pit while their creditors peeped over the rim and laughed. There was no escape—not even death.

'I see.' But she didn't. Not really. From what she had heard the rules were strict. You pay every week. Was there some special reason why the Murdochs were an exception to what had been presented as a rigid rule?

'How much money had you borrowed?'

Vernon Murdoch practically squirmed in his seat. 'Three grand,' he muttered and before they, knowing the interest rates, could exclaim, he defended it. 'The mortgage company was going to repossess the house.' He looked around him. 'This place—it's all we've got.'

And again Joanna could read Korpanski's mind. *So why not get a job?*

Murdoch answered the silent question. 'I can't work,' he said sullenly. 'I have…nerves.'

*And where would we be without them?*

'Josie, your wife?'

'Barmaid,' he said, 'at The Quiet Woman.' He grinned. 'Suits her. She can walk to work and back home again. She likes a drink.' He waved his hand. 'Perfect job for her and I mind the kids, see? Saves on extortionate childminders' fees.'

Joanna studied him. Vernon Murdoch was a jaunty,

quite likeable fellow who would freewheel through his life, quite happily, living on the edge, doing as little as possible—preferably no work. But… She glanced across at the children who alternated between watching her and Korpanski and the huge wide-screen television; he was doing a good job with them, at least. And life with an alcoholic may well not be an easy road to walk. Vernon himself appeared sober.

She stood up feeling she would not find her answers here. She shook Murdoch's hand. 'Thank you,' she said.

Murdoch met her eyes, must have read her verdict and nodded, then spoke over his shoulder to the two children. 'Come on, you two. That's enough telly for today.'

He aimed a broad, cheeky grin at Joanna. 'Shame the park's closed.'

She didn't rise to the bait.

Outside, Joanna looked at her sergeant. 'Well, Mike, what did you think?'

He pursed his lips and frowned. 'I can't see him getting one over on our friend,' he said. 'He hasn't got the balls.'

'And his wife?'

'From the sounds of her she's not going to manage much either before she falls down.'

'No. But we'd better check up on his alibi all the same.'

They knocked on the door of Number 10, Britannia Avenue.

Karen was another pale girl who looked as though life had treated her harshly. She wore big glasses, was very slim and petite and might as well have had victim tattooed across her forehead, there was such an air of having been hard done by, a miasma which clung to the air around her.

She peeped around the door. 'Hello?'

Joanna and Mike introduced themselves and she let them in. The room was small but surprisingly elegant. Painted dusky pink with a cream carpet, there was a pleasant scent of roses. In the window was a small mahogany table on which stood a glass vase with roses the exact same shade of dusky pink as the walls. Classic FM was playing softly in the background and a book lay face down on the sofa. *Suite Française* by Irene Nemirovsky, an Auschwitz victim. An unexpected choice of reading. Would Karen Stanton prove to be more of a fighter than she appeared? Joanna and Mike sat down.

Joanna opened the conversation with the usual questions which Karen answered in a quiet voice, sweetly soft. The real difference between her and the other debtors was that she had kept meticulous records. 'I knew the interest rate was scandalous,' she said, 'but the bank wouldn't lend me any money. I really didn't want to move out of here.' She looked around her with a smile. 'I know it's not great but…it's home and I knew I had to buy Jock out when he left. Here,' she said, handing them the notebook. 'I borrowed two thousand pounds initially from Daylight.'

'Daylight?'

She smiled. 'It's a great name for a money-lending business,' she said. 'I could almost appreciate the humour. Their blog says you see daylight at the end of the tunnel. But the joke is it's really daylight robbery. It would be funny if it wasn't so awful.'

Joanna nodded, speechless for once, and Karen continued, 'I've paid off fifty pounds a week for two years and I'm finally there having given them over five thousand. Not a bad return on their initial investment, is it? In fact,' she said brightly, 'I'd invest in them myself if they ever went public.'

'But you're free now?'

'Yeah,' she said. 'Free. I gave him my last fifty pounds on Wednesday and told him that was that.'

'How did he respond?'

'He started blustering, saying it didn't work like that and I showed him my book and said that I would go to the ombudsman and report him.'

'How much did he mind that you'd finished paying?'

Karen Stanton smiled. 'Quite a bit,' she said mischievously, 'but when I pointed out that they'd doubled their money in two years, that I'd never missed a week, never gone out or made excuses like Josie and Vernon did or even poor old Carly, he didn't have a leg to stand on.'

Joanna was silent for a moment, just beginning to realize how tight this web was. They all knew each other. They could have worked together, plotted their revenge on a person who fronted the business which had appeared to rescue them from their problems only to have dropped them in a worse place. It also dawned on her that of all Jadon's clients that night, Karen was the only one to have had no motive.

'What time did he leave you?'

She narrowed her eyes. 'I've already told your officers.' There was the hint of steel about her now.

'Just for the record, love,' Korpanski said testily.

'About eight thirty, I think.'

'And did you see where he went next?'

'No. It was a filthy night. I settled down and watched the TV for a bit, had a glass or two of wine.'

'Did you go out after that?'

'As I said, it was a filthy night.' She paused. 'Where would I go anyway?'

Time to try a different approach. 'Your daughter?' Joanna began.

'Chose to live with my ex and his current,' she said, her voice carefully controlled. 'Elinor, the woman my husband left me for, has a daughter the same age as Shona. The girls get on very well, apparently. It would seem petty to insist she stay with me just because I'm her mother.'

*So, she lost both her husband and daughter to her husband's mistress. Well, Joanna thought, at least I didn't steal Eloise. She stayed with her mother.*

Karen continued as though realizing perhaps her story didn't quite ring true. 'I admit I was hurt initially. Hurt and angry but I've got used to it now. I'm seeing someone else and things are working out quite well, particularly now I've paid off my debt. I can start to plan a future.' She smiled. 'I have a guy of my own. It's early days,' she added quickly, 'and he's not exactly Johnny Depp but he seems really nice and now I've sorted out my finances we can do things. We can have a holiday together. Have a life.' She gave Joanna a fiercely protective look. 'Had I insisted Shona stay with me she would have resented it and learnt to hate me.' The phrase held an uncomfortable resonance to Joanna. 'As it is…' She stood up, suddenly agitated, then turned around. 'I don't do baggage,' she said sharply. 'I don't hold grudges.'

'Even against Jadon Glover?' It was Mike's contribution and it provoked a startling response. Behind the thick glasses Karen's eyes flashed.

'Even against him,' she said finally.

They left and moved next door.

Frank Widnes' widow proved to be a feisty-looking woman in her early sixties. Her blue eyes bulged. She looked angry.

Joanna faced her with some trepidation. 'You say that Jadon sometimes gave you a week off paying?'

Marty nodded, her eyes as wary as a hunted animal.

'Didn't you worry?'

'About what?'

'About debt.'

'Do you want to know how I racked up the debt?'

Joanna couldn't say she'd had enough of hard-luck stories so she plastered on her interested look. She thought she already knew. In fact, she didn't know the half of it.

'After Frank had hanged himself because of the never-ending debt they persuaded me,' she said bitterly. 'How ironic is that? Give Frank a decent send-off, they said. Have you any idea how much funerals cost, Inspector?'

Thank God, no. And no wonder the woman was so angry.

'A decent send-off costs more than three thousand pounds. So they added it to the original debt.'

Joanna couldn't find any words to respond. Then, inexplicably, Marty's face softened and she continued, 'But yes. Sometimes Jadon didn't call. Maybe he did have a conscience after all.'

'I don't think so,' Mike put in without thinking.

Joanna's response was even blunter. 'Jadon—have a conscience?'

She tried to get inside the woman's mind. 'So the debt was no nearer being paid off.'

Marty Widnes shrugged.

'Debt is part of life,' she recited as mechanically as a religious mantra. 'Don't they say two things in life are certain: debt and taxes?'

It was only as they left the street that Joanna recalled the quote. It wasn't debt and taxes. It was death and taxes.

# FIFTEEN

PC GILBERT YOUNG had been detailed to visit the swimming pool and check out the Murdochs' story that they had attended their daughter's swimming lesson on the Wednesday night that Jadon Glover had last been seen. The woman at the desk was large and lethargic. She spent ages searching through the work roster, finally looking up. 'Yeah,' she said. 'Craig was the lifeguard here that night. You'll find him poolside. And don't forget to wear the overshoes,' she bellowed after him.

Craig was sitting at the top of a small ladder, a slim figure in navy jogging pants and a yellow polo shirt. He was watching the elderly swimmers course their lengths—slowly. This was an over-fifties session.

His grin was neat, teeth even and white, his accent Mock-Australian. 'Hi there,' he shouted down. 'You all right?'

'I just need to ask you a couple of questions.'

'Right you are then,' he responded jauntily. 'I'll just get Steve to cover for me.'

He sauntered along the length of the pool to a room at the top, eagle eye still cocked on the swimmers. He took his life-protection work seriously. PC Young followed him up to the staff room. When Steve had been dispatched Craig perched on the desk. 'Fire away,' he said.

'You know a couple called Josie and Vernon Murdoch?'

'Yeah. They got a couple of kids. Little Ellie's coming on quite well with her doggie-paddle.'

'Can you remember if they were here on Wednesday the fifth? That's nine days ago—a week last Wednesday?'

He hardly hesitated. 'That the night that guy went missing?'

'Yeah.'

'They were as a matter of fact.'

'Right through the lesson?'

'Yeah. Right through till the end. Half six to half seven.'

PC Young felt the tiniest quiver of excitement. All to do with timing, he thought. An hour here, an hour there.

Joanna and Mike encountered the fingertip search again as they left Britannia Avenue and headed for Barngate Street, threading through the play area. The SOCOs were having a problem with the bark. The surface was tricky to work on and hard on their knees. Joanna checked in again. 'Found anything?'

Cornell shook his head. 'Not so far, Joanna.' He scanned the scene, officers on their hands and knees moving forward, picking up all sorts of detritus, cigarette ends, sweet papers, a snapped pencil, a couple of coins, chewing gum.

He looked concerned at the amount of debris he was collecting. 'Are we going to get clearance for testing on all this?'

She shook her head. 'No. Just focus on the cigarette butts and maybe the chewing gum. Apparently he'd have a sneaky drag on Silk Cut. As for the rest, bag it up and wait for developments.' She looked around at the scene, dull and cool. 'Maybe Glover will turn up in the south of France or somewhere and we can chuck the lot away.'

'In your dreams.' Cornell risked a quip. 'Shame we can't bill him ourselves and charge him that fantastic interest rate, let us focus on more important things, eh?'

*More important things.*

She knew exactly to what he was referring. It was common knowledge that Kath Whalley would soon be out of prison. It was also common knowledge who had put her behind bars. Kath wasn't exactly known for her forgiveness. Joanna recalled the rough, tough teenager they had put away for violent theft. Unless Kath Whalley had had a personality transplant the vengeance she had sworn would happen sooner or later. It wasn't guesswork or instinct but something much more certain. Fore knowledge.

She gave a great big sigh and she and Mike carried on their tour, ignoring curious people who were still gathering around the site, which had remained closed to the general public and the children.

The three families at Barngate Street all vehemently denied having seen Jason on the night he had gone missing. It seemed almost pointless speaking to the three clients from Nab Hill Avenue and Joanna was tempted not to bother. But something drove her on and she and Mike turned into it anyway. After the claustrophobia of the other streets, congested with cars, frustrated motorists piling up behind each other, the sound of car horns and driver frustration, in Nab Hill Avenue there was a different atmosphere. It seemed quiet and peaceful, a backwater or a haven depending on your point of view, particularly as a shaft of sunlight turned the wet road into a glistening river of steel. Cars no longer used the street as a rat run, a convenient shortcut to the Newcastle Road, because the road ended in four concrete bollards. It was now a cul-de-sac with fewer cars parked along its sides. There was a feeling of space, a reminder that this was not the centre of a huge city but a small street in a moorlands town. The reminder of surrounding countryside was furthered by the fresh flowers fastened to one of the bollards which bordered the turnaround space at the top. Joanna walked up to them, turned one of the rain-soaked cards over. *To Sam,* it read. *We love you always, Grandma.*

'Do you remember this incident, Mike?'

'Yeah.' His voice was gruff. 'Horrible business. Poor little thing. Six years old. Ran out after a football. I don't honestly think the driver was speeding. It was just one of those things. He didn't have a chance.'

'The driver or the child?'

'Both. We dropped charges against the driver. There was no evidence against him. The car crushed the little chap. He died at the scene of multiple injuries. I think the whole street was traumatized.' His gaze skittered along the row of closed doors. 'They're a close community here, Jo.'

Again, Joanna had that strange sense that these families were connected by a web as sticky and invisible as the Internet. Something else struck her. Was it possible that Jadon's disappearance was connected with this street? With the death of this little boy rather than a result of Daylight's activities?

'Who was the driver?'

'Some guy passing through. I think he was from Macclesfield.'

*A dead end then?*

They stood and looked around them.

Nab Hill Avenue was a small area, only sixteen houses, eight either side ending in the small turning area bordered by the bollards. No chance a car would get through those. There was a walkway through them which, if you turned one way, would lead to Barngate Street. But if you turned the other way it led to the back of Big Mill and from there to Sainsbury's car park. Jadon had vanished from this street or the one next to it. The question was had he come here at all on that last night?

Joanna looked around her, at the row of doors, all closed. It was quiet here, even for a residential area. Even for a No Through Road. At this time of the afternoon where was everyone? Listening from behind closed doors? She looked through her notes. 'Three clients,' she said, reading from the list. 'Erienna Delaney, Yasmin Candemir and Charlotte Parker. All women, Mike.'

'I'm not sure why we're here,' Korpanski grumbled. 'As far as we know our perfect husband never even reached here on that Wednesday.'

'No…?' Joanna was dubious. 'Probably not but there's no harm checking, is there?' She turned to face him and gave an encouraging grin. 'We'd better see if we can winkle some secrets out of our coven of witches.'

Korpanski simply blew out his cheeks. It was his night at the gym and he was anxious not to miss it.

'So,' she said brightly, 'where shall we start?'

'Number six,' Mike suggested, consulting his notes. 'Grandma Charlotte.'

They knocked on the door.

It was opened almost immediately by a slim woman, maybe in her early sixties, wearing leggings and a white sweater, a lot of make-up too dark for her complexion and brown and red striped hair. Her arms bore tattoos and she had three piercings in each ear. 'Yeah?' Her manner was casual, disinterested, uncurious but not impolite.

Joanna and Mike flashed their ID. 'We're looking into the disappearance of Jadon Glover,' she began. 'We understand you were a client of his.'

The woman gave a bark. 'Client,' she said. 'Is that what they call it? Like prostitutes or social workers?'

'Whatever—that's what *we* call it,' Joanna said testily.

'Right, well, he didn't turn up last Wednesday so I can't help you.' Without waiting for them to respond she carried on. 'Yes, it's out of character. Jadon never forgot a debt or wrote it off.' There was little rancour or bitterness. For the first time since Joanna had interviewed the debtors of Daylight—'the light at the end of the tunnel'—this was the first time Joanna had heard someone accept their conditions so equably. 'I heard he'd gone missing, Inspector.' She leaned against the side of the door, half smiling. 'Don't think I'll be wearing a black armband. His place will soon be taken by some other slithering viper.'

Joanna nodded her agreement. 'I expect one of his colleagues will continue to collect their dues.'

'Yeah, so whoever's took him I hope they ask a big

fat ransom from his wife and anyone else who's ben-
efitted from us lots' misfortune.'

This was interesting. 'You think he's been kidnapped?'

Charlotte Parker looked at her as though she was
stupid. 'Well, what else? What would be the point of
knocking him off? No one was going to write off our
debt whatever happened to dear little Jadon. And he
wasn't important enough to hate. This is just about
money, Inspector. Understand? It's why and how it happened. Whoever said it was the root of all evil spoke
the truth.'

Joanna frowned. 'I think it was the love of money,'
she said dubiously. She peered past her into a dark, narrow hallway, stairs rising. Charlotte Parker was obviously not going to invite them in. She had her hands on
her hips, blocking her vision beyond. Joanna caught a
waft of paint. Ms Parker had been decorating.

'Live here alone, do you?' Korpanski tried the charm.

'Yeah, except when my grandchildren come.'

Joanna sensed a chink. 'Were they with you on
Wednesday the fifth?'

'Yeah, up until seven when my daughter, Irina, came
for them after she'd finished work.'

'Right.'

Silence fell. Charlotte Parker was not going to make
this easy for them. She chewed her chewing gum and
met their eyes.

Joanna wanted to prolong the conversation but she
was struggling. 'Had Jadon Glover ever missed before?'

Charlotte Parker shook her head. 'No,' she said.
'Pretty regular, he was.'

'Time-wise?'

'Oh, sometimes early-ish, sometimes later. Any time between seven and nine.' She volunteered the next statement. 'I think sometimes he did Barngate first then us and sometimes the other way round. Varied it, see.'

'Did you owe him much?'

Charlotte Parker looked like she was about to say, 'What's it to do with you,' but she stopped herself. 'Enough,' she said shortly and then, her eyes looking weary, she explained. 'My grandson was diagnosed with leukaemia. We thought he wouldn't live.' She couldn't stop her eyes from filling with tears. She looked anguished. 'We wanted to give him the holiday of a lifetime—take him to Disney in America. Take his mind off things. I borrowed the money,' she said defiantly.

*And what do you say to that?*

It was Charlotte who regained control. 'Stirling's in remission,' she said. Then, biting her lip, 'But not me. There's no remission from Daylight. No let up.'

'How much did you borrow?'

'Four and a half thousand.'

It was again said with defiance, challenging anyone to comment. Joanna had no intention of doing so. She didn't want to alienate this generous grandmother. What good would it do? She couldn't bear to ask how much had been paid back, try to work out percentages and interest rates and in what year she would finally finish paying for trying to distract her grandson from his illness, give him the holiday of a lifetime before he possibly died. It all seemed cruel. But also extravagant.

Joanna steeled herself. She needed to refocus. Somehow in this morass of human tragedy, silliness or profligacy, a man had disappeared. It didn't matter what had led to these people's position with the doorstep money lenders. It made no difference why they had got into debt in the first place or their family circumstances. Her job was not to moralize but to find out what had happened to him. She needed to remind herself if it wasn't against the law it wasn't illegal. Her job was to uphold the law. That was what she was paid for. Not to try and change it. Or even judge it.

'There are three of you in this road who owed money via Jadon,' she said.

Charlotte met her eyes and barked out a laugh. 'Yeah, right lot, aren't we?'

'Do you know the other two?'

She nodded, then grinned. 'Yeah, we're good friends, actually. Got a little club. Share a bottle of wine every now and then. Yasmin. She's one of the good Muslims. Wears a hijab and all that and always in trousers but you ought to see what she wears underneath. Red-hot lingerie. She's a hoot. Turkish.' She chortled. 'Turkish Delight, we call her. Then there's Erienna. She's Irish but don't hold that against her. She's good fun too. Yeah,' she challenged, 'I know 'em. And we're all in the same boat.'

'In what order does Jadon come collecting here?'

She didn't even think about it. 'I don't know. Random, I guess. I've never really asked. Funny,' she said. 'It's Daylight what bonds us but we don't waste time talking about that.'

'So what do you talk about?'

'Dunno. Clothes, make-up, celebrity gossip, the soaps. You know.'

Joanna nodded more to do with connecting with the women than in agreement.

'So he didn't stick to an exact time?'

'Like I said, I don't know.' It was an uncompromising response.

'Tell me,' Joanna said curiously, 'if you think he's been kidnapped why no demand?'

Charlotte Parker shrugged. 'Don't ask me.' She paused then laughed. 'Maybe he's done a runner. He always had a nice big bag of money with him.'

But Joanna's mind was tracking down a different path. Had Jadon been attacked just for the nice big bag of money?

Korpanski stepped forward, breaking into her thought. 'We don't think he's done a runner, Mrs Parker. He was only married a couple of years ago and they seem devoted.'

She snorted. 'Is that so? Glover got married and they're devoted. Nice.' Her voice was mocking.

'Is there something you're not telling us?'

'No. But I've got experience as far as "devoted" couples go.' She scratched the air at the word and fixed the DS with a glare. 'Wives don't hold you down. If you're going to scarper you don't take wives along as well.'

Charlotte seemed like an intelligent woman. Worldly-wise. 'Why would he go?'

'If he'd been stashing away bits and pieces, a bit here and a bit there, maybe it was worth his while to break free. If he wasn't quite as fond of his wife as he had been maybe he wanted to escape without having to pay the price—or explain. Maybe another woman?'

Joanna shook her head slowly. They'd found no evidence that Glover had been unfaithful to his wife. If he had he'd managed to cover his tracks efficiently. But it was certainly an option they needed to consider.

'Is there anything else you can add?'

Charlotte stuck her head out of the door and looked

up and down the street as though wondering who was watching her. Her gaze seemed to stick on the small heap of sodden flowers pinned to the railing.

Still looking at them, she spoke. 'I don't think so,' she said carefully and waited for them to leave, still peering out of the door.

But there was something Joanna needed to know to sharpen her image of events. 'When Jadon collected the money,' she asked slowly, 'did he come inside or wait outside?'

Charlotte shrugged. 'Depended on the weather,' she said, stepping back and half closing the door, anxious to end the conversation.

This time they did.

'So,' Joanna said as they walked along the pavement, 'kidnapped with no ransom demand—or done a runner. I wonder? Leaving behind his car, his wife, his identity, his mobile phone, credit cards? It doesn't seem likely.'

Korpanski kept his eye on her. 'And the other alternative?'

'Someone's taken out their revenge,' she said. 'Come on, Mike, it's a possibility.'

'So which is it?'

THAT WAS EXACTLY the question Leroy, Jeff and Scott were asking themselves. They were fiercely checking the books. Had Jadon been lining his own little nest?

'If he has been,' Leroy said, 'I am going to kill him myself with my own bare hands.'

'And I'll help you,' Jeff said.

'*If* you find him,' Scott said heavily. 'The police aren't having much luck so what hope have we got?'

They bent back over the computer screen.

'RIGHT THEN—NUMBER EIGHT.'

Joanna and Mike stood outside a green painted door and banged. They had to wait a minute for the door to be answered. When it was they saw a young woman with flame-coloured hair and a guarded expression. She looked at them without surprise. 'I had the feeling you'd be along sooner or later,' she said, 'though why you're even botherin' to conduct a search for that piece of shit I really don't know.'

Both Joanna and Mike might privately agree with her but that wasn't the point.

They asked the same questions, got roughly the same answers. Erienna Delaney didn't know in what order Jadon did his visits but he hadn't appeared on the Wednesday in question. It was the first time he'd failed to show. Once he'd been late because he'd had a puncture and another time a black man had arrived, saying that Jadon and his missus were on their honeymoon. Her anger was as hot as the red in her hair and erupted as suddenly and shockingly as a volcano.

She'd borrowed the money because her darn roof was leaking and she didn't think it would ever be paid back as somehow the capital seemed to go up rather than down every time she paid a bit off. There were early get-out clauses and hefty fines if they missed a week. 'Doesn't matter about holidays and such like.'

Joanna and Mike left, feeling dissatisfied. They'd learned nothing but felt they had been swimming against the current. Both women seemed to have built fortress walls around themselves. They were guarded and careful. The only one left now was Yasmin Candemir who lived at Number 4, Nab Hill Avenue. She responded quickly to their knock, a beautiful young woman wearing the hijab as she came to the door. She had lovely teeth, a flawless olive complexion and huge, alluring dark eyes full of a sad expression. She looked demure but not above giving Korpanski a distinctly curious sideway appraisal.

But however exotic her appearance her accent was local and her answers disappointingly the same as her friends. Had they practised this? Got it word perfect? Jadon Glover simply hadn't turned up on the Wednesday. 'No, he didn't turn up,' she repeated. At this she disappeared inside the house, reappearing with a couple of twenty pound notes in her hand. 'I kept the money for him,' she said with a flash of her white teeth and slanting dark eyes. 'It doesn't do to fall behind, you know. They charge extra.' Her tone was coy, challenging. She was, Joanna decided, a likeable character. She nodded her understanding of the situation and Yasmin continued.

'The interest rates are bad enough without adding a single penny to them.'

They didn't even ask her why she'd needed the money. What did it matter? The reasons were legion. It made no difference. The interest rates and penalties were the same. Karen Stanton seemed to be the only one to have climbed on top of the debt which, in view of her personal problems, paid tribute to her intelligence and strength of character. And only one person, Marty Widnes, had ever been given a temporary reprieve. The rest had been subject to the rigid, punitive rules of Daylight.

They left Nab Hill Avenue and retraced their steps, strolling down Barngate Street. Korpanski swallowed the question: so what did that achieve? It seemed that the people, like the streets, closed ranks against outsiders. In Barngate Street two cars had met head to head and it seemed neither would back up. A few faces peered out of windows. Curtains twitched and they passed a couple of shoppers struggling back from town with heavy bags. Finally one of the cars backed up and flashed the other forward and the daily grind continued. The children were coming out of school, most accompanied by their mothers, fathers, grandparents. Some were dashing along on pavement scooters. The children looked healthy and happy but the guardians were watchful of careless traffic or careless children. It was a life where they needed to be careful. Their space was small. There was little privacy. Easy for neighbours to discover your secrets. A supermarket delivery service held up the traffic as it dropped off the plastic boxes full of groceries. They reached the playground, still taped off. The residents were grumbling now, frustrated at having lost their little play area, but the children were content simply watching the scene unfold. A small rim of them were clustered behind the tape, watching every move of the officers, cheering every time a cigarette butt or a scrap of paper was dropped into an evidence bag.

Joanna spoke to Cornell. 'Nearly finished?'

He nodded. 'You can open up the park again.'

'That'll please the little ghouls,' she said, looking round.

Cornell agreed. 'I think they're disappointed we haven't found a headless corpse.'

She was still laughing as she and Mike continued down the hill.

'So,' she said as they walked down Wellington Place, beneath the shadow of Big Mill, 'if everyone is telling the truth, he went missing somewhere between Karen Stanton's house in Britannia Avenue and his clients on Barngate Street.'

Korpanski nodded and they returned to the station.

She studied the whiteboard, trying to see a flaw in the stories, a hole in the alibis, a clue to Glover's fate. Everyone had a reason for disliking Jadon but they all must have known his place would soon be filled. She jabbed a finger against Number 4, Britannia Avenue. 'Who's looking at the Murdochs' alibi?'

'One of the uniformed guys.' Then, as the door opened, 'Talk of the devil.'

PC Gilbert Young was junior enough to still be excited at playing any constructive part in a major investigation. 'They *were* there,' he said, injecting drama into his statement, 'at the pool but the swimming lesson lasts from half six to half seven and the whole family turned out for it.'

The stories were beginning to fragment. Little lies forming bigger holes. 'It doesn't let them off the hook, does it? They would easily have been home before eight. Thanks.'

PC Young gave a sheepish grin.

DC King, a tall lanky guy with long arms, was bent over the computer digging into Glover's past. 'Well,' he said, neatly flicking the keys without hesitation, 'this is an interesting story.' Joanna leaned over him. 'What? Anything interesting?'

He turned around. 'It depends what you call anything,' he said, turning round, 'and interesting.'

Joanna drew up a chair. 'So?'

'I've been looking into his background.'

Her ears pricked up. 'Go on.'

DC King clicked a few more keys. 'It isn't a great story,' he said. 'Jadon Glover spent most of his formative years in a children's home and then he was fostered. I contacted his social worker earlier on and his foster parents to get some background. He was the son of an alcoholic mother and an unknown father, born with foetal alcohol syndrome.' He was reading straight from an email. 'He spent his early years in a children's home in Stoke. When he was seven he was fostered by a couple who were, apparently, quite religious. They obviously rammed religion down the young boy's throat so he became hugely weird, finding all sorts of things a sin including to be in debt.' King looked up at Joanna, who was intrigued.

King continued. 'According to his social services' records he would thank the Lord for all sorts of things and at the same time despise the poor and needy. They describe him as a complex character, a mixture of his foster parents' values and his own rather warped ones together with a possible bit of brain damage from his mother's drinking while she was pregnant. Anyway, in spite of social services' reservations, he stayed with the foster parents until he went to university.' He looked up. 'He really did study accountancy and finance at Durham but was, according to his university assessment, a solitary youth who found it hard to form relationships, and had—and here I quote—'rigid' ideas about virtually everything. I spoke to the foster parents.' He frowned. 'I didn't pick up on much affection there— rather they'd brought him up out of a sense of duty. They said he was unforgiving and controlling. They heard he'd got married but they weren't invited.' King paused, something strange catching in his voice. 'They were very defensive, said they simply tried to bring him up in the way of the Lord. Really?' For the first time since the investigation had begun Joanna was feeling a strange sense of sympathy for the missing man. So these were the things that had formed him. We're all a product of upbringing, genes and pure chance—lucky or unlucky.

'Umm...'

'What?'

'Sounded more of a job to them than real parenting.'

'Well.' Joanna was at a loss. 'Not being a parent myself...' She found it difficult to complete the sentence and hurried on uncomfortably, 'And so the result is our missing man, Jadon Glover, whom all those characteristics fit. I think,' she said slowly, pondering as she spoke, 'I see him a little clearer now. A rather inhibited, contained man who appears colourless enough to merge in with his beige background and appear invisible yet impose all sorts of rules on his wife, including that she give up her job and stay at home. What else was she expected to give up, I wonder?'

She was silent for a moment as she absorbed King's information.

Something about Eve Glover was disturbing her. That plea made so quickly straight to the police when her *perfect* husband failed to return home. That sense of panic. Did she know something relevant?

'Oh.' She stood up in sudden frustration. 'Is nothing in this case simple? Is anyone what they seem?' She was conscious of the sticky web of debt and credit that bound these people as if with rope.

Colclough used to say to her that murders (excepting stranger murders and even then some of those) stemmed from three lines meeting. Time, place and the ever-critical reaction between victim and killer. 'Straight lines cross. Objects collide. The catalyst is incident plus opportunity against this background of disharmony. And always there is an element of chance. Understand?'

She hadn't. Not really, but had nodded anyway.

Perhaps understanding, Colclough had tried to clarify. 'Perhaps something is said which lights the fuse. The situation is already there, the dry tinder combustible material, but it needs the right setting, at the right time, on the right day. Then all the factors combine to cause an almighty explosion.'

And then she did understand—almost. She could picture a situation mulching away like worms in soil. Biological changes causing heat and a chemical reaction.

The question was where did his wife, her past, his work, her work, his background, his character, fit into all this? What had been the catalyst for his disappearance? What was the reagent? Something even more powerful than debt?

And they still did not know what it had resulted in. Hot-blooded murder? Cold-blooded murder? Had Jadon simply taken the money and run away? Or was, even now, a letter being written demanding money for his release? And would Eve pay to have her perfect husband back?

Questions. Still questions. No answers. And now she had run out of ideas.

While she was thinking, Alan King's long fingers continued to dance over the keyboard checking the PNC for current information on the missing man. Still nothing on his bank account and his mobile phone was dead.

'I think,' Joanna said, needing to move, 'I'll have a nosey round his gym.'

Korpanski stood up. 'OK, Jo. Gyms are my home ground. Want me to come?'

'No. Thanks, Mike, but I'll be fine on my own. You stay here. Hold the fort and keep an eye on things.'

'You just want to eye up all those well-muscled guys without a witness,' he said, handing her her coat, laughing and sitting down again.

*7.30 p.m.*

THE GYM WAS TYPICAL—the ground floor of another converted mill, a large board outside boasting weight loss, weight gain, muscle building, body building, rampant success with women, boosted sex drive, everlasting health, cures for high blood pressure, heart disease, lethargy, mood swings and so on. In fact, Pecs promised everything but everlasting life.

Inside it smelt of sweat. The front desk was manned by a woman in a Barbie-pink tracksuit and bouncing blonde ponytail, well-muscled herself, flanked by two powerfully built men. According to the badge pinned to her tracksuit uniform, her name was Sharon. Sharon made no attempt at friendliness but looked Joanna up and down coldly, probably dismissing her fitness level, and glanced up at the larger of her two bodyguards.

Joanna felt affronted. Bugger it. She was into sport, cycling, hiking, swimming. Just not into piling on pounds of muscle that would turn to fat the minute she let the regime slip. And the last thing she wanted was a boost to her sex drive. She smothered the memory, flashed her ID and explained the reason for her visit.

It didn't melt the atmosphere. Sharon gave her a sulky look and said she didn't see how they could help.

'Did he have any friends here?'

'Not really.' The big guy shoved his way forward, answering for her. 'Blokes don't come here to make friends,' he said, truculence oozing out of every pore. 'They come here to work out. See?'

She turned her attention to him. 'And you are?'

'Al Gillingham,' he said, his voice stroppy and confrontational. 'Prop-ri-e-tor.'

She ignored the threat, simply extending her hand, which he took in his big bear's paw. 'Pleased to meet you, Mr Gillingham.'

He grunted.

Joanna tried again. 'Did Jadon have a regular night?'

'Mostly Mondays and Thursdays.' He seemed to ponder over this. 'He'd be in at least those two nights a week, sometimes more, working out, running mainly...' He wafted a hand. 'On those machines over there.'

'Did he chat to anyone?'

Al shook his head. 'He was a loner, Inspector. A loner.' He beetled his eyebrows together and reflected only to repeat his previous opinion. 'A loner.'

She took a quick look at the membership details but saw nothing there that suggested Pecs was anything more than a playground for the big boys.

She left.

In their offices in Hanley, Leroy, Scott and Jeff were having an argument.

Scott was speaking. 'One of us has got to pick up the tab. We can't let them off. We've missed a week as it is.'

Jeff scratched the corner of his mouth. He was getting a cold sore; a sure sign of anxiety. 'Yeah, but we don't know what's happened to him. What if one of them…took him?'

Leroy pressed home the point. 'He hasn't vanished into thin air, Scott. He's gone somewhere.'

'Yeah, but there's no money missing apart from that night's takings. That's hundreds, man. Not thousands. It wouldn't keep our boy for a week with his extravagant tastes.'

'As far as we know,' Jeff put in.

'Listen,' Scott said. 'I've been through those books with a toothcomb. Whatever else Jadon was up to he's been straight as far as the money goes.'

'Well, one of us has to go collecting.'

Reluctantly Jeff Armitage stood up. 'I'll do it. I'll start next week.'

*COME ON THEN, send him into the ring. A change of personnel won't make any difference to me.*

# SIXTEEN

THE HUNT FOR Jadon Glover had gone eerily quiet. With no leads they were struggling to focus their enquiries.

Joanna had had a few tricky interviews with a distraught Eve, trying to explain why exactly the search for her husband had been scaled down. She didn't tell her that they were still asking questions, watching people, observing. They might have scaled down the obvious but covert investigations were ongoing. Digging into backgrounds. She hadn't confronted Eve with Jadon's life story, keeping it up her sleeve. When she related it she wanted to use it to maximum effect.

It came to a head on a visit she made on the Monday morning to Disraeli Place.

Eve was angry. 'But he's still missing,' she protested. 'Are you just going to let things go?'

'I understand,' Joanna soothed, and the fact was she could sympathize with her. Had this been Matthew she would have been both distraught and puzzled. Her life would have been wrecked. But she had to live in the real world with the budget of a stretched police service and they had absolutely no leads—no suggestion that Glover had come to harm. He had simply vanished as though he had dropped beneath the surface of an oily black pool. They had nothing, simply a void. An empty space where his life had been. A man hurrying through the rain was their last possible sighting. Even that wasn't certain.

Yes, it was suspicious. Yes, it was odd but there was no suggestion of foul play anywhere. No one had seen a fight. No one had witnessed a row or a quarrel. There had been no ransom demand. There was no indication of violence anywhere. She'd tried to convey this to Eve. 'We have no reason to suspect that something bad has happened to him.'

'What on earth do you mean?' Some of Eve's petulant temper rose to the surface. 'It's bloody obvious something's happened to him or he would have come home.' Her tone had changed to patronizing. 'So,' she said mockingly, 'if nothing's happened to him, Inspector, where is he?'

'We don't know.' Joanna was close to exasperation. 'We have no leads. People do disappear. We don't always know why. We don't always find them. We have no evidence that anything sinister has happened to him. Believe me,' she said in a surge of sympathy, 'if we'd found anything, anything at all that raised our suspicions that harm had come to Jadon, we would be pursuing it. Believe me.'

And then it was not Eve's anger but her selfishness that appeared. 'And I'm supposed to do what exactly in the meantime with no income coming in?'

That was more tricky. What *did* one do as far as money, life plan and mortgage when one's husband had vanished into thin air? Again, Joanna had absolutely no idea.

Then, surprisingly, Eve showed another side to her character—even more selfish, hard-hearted, calculating. 'Can I have him declared dead then? At least I'll get some bloody life insurance.'

Joanna was shocked by how quickly the loving wife was turning into a calculating, hard-nosed bitch. She looked at her. Who was this woman?

'No,' she said firmly and without compromise. 'There is absolutely *no* suggestion that your husband is dead. I might say we've scaled down operations but we will still be pursuing any leads. We haven't written him off, you know.' She wanted to add *and neither should you*, but she didn't dare. Even the police force had to play at being politically correct these days.

Eve's face seemed to collapse in on itself, crumple like discarded newspaper. 'I don't know what to do.'

Joanna was dying to make a snide suggestion but she'd lose her job. *Why not apply for a pay day loan, Mrs Glover?*

'We'll keep you informed,' she said coldly. 'As I said, just because we've scaled down operations doesn't mean that we've forgotten about your husband. We'll be continuing with background investigations. If anything new crops up we'll be reopening the case, I promise you.' Not least, she thought, because you and I know there is more dirt in this story than meets the eye.

Eve's response was an evil stare. Then, admittedly with dignity, she saw Joanna out, turned back into the house and closed the door quite firmly.

Joanna drove back to the station in a pensive mood. Sometimes non-cases could be trickier than obvious cases. Give me a bloody body on the library carpet any day, she thought, rather than this unsatisfactory case.

She had spoken the truth. She and Mike and a scaled-down team would still be digging away at Glover's details but in the meantime she had plenty of other things to occupy her mind. The entire Leek force had their antennae wafting in the direction of the Whalleys. The insurance companies were digging into Bill the Basher's set up accidents and fraudulent claims and had requested any video evidence the police might have. Mike was looking into this. And Joanna's personal life was far from lacking in drama. She and Matthew had looked around Briarswood again. It was a fine, beautiful place, with lovely grounds and an air of space and elegance, and they were on the verge of putting in an offer. But Joanna felt sad. She felt she would be turning her back on the happiest period of her life. She would have been happy in Waterfall Cottage for ever. It was her perfect home in a perfect village, surrounded by the empty great vastness that was the moorland but Matthew had other ideas and ambitions. When they'd looked into a small bedroom next to the master suite she could see him mentally painting the room in blue with a frieze of little trains chuffing around the walls or else, second best, sugary pink teddy bears. He'd even put his arm around her when they'd stood in the doorway, his green eyes soft as moss, his lips grazing her cheek. 'What do you think, Jo?' It was at times like that she wished she could wave a magic wand and give Matthew everything he wanted.

She'd nodded, bending her head so he couldn't read her face. But she couldn't quite summon up enough enthusiasm for either the house or the situation and she read disappointment in his eyes.

*I'm sorry*, she thought. *I am so sorry*, and felt she would never live up to his expectations. She would always let him down one way or another.

She was letting him down by not being a different sort of person with different priorities and aspirations. However, they did put an offer in on the house and had put Waterfall Cottage on the market. Rory Forrester, the estate agent who'd come round to value the cottage, had been very upbeat about its value as he roamed around, measuring and photographing interior and exterior. 'You have no idea how these rural places are being snapped up, Mrs Levin,' he'd said. 'Some for second homes but plenty of people relocating from London and the South East who want to escape the rat race. They don't come on the market very often. Most stay in the families,' he grinned, 'for generations. We can afford to be very optimistic about the price.' The valuation was a nice surprise but her heart still broke when she saw the For Sale sign being erected. Some things you could do. Others you had no control over. She couldn't change herself, alter her own aspirations.

Combined with these developments at home there were frequent phone calls from Matthew's parents—chiefly his dad—about various properties coming on the market locally and the imminent sale of their own large house. It felt like all change. Matthew's parents seemed to know when their son was in so they timed their phone calls accordingly and didn't usually spend much time talking to her. No one was building bridges here. They'd always blamed her for the breakup of Matthew and Jane's marriage. They'd stayed in touch with their ex-daughter-in-law and still considered Joanna a usurper even though Jane had married again and presented her husband with twin boys, a fact that Matthew had found a bitter pill, while his parents exchanged as few words with her as was minimally polite.

She wasn't looking forward to them living closer.
Unlike Eloise, Matthew's daughter, who couldn't hide
her excitement at having her grandparents nearer. In
fact, Joanna was quite touched at how fond Eloise was
of her paternal grandparents. She had been fond of her
own grandmother but it hadn't been as close as this. It
was, Joanna reflected, one of the nicer characteristics
of her stepdaughter, this bouncing affection she had for
Matthew's parents. Work chugged on as normal but at
home Joanna felt the alien presence of Matthew's parents and Eloise, and even Matthew seemed a different
person these days, more distant now he had his family
around him, and she sensed his anxiety for a son was
compounding. Yes, home life was eventful and Joanna
sensed choppy waters ahead.

So she focused on work. Twelve days after Jadon
Glover had disappeared she held a meeting with the
associated officers to review the case.

His car had yielded very little forensic evidence. A
few fibres from a sweatshirt sold by Tesco's in their
thousands. A blonde hair with no root, which turned
out to be Eve's, and some mud which was found locally
around the town.

The butt of Silk Cut found in the child's play area
proved to have been his. But it was not certain that it
had been dropped on the night he went missing. It could,
conceivably, have been dropped the week before, been
missed by the council workers and discarded on another
day. Like everything else it didn't mean anything. The
council workers weren't absolutely meticulous about
cleaning the area; bark was a difficult surface to clear.
Even if the cigarette butt had been dropped on the night
he went missing it would only mean that Glover had left

Britannia Avenue and approached Barngate Street. He might not have arrived there. Again, it was not conclusive and didn't lead them forward.

They reviewed the list of Daylight's customers, combed through the evidence again, checked through statements. They spent days turning over everything they had but by the end of the week they still had no leads to follow.

And so they watched and waited.

*Friday, 21 March, 1 p.m.*

JOANNA AND MIKE drove up to the moorlands, taking sandwiches and a flask of coffee. She wanted to escape the station, be somewhere anonymous. She wanted to think. Clearly.

Opening the car window let in a blast of cold air which she welcomed as she surveyed the empty landscape. Up here there was an Arctic microclimate. She could hardly remember a hot day here, open to the elements, high above sea level.

'There's something we're missing, Mike,' she said. 'Something right under our noses.'

'Well, I wish we knew what it was.' He was grumpy. He had wanted to chew away on Billy the Basher's bones. Korpanski's wife, Fran, had had a nasty prang in his car a couple of years ago and the guy had been an uninsured driver. Since then he felt decidedly sour-faced about insurance fraud.

Joanna sensed her DS was disgruntled and touched his arm. 'Gut feeling, Korpanski? What's happened to our man?'

He didn't answer straight away but took in the miles

of emptiness—no trees or fields or walls or houses. Just the landscape rolling towards the horizon, the green broken up by dark projections of gritstone. The moorland was an empty area of hundreds of square miles. It didn't exactly help their case along, mirroring the dearth of information they had gleaned.

'What did you want to come up here for?'

'Because…' She couldn't complete the sentence.

Korpanski turned to face her, his chin sticking out. She knew that attitude. It meant stubbornness, that he was about to say something she wouldn't enjoy hearing.

'I think he's dead, Jo.'

Without looking at him, she nodded. 'Me too.'

'And somewhere out there.'

That silenced her. Neither spoke as a buzzard flew across the sun, darkening their windscreen for a moment with its wing flaps. Then Joanna asked the obvious question: 'So where's his body?'

And Korpanski just shrugged but his eyes were scanning the view as though he was thinking, *Out there— somewhere.*

But where do you start?

Added to their frustrations, they knew that the Whalley family was regrouping. Pa had been seen around the town, looking as seedy and suspicious as ever. A couple of uniforms had bumped into him and exchanged 'pleasantries'. The relationship between cop and robber was similar to that of physician and heart patient. A sort of grudging acknowledgment, a mutual acceptance that it was the bum part of the job. Inescapable. Truth was Frederick Whalley had not been looking forward to his psycho daughter coming out either and he had the added responsibility of being her father and worrying what she'd be getting up to. He knew he was getting too old for this cat-and-mouse game and just wanted a quiet life with his Hayley. When PC Paul Ruthin had met Whalley Senior on Leek High Street he had got the distinct impression that Fred would have liked to detach himself from his most worrying family member. During conversation he had assured a sceptical PC that he had absolutely no intention of ever going 'inside' again. But disassociation was not possible in the family of rogues.

'They all say that,' Korpanski had responded gloomily. 'Right up until the moment they get nicked.'

It was true.

They finished their sandwiches and coffee and headed back to the station where DC Alan King was waiting for them. Joanna didn't have to ask whether he had found anything—the detective's sparkly eyes and barely supressed grin told her all. She pulled a chair up beside him as he showed her the sites and the results of the phone calls he'd made.

'Sounds like her perfect husband was a mite controlling,' he said. 'Eve Glover was a single parent mum to a little boy.'

'What? She kept that very quiet.' Joanna was frowning. She had not seen or heard anything of a child. Certainly in that bland home there had been no toys, no children's bedroom, none of the usual paraphernalia. 'Go on,' she said drily, wondering where this was about to lead them.

'When she married Jadon he refused to have the little boy with them.' He paused, his face pained. 'So he was in the care of his grandmother, a feisty alcoholic who took what she called recreational drugs,' King continued with disgust. 'It was obvious she wasn't fit to look after the boy. And that had tragic results.'

Joanna interrupted. 'Didn't Eve go and visit him to check?'

'Yeah, but he was apparently always crying so they didn't really bond. Shit happens,' he said, 'and...'

'I think I know the rest,' Joanna said. She felt sick. She was sensing a connection here, blindly reaching out a hand, remembering. An unfit grandmother. The phrase resonated round and around.

'He died,' King said.

And it brought it all back. Matthew's distress at the little boy's injuries and his throwaway comment that the parents must have been dyslexic to have given him such a name. The chill spread through her body. 'Was the little boy's name Rice?'

King nodded.

Her next question was so futile she already knew the answer. 'The father?'

King simply shrugged.

And she knew. 'Matthew did the post-mortem,' she said. 'It upset him terribly.'

'I'll bet,' DC King said with feeling. Then, glancing over, he added, 'It must be a difficult job.'

'Sometimes.' It was all she could say.

So that was Eve's story. Which threw up the obvious question: how did it fit in with the disappearance of her husband?

Mike was watching and they both knew that at the very least this information warranted a follow-up visit to Eve.

But Eve wasn't at home; neither was she answering her mobile.

*8 p.m.*

SHE WAITED UNTIL MATTHEW was home, had taken a shower and eaten. He kept casting glances at her, unable to guess what it was that she 'needed to talk about'.

'Go on,' he said finally. 'What is it?'

'The little boy you did the post-mortem on.'

'Yeah?'

'The man who's missing, the money lender.'

He didn't even prompt her.

'His wife was the child's mother.'

'What? She entrusted her son to someone so unfit?'

Joanna nodded.

'Why?'

'Because Jadon refused to let the child live with them.'

Matthew could hardly contain his anger. 'She didn't notice he was beaten, bruised, losing weight, cowed? She must be a psycho.'

Joanna shrugged. 'I haven't confronted her with this yet.'

'Well,' he said finally, 'if I were you I'd be looking a bit closer at Mrs Glover.'

She moved next to him on the sofa. 'Thanks for the tip.'

*Saturday, 22 March, 9.30 a.m.*

AS SEARCHES AND THE legal team lined up to facilitate the sale of Waterfall Cottage, on the instruction of Monica Pagett, current address Brooklands Nursing Home, another country cottage came to the attention of estate agents Burton & Shaw. It fell to Rory Forrester to drive out to the moors and value the building and its

surrounding land. He found the cottage easily enough
on that grey Saturday morning. It was the only property
for miles around but even so it blended in so perfectly
with the surrounding moorland he might have missed
it if its presence hadn't been announced by the strange
name, amateurishly painted, on the gate. He stood for
a while, wondering how it had acquired it. Against the
stormy grey of the clouds it seemed to enact a drama
of its own. He opened the gate and looked around. The
neglect of the house was plainly visible, the home of
an elderly lady. Next he assessed its farming potential.
Fourteen acres was a difficult acreage to sell—not big
enough for a farm but too large for a garden. The plan
was to package it up as a small holding and see who
or what nibbled at the bait. Farmers would always buy
land but it wouldn't do for a speculator. There was not
a hope in hell of obtaining planning permission in these
precious and protected wild lands on the Staffordshire/
Derbyshire border. Having completed this part of the
job Rory Forrester turned his attention to Starve Crow
Cottage, surveying it with a professional's eye. It didn't
take him long to assess the building. It was basically a
two up, two down house hardly touched since the early
twentieth century and it appeared to have few modern
amenities. A brief survey revealed it had been built on
poor foundations, no damp course, et cetera, et cetera.
It would have to come down and be completely rebuilt.
That would take time but the Staffordshire Moorlands
Council would grant planning permission—provided
the materials used were locally sourced, the footage
didn't exceed the old one by more than forty per cent
and the design of the new edifice was not 'out of keeping' with the surroundings. In other words it should be

built in the vernacular—no glass-and-concrete futur-
istic angular design to mar the lulling ambience of the
place. The object was to further the illusion that on entering the moorlands the traveller had time-travelled
backwards into the nineteenth century. He smiled to
himself, glancing back at his gleaming Toyota Auris.
Not exactly the Tardis but there was little doubt that up
here time did travel at a different pace.

Already he was penning the phrase: in need of some
modernisation. Any prospective purchaser would read
between the lines, take a look and work it out for himself.

He worked his way through the house, taking measurements and making notes as he went. No mains running water, just a well, no proper toilet facilities, no
electricity, no gas. The garden might once have been
cultivated but no longer. Nettles grew in the corner of
what might once have been a vegetable plot. There were
animal droppings everywhere, even in the front porch.
Broken glass in one of the windows had been inade-
quately stuffed with newspaper. He looked up. Slates
were missing from the roof. It had only been empty for
a month or two but houses need attention—particularly
up here, exposed to raw elements. A tree planted or
self-seeded too close to the building was using its roots
to argue who took pride of place. It was a fight and it
wouldn't be long before nature won. The old lady had
been struggling well before she'd broken her hip.

Forrester took some more measurements and assessed the forty per cent ruling. Someone could build
a very nice and secluded residence here. Through the
bedroom window he photographed the panorama to
prove his point. Then he needed to check the sanitary

arrangements. He stepped up the garden and opened the corrugated tin door. Just a crack. Just enough to make an assessment. As he'd thought—a most rudimentary earth closet dark as the grave. The smell persuaded him not to investigate further. He pulled the door shut behind him.

Time now to step out to the acreage. This was the bit he liked, breathing in pollution-free air, taking giant strides in his wellies through field after muddy field, the only sounds a shriek of a hungry buzzard and the baaing of new-born lambs.

Heaven. He set up his camera, took some shots and stopped. How to market this place was the real problem. Starve Crow Cottage was a rural idyllic fantasy but the reality was grim. It needed pulling down. In winter it might well be cut off by snow drifts. The roads up here were often blocked for days at a time. There really were no amenities and worst of all it was in national park-land so any plans to demolish or develop would have to be run past the national park administrator. As he was listing all these problems the rain came sweeping up the valley—a gusty, hostile warning that up here nature was both king and queen. He climbed back into the car, glad to be protected from the elements but already anticipating trips up here with disappointed would-be buyers. The only thing to recommend it was isolation and peace and, he thought as he swung the car around, a certain lordliness over the landscape.

*Maybe ideal for an artist* was his last thought as he turned back out on to the main road, unaware of what he had left behind.

Instead of switching the car radio on Forrester spent

the journey writing phrases in his head: *In need of...* was the obvious one. *A difficult property to value...*

*Modernisation indicated... Maybe they should put it up for auction.*

And then he looked around him at a view which even on this sombre day could only be called majestic. And he rephrased his vocabulary.

*A unique opportunity. Fabulous views. Unchanged for centuries. Unspoilt. Untouched. In its raw state.* He revised his asking price and added, *Acreage plus potential.*

An auction could draw them in. Let them slug it out!

HE SPENT THE afternoon putting the details of Starve Crow Cottage and fourteen acres of virgin moorland on the Internet site that dealt with small holdings and attracted would-be farmers as well as people who wanted to open kennels and catteries, have horses and other such country pursuits. By 5.45 p.m. he was ready. He pressed the button and off it went into the ether.

COINCIDENTALLY, AS WATERFALL COTTAGE and Starve Crow Cottage joined the market under the capable hands of Burton & Shaw, Dr and Mrs Peter Levin, Matthew's parents, found a lovely bungalow and completed the sale of their own house.

Matthew and Joanna's offer just needed to be accepted on the Buxton Road property and Waterfall Cottage sold and it would be all change.

And Eloise now had a boyfriend called Kenneth, a strange, bespectacled medical student in the same year as her. He was quietly intelligent and both Joanna and Matthew were finding him hard to get to know. He had a curious smile, part mocking, part cynical, and neither of them was quite sure what it meant. Was he smiling *with* them or *at* them? Even Matthew, who was the most indulgent father ever, wondered aloud whether Kenneth was being patronizing.

'Do you think,' he demanded one evening after they had left, 'that all the way home he's making negative comments about us? Taking the piss, Jo?' He looked so hurt she felt sorry for him. 'Who knows?' she said gently. 'Anyway, it mightn't last.' Truth was she wasn't sure she liked Kenneth any more than she liked Eloise.

She was glad Eloise had another male to command her attention but she could see that Matthew's discomfort with his daughter's boyfriend was making cracks in their relationship. He was less confident with his daughter, slightly guarded.

She hadn't yet tackled Eve Glover with her newly acquired knowledge and Matthew and she hadn't discussed it further. She knew the subject of the little boy's death dredged up disturbing memories but privately she spent some time trying to work out where the little boy with the strange name fitted in with Eve and Jadon's lives and his disappearance. Did Eve blame her husband for her son's murder? Or was she completely heartless? She certainly had a reason to hate her 'perfect', selfish husband. So she remained silent. For now.

*Wednesday, 26 March, 8 p.m.*

LEROY AND JEFF WERE doing the Wednesday round together. Though they wouldn't have admitted it there was something about retracing their vanished friend's footsteps that made them uncomfortable so they had

decided two was safer than one. They had uneasily
mocked themselves for such a wimpy attitude but they
were spooked by Jadon's disappearance. This falling
through a black hole was unnerving. To know nothing was worse than the truth spilling out—whatever it
was—at least they'd know what had happened. But for
now they grudgingly fell in with working together. Just
on Wednesday evenings. Just in that area. And the folk
who inhabited the five streets appeared to be behav-
ing themselves and paying their debts on time without
demur, handing over the money with nothing more than
a sullen, sometimes mocking look. But every time they
knocked on a door they were aware that one of these
people was the last person to have seen Jadon alive.

It wasn't much better when they knocked on the
doors of Barngate Street and Nab Hill Avenue, threaded
through the passageway between the two rows of
houses, walked swiftly behind Big Mill or cut through
the children's play area. Even on the bright, pretty
nights of early spring they constantly checked behind
them, wondering if someone was watching.

*I'm waiting. Waiting to pick you off one by one.*

*Thursday, 27 March, 10.30 a.m.*

JOANNA HAD BEEN LOOKING forward to this encounter,
to confronting Jadon's wife, puncturing Eve's Teflon-
coated character and seeing her reaction. And with that
reaction she wanted to assess what bearing Rice's death
had on her husband's disappearance. As she drew up
outside the house in Disraeli Place she reminded herself
of the first rule of policing. Suspect 'coincidences' and
apparent anomalies. Only Eve could thread the stories

together and Joanna was buzzing to know a little more about this strange case so she sat outside for a moment and wondered.

Finally she left the car, walked up the drive and knocked on the door.

Time to flush her out.

THE LONGER EVE was without her husband the more she appeared to regain her true self. She looked cool and collected as she opened the door, her perfume wafting out into the street. 'Inspector,' she said, apparently surprised at the intrusion. Then, maybe, with her second sentence, her facade was punctured. 'Have you heard anything?' The gaze in her china-blue eyes was transparent.

'I'm sorry,' Joanna said, 'no, we haven't. Might I come in? I have some more questions. It's possible they might distress you.'

She knew. Straight away the look was there, deep in her eyes: guilt, fear, anger.

She nodded. 'I think I know what this is about,' she said quietly. 'Come in.' She turned to her side, flattened herself against the wall and Joanna threaded past her.

Joanna wasn't going to play any games any more. As soon as they were seated she came straight out with it. 'I know about Rice,' she said bluntly.

But if Joanna was in no mood for playing around, neither was Eve. A quick gasp was the only sign that she had heard. Then her face hardened. 'It doesn't have anything to do with Jadon's disappearance,' she said, her eyes full on her, her tone blunt and uncompromising. No grief there either.

Something deep inside Joanna felt vicious then. Matthew wanted a son so badly. She hadn't at first wanted a child at all but at that moment she wished she could tell him that she was pregnant. He would, she knew, be a loving and caring father. Just look how he was with that she-devil Eloise. And here was Eve, hardly grieving for her own little son, while Jadon, admittedly not the father, had tried to deny his very existence.

'I only have your word for this,' Joanna said, folding her arms to hold in her own emotion, 'but it strikes me as a very important factor in your husband's disappearance.'

Eve looked panicky and alert. 'How so?'

Joanna leaned forward, trying not to breathe in the cloying perfume that reminded her of honeybees buzzing around, ready to sting if you moved too near. 'You must have blamed him for your child's murder.' She was not going to wrap the facts up in the cotton-wool blanket of euphemism.

'It wasn't Jadon's fault. It was my mother.'

'And you thought she was fit?'

'I didn't realize how *unfit* she was.'

'Didn't you notice that he was losing weight, bruised, battered and frightened?'

'He was just miserable.' Eve almost spat the words back at her.

'Nevertheless,' Joanna pursued the point, 'Jadon was, indirectly, responsible for your son's death.'

As Eve failed to come up with anything Joanna drove the point home. 'Had Rice lived with you and Jadon, presumably your mother wouldn't have assumed the role of grandparent.'

But instead of looking guilty or grief-struck, Eve

looked angry. 'And all the time,' she said, her face set, 'he was lying to me.'

'Yes. Your mother is in prison for the cruelty she inflicted on your son and will be brought to trial.' She gave Eve a few minutes to let the statements sink in before she went for the full frontal. 'Did *you* have anything to do with your husband's disappearance, Mrs Glover?'

'No.' She gathered herself enough to blurt out an angry, 'How dare you?'

'Do you know who did?'

Again, a defiant and explosive, 'No.'

'Do you know *where* he is?'

Eve shook her head.

Joanna wanted to insert a narrow, sharp blade to open up the cracks. 'Jadon wasn't quite the perfect husband, was he? At least, not for someone who already had a child.'

'It was my mother who…' Her voice trailed away.

'Jadon was controlling.'

Cornered, Eve defended herself. 'If I hadn't wanted that control, if I hadn't loved him I wouldn't have put up with it.'

'Was he worth the cost then?' Joanna asked, partly out of curiosity.

'I thought he was.' The words and the manner in which she spoke them were stilted.

How things had changed.

'Eve, do you know what's happened to your husband?'

Eve simply shook her head, her eyes blank, devoid of any emotion.

Joanna left. She had an appointment.

*11.30 a.m.*

'Mrs Levin.' The doctor, male, in his fifties, appeared unsympathetic and impatient. 'You really can't expect things to happen so quickly. I suggest you relax, find a little patience from somewhere. Keep trying. Your husband already has a daughter. We know he's all right and you have had one previous pregnancy.'

*That ended in disaster.*

The GP was anxious to end the consultation. He even glanced ostentatiously at his watch, holding his forearm out in front of him stiffly. 'Come back in six months if nothing's happened and I'll run some tests. As it is you're being just a little premature.'

His patient smile was unconvincing. She left. He couldn't be expected to know what this meant to her.

She sat outside in the car, reflecting. She knew exactly how Ann Boleyn had felt—desperate. But at least she'd produced a decent daughter. She smiled—at least *she* wasn't about to lose her head. Only, maybe, her husband. Riding on the back of that was another thought: if Matthew had doubted she could bear him a child— the son he so desperately wanted—would he still have married her?

She leaned forward, resting her forehead on the steering wheel.

The phone dislodged her from her uncomfortable thoughts.

*She had a compulsion, something almost as powerful as an electro-magnet, drawing her back there again. It was the stupidest thing to do. But however much she advised herself against going there... Leave it alone. However dangerous it was, she knew she would return.*

*'Just to make sure,' she told herself.*

*She had recurrent nightmares. She'd close her eyes ready for sleep and the name would be there, roughly drawn, free hand, on a block of wood fixed to the gate by wire. Starve Crow Cottage. In her dream she opened the gate and walked through, feeling no cold and no weight. She simply glided along the path towards the cottage. She pushed open the door of corrugated tin and looked.*

*And in her dream, just before she woke, a hand beckoned to her.*

*It was lucky she lived alone or someone would have heard her scream.*

*When she woke, she was more rational.*

*She justified her actions but underneath she was puzzled.*

*She had never expected to have a conscience, never expected to feel remorse. He was a shit. A greedy, cheating bastard. The trouble was that when she thought about it she still got angry. And when she was angry she wanted to get them all. Destroy the entire business. Pay them back the misery and unhappiness they had inflicted on her and her friends. Shit. It was awful. She fought the instinct—focused on work, on friends. Anything but that.*

*But still the hand moved.*

*She read the papers obsessively. Nothing found. Nothing found. She scanned the columns. There was no mention of him. Since a column inch or two on page three of the* Leek Post & Times *two and three days after he had gone missing there had been no mention of him.*

*He had been forgotten about. People slide from the front page to the back, from headline to obituary. No one was looking for him. She could almost feel sorry for him. No one loves you, Jadon. No one.*

*But he continued to invade her mind. She knew that the power drawing her back would win in the end.*

*'You all right?' her friends asked and she just smiled and made some silly joke about the time of the month.*

*And yet, even so, she found herself in the car on a Saturday morning, following the same road. When she reached the cottage the sun was on the gate. She looked, shielded her eyes and looked again. No, it couldn't be. Her heart skipped a beat. This was, surely, another part of her bad dream?*

*She looked yet again. And saw, with the clarity of fierce daylight and an unblinking sun, hammered into the ground, a For Sale sign. Solid and uncompromising as any statement.*

*The property was for sale. It would soon have visitors. Potential buyers. Perhaps someone would decide to develop the cottage, dig up its secrets... She covered her face with her hands.*

*She had relied on his staying hidden. Now it was just a matter of time.*

Leroy, Jeff and Scott had come to the same conclusion.

'Our business has to keep going, mate. We can't live on fresh air. You need to do this on your own now.' His slap on the back was meant to seem friendly but Jeff read it for what it was. A threat. You take over Wednesday evenings alone.

'Yeah.'

And so the rounds began again, Jeff Armitage taking

over the Wednesday evening pick-up—alone this time, following the same route that his predecessor had, parking at Sainsbury's, taking the money from the families in Mill Street, walking up the hill, calling in Wellington Place then Britannia Avenue, crossing the children's play area to Barngate Street then down Nab Hill Avenue and back to Sainsbury's. But every Wednesday when he followed that same route he felt apprehensive. Without an answer or an explanation as to what had happened to Jadon he couldn't know something bad hadn't happened. He didn't want to drop down the black hole. Like him.

Time went by.

# SEVENTEEN

*Sunday, 30 March, 11 a.m.*

IT WAS HARD SHOWING people round the little cottage where they had been so happy. Each room had memories sealed into its walls, love-making, conversations, wedding plans, even arguments. As she showed the first couple around Joanna felt slightly resentful, as though she had been coerced into this. She wasn't sure she wanted to leave Waterfall Cottage at all. In the end it didn't matter anyway. They didn't like it.

Too small; sloping ceilings in the bedrooms (gave them a poky look and made them feel claustrophobic); proximity to the church (we'll be woken up by the bells on a Sunday morning); the yellow paint in the hall (change it).

And so as they walked through her life, from room to room, picking the house apart, criticizing and insulting, she wouldn't have sold to them had they offered twenty thousand over the asking price.

A second couple, seen two hours later, worried about being snowed in in the winter. Yeah, it happens—no one dies. Her hostility was compounding with each negative couple who toured Waterfall Cottage. She and Matthew loved the place. They had from the first moment they'd bought it from a local shepherd.

When Matthew finally came home from a day on call, eyebrows raised, she felt deflated. A failure.

A third couple seen that evening wanted it as a *second* home. They already had a house in London and a flat in Spain but needed to escape 'to rural England'. Joanna felt even more insulted. Patronized. The Staffordshire Moorlands were not a theme park but a real place for real people with real life everyday struggles and Waterfall Cottage was part of that. A home—a real, live home. Not an escape to a perceived idyll.

And then, in the evening, along came a couple so much in love, so starry-eyed with each other and the cottage that Joanna felt almost jealous. She watched their eyes meet, their hands lock as they cooed and exclaimed, as she and Matthew had once done, over the original features, the blackened beams, the arched windows, and she sighed for the past. The things we lose. She watched in the mirror over the mantelpiece as they exchanged a kiss.

By Monday the young couple, both teachers in different schools in Leek, were the ones to make an offer but were, apparently, four thousand pounds short for the deposit. Joanna wasn't sure whether she was pleased or not. She just felt numb and the waiting game continued.

Work was a welcome distraction—particularly when in early April Matthew's parents came down for a week, staying in a bed and breakfast to secure their property and plan for any work to be done before they moved in. Naturally Eloise came over most nights with Kenneth, whom Joanna was beginning to welcome as another outsider. Kenneth was the one who made conversation seem less like a chore and she began to warm to him, reading shyness behind his awkward smile, unease and insecurity when he challenged both Matthew and Eloise on medical matters. He was obviously a pedant, stripping any issue right back to its core. He sat at the kitchen table, frowning as he combed through the house details, even helped Joanna with the washing up, the pots and pans that wouldn't fit in the dishwasher, while the others sat in the dining room, poring over house details and sums. When they were alone Kenneth chatted easily to her and when Eloise joined them, draping her arms possessively around his neck, he seemed impervious to the barbed comments she directed towards her stepmother. He was tall and skinny rather than slim, with loose, gangly limbs that didn't seem quite coordinated. He had beautiful hands with long, sensitive fingers and talked about being a children's thoracic surgeon, a comment to which Matthew listened without responding. She watched his reaction to the youth, his appraisal of his comments. Kenneth wore thick glasses and had a pleasant, slightly hesitant manner. But what Joanna really liked about Kenneth was the effect he had on Eloise. Eloise, who had always been so difficult and hostile towards her, suddenly seemed to have grown up, her resentment towards Joanna ameliorating into something else. Not quite friendly but certainly more tolerant—or truthfully, less intolerant. She even gave Joanna the odd smile and did not seem quite as determined to cling to her father like a sprig of particularly poisonous and tenacious bindweed. Together with Matthew's parents, Joanna invited them over for supper one evening and cooked a lasagne and tossed a salad, feeling awkward as she served the meal because she didn't even know what to call Matthew's parents, her in-laws. Peter and Charlotte seemed far too informal for the stiffly mannered retired doctor and his wife. Mum and Dad, mother and father—none seemed appropriate. So she simply served the meal as though she was a dumb waitress with a *risus sardonicus* papered over her mouth. Only Kenneth offered to help with the clearing up, leaping to his feet and picking up the dishes before helping to load the dishwasher then picking up a tea towel when Joanna rinsed the wine glasses. When they'd finished he gave her an awkward but companionable smile and they re-joined the others, who were still poring over papers scattered across the table. She felt quite resentful as none of them even looked up. Their discussion was patently too lively for distraction.

Strange. And if she and Matthew had a child where would he or she fit in? she wondered. Would the child be the new focus of their attention?

Later, she and Kenneth sat on the sofa, finished the bottle of wine and watched; bystanders while the others remained at the now cleared dining-room table. Matthew glanced over once or twice, tight-lipped, and she knew that later, when they were in bed, he would accuse her of not making an effort with his daughter and parents. It was an old argument, one neither of them would ever win. But Kenneth caught her eye and grinned and she had an ally in the room. Maybe, she thought, looking around, it would all work out—somehow—in the end.

*C'est la Vie.*

*C'est la Mort.*

And of Jadon Glover, there was no sign.

*Wednesday, 16 April, 7.30 p.m.*

LEROY WAS AWAY. He'd gone to Spain for a fortnight's break to stay with a friend, and Scott was having a well-earned night off so Jeff was left holding the fort, or the baby, or whatever. Anyway, he was the one picking up the money that night. Alone.

The supermarket was busy. Easter fell at the end of the week, Good Friday just two days away, and people were stocking up, buying their chocolate eggs and simnel cakes, picking up chickens and turkeys, steaks, burgers and sausages, lagers and beers. Plenty of stuff to throw on the barbecue and celebrate a few days off work. The weather forecast was promising and the mood optimistic. Spring creating a spring in their steps. Finding a space in the crowded supermarket car park, Jeff parked up. When he'd done his rounds he'd pop in and pick up a couple of chocolate Easter eggs too.

It was funny, he thought as he locked his car, how quickly they'd forgotten about Jadon. The waters had soon closed over his head, as though he'd ceased to exist, had never existed. Rumour had it that these days Eve was swanning around in a brand-new silver Mercedes E-Class. Rumour also had it that she and Robertson had been seen around together. She didn't seem to be wasting her time grieving for her missing husband so why should they? He, Leroy and Scott had spent a whole day going right through the books. There didn't seem to be any money missing, apart from the eight or nine hundred Jadon should have been carrying the night he'd disappeared—so why should they bother? Particularly as the police didn't seem to be doing anything.

The further away from that rainy March night they

moved the less real it seemed. It was fading into a memory, bleached and faded, something that might or might not have happened, something to be folded and placed in a drawer. One of those puzzles that would never be solved.

Jeff Armitage left the bustling supermarket car park and almost instantly it was quiet. He turned to the left, walking quickly. Mill Street appeared deserted. The shops here were shuttered and dark. He quickened his pace. Maybe they were all at the supermarket. He knocked on the first door. Maybe they'd have sold out of Easter eggs by the time he got back. The door opened.

'Huh. I might have known the Easter spirit wouldn't touch you.'

He'd learnt not to react but met her eyes steadily. 'Forty quid.'

She slapped it into his palm.

He walked to the next house. But as he lifted his hand to knock it was pulled open.

He performed the same action six times until he'd collected all the money owed from Mill Street—for this week. Astrid Jenkins always left her door unlocked and the money on the table, placed there by her carer.

He prepared to cross the road. There was a Gatso speed camera here, at the bottom of the long, straight hill, so the traffic was always moving nice and slowly, just under thirty miles an hour. He ran across the road which brought him to the base of Big Mill. He looked up at it uneasily. In his mind it was a dangerous eyesore. He scuttled past it. He didn't like the place. It had a bad feeling. They ought to pull it down or develop it, he muttered to himself. Do something with it, anyway. Not just leave it like that. A hazard. That's what it was.

A magnet for druggies and thieves. He averted his eyes from the broken windows and hummed to himself to melt away the spooks.

He turned into Wellington Place next. No one misbehaving here today. All doors were opened, all money sullenly handed over. Carly was a bit more polite than usual. She was a nice girl was Carly. And her bloke wasn't a bad sort either. Not really. Carly even managed a tight little smile when she gave him her money but her overwhelming expression was one of sadness; grief like a grey wash running down her face.

He threaded round the back of Big Mill, sensing its shadow filtering out the last vestiges of sunlight. If possible the back was even worse than its front. It was a neglected area, dank even on this bright April evening. People had chucked rubbish over the railings. The railings themselves had been bent apart to allow miscreants to squeeze through. Jeff tutted to himself, quite ignoring the fact that as a boy he would have been one of those miscreants himself—probably one of the ringleaders. He hurried along Britannia Avenue, puffing after the steep climb towards the top. He was panting when he arrived, took a deep breath and knocked on the first door. 'Hello, Marty,' he said jauntily. 'How are you doing?' No truce for her this week.

The stare she gave him was not so much nasty as disturbing. She seemed to be looking right through him as she handed the money over without speaking, merely fixing her eyes on him as though she knew something he didn't.

*Like, maybe what had happened to Jadon?*

'Thanks,' he said uncomfortably, putting the notes

carefully into the roll, slipping an elastic band around it then fastening it into his case.

He walked fast.

He'd felt uncomfortable and uneasy earlier. Now the feeling was compounding.

He didn't know exactly when he woke up to the fact that something wasn't right, that he was on the edge of something, teetering over.

Jeff was not blessed or cursed with much imagination but he could imagine himself in Jadon's shoes, stepping along this very road on that rainy night, raising a hand to knock on doors and demand his money, the street as quiet as it was now, the people not at the supermarket but hiding, opening their doors reluctantly only to hand over the part payment of their never-to-be-paid-off debt before giving him a look of hatred and slamming them shut again.

Josie Murdoch slapped the money into his hand so hard it almost hurt. He frowned at her, wanting to say, 'There's no need to be like that. We did *you* the favour in the first place, you know. You and your old man were desperate. Glad enough then to accept our terms and grab the money with your sticky little paws.' He'd half got the speech ready but by the time he'd got two words out he was speaking to a door.

Nobody liked him.

Next was the bit he dreaded, crossing the child's play area into Barngate Street. It was a dull evening and the police tape still made the area out of bounds. One of the swings was moving but there was no one on it. He stared at it. To and fro. Not possible, he thought. There was no breeze tonight so why would it move? He stepped towards it, wondering.

The jumble of streets and houses lay ahead of him, around him like a maze, but there was little sign of life. Most families were inside their houses, a few children standing on their doorsteps, a couple of faces watching from windows. Jeff was thoroughly spooked now. He was slipping away from the real world into that place—the nothing place wherever Jadon was. The parallel universe where no one would find him. No one was taking any notice of him. He was invisible.

He looked around him at the darkened windows and thought he saw a light in one, someone moving, watching him. Then he realized it was simply the reflection of the early evening sun and the person was himself. Invisible no longer. He told himself off for being skittish and twitchy, acting like a big girl's blouse. He stood still and lit a cigarette.

How lonely, he suddenly thought, can it be, walking along a street of ten or twenty houses and yet see no one and be seen by no one? Was he already living in Glover's parallel world?

Bad thoughts.

The roads were still quiet, the crowds still out shopping for their Easter eggs. The sun had dropped behind the buildings so the shadows were long. Even his. He looked down and smiled. He looked like the man on stilts you see at the circus. Long, long legs.

He was impatient now to finish. He wanted to go home. He looked to the front. Just two more streets, Barngate and Nab Hill Avenue, cut back through the play area towards the bottom of the hill, take the short path behind Big Mill and you'll be in Sainsbury's car park, my son. Then home sweet home.

Never had he yearned so much for people, for the

crowded sociability and reassurance of normality—
a supermarket car park, home. *Safety in numbers.* He
wished a few more people were around—at least a few
more than these two boys kicking a football around
aimlessly. He felt he was being watched.

*THIS TIME I SHALL not hide behind my own front door—
I'll choose an anonymous spot. I know I cannot hide
the body in the same place. It will not remain hidden
much longer. Soon people will be there, looking, digging, photographing, planning. Finding. No. This time...
Let's do it out in the open. Shout it from the rooftops.
Leave him there for all to see, not drop him down in the
cesspit, even though that is where he belongs...*

THE SUN HAD dropped behind the row of roofs. Jeff Armitage glanced around him, along darkening streets;
even the parked cars seeming a sinister hiding place.
The two boys kicking the ball didn't appear to be taking any notice of him or anyone else who just might be
hiding—in the passageways, behind parked cars, along
the darkening streets.

He quickened his pace. Never before had he felt so
reflective dealing with his clients. He'd never really
thought about them. Not as people, anyway. Neither
had he thought about the circumstances which had led
to their debt. He stopped and lit another cigarette. Each
one of them handing over their money seemed to display the exact same emotion: hatred and resentment,
which wasn't fair. Daylight had been a solution of a
sort. They had lent them money at a time when they had
needed it. They had been on their beam ends. Bloody
desperate, and Daylight had come along like the Good

Samaritan. That's what they'd done. Handed over the cash. In notes. No cheques or questions. *Cash in their desperate hands*. They'd turned up day and night with money. Twenty-four bloody seven.

*Any time, any place.*

Their clients couldn't expect that little service to go unrewarded. He dragged hard on his cigarette. They weren't a sodding charity. And yet each one of them opened the doors with spite and hatred and a certain knowing look, as though they awaited his fate like watching Christians being thrown to the lions, waiting gleefully for him to be gobbled up, or fall into the black hole like Jadon. Simply cease to exist. What was he saying? He took another drag on his cigarette and told himself off for being fanciful. It wasn't like him to think like this. He was a man of action. That was what he was. He didn't worry about what people thought of him and he didn't have post-mortems. It was business. Just that, and he was a businessman. They had costs and wages to pay, premises to rent, loans to pay back. It wasn't as though they were rich men themselves, rolling in money. They too had had to borrow to get started.

The two boys were still kicking the ball around when they were joined by a third person, someone in a hoodie and tracksuit bottoms, hands in pockets, head down. It was hard to tell whether it was a woman or a man. Certainly someone slight. Small woman, very small man. Jeff took no notice and carried on walking, slowly now as he puffed on his cigarette, still lecturing himself.

Jeff, he was saying, get a grip. You can't suddenly develop a conscience, start justifying what you do—as though you have to. Not now. This is the way you live.

This is the job you do. This is the service you provide in this expensive, complicated world we live in.

Suddenly he stopped, struck by something. She or he was still there, hood pulled up right over his or her head. Almost his last thought was that it was like a monk's cowl. Then he felt the push, frowned and looked down. Why hadn't he felt any pain when blood was pumping out of him? Confused and bemused, he tried to call out but the two boys were still engrossed in their aimless football.

It brought back tear-jerking memories. Him and his brother kicking a ball and waiting. Dad somewhere, probably in the nearest pub, mum somewhere else, probably trying to fix the washing machine—broken again. No money. Never any money.

He looked at the monk figure, questioning. Then he felt the thrust again and knew he was going to die very soon.

'No!' he said, tried to peer through the haze, to appeal to the children. Then he fell heavily, his mouth tasting the bark on the ground. The monk figure dropped the knife.

*Done. It is done.*

# EIGHTEEN

*Wednesday, 16 April, 8.10 p.m.*

THE BOYS HAD sauntered over to the man lying on the ground, staring silently for a moment before they realized what they were looking at.

'Oh my God,' Iain said. 'He's dead.'

Bob was his brother, only five years old to his brother's six and a half. He simply stared, open-mouthed.

Then they did what any normal pair of brothers would do in this situation. Ran for home, yelling as they went: 'Mum! Mum!'

Petula Morgan of Number 12, Barngate Street took a bit of convincing that they were serious, followed them out to the slide (where they weren't supposed to be, this late) and saw what they had—the huddle of clothes on the floor drenched in blood. She fished her mobile phone out of her pocket and dialled, her hand shaking, her eyes glued to the person lying on the floor. She knew instantly who it was. She'd had the money by the door ready to hand over. She pulled the boys tightly to her.

Police were there within minutes. A squad car burst noisily and visibly on to the scene, siren blaring, lights flashing. Petula had never felt so glad of its presence. It was only when the officers ran from their cars that she unglued her eyes from the man, looked around and wondered.

PCs PAUL RUTHIN and Gilbert Young had been cruising near the area when the call had come in. Hearts pounding, they had looked at each other, switched the blue light and siren on and screamed their way across the sleepy town to the children's play area. It didn't take a trained eye to see that the guy was dead. Lying on his front, face in the ground. Ruthin felt for a carotid pulse and found none. He too was on his phone in minutes. Then they waited.

Joanna was at home, starting to pack things up in boxes and mark them with a thick black felt-tip pen. The young couple had come up with three and a half thousand out of the four (hopefully not acquired from a doorstep money lender) and neither she nor Matthew had had the heart to turn them down again. The pair had reminded them so much of their own past. Romantic and idealistic. So in effect Waterfall Cottage was sold and she was feeling bereft, as though she had lost a piece of herself. She was sealing the first box and writing BOOKS on the top when the phone rang.

As soon as she heard the words body, children's play area, and the location—between Britannia Avenue and Barngate Street—she knew it would be one of them. She just didn't know which one.

'Wait there,' she said. 'Get a forensic tent and lights. Touch nothing. Wait for me. I'll be there.'

'Matt.' He was outside, collecting up gardening implements. 'A body's turned up. I think it's connected with Jadon Glover's disappearance.'

He looked interested. Since establishing a connection between the case of the battered child that had upset him so much and Joanna's current investigation he had felt a part of it.

'You want me to come?'

'Actually, that'd be really helpful. It looks like he's dead so if you could certify him and we can clear things with the coroner, move the body, it'd make things happen a bit quicker.'

'OK. You're on.' Since convincing her that to move was the right thing Matthew had been in a very conciliatory mood. She could have asked for the moon and he would have had a good go at getting it for her.

They were in the car, heading for the crime scene when he looked at her. 'They have to be connected?'

'Have to be, Matt. Unless Jadon has kept himself hidden, coming out to murder one of his colleagues.'

His hands gripped the steering wheel as he manoeuvred out on to Ashbourne Road and headed towards Leek. 'Pretty unlikely, Jo.'

He turned to look at her as a lorry thundered up behind them. Too close.

'I have to consider all possibilities.' She glanced at him. 'You're always advising me to keep an open mind.'

'I didn't think you listened to my advice.' His face was humorous.

She matched his humour. 'I don't make a habit of it but every now and then you make a sensible suggestion.'

His response was a smile and a nod and she spoke her thoughts out loud.

'I'm betting it's one of the other money lenders.'

'You think it's the same guy as whoever abducted Jadon Glover?'

'Or woman—yeah. I'd take a running bet at it.'

'Right.' He smiled at her. 'Different MO though.' As she had picked up some of his medical phrases, he had picked up on copper-speak.

Murder attracts attention. How so many people knew what had happened so quickly was beyond Joanna's comprehension. She only knew that bad news travels faster than the speed of light, permeating through narrow streets, from living room to living room. Phone lines, text messages, gossip flashing from door to door.

They'd arrived. Why do people do it? Just come to stare at a dead man? Simply to share in the excitement, have a bit part in a real-life drama?

Matthew parked the car and together they threaded their way towards the area. The two constables had already erected a forensic tent to give the dead man the dignity of at least not starring in his very own snuff video.

'Familiar ground this,' Joanna said as she stepped over the bark, keeping to the marked access route. Already combed for signs of a man who had vanished off the face of the earth, she thought. And all we found that time was a cigarette butt.

Phil Scott met her. 'Thought I'd bring the pathologist with me,' she said. 'Save a bit of time. And he wasn't doing anything useful at home anyway.'

Matthew touched her shoulder. 'Don't go pushing your luck now, Jo,' he said softly and the intimacy in such an environment made her shiver.

The light was going fast. In forensic suits and wearing gloves and the most unbecoming hats you could imagine, they approached the tent. Their man lay face down, head pressed into the ground, in a dark pool of blood. He was dressed in a suit and still clutched his leather man-bag. She watched Matthew go through the paces. Feel for a pulse. Roll him over. And now she

could see who it was. Jeff Armitage had met his end.
Matthew looked up at her.

She nodded. 'Jeff Armitage,' she said. 'One of the
Daylight boys.'

Matthew carried on then. She watched as he went
through the paces, took his temperature and then an
ambient reading, listened for a non-existent heartbeat,
touched the skin, looked at fingernails, hands and lips,
checked pupil reaction and searched for obvious injury,
in this case only too easy to spot. Five separate and large
blood stains had seeped through his cheap suit jacket.
One of the areas was just over his heart. As Joanna
watched Matthew do the necessary she knew something else. Jadon Glover's body was out there somewhere. They simply hadn't found him yet. She watched
Matthew take notes and followed his line of reasoning.
The wound low down, somewhere near his liver, had
probably been struck first, the one higher up second and
as the man lay dying on the floor he'd suffered three
more—to make sure. Ending with the heart.

Matthew looked up at her. 'You'll be reopening the
case.'

'Yeah.' She tried to smile. It was a brave attempt
which didn't fool her husband for a moment. 'Well, we
never really closed it.'

He simply nodded. 'OK—I'll leave you here then.'

'Yeah. One of the cars will run me home later. I'll
ring the coroner, Matt. Thanks. You get off home.'

'Yeah. See you—much—later.' He gave her a sterile
peck on the cheek and left her to begin. It was going
to be a long night.

'OK,' she said, addressing PC Gilbert Young, their
newcomer from Stoke, 'who found the body?'

'Two little boys, age five and six, from Barngate Street.' Beardmore glanced at his notes. 'Number twelve.'

Joanna looked up. 'Are they OK?'

'As far as I know. We haven't had a chance to…'

'No worries. I'll go myself.'

She knew the geography of this area already, only too well. She crossed the road and made her way down Barngate Street to number twelve. All the lights were on. She knocked on the door and heard voices inside. She knocked again.

The woman who came to the door looked pale, shocked and slim, with long rats' tails of thin, straggly blonde hair. She looked worried and frightened, dressed in maroon leggings which emphasized her skinny legs, a sloppy grey sweater and slippers. She looked resigned when Joanna said, 'Police.' As though there was no fight in her. Joanna felt sorry for her. She looked like a victim—even without this newest curse.

'The boys?'

'They're in here.' The woman moved a step closer and spoke quietly, conspiratorially. 'I'm Petula Morgan,' she said, 'their mum. They're only five and six and a half. They don't really know or understand what's going on or what's happened. Please, go easy on them. I don't want them traumatized any more than they already have been.'

'That's all right,' Joanna said. 'I understand.'

But she hadn't finished. Petula moved closer, still seeking more reassurance. 'Are you a mum?'

'No, I'm not.' As always Joanna's hackles rose at the question.

'I don't suppose I can request…?'

'I'm the senior investigating officer in this case,' Joanna said crisply. 'I think you can trust me to treat your sons with consideration.'

Inside, she was fuming. Why did mothers believe that they had the sole rights to relate to children? What special powers did they think arrived in the lap of motherhood?

'OK,' Petula said with dragging reluctance. 'They're in here.'

Joanna walked into the small sitting room. Two small boys were sitting on the sofa. A woman in her late forties looked up. Warily.

'P-o-l-i-c-e,' Petula mouthed to her and the woman nodded an, *I thought so.*

Petula ushered Joanna to a spare chair and asked if she wanted a cup of tea. 'Please,' she said, thinking, *let's make this as normal as possible.*

She grinned at the two boys who were watching her nervously. 'Hi, boys,' she said cheerfully.

Neither of them smiled but took their cue from their mother while the older woman—grandmother?—went to make the tea.

'Were you on the swings tonight?' She asked the question casually.

The older one gave a slow, considered shake of his head. 'We was just playing football,' he said defensively.

Damn. She should have recognized the red and white shirts of Stoke City. She recovered her lines. 'On your own?'

The older boy nodded and his younger brother mimicked with a serious dip of his head too.

Joanna tried to get the right balance of interest without obvious nosiness. 'Often play there, do you?'

Again, two solemn shakes of the head with a couple

of swift glances at mum, checking. They knew they shouldn't have been there. Not that late.

'But tonight you came running back for your mum.'

The older one put a warning arm on his brother's shoulder.

'So what's your name then?'

'Iain—spelt funny.'

'Makes it a bit different from the usual, I suppose.'

The attempt at chumminess drew no response. Iain simply shrugged. 'And your brother's name?'

The younger one took charge of this. 'I'm Bob,' he blurted out.

'OK, thank you, Bob.'

Bob gave a beatific smile and settled back into the sofa.

Grandma returned with a cup of tea and sat between the boys. Bone china, Joanna noted approvingly. Nice. She took a sip. 'So, boys,' she said, focusing on the tea. 'Tell me what happened tonight.'

'We didn't really see anything.' Iain had a sudden interest in his nose, rubbing it and surreptitiously sliding a finger inside. His mother frowned and he dropped his hand into his lap. Joanna did not want to think what might be on the end of it.

'No.' His brother, undistracted, echoed. 'We didn't really see anything.'

'But a man was on the floor.' Joanna eyed them as she took another sip of tea. 'Was anyone else there?'

'Someone,' Iain said importantly.

'Anyone you know?'

'I'm not sure.' Iain was dragging this one out to the admiration of his little brother. She turned to him now. 'Did *you* know who it was?'

Bob sadly shook his head. 'No,' he said, 'I didn't because she was wearing...' Hand to mouth to smother a giggle, as though it was a forbidden word, '...a hoodie.'

A woman and a hoodie. It was a start. After the complete void of Jadon Glover's disappearance it was at least something tangible. She made it into a game. I-Spy. Twenty questions. 'Was it...someone who lives in this street?'

Iain put a considering finger to his chin. 'I don't know,' he said, deliberating over the words.

His mother, Joanna noted with approval, was saying nothing. Not encouraging or discouraging, not threatening, making promises or asking her own questions. Simply leaving the boys to respond to the police on their own.

Joanna narrowed her eyes and pretended to guess. 'Was it a red hoodie?' She tried to look pleased with herself.

The boys looked at each other, frowning now.

It was Bob who answered, speaking very slowly. 'I think it was blue.'

More guesswork to narrow the field. 'Dark blue? Like the night sky? Light blue like the sea on a sunny day or royal blue like on the Union Jack?'

But it had gone far enough. Grandma's arms tightened around the pair of them. 'I'll stay tonight, pet,' she said, ignoring Joanna. The boys' mother flashed her gratitude. The interview was over.

Joanna stood up and Petula followed her out to the hall. 'You have a fine pair of boys there, Mrs Morgan.' She was surprised to pick up on a note not only of truth but of envy in her voice.

Petula looked both delighted and proud as she nodded. 'Thank you, Inspector. All my own work,' she said. 'Father didn't want to know. We struggled when Iain was born, but when Bob came along eighteen months later it was curtains. Luckily I've got Mum.'

It flashed through Joanna's mind again how lucky she was. Matthew would never abandon either a son or a daughter—let alone two children.

Another phrase resonated. *Luckily I've got mum.* Eve had had her mum. Joanna's mother was hardly grandmother material although she wasn't bad with her sister's two, Daniel and Lara, who were growing up so fast. But Joanna knew her mother would never treat a child ill. Unlike Eve Glover's mother.

She gave Petula a card. 'If they say anything more that might help us find the killer, please get in touch.' She was surprised at how calmly the woman was taking this. Her boys had witnessed a violent murder. Had this been a movie the boys would have been under police guard in case they did remember anything and the killer came back for them. After all, it looked as though this was the work of someone who had already killed twice, because Jadon had to be dead too. They simply hadn't found his body yet. Jeff Armitage's murder was not the first but the second and it wouldn't take the residents long to reach the same conclusion. From there it was only a small step to the residents of these streets getting twitchy and asking for extra police patrols. She half expected Petula or Grandma to also ask whether it was safe for the children to play in the recreation area. The answer was surely no. Even after the restrictions had been lifted would it ever be safe again? Only if there was an arrest. But neither of these questions was asked, which she found surprising. The two women's focus was completely on the two boys, apart from a brief, conspiratorial glance at each other.

For now she had to face her own problems. Rush would soon be breathing down her neck and he would want results. It looked as though the murder of Jeff Armitage was the second in a connected crime—and they'd not even managed to solve the first one.

They'd not even found his body.

# NINETEEN

THE ROUTINE WAS SO automatic Joanna hardly had to think about it. They would work through the night, isolate and guard the site, pick up any evidence that might be significant. Check the CCTV. The coroner was informed and Jeff Armitage's body was removed to the morgue. Matthew would perform the post-mortem in the morning.

In the meantime, they started digging into Jeff Armitage's life.

He turned out to live in a semi at the other end of town with a guy called Arnie. Whether his name was Arnold or this was a pseudo name connected with his famous namesake Joanna didn't know but she dispatched one of the PCs to interview him while she started collating the evidence. The area would now be under even closer surveillance. Unfortunately the children's swings and the slide were not covered by CCTV, only the approach to the area. They would be able to see people coming and going but not the actual assault. Had it been better placed maybe, just maybe, they might have got some useful information. As it was they had nothing to go on.

*9.30 p.m.*

JOANNA RETURNED TO THE station, thinking. They needed to shift this investigation, change gear. Find Jadon's body or Jadon himself. It wasn't beyond the realms of possibility that he was still alive, a ghost haunting Leek town who had taken his revenge out on his colleague. It was a possibility they couldn't discount—not just yet. The boys had said they had thought it was a woman but Glover was not a big guy. Slightly built, in a hoodie, it was possible the boys had been mistaken.

But the crimes couldn't have been more different. If one killer was responsible for two deaths he or she had certainly changed gear. Armitage's body had been left in full view. No attempt had been made to hide it or conceal the crime. It was the opposite of the mystery that surrounded Jadon Glover's fate. Was it even possible the crimes were not linked?

No. Too much of a coincidence.

Too many questions, not enough answers. In fact, Joanna grimaced, they had no answers.

Nothing except an angry motive.

The question burned into her mind: why hide Glover's body so successfully but make no effort to conceal Jeff Armitage's murder? Where was he?

She allowed her mind to wander here and there. Thinking time was important. She tried to imagine Jadon's fate. Bodies buried showed up as fresh earth even out on the moors. Bodies left out even at this time of year tended to decay, attract flies and, without putting too fine a point on it, stink, so where was he?

SHE FINALLY MADE it home at 1 a.m. Matthew was fast asleep and she made a real effort not to disturb him. She almost succeeded until she lowered herself into the bed and pulled the duvet around her. He murmured, threw his arm out and turned towards her then sank back into sleep.

*SHE WAS HAVING a nightmare. One she had had before. It always began in the same way with the smell of paint. It made her nauseous because she knew what came next. The car. The windscreen wipers whispered before they turned into fingers grappling through the windscreen, trying to reach her. She drove on. A great black skinny bird flew over cawing and croaking in desperation. She was pulling something heavy, tugging it towards... The door was difficult to move, rattling and clanging into the night, but she managed it and, pulling him inside, pushed him down the hole. But the nightmare was not over. As she retreated and tried to close the door behind her she could not resist one last look. And that was when she saw it. His hand moved.*

*That was when she woke screaming and knew.*

*She never would be free. She could remember him saying it to her and disagreeing but in the end he was right. 'You will never be free.'*

*Thursday, 17 April, 7 a.m.*

HE WOKE HER GENTLY, still damp from the shower, a towel wrapped around his waist. He handed her a cup of coffee and she sat up, thoroughly awake now. 'You're early.'

'Yeah,' he said, sitting on the side of the bed. 'I, umm… I have to go to court this morning but I can do the post-mortem on your man this afternoon. Is that any good?'

She sat up. 'Yeah. Great. Thanks.'

He delved into the wardrobe and took out his suit while she watched him. There's something sexy about watching a man dress for the formal background of court. Particularly Matthew, who usually went to work in chinos, cords or jeans with a sweater or jacket.

He was, at best, a casual dresser.

But not today. He looked like a solicitor in a grey pinstriped suit, pale blue shirt, maroon tie. She beamed up at him. *Wise choice, Piercy.*

'What's the case?'

'It's the little boy,' he said. 'Eve's son. The one whose grandmother "looked after" him while she was busy being the perfect wife to the perfect husband.' He bent and kissed her and she breathed in the sharp scent of aftershave. 'There's not much doubt about the verdict. Whether Eve Glover will come in for criticism I don't know.'

'And does it have any bearing on my case?' She sat up, hugged her knees. 'I suppose it would give Eve a reason to attack her mother—if she'd cared about the child.'

'It might also give her a reason to go for her husband.'

'Yeah,' she said. 'I've thought of that.'

She finished her coffee and touched his arm. 'Poor kid. He didn't have much of a chance, did he?'

'No. I hate these cases, Jo.' His eyes looked troubled. Stormy green. She put a hand on his arm. 'I know, I know. But just think of all the children who *are* loved and wanted and precious. Focus on those, Matt.'

He smiled, gave her a peck on the cheek and stood in front of the mirror to brush his hair. Matthew always finished with a comb-through with his fingers which gave him the tousled look that suited him so well. Jo-anna smiled to herself then climbed out of bed too. 'Will you ring me when you know what time the post-mortem on Jeff Armitage will be?'

'Yep.' He was downstairs, already eating his breakfast. Time for her to get in the shower, get dressed and face the day. And she had the feeling it would be both long and difficult.

*8.15 a.m.*

RUSH WAS WAITING FOR her, almost ambushing her as she walked into the station. He didn't say anything but motioned, with his head, towards his office.

Once inside he wasted no time getting to the heart of the matter. 'I take it you're of the opinion that these two cases are related?'

'Yes, sir. I can't think they're random. Too much of a coincidence.'

'So just fill me in, will you?' There was just the faintest hint of sarcasm in the question.

'The body of Jeff Armitage was found by two young boys yesterday evening. They were witnesses to the crime.'

He held up an index finger to halt her—right there. 'Have they been able to give you any details?'

'They're five and six-and-a-half years old, sir. They have said that the perpetrator was a woman wearing a blue hoodie and tracksuit.'

'Right,' he said, his mouth thin with disapproval. 'CCTV?'

'A bit vague, sir.'

'And the other one?'

'Jadon Glover, sir. He hasn't turned up. We haven't found a body and have no further evidence. He seems to have just dropped off the radar. We've done some pretty thorough searches in the surrounding area but haven't come up with anything.'

Rush was silent for a moment. Then he said, 'His car?'

'Still impounded, sir. But we found nothing.'

'And his wife…?'

He must have sensed her hesitation because he stared at her. 'His wife?' he repeated.

'There is an issue with his wife, sir.'

His eyebrows lifted to prompt her. 'Well, go on, Piercy, or am I to be kept in suspense?'

'She had a little boy, sir. When she married Jadon Glover he did not want the little boy around so he was parked with Grandma.'

'On a permanent basis?'

'Yes, sir.' For some God-knew-what reason she found herself defending Eve. 'I think she visited him when Jadon was at work.'

'And?' He was a man of few words.

'The grandmother was…unsuitable, sir.' She paused. 'The child was neglected and worse. He died. Matthew, my husband, did the post-mortem. The child was treated cruelly. The grandmother is in court today.'

Rush's eyes burned into her face. 'That gives the child's mother,' he said very slowly and deliberately, 'prime motive. Surely?'

How could she get this one across?

'I would have thought that, sir, except that she didn't seem to have really bonded with the child. She didn't seem to care, sir.'

Even Rush was silent at that. He dismissed her with a tight-lipped, 'Thank you.' She was almost at the door when he fired his Parthian shot. 'Try and get a result this time.'

She would have loved to have banged the door behind her.

*You think I'm not doing my level best?*

Korpanski was already in, working on the computer. He swivelled around as she entered, her face reflecting her dark mood. 'Ooops,' he said.

She took her ill humour out on him, saying sourly, 'Thanks for the helpful comment, Mike.'

He simply grinned at her, unruffled.

She sat down. 'We have a problem.'

'Yep. So what have we got?'

'A second money lender killed. And it looks very much as though Jadon met the same end.'

'Except…' Korpanski frowned, adding unnecessarily, '…we don't have a body.'

'I've called a briefing for nine. Matthew will do the post-mortem on Armitage this afternoon. He's in court this morning. It's Eve's son's case. Granny's in court. We've got to go back to house to house, Mike. I'm convinced the killer is one of our debtors and I'm also convinced that they killed Jadon as well. Our killer is from one of those streets. Most likely either Britannia Avenue or Barngate Street but possibly one of the others. Someone from Mill Street or Wellington Place could have followed him or one of the three people from Nab Hill Avenue walked down to meet him. It's even possible he varied his order that night as he sometimes did, visiting Nab Hill Avenue first. Our crime scene, Mike, is somewhere in that vicinity. Considering the foul weather the night Jadon was killed he probably stepped inside the house. And if the killer used a knife there will be blood.'

'Can't argue with that,' he agreed.

At the same time that Joanna was briefing her force Matthew was in court, giving evidence.

'I performed the post-mortem on Rice Sutherland on the morning of March the fifth at the mortuary. I also performed X-rays. There were forty-four separate injuries in total…' He listed them and responded to a question: 'No, it's not possible that these injuries were accidental.' He anticipated the next question by adding, 'And Rice did not have an underlying condition that would have made him susceptible to fractures. The injuries had been sustained over a long period of time, probably since Rice was a few months old.'

IN ANOTHER PART of Leek, Kath Whalley was holding court. 'I will get her,' she was saying to the gathering, a combination of family and old cronies. The Whalleys didn't really have friends.

'But it'll be in my own time. I want her vulnerable. I want her to suffer. I've waited for this chance, planned it every day I was inside. I am going to make her regret ever tangling with me.'

Fred sat, impassive. It went against the grain but he needed to warn the detective. She needed to be on her guard.

And in yet another part of the small town Rory Forrester was packing his wellies into the boot of his car. Later on today he had a job to do. What he called a 'Good Life' couple wanted to take a look round Starve Crow Cottage and it was his happy task to show them around. Later. With April had finally come warmer weather. And with warmer weather came the flies and the putrefaction accelerated.

*9.45 a.m.*

JOANNA WAS KEEPING THE briefing factual yet at the same time inviting ideas.

'It is highly suggestive that Jeff Armitage's murder is connected with the disappearance of Jadon Glover,' she said. 'Here we have two options: Glover is either dead, in which case his body has not been found—or he is alive, in which case is he implicated in the murder of his colleague?' Honesty forced her to add, 'I think that's highly unlikely. I believe Jadon Glover is dead and we have, so far, failed to find his body.'

A small thought wormed its way into her mind. Perhaps it had been important that Glover's body was not found for one of two reasons. Either the implication of his killer—possibly his wife, given what they now knew. Or if his body had been found was it possible the perpetrator might not have had the chance to get at Armitage? While Glover's was a disappearance, a full-blown murder investigation was something else. Arc lights would be turned on the crooked streets of Leek. No chance for another street stabbing.

Instinct told her she had just put her finger on the button. Police training pushed her towards caution.

The officers were silent. Questions might be asked but where were the answers? A few of them sighed. They needed evidence.

Joanna tried her best to encourage them. 'So keep

an open mind. We need to continue with the house-to-house enquiries and take any witness statements. Find out who Armitage visited last night, how much money he had on him, check his mobile phone, computer records, try and get in touch with his two remaining colleagues. See if anyone apart from the two young boys saw anything. In the meantime, DS Korpanski and I will be visiting Eve Glover—again. Hannah…' she addressed DS Beardmore, '…you've done some child protection training, haven't you?'

'Yes.'

Without warning it flashed across Joanna's mind the difficult time Matthew would be having at this moment recounting Rice's injuries to the court. She'd been at these sessions herself and winced at the graphic detail of cruelty and suffering. She shook herself.

*Focus on the job, Piercy.*

'I wondered, Hannah, if you'd mind speaking to the two boys again. These are, potentially, important witnesses. Their mother and grandmother seem to be around most of the time so they can sit in.' She risked a smile. 'Make sure you're not breaking the rules.'

Hannah Beardmore smiled her response. She was not a rule-breaker.

Joanna addressed the entire room then. 'We'll be searching the four streets for some forensic evidence, focusing mainly on Barngate Street.' She turned to Mike. 'Keeping the three women from Nab Hill Avenue in our sights.'

Korpanski nodded.

Her next sentence was dragged out reluctantly. 'And I suppose, whatever our personal opinions, we'd better warn Jeff's colleagues.'

*11.30 a.m.*

JOANNA WAS HAVING TROUBLE tracking Eve Glover down. She wasn't on her landline which put her straight through to answerphone; neither was she answering her mobile phone. She left messages on both and for a moment had a tingling feeling.

What if Eve was with her husband? Holed up somewhere? And then she answered her own query. Eve was, obviously, sitting in court, listening to the injuries her own son had sustained from her mother.

Of course she wouldn't be answering the phone.

*12.15 p.m.*

MATTHEW HAD FINISHED GIVING evidence and had returned to the front row as the coroner delivered the verdict of culpable homicide. Now it would be up to the police and the courts to bring the case to court. Matthew's role was theoretically over. If Rice's grandmother pleaded guilty there would be no need for him to recount the child's injuries again. But as he left the court he knew that for him the scars would remain, deep inside him. These cases brought their own particular sort of sickness. The memory of that small boy with distorted limbs, injuries that must have been agonizing, signs of neglect everywhere from decayed teeth to severe malnutrition, even lumps of hair pulled from his scalp, would stay with him, invade his dreams and lie at the back of his mind. Gradually, over months, they would fade.

And then there would be another—and another.

After court had been dismissed he sat very still in

his car, glad of the silence and of being alone. He felt terribly depressed. No child should be brought into the world unless it was desperately wanted by *both* parents, not just one. He couldn't do this on his own. He couldn't love any child enough for both of them and he knew Joanna didn't really want a family. She was happy with him and her career. Maybe he should have recognized that from the start and been content. She had to want a child and love it too. Had he been able to, he would have rung Joanna right now and shared this thought, spent time discussing their future. He fingered his phone but in the end returned it to his pocket. When he saw her this afternoon it would not be private but public. No time. No chance for a talk. How many couples are destroyed by this?

*PUT THE KNIFE through the dishwasher twice on the hottest wash and no forensic laboratory will find even the most microscopic trace of blood. The wonders of modern science and machines.*

DS KORPANSKI HAD been dispatched to speak to Jeff Armitage's partner, Arnie, who turned out to be nothing like the muscle man he'd expected but a small, wiry man in his late twenties with a whisper of a voice. Mike treated him with respect but it was soon obvious that Jeff Armitage had kept his private and professional life far apart. Arnie knew nothing of value about his partner's business dealings. He seemed frozen. Paralysed with grief.

DS Hannah Beardmore had quickly put the boys, their mother and grandmother at their ease. She was so motherly herself. Her plump, maternal figure, gentle voice and patient manner melted their fears well away. Also she spoke in the slow pace natural to native moorlanders.

She accepted the proffered cup of tea, admired the boys' shaky Lego models, sat back and, quite casually, asked if they remembered anything else about the lady who pushed the man to the floor.

It had been decided not to tell the children what it was they had witnessed. They were young and vulnerable and might be damaged by the knowledge. On the other hand, they were potentially valuable witnesses. Not only had they witnessed the crime but they had actually seen the killer, so anything they could remember would be useful. They regarded her with round eyes as she told them that they were being very helpful.

It was Bob, the younger boy, who dug his brother in the ribs. 'She dropped something,' he said. 'The lady dropped something. I heard it...' His brother turned to look at him, surprised perhaps that his brother could remember something he could not.

Then he seemed to remember. 'It tinkled,' he said, 'like money.'

His brother gave a solemn nod while Hannah Beardmore listened.

# TWENTY

FINALLY MATTHEW ROUSED himself from his stupor and rang to say he would be starting the post-mortem at two—if that was OK. Joanna agreed to attend as well as two uniformed officers to collect any evidence.

When 2 p.m. came and she'd arrived he was already in his scrubs and seemed a little distant, avoiding her eyes. No kiss. 'Matt,' she said, putting her hand on his arm. 'Did the court case go OK?'

'Yeah,' he said, fiddling now with his facemask; a useful concealer of facial expression.

'Is everything OK?'

'Yeah,' he said again, then, unable to stop himself, he grabbed her elbow. 'When are we going to be able to talk, Joanna?'

She knew she couldn't give him a definitive answer so shrugged.

'I thought so,' he said and turned away from her to face the corpse being wheeled into the PM room while she fumed. What did he expect? He knew full well she was in the middle of a serious case—probably two murders, not even just one. It simply wasn't fair for him to make demands on her. So she stood, resentful.

As they wheeled him in Joanna started. She should have been used to it by now but one never really grew accustomed to this sight.

Jeff Armitage was still dressed in his blood-stained

chain-store suit, shoes on. His man-bag had already been looked at and saved. It had contained nothing particularly interesting or helpful: money, books, mobile phone. Nothing to hint at his killer. The clues would all be here. On his body.

While his clothes were being cut off and bagged up, along with fingernails and hair combings—all the trace evidence gleaned—Joanna watched and worried as she studied her husband's face. She knew Matthew so well. He was deep and stubborn. She knew exactly what he wanted out of life and she could go along with it. So far. What she couldn't provide was to want those same things herself with matched enthusiasm; neither could she magic up a pregnancy.

And then there was Eloise, who always drove a wedge between them wilfully and skilfully. Joanna had learned to deal with this by limiting contact with the girl and keeping her distance when they did meet up. It worked—up to a point. If anything Eloise's boyfriend, Kenneth, had made the situation a little easier. He bore Joanna no grudge, felt no hostility towards her and was simply amiable and polite. Neutral. Unlike… Her mind drifted on.

Matthew's parents. Their arrival had driven the wedge a little wider, pushed it in deeper. Perhaps, Joanna reflected as she took her place at the side of the mortuary table, had she become pregnant, the hostility would have melted away. But, so far, that hadn't happened. And so the situation between her and Matthew's family remained uneasy, a sort of skirting around each other, like wrestlers in a ring, waiting for the first body encounter. As for her own family, her mother and sister (married, with two kids), they had never been close. She had been too much of a daddy's girl and when he had gone frost had formed between herself and her mother and sister. Ironically they both simply adored Matthew. Lara, her niece, treated him as a favourite uncle. Even Daniel, her nephew, sparred with him and played football. On their infrequent visits, she would watch them and know: this then would be how Matthew would be with his own son—if he ever had one. And her mother never missed an opportunity of reminding her of this. Typical of her mother to poke her nose in when she was ignorant of the facts.

Joanna watched him work, taking measurements, making observations into the video recorder, tousled blond hair the colour of damp sand, face completely absorbed, half hidden by the mask he tended to tuck under his chin. He had long lashes over green eyes that magically changed colour according to his mood, from the dull green of seaweed in a rock pool on a dirty grey day reflecting disapproval to a bright mischievous, elfin brilliant colour. How had their blazing passion for one another withered to this? And—watching his nimble fingers begin to tease out Armitage's body secrets—how could they rekindle that love? A holiday? No—Matthew wanted this house, Briarswood. There was only one answer and it was, it appeared, beyond her capability, whatever the doctor said. Relationships. She sighed. They were too complicated. At what point, exactly, had she lost control of her own life? Like Eve who, with her glamorous Italian wedding, had lost her son.

And then Matthew lowered his facemask, looping it underneath his chin, looked across at her and she remembered exactly at what point she had lost control. At this exact point when his eyes had crinkled and he had smiled at her, warmth lighting his face. She smiled back at him and felt heat trickle back into their relationship. They did love each other. Then he bent back over his work and her eyes too returned to the body of the murdered man. They also had this in common, their work.

Jeff Armitage was small and wiry, his body, even in death, muscular, tattooed and toned. He lay naked, exposed. Matthew made a cursory examination of his brain but it was patently obvious that the main focus of the post-mortem was to photograph and examine the five stab wounds to his chest.

The amount of contusion and bleeding around each one was the clue to the order of the assault. She'd watched enough post-mortems to know this. First of all, Matthew photographed the wounds. Then he took measurements of the superficial injury. Because of the skin's elasticity the wounds tended to be smaller than the size of the blade and he took this into account. But the depth of the wound was a firm indicator of the length of the blade so he inserted a probe to measure its depth before he began to explore beneath the surface and assess damage to the deeper structures. In some cases one could perform a virtual post-mortem using a CT scanner but this was a new technique and not ready to be used in a murder case. This one needed the old butcher's slab of a post-mortem table and the sharp eyes of a pathologist. Matthew pulled his face-mask back up over his nose and mouth.

'Twenty centimetre blade, width three to four centimetres. Sharp and pointed,' he said. Then, looking directly at her, his green eyes gleaming, he said, 'Think kitchen knife. Carving knife.'

She could tell from the way that his facemask was rucked up plus the crinkles around his eyes that he was smiling at her again. They would be all right. They loved each other enough to weather the storms ahead.

His attention returned to his work. 'Wound one,' he spoke directly into the video camera, 'extended into the liver and caused extensive bleeding in the upper hepatic edge.'

He worked again, cutting, exploring slowly and rhythmically, getting into his stride as he became more absorbed. 'Wound two nicked the aorta, again causing extensive bleeding, blood spurting but internally.' His gloved index finger was probing around.

Joanna interrupted. 'Would the perpetrator have been blood soaked?'

'Possibly.' Matthew screwed up his face as he scooped up a handful of what looked like dark red tripe. 'It's just a nick. The pressure in the aorta is'—he sucked in a breath—'impressive, to say the least. But really I can't say, Jo. Maybe, maybe not. Probably. Certainly there was extensive loss of blood but most of that seems to have been contained in the peritoneal cavity so don't go looking for someone walking up the street soaked in blood. No *Nightmare On Elm Street*.'

She smiled. He always managed to put a lighter note on what was undoubtedly a grisly business.

His hands were still for a minute, his eyes, now resting on her, warm and friendly and she felt reassured. She smiled back at him. There was a moment between them, nothing more.

But it was enough. It was precious and now she was happy and confident again.

Then he turned his attention to the other three

wounds inflicted in the chest and for this he needed to split the sternum. This was done with…think cheese wire, and the grating noise turned her stomach.

'Wounds three and four both entered the lung. Three on the right upper lobe and the skin area is wider.'

*Two knives?*

He was frowning, then supplied the logical explanation. 'Maybe he moved. Twisted away. The fourth blow was inflicted to the left lower lobe and missed the heart by—' Matthew blew out his cheeks, inflating the face-mask as he measured, 'A centimetre. No more. Then the fifth blow was hey bingo. Straight into the left ventricle.' He turned to Joanna. 'He would have bled to death from strikes one or two but it would have taken a while. Maybe half an hour or so.' He couldn't resist a touch of black humour. 'Had the later blows not been inflicted he could have texted you the identity of his killer.'

She could have punched him even when he turned around and said, with a flourish, tugging his facemask off, 'So there you are, Jo. Cause of death shock due to blood loss due to multiple penetrating wounds entering the liver, aorta, lung and finally the heart.' He held his gloved hand up in warning. 'And before you even speak, it's not possible for them to have been self-inflicted so we're looking at a homicide.'

She defended herself with a smile. 'I wasn't even going to say it.'

'No, but it's as well to have all eventualities ready in case defence brings it up.'

'Defence?' She felt despair. 'For that I need a suspect, Matt.'

He put a hand on her shoulder and gave her a light kiss, his eyes warm now. 'I have complete faith in you.'

'I wish *I* did.'

But as she left the mortuary she switched her phone
back on.

*4 p.m.*

RORY FORRESTER WAS ENJOYING driving across the moorland. He switched the radio off, opened the window
and drank in the sweet air, the isolation and the complete and utter beautiful silence. He had full appreciation of the majestic beauty of this area, particularly as
he came from inner city Birmingham.

He could pick out the cottage from a mile away.
Starve Crow Cottage sat in splendid isolation, miles
from anywhere, on a ridge too high for trees. He was
meeting the couple here, a pair who had made money
in IT and now wanted a taste of the good life, or so they
thought. In Forrester's mind the reality didn't always
live up to the fantasy. Life out here could be tough.
Still—their decision. His role was to sell them the idyll.

He was still smiling as he opened the gate and
moved his car on to the track, off the road and glanced
again over at the sad little cottage, his mind echoing his
initial impression. *Would benefit from modernisation*...

As he shut the gate behind him his eyes rested on
the rough, hand-painted sign.

Starve Crow was about the ugliest, most repulsive
name for an abode he'd ever met. Now... Roaming Hills
or Moorland View. Something on those lines. Nothing
too twee—no DunRoamin' or silly jokes Llareggub.
But definitely not Starve Crow with its inference of
witchcraft. And yet—as he scanned the empty land-

scape, listening out for a sound—one could almost believe in witchcraft out here.

He pulled his wellies on, glanced at his watch. The
couple were late. Maybe, in spite of his instructions,
they couldn't find it.

*4.10 p.m.*

JOANNA WAS HOLDING A briefing, pooling everyone's
observations. Up on the board was a map of the surrounding area. She looked at it trying to divine where
their killer was and where Jadon Glover's body could
be. Or was it possible that he was the killer, stalking
and then murdering his mate? Without a body she was
aware that she could discount no theory, however im-
probable it might be.

But surely she could discount this one?

The boys had firmly said their perpetrator was a
woman. Could Jadon Glover have been mistaken for
a woman?

She wasn't convinced.

Looking at the pictures of the dense tangle of streets
on the southern edge of Leek she believed their killer
was in there and, she guessed, one of the people on
Daylight's list of clients. So what was so hard about
this?

The lack of a body—that was what was making this
case difficult. But now she had Jeff's.

She emphasized this point as hard as she could and
then wondered. Could she be wrong? Was it possible
that it was someone outside their current list of victims?
Either someone who had broken free of the doorstep

lenders' stranglehold like Karen Stanton or someone who had watched another's suffering?

But she had to suggest one route or another. 'Focus on this area and on these people,' she said, sketching out a circle and a list behind her without looking like a TV weather girl, she knew the names and the area so well. She stopped for a minute, frowning, turning now to the map of the wider area. Jadon Glover's body was somewhere out there. Was this really such a straight-forward case? Or was the reason they had made such a mistake in Glover's disappearance because they had underestimated it? Thought it simple when it was, in fact, complicated? And where did Eve and her sad little son fit into all this?

She addressed the officers. 'We still haven't ac-counted for Jadon Glover's disappearance,' she said. 'Think body but keep an open mind, please.'

She was glad that the two small boys had both said that their perpetrator was a woman. Surely it narrowed the field?

Watching the officers file out, she tried Eve Glover again. Not surprisingly Eve sounded flustered and upset.

'Could I come and talk to you this evening?'

'All right. All right. I'm usually home by six-ish. I don't suppose…?'

There was no need for her to finish the sentence. 'No. I'm sorry. We haven't made any progress on your husband's case.'

She put the phone down, unsure whether Eve Glover knew anything about her husband's colleague being found murdered. Interesting. It always helped to assess your suspect's reaction when it was you who dropped the bombshell of bad news.

PC DAWN CRITCHLOW was outside Number 3 Britannia Avenue, frowning, trying to recall why the name was so familiar and why it rang a muffled bell until Karen Stanton opened the door to her knock. 'Hi there,' she said. Then Dawn remembered. Karen had been the teaching assistant to the second two of her four children. Karen recognized her at once and seemed unsurprised at the visit. 'Oh, hi there, Dawn,' she said. 'Nice to see you. I suppose you've come about…?'

'Yeah.' Dawn explained her mission. Karen was at once friendly and cooperative. 'Come in, come in,' she said. 'What a weird business, Jadon running off like that.'

Dawn interrupted. 'Is that what you think happened?'

'It's the general feeling. His wife…' Karen's voice tailed off. 'Maybe I shouldn't be saying this but…'

'Do you know Eve Glover?'

'Not well but I do know her a bit.' She didn't explain how.

Dawn put a hand on her arm. 'If you want the streets to be safe then you need to help us all you can.'

Karen lowered her eyes and then Dawn remembered what it was that had triggered her memory. During the briefing it had been mentioned that Karen was a carer for a lady who had had a stroke. Nothing more than that but for some reason she wanted to know more.

'You double up on jobs now?'

Karen smiled and nodded. 'It isn't much of a job,' she said. 'I enjoy it too much. I look after a lady who lives in Mill Street.' Then as Dawn made no comment, simply watched her, she added, 'She had a stroke a year and a bit ago.' A pause. 'I just help her get up, have a bit of a chat and put her to bed.'

'What time?'

'Half eight or so.'

And then, inspiration. 'Is her name Astrid Jenkins?'

'Yes.' Karen's smile was so warm and friendly Dawn almost didn't want to continue. But when Karen had nodded she had read guilt in her face. She'd been caught out. One to save for the evening briefing.

JOANNA WAS ALONE in the station, enjoying the silence, the time to think. To evaluate. What did they know?

Jadon—vanished off the face of the earth. His colleague now murdered. She left her seat to study the map of closely-knit streets, to its right the list of names of the people who owed money to Daylight. Then, not a debtor but connected, there was Mrs Eve Glover and the tragic consequence of her husband's refusal to include her son in their marital home. And there was the tenuous connection with Robertson. Hang on a minute, she thought. She'd bet a dollar that he'd financed the entire operation of Daylight and was creaming off his little cut. No wonder he was doing so well when accountants across the city were rapidly losing their status because many people these days filed their tax returns online.

Perhaps it was time to make contact again with the two remaining partners in Daylight and squeeze this little bit of juice out of them.

Wherever that might lead.

*5 p.m.*

AT STARVE CROW COTTAGE the couple from London had just turned up. Forrester knew they were wrong for the place the minute they climbed out of the car, wincing at the chilly wind, the man stepping straight into the mud with handmade Italian brown leather 'country' brogues. They stood for a while, the woman struggling to find the right words. 'Gosh,' she hit on finally. 'So this is it.' She looked around, almost in despair at the vast landscape.

For once, even Forrester couldn't find his spiel as they both turned towards the cottage, which on this lovely spring day managed to look even more of a wreck. 'Maybe,' said the woman, who was dressed in a pair of loose-fitting trousers and an expensive-looking camel coat which she was wrapping round her as though it would protect her from all this fresh air, 'this isn't such a good idea?'

Her partner put his arm around her. 'We'll start again,' he said. 'Knock it down and rebuild.' He gave an embarrassed grin at Forrester. 'Rename.'

Forrester cleared his throat. 'There are, umm, restrictions on any rebuilding.' He said hopefully, 'National Park?'

They both stared at him and he wondered where to begin. His job was to sell Starve Crow Cottage. By hook or by crook, but not to them.

The look on the woman's face as they toured the inside was a picture. A mixture of disgust and a desire to show her partner—husband?—how much of a pioneering spirit she had.

It was almost funny.

*5.10 p.m.*

JOANNA PICKED UP THE phone and dialled Scott Dooley's mobile number, introduced herself and gave him the news about Jeff.

He was shell-shocked. Apparently no one had told him; neither had he switched on the news, picked up a paper or caught up online. At first he was audibly nervous, his voice high pitched and wavering, but as he absorbed the news his attitude changed and he became aggressive, almost predictably, towards her. 'And you still haven't found Jay, have you? You don't even bloody well know what happened to him.'

Joanna didn't want to admit it but it was true. 'Not so far.'

So then he changed again to become scornful. 'So you think you and your bunch of monkeys will have any more luck sorting out who killed Jeff?'

There was only one way to deal with this attitude. Ignore it. Float over it. But it stung. 'Is there anything you think might help us find out what happened to your colleagues?'

'So you think it's the same person?'

Now she could afford to be scornful. And rude. 'Well, it's a bit of a bloody coincidence, don't you think? One of your mates murdered, the other disappeared off the face of the earth?'

His silence was eloquent. She could almost watch the cogs of his thought processes cranking round.

*Was Jadon the killer? Is he some sort of psycho killer stalking us? Am I going to be next? Or Leroy?*

She let him stew for a bit. Let him have the agony of not knowing.

Then he found his stride and blustered. 'I can't believe you're making such a pig's ear of this. Jeff was killed right under your bloody noses.'

She couldn't argue with him but she could *use* his anger. Angry people are often careless in what they say.

He continued with his rant. 'And you haven't tracked Jay down. He must be somewhere.' His anger was turning into paranoia. 'How safe are *we*, Inspector, with you and your bunch of morons meant to be guarding us?'

Whew. *Morons?* It was an expression of disgust.

'I'll be honest with you, Scott,' she said calmly. 'It seems that someone is targeting you and your'— meaningful pause as she chose the right word—'outfit. Maybe they think that the interest rates you're charging are a little'—another pause—'excessive?'

Now he was defensive. 'Who else would lend that bunch of saddoes money?' he asked scornfully. 'They haven't exactly got a good credit rating. The banks are not going to be queuing up to chuck good money after bad. It's *our* money so *our* charges, little lady, or nothing.'

'And don't you just capitalize on that,' she said.

'Sweetheart.'

She winced.

'*Inspector, love*, you don't exactly gain a huge fan base doing this little service to the community. We know that.'

'It was a woman,' she said suddenly and knew from the silence on the other end that this had hit home.

'A woman?' Shock.

'That's right.'

And then Scott recovered. 'It doesn't exactly narrow the field.' But now his voice was humble.

'Slightly built.'

He was back to furious now. 'I've got one dead mate and another gone off the face of the earth, probably dumped somewhere down a hole or out on those fucking moors. I don't exactly feel safe right now and I don't think Leroy's taking out life insurance either. And all you've got is a slightly built woman. A real help; only excludes the real fatties. And blokes. Whose side are you on?'

'I'm on the side of justice,' she said calmly. 'I want to find out what's happened just as much as you do. And I have a duty to protect both you and your colleague as well as the general public. If you think of anything that might help us discover who it is that's responsible for Jeff's murder perhaps you'll get back in touch with me?'

'Ah, yes.' At last he had found humility and some curiosity. 'How did he die?'

'He was stabbed. Five times. The last one pierced his heart.'

From somewhere he dredged up one last attempt at humour. 'Didn't know he had one.'

Even she couldn't help but smile at that.

'Find Jadon,' Scott said, finally practically spitting the words down the phone. 'Please?'

When the conversation had ended Joanna sat, thinking. The phrase was resonating through her head. *Find Jadon.*

*I wish*, she thought and dialled Leroy Wilson's mobile number. She could tell from the ringing tone that he was abroad and from the lazy way he responded to her introduction which soon changed to a sound as taut as a violin's 'E' string when she spilt her news. 'What?' It was more of a squawk than a question.

She repeated her information and asked where he was. 'Spain, love. And getting the next plane back.' The words held a threat. He obviously had no time to waste on arguments or recriminations. She asked if he would come and see her on his return and got a tight, 'If you insist.'

She put the phone down, sat back and looked at the list of characters on the whiteboard, mentally walking through the list of facts they already had.

Back to the beginning. For some reason she thought it was all about area, about the cramped terraced houses, tiny yards out the back, no room for cars, doors opening out on to the street. Nothing private. Except from this very populated part of town Jadon Glover had, somehow, vanished. In her mind she walked through the streets, seeing it all, even the bunch of flowers left at the scene of the child's fatal accident which had led to the closing off of Nab Hill Avenue. The dire financial circumstances of the clients or, more truthfully, victims of Daylight.

Park the car and walk along the pavement to Mill Street and the six families, each one of whom has an alibi. Cross the road, watched by the huge, derelict mill, such an obvious choice for both murder and concealment of the body. But no. Holmes and Watson had found nothing there and the sniffer dogs were adept at scenting out any corpse. They had not even picked up the scent of blood in the five floors of the empty, cavernous building. So…

Wellington Place. She pictured the cramped row of terraced houses then returned to the wet night, Jadon Glover collecting the money while people sat in their homes and waited, twenty pound notes in their hands, ready to hand over. She sensed their injustice, their anger, hatred and fury as they gave him their hard-earned cash, knowing they were providing him and his associates with their greedy living.

And as they paid off this loan other crises would present themselves. They were already up to their ears in financial trouble. Strapped for cash. She might not like Dooley's sour words but he was right. No bank would have lent them money. They would have lost jobs, cars; their lives would have grown harder and harder. People like Paul Ginster and Christine, Carly Johnson and Stuart Madeley.

Her mind turned to Britannia Avenue, the Murdochs' drunken and defiant state. Out or rather hiding that night, they simply hadn't wanted to pay. Probably spent the money on more booze or fags. Karen Stanton, alone, it seemed, in breaking away from the money lenders. Marty Widnes and the one indication that possibly Jadon Glover had had a conscience?

Mentally she crossed the children's play area, hearing the crunch of the bark beneath her feet, feeling the chill of the slide, watching the empty swings bob to and fro.

And then there were the three women from Barngate Street, the two little boys and their mother and grandmother, Sarah Gough with her troubled son. But in her mind what she saw now were the flowers—the little boy who had run out on the road, the motorist who had failed to see him and the tragic consequences, the flowers still laid on the pavement and the council doing what they could by blocking the top of Nab Hill Avenue off to traffic, making it into a cul-de-sac. Joanna grimaced. Kind of a reflection of the lives caught in Daylight's sticky web. And yet…

*6 p.m.*
*Starve Crow Cottage*

IT WASN'T UNTIL THEY'D both asked delicately about the amenities that everything fell apart. Rory Forrester led them up the garden path, trying to work out how best to present it, dreaming up estate agent speak for this, a drop into a hole in the ground. He was just opening his mouth to say *basically, there are no amenities,* when the woman screamed.

'It's a hand!'

JOANNA WAS STILL mentally at Nab Hill Avenue. She sat up straight. She was wrong in that judgement. Charlotte Parker, Erienna Delaney and Yasmin Candemir were not victims. They were survivors. Bonded sisters. They did not seem ready to be crushed underfoot by Daylight. They almost seemed to be laughing, hands on hips, mocking them as they slugged down their celebratory wine. Not drowning but waving.

And then into the melting pot she chucked the outsiders, Eve Glover and Karl Robertson. If she was right it was Robertson who had financed the entire project. So, in a way, Glover *had* worked for him. Not outsiders then, but on the periphery. What had Johnston and Pickles to do with it?

Her instincts, if not screaming, were whispering innuendoes in her ear.

*One of them. It is one of them.* Their murderer's name was here, on the board.

Wandering quietly and softly through events and their geography had helped to clarify her picture.

Hannah Beardmore popped her head round the door.

'I've just seen the boys,' she said. When she related the bit about the perpetrator dropping something metallic, Joanna sat up. 'Get up there,' she said, 'and share that little titbit of information with the SOCOs. Tell them to look out for a coin, a button, an earring, a key. Anything.'

'Happy to.'

She sat back in her seat, wondering if this seemingly small nugget of information might lead them at last to an answer or if it was another blind alley. The door opened. Korpanski was back, filling the small office with his bulky presence. He grinned at her and rested a friendly hand on her shoulder. 'Solved it yet, Jo?'

She smiled up at him, fond of the burly policeman with his impressive physical presence. 'Not yet, Mike,' she said. Then, 'Can I run something past you?'

'Go for it,' he said, dropping heavily down into his chair, making it squeak and slide in protest.

'We've been assuming it's one of the debtors?'

'It seems logical,' he said cautiously.

'But there are difficulties with that theory.'

'Such as?'

'Let's go back to that night. If Jadon was murdered on the street someone would have seen something? The doors open right out on to the pavement.'

'It was a filthy night, Jo.'

'And if he had been stabbed too—and we know that in general killers tend to favour the same murder method. I mean, the assault on Jeff Armitage didn't look like our perp's first stabbing, did it? She hit vital organs. Right out there. Shows a bit of confidence, don't you think?'

'If you say so.'

'So if Jadon was murdered we can make a guess that

he was stabbed. But if that had happened either on the street or on the children's play area—where Jeff was killed—we would have found some trace evidence.'

'Go on.'

'I was wondering… Was he abducted first?'

He seemed unconvinced. 'What—he gets in a car with one of the people who owe him money?'

'What if she said she needed to get to an ATM?'

'It's possible, I suppose, but I can hardly imagine him falling for that one.'

'Hmm. Well, it was worth a try.'

The DS was quiet for a moment. Then, slowly and tentatively, he spoke. 'We didn't know him, Jo, but I can't see him walking into a trap. He must have known that people may well wish him harm. He'd be too canny to let himself be abducted.'

She gave a deep sigh. 'So many blind endings, Mike. Big Mill, for instance. Goodness—it would be the star of any TV murder mystery. And—nothing. Then there's the people he was visiting that night. They must have all hated him. *Hated* handing over the money. Again—nothing. So what I'm asking is how *did* it happen?'

He thought about it for a moment, screwing up his face in concentration. Then he sat forward, frowning and shaking his head. 'Try this for size, Jo,' he said gruffly. 'He's lured *into* the house. Maybe using the weather as an excuse. He's killed *there* and his body dumped.'

And now she was slowly nodding her agreement too.

'The thing is, Mike,' she said, 'where?'

That was when, right on cue, the call came in.

# TWENTY-ONE

SHE'D ALWAYS KNOWN this call would come. Somewhere, deep inside her, she must have suspected that Jadon Glover's body had been hidden in some tiny little rathole, somewhere in the vast expanse that was the Staffordshire Moorlands. Right on their patch.

And when she learned the location she realized she knew Starve Crow Cottage. She and Matthew had often walked the high trail, starting from the Roaches and crossing the boggy, high part of the moorland towards Royal Cottage, wondering if the story that Bonnie Prince Charlie had stayed there in 1745 was, in fact, true. So many place names in the moorlands were the result of fables.

They had passed the neglected house, read the name on the gate and wondered, made up stories to its origin without knowing the truth. They had seen smoke coming out of the chimney and wondered who lived there.

Now they knew.

*7.30 p.m.*

SO THE CLIMB UP to the high ground was a trip along memory lane but at the same time a place which would forever now be spoiled, the memory of those idyllic walks replaced by an image of an ugly murder, its resting ground the most sordid.

She and Matthew never had found out where the grotesque name had come from. Now she was about to learn. Mike had dug around just before they left and filled her in on the story as they drove out to the moors.

'Really?' she said, recalling the smoke coming out of the chimney. 'And does anyone live there now?'

Korpanski shook his head. 'Apparently not,' he said. 'The old lady, Monica Pagett, broke her hip six months ago and has never been back. She's in a residential home.'

'That must be hard after living out here.' They were climbing into the chilly spring mist, the sun setting to another cold spring night.

Korpanski looked at her. 'Hard? You mean easy,' he said. 'She's in a nice warm home, with a hot shower room en suite, meals provided. No wood and coal to get in. No fires to light.'

'And I bet she hates it,' Joanna said, taking in the wide expanse.

Korpanski shrugged. 'Don't know as to that, Jo.'

But Joanna had watched her own grandmother dragged kicking and screaming away from the terraced house where she had lived all her life and knew home was home so she felt some sympathy for Monica Pagett.

Social services made these decisions. They took over a person's life and deemed what was appropriate and what not.

How much, Joanna wondered as they approached the bleak scene, had these events also sealed Jadon Glover's fate? Their killer had not come here by chance. Either they had known Mrs Pagett and her circumstances and property or they had happened upon it one day while hiking in the moors, as she and Matthew had done. The name and the location would always stick in the mind.

Something else stuck in her own mind. Just before they'd left she'd had to ring Eve to tell her that she was unable to come as something had 'cropped up'.

And Eve had guessed.

'Is it Jadon?' Her voice had been little more than a squeak. 'Have you found him?'

Joanna had kept her voice neutral. 'I can't tell you, Mrs Glover. I don't know myself. As soon as we do know anything for certain I will be in touch.'

There had been a sniff, followed by silence.

THE SCENE THAT greeted her as she climbed into the moorlands and reached the cottage was straight out of Dante's *Inferno*, a sullen, leaden sky now throwing reluctant shafts of light, hardly illuminating cars, and a group of people all tensely waiting for her. Korpanski was at her side. Quiet, for once, his square face serious. He didn't look at her.

They followed Rory's footsteps skirting around the back of the cottage, using the concrete slabs as stepping stones across a sodden, muddy patch of grass. As they walked behind Forrester they sensed that the white-faced estate agent was not going to show them in person to the end of the path. He merely indicated with his arm, stood back to let them pass and looked as though he was going to be sick.

With the corrugated metal door wide open the smell was apparent from eight feet away, flies buzzing towards the site. Joanna braced herself. No corpse was a pleasant sight but this promised to be particularly repulsive. Time isn't kind to bodies.

Privy shelters had been built in single bricks with no windows, little more than a pill box with a corrugated tin roof under which a savage wind was now blowing as though the elements were venting their fury on the scene. The door, too, was of corrugated tin. It was the most basic of earth closets, a wooden toilet seat set in a box which soaked straight down into a pit in the ground below. Behind her, Korpanski tried to make a joke of it. 'Enough to give you constipation.'

She grimaced. It was the closest she'd get to a smile.

The body had been eroded by insect life, sticking out of the wooden toilet seat, the face eaten by rats but still discernible—eye sockets, teeth, jaw, hair. Even in disgust at the sight Joanna couldn't help reflecting that for the dapper 'front guy' of Daylight, be-suited, mobile phone, tablet, 4x4, this was an ignominious burial. Someone had wreaked their revenge with a vengeance and spite and dumped his body where they thought he belonged. But then a closer look inside the privy made her heart hammer in her chest. Glover—if it was Glover—had his hand up. *He'd tried to get out?*

She looked in despair at Mike. 'Shit,' she said, appropriately. 'He wasn't dead?'

Even Korpanski's face paled. 'We need Matthew,' she said, 'and some SOCOs.'

And that meant withdrawal and the inevitable wait.

*8 p.m.*

THE TEAMS ARRIVED WITHIN half an hour—practically a record, particularly out here in the middle of nowhere. She had taken a brief statement and some details from the shocked couple who had taken shelter in their car.

At a guess they wouldn't be making an offer on Starve Crow Cottage. Rory Forrester was sitting in his car, head in his hands, talking into his mobile phone. Joanna heard some of his words.

'Police… Sealing it off… No chance.'

She could almost have felt some sympathy for him. But she had a job to do too.

The SOCOs were soon busy, taping off access routes, taking pictures, soil samples, setting up arc lights. Joanna was glad to see that Mark Fask was heading the team. Efficient and thorough, they needed him.

Matthew took a little longer to arrive. Just after nine she saw his maroon BMW slide in next to the squad car and waited while he donned his paper suit, hat, gloves and picked up his equipment. It was a routine she knew so well she could have choreographed it herself.

He strode towards her, long legs making short work of the two hundred yards between them. His eyebrows rose as he took in the toilet. 'Wow,' he said, grinning. 'Not exactly the Ritz.' Then, 'You OK, Jo?' He knew how squeamish she was. And this scene was making her particularly so. Even more than usual. But she nodded and he patted her arm.

At that the wind rose and screamed around the buildings like a mad banshee. Or perhaps it was the spirit of the crow who had starved to death vainly waiting for his owner to come home and feed him.

Matthew walked along the path and slipped inside the privy. He stood for a moment, observing, thinking but not touching. From the outside Joanna saw his head move forward and then he began work: collecting samples, bagging up the hands, taking ambient temperatures. He stood back, the door now propped ajar, and confirmed Joanna's worst suspicion.

'He wasn't dead when he was put in here,' he said. 'He tried to get out.'

She was chilled. It was an Edgar Allan Poe nightmare, a dying man scrabbling, his body stuck in that filthy pit. She forced herself to focus. 'Cause of death?'

His eyes were bright as they rested on her. He had the merest wisp of a smile. 'Not a chance, Jo. Not till I get him out of there which...' he looked around, '...if the SOCOs don't mind, I'd like to do now?'

Joanna made a quick check. Once the body was pulled out of the privy some evidence would inevitably be lost, the position of the body being the most important. She consulted Fask and he nodded.

They laid the body on an open body bag, all wearing masks against the stench. Putrefaction plus a long douse in a used privy made for quite a bouquet. Joanna met Matthew's eyes over his mask and knew they were both thinking the same thing: bath. A nice, hot, fragrant bath, soaping each other's backs until they had erased every tiny element of decay from their skin and replaced it with perfumes.

Now she could look at the remains, mainly the clothes, Joanna could see it was—or had once been— Jadon Glover, Eve's perfect husband. But looking at the state of him now—predation, probably insect and rodent, as well as putrefaction—she did not fancy asking Eve to identify him. She looked worriedly at Korpanski. *Someone* was going to have to identify him. Maybe Leroy or Scott—someone with a very strong stomach. Otherwise it would be down to clothes and DNA. What effect would seeing what had happened

to their mate have on his two remaining colleagues?
Would it be the end of Daylight? Would the two remaining personnel cut their losses and run away? Fast?
Had the crimes succeeded in their objective? Or would
greed win over fear?

Matthew took a watch from the body's wrist, handed
it to her and she put it in an evidence bag.

'This might help with identification,' he said. 'A bit
less traumatic than the entire thing.'

She nodded. 'Thanks, Matt.'

THE CAUSE OF death looked very much as though Jeff
Armitage and Jadon had shared the same fate. There
was the dirty rust of blood in a few places on the suit,
holes in the fabric and marks on both hands which even
Joanna could read as defensive; a vain attempt to protect himself from an avenging angel. Then she looked
around her at the bleak crime scene—and what lay underneath.

Fask nodded, reading her mind. 'We're going to have
to dig the entire place up,' he said, 'in case…'

Yeah, Joanna thought, still taking in the scene. The
possibilities were enormous. The weapon, his missing
mobile phone, another body, even?

*10 p.m.*

SHE OWED IT TO Eve Glover to let her in on the news
and that meant leaving the scene. She didn't envy the
coppers who would have to stand guard here all night.
They'd need their thermal underwear.

She and Korpanski returned to the car. Rory Forrester and the would-be buyers were long gone.

Outside Number 8, Disraeli Place stood the smart silver Mercedes E-Class. Eve looked at Mike, who shrugged and grinned. They might not know yet who had killed her husband and Jeff Armitage but at least they had anticipated this one.

'Let's burst in on them.' It was Mike's mischievous suggestion, his mood lighter now they had left the crime scene.

But as she was shaking her head, down the path walked a very jaunty Karl Robertson, comb-over blowing in the brisk breeze, a young man's spring in his old man's step. He looked like the cat who had just drunk an entire saucer of cream and was anticipating a lifetime ahead of such luxuries, so pleased with himself he didn't notice the two detectives in the waiting car. He reversed out, his manoeuvres jerky and excitable, and burst down the street, wheel-spinning out on to the road back towards Leek and Hanley.

'Well,' Joanna said, 'confirmation of our theory? Come to comfort Eve after her day in court? He looks pleased with the state of play.' She frowned. 'Is he married?'

Korpanski gave her a quick glance. 'And that has exactly what significance?'

She didn't answer. And now Korpanski was being particularly stolid and pedantic. 'Let's not jump to conclusions, Jo.'

'Well,' she said reasonably, 'look at it this way. I've been working it out. It takes money to set up a business like Daylight. Jadon and his pals had to have the capital to lend out in the first place. Someone put up the money. That's why Jadon could say, with impunity, that he worked for Robertson. It wasn't such a lie after all. Robertson put up the money and I dare say he took a cut of the profits. So, in a way, Jadon was telling his wife the truth. He did work for Robertson, who is much more involved than we've suspected.'

He looked at her, hardly bothering to comment.

She nodded. 'So did *she* know? Or more relevant how much *does* she know now and how much more does Karl Robertson know?'

He was half out of the car. 'One way to find out.'

'Remember,' she said as they approached the front door, 'Eve has a very good reason for hating her perfect husband.'

He knocked.

Eve looked calm as she answered the door. Calm but frightened. She was neatly and neutrally dressed in a black skirt and white sweater which fitted well and looked expensive. She was wearing perfume and looked nothing like a woman who's spent the day in court listening to the injuries her mother inflicted on her murdered son. Neither did she look like a woman whose husband has been missing for the past few weeks. She looked—Joanna had to admit it—serene. Nothing like the woman in hysterics who had screamed down the phone that her perfect husband was three hours late home from work.

So, what had changed? Was she on medication?

Her eyes skittered between Joanna and Mike but she said nothing, asked nothing.

It was Joanna who spoke first. 'Can we come in?'

Eve nodded, her eyes now asking the questions. Who? How? Why? Where?

Joanna and Mike waited until she had sat down on the sofa. Neither fancied catching her if she fainted.

And the news was not good. Joanna had to remind her-self that this woman was a possible murder suspect. At best she had stood back while her mother had systematically abused her son and not lifted a finger to prevent his murder. And now, far from sitting at home with nothing to do or grieving for husband and son, she had simply renewed a friendship with Robertson. So both had apparently played a double game. Because of her husband's selfishness she had entrusted the little boy to her psycho, alcoholic, druggie mother. Surely Eve must have known? But if she had wanted Jadon she had been left with no choice. Because…

These thoughts flitted through Joanna's mind while she waited for Eve to ask the question. Her eyes did.

'We've found a body,' Joanna said, 'in the grounds of…' no need to go into detail, '…a remote cottage in the moorlands.'

'Is it…?' She spoke as though terrified of the answer.

'We don't know for sure yet.' Joanna tried again to puncture the look of utter confusion on the woman's face. 'You understand that we have to identify this person?'

Eve must have understood something of the degradation of a body left in the open. Her terror compounded. Her hands gripped the sides of the sofa. 'You want me to…?'

She was so white that Korpanski jerked forward ready to catch her while Joanna was convinced this was no act.

'No, we have other ways. If it is Jadon he's been dead for a little while.' Something of Joanna's better nature took over. 'We have other ways,' she said again, even more gently, 'and as soon as we're sure we will let you know.'

'Did someone kill him—like Jeff?'

*So she knew about Jeff's murder.*

'Was it an accident?'

'There will be a post-mortem tomorrow,' Joanna said awkwardly, 'but I have to warn you that the way the body was positioned and the fact that Jadon's car was left in Leek means that at the moment we're treating the death as suspicious.'

She did not want to go into detail. Not at this stage. And she would spare her the ugly facts—for now. They'd almost certainly come out in the coroner's report.

*Wait.* It had always been Colclough's advice. *Wait until you're sure.*

To which she added a little mantra of her own. *And don't forget the person you're talking to may well be your perpetrator.*

'We'll keep you informed, Eve,' she said. 'Do you need anyone to stay with you?'

Eve shook her head.

After a pause Joanna decided to toss a pebble into the pond and see where the ripples reached. 'Difficult times for you, Eve, what with your son and Jadon.'

Eve simply shook her head, despairing. 'I didn't know what she was doing. I swear I just thought he was a miserable child.' She dropped her face into her hands.

Joanna shot Mike a swift questioning look.

'I seem,' she said, lifting her head, 'to have made all the wrong decisions.'

*Now was the time to...* 'I expect it's good having an old friend over,' Joanna put in innocently.

To her immense satisfaction, Eve looked startled.

'Sorry?'

'We saw Mr Robertson leaving the house earlier.'

Eve had to think quickly to supply an explanation but her eyes were very wary. Watchful, even.

Korpanski's face was set.

'He's been a support,' she said quietly.

Mark Fask rang her as she and Mike headed back to the car. 'I'm going to have to hire a digger,' he said. 'This is going to be a very difficult crime scene.'

Just give me an easy one, Joanna thought and started to plan what she would say to Rush. She had to at least inform him of the turn events had taken. He hardly responded over the phone and guaranteed her a sleepless night by inviting her to stand on his carpet at eight in the morning.

*Friday, 18 April, 7 a.m.*

SHE WOULDN'T HAVE SLEPT anyway, and Matthew was equally wakeful. They shared a coffee then she headed for her car and back to the station.

Rush was already in his office scowling into a computer screen. Without looking up, he said, 'Give me some good news, Piercy.'

And when she didn't respond he followed this up with the tightest of smiles. 'OK, something nice and cheap then.'

How could she put this? 'The body we believe to be that of Jadon Glover's, sir. It was found by accident—coincidence. To put it bluntly, sir, it was stuffed down an old-fashioned earth closet some fifty yards up the garden path of a remote cottage. The property is empty as the owner is currently in a nursing home in Leek.

She broke her hip a couple of months ago and recently decided she won't be returning to her home so the cottage has been put up for sale.'

'Go on.'

'A couple were viewing it.' As succinctly as she could, she described the way they had found Jadon Glover's body.

Even Rush, for once, was speechless.

'We're going to have to investigate the cesspit.'

Rush frowned.

'With a mechanical digger, sir.'

'Post-mortem?'

'Planned for tomorrow, sir.'

She knew she had to tell him. 'There was evidence.' No, there wasn't. Not yet. 'We believe,' she began. Then substituted that for, 'It looks as though…'

Rush's pale eyes locked into hers. 'What are you trying to say?'

'It looks as though he might have been still alive when he was stuffed down the toilet. His hand was grasping the wooden toilet seat.'

Rush's mouth opened but nothing came out for a moment…two moments. Then, 'He's been there for how long?'

'Probably since the night he disappeared. That's over seven weeks, sir.'

'And this place…' he asked delicately.

'Starve Crow Cottage…'

Rush looked up, startled. She'd forgotten she had omitted to tell him the bizarre name of the smallholding.

'Really?'

'Yes, sir.'

'Suspects?' And as she was silent he barked, 'Please,

Piercy, at least give me some suspects.' He was waiting for her response.

She knew she had to be honest. With a drowning sense of failure, she said very quietly, 'There's no one specific in the frame at the moment, sir. Enquiries are…' Her voice trailed away.

'And Mrs Glover?'

'I'm keeping her informed.'

Rush pressed his thin lips together and was silent, which made Joanna fidgety. He was one of those people whose silences are more sinister than any words they could have said.

His face, normally taut, sagged and he nodded. 'You'd better get back out there.'

She escaped as quickly as she could.

JOANNA HAD KEPT the watch back—not quite sure why, perhaps to give her another opportunity for storming Eve's defences. Her eyes were dry and clear as she looked and nodded. 'It is his,' she said and already there was a calculating look on her face. Joanna almost shuddered. She had rarely ever met anyone quite so cold. The two people nearest to her had both had terrible deaths. And yet here was Eve, in the centre, icily calm, controlled and detached from the mayhem that surrounded her.

She offered her an officer for company which Eve politely declined. At a guess, Joanna thought as she left, Robertson would soon be winging his way across to her.

AT BROOKLANDS STEPHANIE BUCANNON was listening to the news on Radio Stoke. She listened to the account of the body found at a cottage, its location and only stopped when she heard the name.

She went straight into the sitting room. 'Monica,' she said softly.

Monica Pagett looked up, her face softening when she realized who it was. 'Hello, my dear,' she said.

Stephanie sank to her knees beside the chair. 'You're not going to like this,' she said and related the story. The nonagenarian listened without comment until she reached the end. 'How dare they,' she said, looking up. 'How bloody well dare they use my home to dump off some…'

'The poor man,' Stephanie said.

But Monica had already jumped to the practical issue. 'No one will want to buy it now,' she said, then touched the carer's hand. 'Oh, I do wish I hadn't broken this silly old hip. This…' She met the nursing assistant's eyes, '…would never have happened.'

'Oh, Monica.' The girl's affection shone through. 'You are a case.'

But Ms Pagett had not quite finished yet. 'If I hadn't broken my hip I'd still be there.'

'But maybe *you'd* have been in danger.'

'The only thing in danger would be someone who came trespassing on *my* land and *my* property.' Then she cackled loudly. 'And that bloody bird,' she finished. 'I hold him responsible. I'm glad the silly old thing did starve to death.'

Stephanie put her arm round her and kissed the lady's cheek. 'You,' she said, 'are a head case.'

And Monica joined her in laughing.

*10.30 a.m.*

THEY HELD THE BRIEFING in the station's main building, the assembled officers now numbering over a hundred.

Two savage murders in a small town commanded man power. Even Rush with his head full of figures couldn't argue with this one. The world's press had somehow found the story and the gruesome place where Jadon's body had been left. Starve Crow Cottage and its isolated surroundings was worthy of a headline or two, even without the added fact which had inevitably leaked out that his body had been dumped in a primitive privy. Thank goodness the full story had remained off the paper's pages. But the pictures that graced the country's headlines were enough to remind people of another moorland location near Manchester, a place which would always bring a shudder—Saddleworth Moor.

'It's nothing like it,' Joanna said disgustedly, tempted to throw the paper in the recycling bin. 'No similarity between the cases at all.' But the following line was still sobering: *Are there any more bodies out there?*

'I hope not.'

Too much information was being collated, shared and pooled. It was difficult to sort the wheat from the chaff but the sticky threads continued to join together.

'For now,' Joanna said, 'we'll assume that the body found in the cottage toilet is that of Jadon.' She looked around the room. 'So...?'

Dawn spoke first. 'Karen Stanton,' she said, 'is a carer for Astrid Jenkins, the lady who lives in Mill Street. She puts her to bed at around eight thirty every night.'

Joanna physically sketched in the line between the two women. 'Which puts her,' she observed slowly, 'passing Jadon Glover at around eight thirty. Did she see him again?'

PC Dawn Critchlow shrugged. 'She says not, Joanna,' she said. 'She said she didn't go out again that night.'

'Is that the truth?'

Joanna glanced at Korpanski and saw him stiffen. 'OK, Dawn,' she said. 'Thanks.'

They all stared at the map and wondered.

Joanna spoke aside to Mike. 'We need to talk to Mrs Stanton,' she said, 'and find out why the lie.' She turned again. 'Perhaps she knows something.'

Korpanski spoke up, stating the obvious. 'She was the one person who didn't have a motive anymore. She'd paid her debt off.'

'Maybe.' Joanna's mind was tussling with this. 'It's possible,' she said, 'that she was just furious at the money she'd already given.'

Korpanski nodded but he looked unconvinced.

Joanna turned back to the board and drew a faint line between Astrid Jenkins of Mill Street and Britannia Avenue.

What were they still missing?

She threw the question out to the roomful of officers. And then it hit her. As soon as everyone had left she looked at Mike. 'Guess where we're heading.'

Karen Stanton sat on her sofa in her neat room, her back ramrod straight, expressionless. Calm, collected and very much in control.

'I didn't mention the fact that I'd gone out later that evening because it wasn't relevant,' she said.

'You could have let us be the judge of that,' Joanna said, her voice hard. Then, 'Tell us the route you took down to Mill Street?'

Karen was hesitant. 'I crossed the play area,' she said

slowly, 'threaded behind Big Mill and crossed the main road towards Mill Street.'

'What did you see?'

Karen licked her lips.

'Mrs Stanton,' Joanna said steadily, 'tomorrow I shall spend the morning watching the post-mortem on Jadon Glover. I have just come from his wife. We have yet to enlighten her on the exact circumstances of her husband's death but it will all come out in the inquest. It is a gruesome story, I can assure you, so help us.'

Karen's eyes were wary. Joanna tried again. 'And only a few days ago I watched another post-mortem on Jeff Armitage.'

Karen Stanton couldn't prevent her lip from curling in contempt. Joanna had planned to say the second murder could possibly have been prevented but she could see there was no point.

Karen knew something but she wasn't telling.

They left. She spent the rest of the day closeted with Korpanski, combing through various possibilities.

By late evening she had a worm of an idea. Nothing definite, little more than a tiny thought, a faint glimmer of flickering candle light at the end of a very long tunnel.

It was late when she stood up stiffly, stretched out her arms and yawned. She rested a hand on her sergeant's shoulder. 'Well, Mike,' she said, 'at least now we're starting to ask the right questions.'

He grinned at her. 'I'm knackered,' he said. 'I can't think straight anymore.'

She nodded. 'We both need a good night's sleep. See you tomorrow.'

*Midnight*

IT WAS LATE WHEN she finally arrived home. Matthew was asleep on the sofa. He hated going to bed without her and would delay the moment as long as he could. She woke him with a kiss. No whisky breath this time. 'Were you dreaming?' she asked fondly.

'Maybe.' He was still sleepy.

'About tomorrow's little job?'

Even that didn't dent his sleepy grin. 'Again, maybe.'

Although it was late she poured herself a glass of wine and sat down next to him.

He rallied slightly. She was tempted to flatten his hair which was sticking up like an errant schoolboy's. And then she thought not. Leave him looking like a sleepy Just William.

'Anywhere near finding out what happened, Jo?'

'No,' she said. 'Frankly, no. It's like someone's unpicked a patchwork quilt and I'm trying to stitch it back together with no idea of the final pattern. Lots of little fragments, anomalies, some of them quite promising but I can't make sense of it. Korpanski and I have spent the day working through everything we know.' She gazed into the fire. 'I know it's to do with debt. Money. I know it's to do with revenge but Jadon Glover was a complex character.'

'And Eve Glover?'

'There seems so little passion there that...' She looked at her husband. 'I just don't think she cared enough—either about her husband or her son. She's almost detached from it all. Murder is a crime of emotion, jealousy, greed, hatred, love. Eve only seems to care about her own creature comforts. She's almost a psycho in that way.'

'Wow,' he said, taken aback.

She was silent for a moment. From the beginning she'd assumed that the origin of this murder and ignominious disposal of the body had arisen out of one of the stories of hardship and exploitation, of greed, poverty and desperation. But she had always wondered…

There were other factors in this case.

Karen Stanton had to be shielding someone. She had concealed the fact that she had been out and about that evening at about the time Jadon Glover had been abducted.

There was the other murder of the little boy.

There was the fact that Daylight had been backed by a friend of Glover's wife. He'd turned up pretty quickly to 'comfort' the grieving widow.

And then there were the flowers placed at the end of Nab Hill Avenue, the tragedy that had sealed off a road, turning it into a cul-de-sac. She was silent for a moment, feeling chilled in spite of the warmth—almost stuffiness—of the room.

'Penny for them,' Matthew said cheerily and she looked up.

'If I've been wrong about the motive for the crime what else might I have been wrong about?'

'I don't know,' he said, yawning, 'but I've got a busy day tomorrow.' He sneaked in closer. 'Shall I tell you what I'm doing?'

'I'd rather not.'

'To be honest,' he said with a wicked grin, 'I'm doing a post-mortem on a very unsavoury corpse and watching me with an eagle eye will be the scariest detective inspector in the entire Leek Police Force.'

'I'm almost sorry for you,' she scoffed, 'being exposed to that.' But he was right. Tomorrow promised to be a very busy day. Joanna only hoped it would provide them with some answers.

# TWENTY-TWO

*Saturday, 19 April, 8.30 a.m.*

THE POST-MORTEM had been scheduled early so it made sense for Joanna to travel in with Matthew and meet the other members of the team at the mortuary. She could hitch a ride back to the station with them. As expected, with such a gruesome discovery set against a dramatic backdrop, there was no shortage of media interest, even a reporter from *The Sentinel* hanging around outside the mortuary. But they were all out of luck. As Matthew pressed in the keypad numbers Joanna crossed over to Richard Corby. 'Come on,' she said, 'you know I can't tell you anything yet.'

'Maybe in an hour or two?' He sounded hopeful.

The relationship between the police and the press was always tetchy, but she had learned not to let her irritability show. The press knew the police needed them to spread the word. They were better as allies than enemies but even so. 'You can't expect me to give you any details.'

'Can you just confirm that the body found...' the reporter made a great show of looking down at his notes for accuracy, '...in a remote moorland location known as Starve Crow Cottage is that of the missing man,' another glance down, 'Jadon Glover?'

Joanna forced her face to remain blank. 'We'll be making a statement later, Richard,' she said. 'You don't need to hang around here all day. There's nothing here for you—not yet anyway.' She put a friendly arm on his shoulder. 'As soon as we've got anything we'll be calling a press conference. I'll let you know.'

'OK.' He turned to go but another reporter, a small girl with hair the colour and texture of dried straw, must have been short of column inches. 'At least tell us if he's been identified yet?'

'Not formally, no.' Joanna had learned over the years to measure each word she uttered to the press. Careless statements or ill-advised phrases could look terrible in print—or worse, speech marks—and they could easily be tracked back to her and misconstrued.

Focusing on identity, Joanna was thinking of the state of the corpse. Who could possibly identify him as the dapper and confident man who had parked his car in a supermarket car park a few weeks ago and had such control over his own and other people's lives?

Richard Corby turned around, gave her a hard look and took a step nearer. 'You *know* who he is,' he said under his breath, 'and so do I. So when can I go public on this?' He tried to encourage her to spill the beans with the sweetener, 'Maybe rope Joe Public in on the investigation?'

But she wasn't tempted and shook her head. 'You know the rules, Richard, as well as I do. We'll have to use fingerprints and DNA,' she said. Then added under her breath, 'Off the record, just remember if it is Glover he's been missing for seven weeks. The weather's turned warm and this person wasn't exactly buried six feet under in a lead-lined coffin.'

He looked even more interested. 'So how was he buried?'

She said nothing.

He took the inference and measured it. 'Bit of a mess then?'

'That,' she said, 'is an understatement.'

'Rumour is,' he responded, eyebrows folding in on themselves and turning his back on his fellow members of the profession, who were watching with curiosity, 'that he was found with his head sticking down the outside lav.'

'I couldn't possibly comment,' she said. Then added curiously, 'Where *do* you get your information from?'

He simply grinned. 'Keep in touch, Inspector Piercy.'

'Yeah.' It was good-humoured banter. They both knew the rules of engagement. As for the others, she wasn't so sure and the last thing she wanted was to be hauled in front of the IPCC—again.

She entered the mortuary.

Over the years Joanna had learned the trick of dealing with less savoury post-mortems. She would dab Chanel perfume—not eau de cologne but proper perfume—on her wrist, ready to sniff when the mixed scent of gore, formalin and in this case putrefaction got too nauseating. She kept her breathing shallow and usually ate a light and anti-nauseous breakfast of dry toast. When the going got too tough she would simply look away and Matthew would describe the details she needed to know. The rest he would leave out. That seemed to work most of the time, sparing her feelings. As SIO she had to attend the post-mortem and sign out the evidence bags, but sometimes she would rather have been anywhere but here, in this clinical room, fans turned up to maximum but never enough.

As Matthew began with the initial assessment her mind started drifting, aimlessly floating like a helium balloon without a weight through the various crime scenes connected with this case. She was transported elsewhere, back out on to the chilly moors, walking the cramped streets of Jadon's Wednesday night patch. Even stepping through Big Mill with its ghostly clatter of ancient machinery long gone. She realized now why she had been so distracted. There had been so much going on in the teeming streets of Leek, so much hidden behind the closed doors of the terraced houses and so many stories of poverty and debt, of heartbreak and happiness, of parsimony and profligacy, stories which had cost happiness and ultimately lives like Frank Widnes. Now all these stories and dramas floated through her mind, bunches of flowers and dead children mixing together like a bizarre Chagall, and they started to form some sort of pattern—an order. The patchwork quilt was re-stitching itself, pieces finding their correct order and place. It wasn't that she hadn't noticed all this. She had. Her eyes had taken it in. But she hadn't paid it enough attention, thought deep enough about it or understood its significance.

*Now* she couldn't understand why she hadn't recognized their true worth.

'You OK?' Matthew certainly was. In a long waterproof apron, mask, gloves, with his hat on, he was in his element, his eyes bright with the work ahead of him, that puzzling out of events and their correct sequence.

'Yeah.' She looked up. What remained of Jadon Glover's clothes had been cut off and bagged up. He lay there, naked, in an advanced state of putrefaction. Blow-flies, rodents and degradation had all done their worst. Joanna corrected that thought. Not their worst or their best, only what came naturally in their quest to survive. Whatever Jadon Glover had been like in life—dapper, deceitful, selfish, smart, in death he was…disgusting.

She shelved her thoughts. No use sinking into thought now. She needed all her attention. All her wits.

As Matthew began his detailed analysis of the state of the body and its internal organs her thoughts took a journey of their own, back to the wedding photograph of Eve and Jadon. There was so little resemblance between the smiling, confident groom and this thing lying on the table. Her mind moved on to the little boy, Rice, who was missing from the wedding. But her mind was blocked with the images of small bunches of flowers tied around the lamppost. The tragedy had been a couple of years ago but someone was still bringing fresh flowers and not for Rice Sutherland. She'd noticed. The ribbon was fresh, as were the blooms. Not silk ones, attached a month or a year ago to bleach in the sun and be soaked by the rain, catch flakes of snow, attached only to be abandoned and forgotten. These flowers had been put there less than a week ago. Roses and lilies; expensive in an area that did not allow a large budget for such luxuries. Someone was caring for the site. Who? Someone from Nab Hill Avenue or the surrounding streets? Did it have any connection with current events? She knew now it was one small fact that she had over-looked and shouldn't have done because she couldn't answer her own question.

She glanced across at Matthew, wondering whether he'd noticed her lapse of attention, but he was too absorbed. He'd pulled his mask up over his nose and mouth but his eyes were firmly focused on his fingers which worked and probed, measured and asked digital questions. He made notes partly speaking into a recorder, sometimes writing on a tablet, sometimes taking photographs. Currently he was frowning as he examined an internal wound in something that looked like a piece of rotten meat.

'OK,' he said, finally looking up. 'Again, cause of death stab wounds to the abdomen and chest but he didn't die instantly.' He tugged his facemask down. 'Your killer's getting better at her job,' he said.

'Her?'

'Probably. It wouldn't have taken much force. And aren't most of your debtors women?'

She nodded then asked the million-dollar question. 'When was he stabbed?'

'Probably,' Matthew said, considering, 'around the time he went missing. We'll need some help from the forensic entomologist. I've already given Tim a ring. He'll be able to pin down a time span better than I can.'

And now for the worst question. 'How long was he alive in that stinking place?'

'An hour—two hours at the most.'

'Conscious?'

He nodded. 'He must have been. It looks like wood and old faeces under his fingernails.'

It was a terrible thought. She was distracted by Mark Fask who had been busy bagging up the clothes. 'We got a notebook here, Jo,' he said. 'It's a bit soggy and smelly.' He held up an evidence bag.

'Are you going to be able to read it?'

He nodded. 'I think so. We'll dry it out first and take a look through.'

'Yeah—good, thanks.' She wished she could rid herself of the nightmare picture of those hands scrabbling at the edge of the wooden lavatory seat, trying to lever himself out of the cesspit, mortally wounded. In photographs she had seen for herself how well muscled Glover had been due to his regular visits to the gym. Fitted up by Pecs, he might have managed to lever himself out of the toilet but it would have been a waste of effort. There was no one who could help for at least five miles in any direction. Only his killer had known he was there at all. He might even have crawled to the road but how much traffic passed? It was too remote. From the time his killer had planned where to dump his body he was doomed even if he was not quite dead. Surprised at her reaction for a man she had perceived as thoroughly callous, she felt nothing but pity. But Glover, she tried to tell herself, was a greedy, hard-hearted bastard who fed on the poor and needy. Then she remembered Marty Widnes of Britannia Avenue and half revised her opinion. He had shown her pity. Pity or rather guilt? Whichever, it was disproportionate when it was Daylight who had impacted on her husband's suicide but it was still pity. Of a sort.

Matthew tapped her shoulder, breaking into her thoughts. 'I'm all done,' he said, jaunty as he peeled his gloves off and released himself from the long apron. 'You'll have my report by tomorrow morning, Inspector.'

She nodded then smiled at him. 'Thanks, Matt. I'd better go,' she said. Then, knowing that the SOCO and two junior officers were surreptitiously watching them, she touched his cheek with her index finger. 'I'll see you,' she said and he nodded, his eyes bright and resisting asking the question: when?

She hitched a lift back to the station with Jason Spark. On the way she received an unexpected phone call. 'Joanna?'

'Yeah.' She waited, thinking: caller, identify yourself.

'Baxter here.'

She was floundering.

'Cornell. SOCO. Work with Mark Fask.'

She was all apologies. 'I'm sorry, Baxter. I just didn't recognize your voice—or your number.' Already she felt her pulse start to trot, its speed increasing. She knew the SOCOs. They would be busy combing the crime scene. They wouldn't be wasting time ringing her unless they had something important to tell her.

'We've done some digging,' he said, 'excavating the cesspit. We've come up with a mobile phone.' Pause, 'In a very degraded state.'

'Jadon's?'

'We haven't confirmed yet with his service provider but we think so. It's a 4G model.'

'Can you get anything from it?'

'We'll try,' he said. 'There's another thing.' He hesitated, then added uncertainly, 'Ma'am.'

She winced and waited.

'We've been taking some soil samples from around the cottage. The soil there's pretty unique. It has a high peat content and because of the altitude of the moorlands it's low on minerals and salts. They leach away,' he explained helpfully.

'And that means?'

'Not trying to do your job for you, Inspector, but no

one brought Jadon all the way up here in a wheelbarrow, did they?'

She'd got it. 'Wheel arch samples.'

'Unless they got their car valeted and, if you ask me, the people who were in hock to Jadon Glover weren't the sort to blow a fiver on having their car cleaned up.'

'Thanks.'

But when Cornell had hung up Joanna was still left with nothing but questions. What had Jadon and Jeff's murders really achieved? Would it be the end of Daylight? Would the debts be wiped out? She didn't think so. Robertson would have his money, Eve too. Were the other two 'directors' in danger now? Should they be protected? Yes, until they'd made an arrest. Where did Eve fit into all this? Matthew, she reflected, had been right. Rice should probably have been Rees. Poor child—she'd even got his name wrong.

So she let the objects spin around her mind. Where did Karl Robertson fit in? Where did the murder of Rice fit in, if at all? And then there was the other child, the one who had run out into the road after a football. The child whose death was still commemorated with fresh flowers every week. Was the accidental death of that little boy part of this or not? Why had Karen Stanton concealed the truth?

Still questions.

Her phone rang again. Barraclough, this time.

'Didn't the children say that the lady who killed Jeff Armitage dropped something?'

'Yes. Something metallic.'

'We've found a metal button. It just might be—on the other hand...'

Killers had been convicted on something as small

as a button. She felt a faint glimmer of hope. 'Do we know when it was dropped?'

'Put it like this—the area's been sealed off since Glover's murder. It was only reopened last week.'

So, not great, but something.

She didn't have to instruct him to bag it up, tell him that from small acorns, etc., etc. He was an experienced SOCO who drank in every word at the briefings. He knew what to do without any prompting from her.

For now her focus was on the child who had met his death on Nab Hill Avenue and the flowers laid there so carefully.

And as if to echo her starting point Baxter Cornell rang again just as she was returning to the station. 'Joanna,' he said urgently.

'Speak.' She felt excited. Cornell wouldn't have rung had he not had something important to say.

'We've started drying out Glover's notebook,' he began.

She was impatient to find out more. 'And?'

'He kept a handwritten record of his visits.'

'As well as on his tablet?'

'Yes.'

'Anything from the night he died?'

'Yes. He broke his routine.'

She waited.

'He went to Wellington Place and then Britannia Avenue. Ticks by everyone's name except the Murdochs. Big cross there.'

'And then?' She was so eager she pulled over by the kerb to listen closely.

'Then he went straight to Nab Hill Avenue, not Barngate Street.'

Instinctively, as though ringing an expensive wine glass, Joanna knew what it was that Karen Stanton had seen and why she had concealed it.

At last, a focus. A channel narrowing down the field.

'Do you know who he visited first there?'

'No. There's no entry for Nab Hill Avenue. He's opened it and underlined and that's where it ends…' he hesitated, '…with a streak of blood. It must have been in his pocket and then fallen out when…'

He didn't need to say any more.

'Nab Hill Avenue…' She recalled the three women. A coven, Mike had called them. 'Narrows the field a bit.'

'Looks like it.'

'Whoever killed him,' she was thinking out loud, 'almost certainly wouldn't know he kept parallel records. They would just have thought the entries were made on his tablet. Thanks.' She'd known as soon as they'd found Glover's body that it would yield clues. That was why the killer had hidden it so well—in the grounds of a cottage they must have thought was abandoned. Now corroborative evidence would come thick and fast. Cornell was right to focus on the car that must have been used to dump Glover's still-living body. But there would be more to find—a murder scene. She felt the quickening that accompanied the first hint of light after a very long night. At times she had wondered whether they would ever find Glover—not knowing whether he was dead or alive. After Jeff's murder she had even wondered whether it was possible that Glover had murdered his partner. But now they had found Glover's body there was a trail to follow. And it led to Nab Hill Avenue, a significant dead end.

She called the station and gave Mike a potted version of Cornell's information. 'Dig out the files of the child who was killed in Nab Hill Avenue,' she said. 'Find out if there is any connection with the three debtors who live in the street.'

'Will do, Jo.' He paused. 'You think that's where this all ends?'

'Someone is putting flowers there,' she said. 'Fresh ones, every week.'

# TWENTY-THREE

*Saturday, 19 April, 2 p.m.*

JOANNA PULLED UP outside Brooklands Nursing Home. It was a large, Victorian house with a flat-roofed modern block built on to the back. She rang the bell.

A plump, middle-aged woman answered and, responding to Joanna's query, showed her into a room on the first floor and a woman sitting in a high-backed armchair. She looked up with alert blue eyes as Joanna introduced herself.

'I wondered if you'd want to come and talk to me,' she said crisply as the nursing assistant closed the door behind them and Joanna sat down opposite.

Monica's hands gripped the blanket that covered her knees. Her knuckles were lumpy and arthritic. 'Bloody cheek, that's what I call it.'

'Take me through events,' Joanna said. 'When did you break your hip?'

Monica laughed and touched her short straight iron grey hair. 'February,' she said. 'Slipped on a patch of ice going to the privy. I was lucky I made it back to the house.' Her sharp eyes bored through Joanna's. 'Crawled, I did. I'd have frozen otherwise. I wouldn't have been found.'

How long might she have laid there? It was the question she could not, should not ask. Monica answered it for her anyway.

'Days,' she said, 'maybe weeks.' She laughed, a dry, witch's laugh. 'Probably within the year.'

'Did anyone ever come to visit you at the cottage? Who knew of the existence of your…toilet arrangements?'

'Dunno,' Monica said. 'Hikers maybe, people passing and such like.'

'Did you have visitors?'

Her eyes were sharp as she responded with a shake of her head.

'So you went to hospital?'

Monica nodded.

'And then—'

'Here.'

'You put the cottage up for sale and so…'

Monica leaned forward. 'Still call it a bloody cheek, dumping him in my private…' Then, mercurial, she cackled. 'Know how the cottage got its name?'

Joanna spent the next half hour listening to the story of the Starving Crow.

And then Monica told her another story—of a woman who had been out walking her neighbour's dog and had asked if she could use the lavatory.

'I felt embarrassed,' she said, 'but the woman didn't seem to mind the rudimentary loo.'

*4 p.m*

MIKE WAS READY FOR her when she arrived back in Leek, everything spread out on the table. 'The child's name,' he said, 'was Stephen Gorling. He was just four years old.'

'What was he doing in Leek?'

'Staying with an aunt who lived in Nab Hill Avenue while his mother had a weekend away with her new boyfriend. He saw a car outside and thought his mother had come back so he ran out into the road.'

'I thought he went out after a football?'

'That's the story that was put around but that was initial conjecture. The reason that came out in the inquest was that he ran out thinking it was his mum. Stephen's mother drove a large black Mitsubishi.'

'But, wait a minute, that wasn't the car that hit him?'

'No. It was the car behind the Mitsubishi but it was that, apparently, that was the reason he ran out into the road—or so his aunt said. He shouted, "Mum's back." Put that together with the fact that the accident happened on a Wednesday evening. But there was no mention of Glover.'

She looked at Mike. 'It seems a bit harsh to hold him responsible for the little chap's death if he had nothing to do with it. He can't help it that he drove the same car as the child's mother.'

'Well, those are the facts,' Korpanski said. 'It all happened on a Wednesday night which was his night for collecting money in that area. In those days, before Nab Hill Avenue was blocked off, he used to drive up the roads and park where he could. Of course, the new Sainsbury's wasn't complete then either. When Sainsbury's opened up and simultaneously the council, in response to parents' pressure groups, blocked off Nab Hill Avenue, making it into a dead end, he started parking in the supermarket and walking his round. It just made things easier for him. Had Glover not been skulking round the streets the little boy wouldn't have been run over.'

It was, at best, a tenuous connection but… 'Who was the aunt?'

'Erienna Delaney.'

'Shall we head over there? Now.'

# TWENTY-FOUR

AND SO THEY funnelled back to Nab Hill Avenue.

The street was dark and menacingly quiet as they entered. The terraced houses seemed to be holding their collective breath, waiting for the denouement. As they walked up the street nothing stirred except a small shivering of the cellophane wrapping around the flowers. Pink and yellow tulips today. Joanna took a look at Mike. She wasn't an imaginative person but she felt spooked. Something here wasn't right. Even Korpanski was looking around him, all his senses fully aware, his glance shifting from left to right with nervous, jerky movements. She drew in a deep breath and kept walking. One step at a time. She knew one aspect of this environment which was making her uncomfortable. After the noisy battle to get through the other streets, this one was eerily quiet. As they approached number eight the door flew open and Erienna Delaney was standing there. She must have been watching their approach. Her face was calm but hostile, her eyes wary. She stood back to let them enter her house without asking a single question or speaking a single word. The silence didn't feel right. In fact, nothing felt right. Joanna was glad she had not come alone. There was something reassuring about Korpanski's sheer bulk which practically filled the narrow hallway.

They followed her into a small, neat sitting room

which held the faint scent of the White Company's *Flowers*, one of Joanna's favourites.

Erienna spoke first as she sat down in an armchair. 'I suppose,' she said, her eyes still fixed on Joanna, 'you've come to ask me about Stephen.' A wry smile creased her face. 'And I suppose you've put two and two together to make six.'

Joanna was surprised. She had expected Erienna Delaney to assume they had come about the two murders. Instead she had tugged the rug from under their feet by moving straight to her nephew.

Erienna looked from one to the other, waiting for them to catch up. And then, before they could make any response, she spat, 'I'm not that feckin' stupid.'

Joanna waited. If Erienna had something to say she was prepared to listen.

'It was just circumstances,' Erienna said. 'Not *his* fault.' Her face changed again. 'And not Stephen's either. Sometimes you just have to accept things are just fate and that's that. Maybe Stephen dying like that meant that the council blocked off the road and, who knows, it's possible it's saved some other poor child's life. But I can tell you…' She folded her hands across her lap. 'I had nothing to do with Jadon Glover's death.'

Joanna glanced at Mike, trying to keep her expression neutral. *She would say that, wouldn't she?*

'Did he call here on that last Wednesday night?'

Erienna's expression changed again and Joanna realized she didn't know how to answer this. The Sisterhood was sticking together. Joanna prompted her. 'The truth, Ms Delaney?'

Erienna Delaney was no coward and no slouch either. She didn't answer but sat motionless.

Joanna felt her attitude harden. 'There have been two murders,' she said. 'Two men have been brutally killed.'

Erienna Delaney's shoulders shuddered. But she still needed a shove in the back.

'You understand?' Joanna said. 'Jadon Glover's body was tipped down a toilet. He was still alive at the time.'

She waited for that to sink in before continuing. 'The pathologist believes he possibly lived for up to a couple of hours, fatally wounded with his head stuck down an earth closet, trying to heave himself out. You understand? Now I don't like or condone the way Daylight conducted their business but I can tell you this was a horrible end to a man who had been married for just two years. His wife was distraught. She called him a perfect husband.'

Erienna snorted and even as Joanna spoke she recognized the hollowness of the phrase. Erienna's eyes flickered. It was the only sign that she had heard but her shoulders tensed and she looked as wary as a cat.

'Look,' Joanna said, 'I really don't want to have to bring you in to the station for questioning but make no mistake, Erienna, I will if I need to. I will get to the bottom of this. DS Korpanski and I will be making an arrest and we will be charging you and your less guilty friends as accessories and obstructing the police in the execution of their duties.'

Delaney was still dumb and immobile.

So Joanna continued, 'We have you three in our sights. Now I suggest you share a glass of wine or whatever you usually have with your cronies and then come back and tell me the truth.' She felt her face harden. 'One of your mates is a killer. Make no mistake about that. Watch your back, Ms Delaney. And by the way,' she added, 'we do have some forensic evidence from the crime scene.' She deliberately did not specify which crime scene. Maybe the dropped button found by the SOCOs would lead nowhere.

She and Mike left.

She stood in the middle of the street. 'Behind one of those doors, Mike,' she said thoughtfully, 'is a crime scene waiting for us to unpick its secrets.'

'And you think we'll flush them out?'

'Oh, yes,' she said, turning to him. 'I'm sure.'

# TWENTY-FIVE

*Saturday, 19 April, 8 p.m.*

THEY HAD RETURNED to the station, waiting as reports were now coming in thick and fast. Whether the coven was going to come forward or not, Joanna was gaining evidence and she started drawing up a list. She would, if necessary, apply for a warrant to impound the cars of all three women and to search their properties. They would find blood or mud, a hair or a thread. Something.

During the briefing she brought the team up to speed with the finding of Glover's notebook, the facts surrounding the death of the little boy on Nab Hill Avenue and the story of Erienna Delaney.

No one could dispose of crime evidence that completely. With modern techniques and microscopic eyes they would find specks of blood, fingerprints, soil, plant life, blood, a weapon, evidence. It was simply waiting for them to pick it up. Connect the body with the crime scene.

Of course, a confession would be nice but it wasn't absolutely necessary. It would simply make it easier and cheaper to send whichever person had struck the blows to prison. Joanna sat at her desk, her eyes unfocused on the screen. In her heart she knew who it was.

She fingered the evidence bag containing the one metallic button.

Monica Pagett had described the person who had asked if she could use her lavatory one day nearly a year ago. It only needed them to show her a photograph. Thank goodness for the sharp eyes and acute memory of that particular ninety-five-year-old. It wasn't Erienna, or Yasmin.

It was Charlotte Parker. For her money it was 'grandma' who had stuck the knife in. From the time she had met the steely woman with her tough, independent character she had recognized something in her. Something which resonated with herself. She was uncompromising. Unforgiving. Unforgetting.

'We've got no evidence, Mike.'

'Up to us to find it then.'

'Something else… How could she have man-handled Glover's body along that path?'

Korpanski simply shrugged.

'How would she know the cottage was empty—that Monica wouldn't just return one day?'

Again Korpanski shrugged but this time he had a suggestion. 'Perhaps she had a friend who worked in the hospital and found out that way. Leek's just a small town, Jo.'

And so for now the cramped streets with their stories and their secrets would remain. Their debts would be picked up again—just by someone else. They would never quite swim above them but would remain struggling for breath and the sharks would swim as the vultures hovered, ready to pick bits off. They would always be the underbelly. She gave a loud sigh and Korpanski looked up. 'You're not feeling sorry for them, are you?'

'Of course not.' She was indignant. 'God, Mike, I

saw his body as well as Jeff's. I saw the savageness of the assaults as well as the suffering of Jadon. And Jeff—well, it was pathetic.'

'Hmm.' He returned to his screen but when she stayed motionless he too gave a sigh and turned away. 'So what's in your head?'

'Just sadness,' she said. 'That's all. I just feel sad at the life some people have.'

'Hang on a minute, Jo,' he said, 'it could be worse, you know.'

'How?'

'They're not in some war-torn place, having bombs dropped on them and their families slaughtered.'

'No,' she agreed, 'but they live this grey life, this everyday struggle.'

'You need an arrest,' he said, 'a confession, a nice clean court case and a holiday with your husband.' He winked at her. But she sat still, frowning. Korpanski, however, had already turned back to the computer and missed her frown.

*Sunday, 20 April, 8.30 a.m.*

IT WAS THE FOLLOWING day, a Sunday—a good day to find everyone at home—when Joanna received the warrants to search all three homes beginning with their hot favourite.

Charlotte Parker watched as Mark Fask and his team scrutinized her house. She leaned against the wall, watching them from the narrow walkway. Without a word she kept watching them as they brushed fingerprint dust, saw them mark and photograph various points along the wall, take samples from the floorboards, swab the back of the front door and the sitting-room door, inspect her wheelie bin. She watched, resisting attempts to encourage her to leave the scene, simply moving out of the way when the SOCOs drew too close. Her expression was inscrutable as her car was put on a low loader. After an hour and a half, she picked up her coat from the back of the chair and her mobile phone and walked out, speaking into it as she went.

Fask caught the first sentence.

*'They're here now.'*

## 11 a.m.

JOANNA WAS AT HER desk, fiddling with her biro, too agitated to concentrate. Tensely she was waiting for a phone call. She jumped when it finally came through.

'Yes?'

Korpanski looked across at her.

'Right. I'm on my way.'

And in that one short sentence DS Mike Korpanski caught it—the whiff of excitement. Something at last was happening.

Joanna was standing in front of him. 'Well,' she challenged, 'are you coming or sitting here?'

He too was on his feet.

'We have lift-off,' she said. 'That was Charlotte Parker. She's at the front desk.'

Whatever Korpanski had been expecting he had not anticipated this.

JOANNA FACED THE woman across the table and studied her. Parker returned her gaze and similarly studied the determined woman who sat opposite.

The DI looked calm and she, herself, felt similarly so.

She had been cautioned and remained focused on the questioning blue eyes which remained curious, the gaze steady and her face impassive, hands resting on her lap.

Then Charlotte Parker gave her a small, friendly smile. Almost apologetic. It took Joanna aback. She leaned forward. 'I think I understand.'

It was meant to sound conciliatory but Charlotte Parker took it coolly. 'Do you?' It was a challenge.

Joanna recalled something Colclough had once told her.

*When a suspect is ready to confess, whatever the crime, let them talk—and talk—and talk until they run out of words.*

Charlotte folded her arms and frowned. 'This is hard to explain,' she began. She started looking around her. 'It wasn't even born out of hatred, Inspector. Not really.' She leaned forward. No solicitor at her side. She'd refused one. She tossed her tiger-striped locks as a gesture of complete freedom. 'What's the point of trying to justify my actions?' she said. 'It's not going to get me off. It's time,' she said, closing her eyes wearily. When she opened them it was to ask a seemingly unrelated question. 'Have you ever had rats, Inspector?'

*Let them talk.*

'No. Mice a couple of times if the weather's been particularly wet or hard but no rats.'

'There's an instinct inside you,' Charlotte Parker continued as though she hadn't heard. 'An instinct to rid yourself of it. No matter how. That's how I felt about Jadon Glover. Every Wednesday. Every bloody Wednesday...' she was knocking her palm on her forehead, punctuating the words, '...he'd be there knocking on the door. Bang, bang, bang, bang...' She put her hands now on either side of her head. 'He *knew* we were vulnerable, defenceless. Poor as church mice and still he came week after week, bleeding us dry.'

'Are you saying he took pleasure in that?'

Charlotte looked up. 'Jadon, take pleasure? Don't you understand, Inspector? He had no emotions. Not pleasure, not malice. No feelings at all.'

'But he did,' Joanna insisted, for some unknown reason feeling bound to defend Glover. 'He missed calling on Marty Widnes a couple of times.'

'Guilt,' Charlotte said, folding her arms. 'He hounded poor old Frank to death.' She smiled. 'It started with me getting taken short out on a hike one day, seeing the house. So remote. And then as though it dropped into my lap, by chance I mentioned it to a friend and she told me about Mrs Pagett being in hospital, told me she'd never return home.' Grandma Parker smiled. 'Told me the old lady was stubborn as a mule. *She'll die before she'll ever sell that place.* It seemed like…an invitation.'

Joanna nodded.

'Had Monica Pagett not decided to sell Starve Crow Cottage I would have got away with it, wouldn't I?'

'Possibly, temporarily.'

'You'd never have found his body, would you?'

'One day,' Joanna said, 'someone would.'

Charlotte 'Grandma' Parker was silent for a moment longer before asking, 'Why did you home in on us?'

'Sorry?'

'How did you know to focus your search for evidence on Nab Hill Avenue?'

Joanna had to be honest here. She would like to have said she had worked it out, even that Karen Stanton had seen Glover turn to the right, into Nab Hill Avenue not

Barngate Street, but she hadn't and the truth would all come out in court. 'Glover kept a notebook.'

'I know. An electronic one.'

'No, not an electronic notebook—at least, not only an electronic one. He also had a small, handwritten thing that he kept in his breast pocket. When he'd completed a street he filled it in.'

'The sneaky bastard,' Charlotte said softly to herself. 'The sneaky little bugger.'

What could Joanna say except, 'Quite.' She continued, 'He'd already written the headline "Nab Hill Avenue" so we knew he'd changed his order the last Wednesday he was alive. We knew he'd come to one of you.'

'So why start with me?'

'I thought you were the most likely. And this.' She held up the evidence bag with the button in it.

Charlotte Parker's laugh rang into the room. 'Oh, you, the police,' she said. 'That isn't even mine.'

'But we got there in the end.'

Charlotte's nod was almost a grudging tribute.

*Sunday, 20 April, midday*

SHE WISHED SHE COULD have made a better job of breaking the news to Eve Glover that someone had confessed to her husband's murder and they would be charging her, but she had an overwhelming feeling of regret. She wished she could have charged Robertson with financing what surely should have been an illegal operation. She wished Eve's son had not died in such a brutal manner. She wished the Mitsubishi had not roared up Nab

Hill Avenue, deceiving a little boy into believing his mother had returned.

She wished she could pay off all the debts. She wished Frank Widnes had not hanged himself. She wished...

And as her prosaic mother would have said, 'Wishes don't pay bills.' No, Mum, and wishes don't bring back the dead either.

She had a brief meeting with Leroy Wilson and Scott Dooley and suggested they try a change of career plan but had little hope that they would follow her advice.

Eve was eerily calm as she broke the news and Joanna felt admiration for her iron control. She had, in the end, lost both husband and son. And what, Joanna thought as she closed the front door of Disraeli Place, could be more precious than that?

Then her admiration and sympathy abandoned her. A car pulled up and Karl Robertson climbed out, red flowers at the ready. Joanna realized it was not sympathy that Eve deserved but recognition. She was a survivor.

Robertson met her halfway along the drive. She'd never asked what his marital state was—divorced, single, separated or still happily and blissfully married to a Mrs Robertson. 'I've come over to help Eve plan the funeral,' he said, 'and to reassure her...' fat chins wobbling, '...that she will be looked after.'

Was Eve Glover really one of those women who just had to have a man around, even one who had probably set her husband (supposedly adored, supposedly perfect) on the business path which had ultimately led to his death and was probably using her in a different way, a sugar babe bit-on-the-side?

Joanna despaired of such women.

In a dry voice she related the facts to him and said that the coroner would soon release the body for burial. 'And,' she couldn't help adding, 'that of his colleague, Jeffrey Armitage.'

'Right.'

She clocked off at eight. She'd had enough of the world and its tacky little problems. She and Matthew had a leisurely Indian at Abdul Spice and that night she slept for a full eight hours.

# TWENTY-SIX

*One month later*

JOANNA STARED AT the pregnancy test. Pregnant! Written in blue. It shouted it from the tiny stick from the bathroom into the empty bedroom, down the stairs like a puff of blue smoke—or pink. She kept staring at it, hardly able to believe the fable, as many women must have done before. What did this mean? It was already growing inside her. Tiny cells multiplying. Fast. Two, four, eight, sixteen…

She put her hand on her stomach and felt absolutely nothing. It was flat. Someone had once told her they started off like this—invisible. Even after six weeks the cells were a tiny clump no bigger than a fingernail. She looked at her own fingernail then at her face in the mirror. Did she *look* different?

Yes, she did. There was a glow about her. A glow of knowledge, a glow of success. A glow that knew Matthew would be overjoyed. She couldn't wait to tell him. She pictured his face, boyish, excited, hand ruffling his hair as he habitually did, almost to suppress exuberant, bubbly news from bursting out of his scalp. And that's what this was. The very best of news.

In a month they would be in their new house, well in time to decorate a nursery and prepare for this child that Matthew had so wanted. Then she caught sight of her face in the mirror, only this time she was not smug and jubilant but anxious. What if?

Korpanski had told her she'd love the little thing the second it was born. Before then, even. Would she? She was very unsure of this. She was not maternal. She was doing this for Matthew, for the man she loved.

Then other considerations crowded in. How would Eloise greet the news? Was she sufficiently absorbed in Kenneth to skate over an event which would alter her importance and status in her father's eyes? Or would her hatred for Joanna combine with jealousy of anything which might replace her in the pecking order and her father's attention?

And Matthew's parents? How would they respond to a child they might regard as a bastard? Oh, yes. She had heard them. 'Should be still married to Jane.' There were struggles ahead and like most news it was at the same time both good and bad.

Downstairs, she could hear Matthew humming. He was making them both some coffee. An entire cafètiere. She could smell it wafting up the stairs, rich and pleasant. She gripped the test stick which told the first chapter in such a significant story—a story of life. She moved towards the bathroom door. If there was one thing she knew without doubt it was that in a couple of minutes Matthew Levin, doctor, pathologist, husband, would be the happiest man on the planet. He would want to laugh and shout and sing. And tell everyone. Share the wonderful news. If Matthew could climb the tower of St Edward's Church and ring the bells he would.

It was the only thing she knew for certain.

She wanted to crawl back into the bathroom, lock the door and think.

But she couldn't, wouldn't deny him this. Not for one more second. She went downstairs, into the small, oh-so-familiar kitchen. He was in a blue towelling dressing gown, feet bare, honey hair morning-tousled. He looked up at her and he knew.

He already bloody well knew.

'Jo?' he said uncertainly and took a step towards her. Then his arms were around her and she felt the warmth of his body, the musculature of his arms, his legs, his face wet with tears. 'Jo,' he said.

And in Morgan Street the banners were still up. 'Welcome home, Kath.'

\* \* \* \* \*